German Stories
of Crime and
Evil from the
18th Century to
the Present

DOVER DUAL LANGUAGE

Deutsche Geschichten
von Verbrechen und
Bösem vom 18.
Jahrhundert bis
zur Gegenwart

Edited and Translated by
M. CHARLOTTE WOLF, Ph.D.

DOVER PUBLICATIONS, INC.
Mineola, New York

ACKNOWLEDGMENTS

Karin Holz: "The Last Trick" ("Der letzte Stich") by Karin Holz, from *Regensburger Requiem: Kurzkrimis von der Donau,* KBV Verlags- und Mediengesellschaft, GmbH, Hillesheim, 2013. Reprinted with the permission of the author.

Iris Klockmann: "The Kiss of Death" ("Der Kuss des Todes") by Iris Klockmann, first published by Dover Publications, Inc., 2015. Printed with the permission of the author.

Bibliographical Note

German Stories of Crime and Evil from the 18th Century to the Present / Deutsche Geschichten von Verbrechen und Bösem vom 18. Jahrhundert bis zur Gegenwart, first published by Dover Publications, Inc., in 2015, is a new selection of German stories reprinted from standard editions, unless otherwise noted, and accompanied by new English translations prepared for the Dover edition by M. Charlotte Wolf, Ph.D., who also made the selection and wrote the Introduction and author biographies.

Library of Congress Cataloging-in-Publication Data

German stories of crime and evil from the 18th century to the present = Deutsche Geschichte von Verbrechen und Bösem vom 18. Jahrhundert bis zur Gegenwart : a dual-language book / edited and translated by M. Charlotte Wolf, Ph.D.
    p. cm. — (Dover dual language German)
In English and German.
    ISBN-13: 978-0-486-79658-1 (paperback)
    ISBN-10: 0-486-79658-2
    1. Detective and mystery stories, German. 2. Detective and mystery stories, German—Translations into English. 3. German fiction. 4. German fiction—Translations into English.
    PT1340.D4G57 2015
    833'.0872—dc23

2015000852

Manufactured in the United States by Courier Corporation
79658201   2015
www.doverpublications.com

CONTENTS

iii

"A Native American elder once described his own inner struggles in this manner: Inside of me there are two dogs. One of the dogs is mean and evil. The other dog is good. The mean dog fights the good dog all the time. When asked which dog wins, he reflected for a moment and replied, 'The one I feed the most.'"

George Bernard Shaw

INTRODUCTION

From "alibi" to "warrant," most adults and adolescents in the western hemisphere have grown up with a vocabulary that pertains to the world of crime, either from reading crime fiction, from crime shows on radio and TV, from full-length movies on the big screen, or even from the daily newspapers.

The roots of modern crime fiction are often attributed to Anglo-American writers such as Edgar Allan Poe (1809–1849), Sir Arthur Conan Doyle (1859–1930), Edgar Wallace (1875–1932), Raymond Chandler (1888–1959), Agatha Christie (1890–1976), and Dorothy L. Sayers (1893–1957). Many regard 1845 as the year of birth of the modern detective story,[1] when Poe's hero C. Auguste Dupin solved—on paper—the puzzling murders in the Rue Morgue by using a mixture of analysis, calculation, and imagination.

The Origins and Development of Crime Fiction in Germany

However, few American and British readers know that since the late eighteenth century, Germany too has had a richly developed tradition of crime fiction that parallels and even predates Edgar Allan Poe's "Murders in the Rue Morgue."

August Gottlieb Meißner (1753–1807) is generally recognized as the father of the German crime story genre.[2] His story

---

[1] Horst Bosetzky and Felix Huby, eds, *Nichts ist so fein gesponnen: Kriminalgeschichten aus erlesener Feder* (Meßkirch: Gmeiner Verlag, 2011) 9.

[2] August Gottlieb Meißner, *Ausgewählte Kriminalgeschichten. Kleines Archiv des achtzehnten Jahrhunderts,* ed. Christoph Weiß (St. Ingbert, Germany: Röhring Universitätsverlag, 2003) 9.

in this anthology, "Die Edelfrau unter Mördern" (included in this collection; English title: "A Noblewoman Amongst Murderers"), is based on a true event and contains many of the classic elements of a traditional crime story—a gang of bandits, a beautiful damsel in distress, a crime committed, and an unforeseen "happy ending."

The Saxon writer Christian Heinrich Spieß (1755–1799) earned his reputation as the founder of gothic novels.[3] His story "Marianne L.," also in this anthology, is a riveting account of a violent crime, including a detailed and step-by-step description of the investigation, the discovery of the circumstances that led to the crime, and the successful conclusion of the investigation.

German poet, philosopher, historian, and playwright Friedrich von Schiller (1759–1805), a close friend of the great writer Johann Wolfgang von Goethe, is not generally thought of as a crime-fiction writer. Yet his story in this anthology, "Der Verbrecher aus verlorener Ehre" ("The Criminal Of Lost Honor"), is another thrilling example of an eighteenth-century crime story.

Probably the best-known crime story to German readers (not included in this collection) is "Das Fräulein von Scuderi" ("Mademoiselle Scuderi"), a story from 1818 by the influential Romantic writer E. T. A. Hoffmann. The protagonist is an elderly noblewoman held in high esteem by French King Louis XIV and his mistress, Madame de Maintenon. A reluctant and somewhat uncharacteristic investigator, she manages to solve a series of violent attacks on mostly wealthy lovers that occur when they are en route to their mistresses.[4] The tale is widely regarded as one of Hoffmann's best, not only because of its suspenseful plot, but also for its vivid descriptions of life, places, and people.

The German story with a style most similar to Poe's famous account of the Rue Morgue murders is "Der Kaliber" ("The Caliber"), written by the eccentric German playwright Adolph

---

[3] "Freibergs vergessener Poet." *FreibÄrger: Freibergs alternative Zeitung.* No. 36, Oct/Nov. 2005: 1.

[4] J. M. Ellis, "E.T.A. Hoffmans Das Fräulein von Scuderi," *The Modern Language Review*, vol. 64, 1969: 340-350.

Müllner (1774–1829) and published in 1828 (not included in this anthology). American literature professor Barbara Burns calls it "the first German detective story."[5] It begins with a magistrate being confronted with a murder case and the perpetrator readily admitting to the crime. However, the magistrate has doubts about the circumstances that led to the offense and decides to keep investigating. It turns out that he was right to doubt, with the final proof being a piece of evidence that he unearths.[6]

All of these stories were hugely popular in German-speaking countries during the eighteenth and nineteenth centuries. Some were published even earlier than Poe's famous tale, which challenges the popular perception that his was the first detective story ever.

The Popularity of Crime Fiction

A look at the history of Western crime fiction suggests several distinct but often overlapping themes and motifs that engage different segments of the reading public, and latterly of the viewing and listening public also.

1 Moral Instruction

This is perhaps the oldest purpose of writing fiction, dating back to the days when the Church dominated Western intellectual life, when a morality message was one feature used to distinguish "good literature" from "bad literature." (The first book to be printed in Western culture was, after all, the Bible.) August Gottlieb Meißner's story in this anthology, "A Noblewoman Amongst Murderers," illustrates this purpose well.

---

[5] Dieter Paul Rudolph, "Eine klitzekleine Geschichte der deutschen Kirminalliteratur," *Krimi-Couch, de.*, June 2014, 1 Aug. 2014 < http://www.krimi-couch.de/krimis/dprs-krimilabor-eine-klitzekleine-geschichte-der-deutschen-kriminalliteratur.html>.
[6] Rudolph, "Eine klitzekleine Geschichte der deutschen Kirminalliteratur."

The Church started to lose its monopoly on intellectual life with the onset of the Renaissance and lost increasingly more during the Age of Reason, allowing more secular approaches to the arts and sciences to begin to emerge.

2 Intellectual Challenge: The Whodunit

The classical whodunit starts with mystification and ends with the uncovering of the reason(s) for the crime, the details of the crime, and the name(s) of the criminal(s).

A crime has been committed (someone has been murdered), or perhaps is just suspected (someone has disappeared), and an investigation starts. At the outset, the crime puzzles both the reader and the story's characters. Step by step, the circumstances leading up to the crime, and the clues left behind, are unveiled, until the mystery is solved and (usually) the perpetrator receives his or her just punishment—the often-overlapping "moral instruction" component of the tale.

At this end of the crime-fiction spectrum, the detective has to reconstruct the crime and the events leading up to it in order to solve it—what the German philosopher Ernst Bloch called the reconstruction of the "untold story."[7] The detective is called upon to uncover the motives that led to the crime, along with the methods and opportunities available to possible perpetrators, in order to reveal and convict the criminal.[8] Such stories often are characterized by changes of scene, flashbacks, "red herrings," dead ends, surprise developments, and step-by-step disclosures.

In this anthology, a classic example of this type of crime story is Balduin Groller's "Der große Unterschleif" ("The Great Embezzlement"), with the detective representing a German adaptation of Sir Arthur Conan Doyle's famous detective, Sherlock Holmes.

---

[7] Ernst Bloch, "Philosophische Ansichten des Detektivromans," *Der Kriminalroman: zur Theorie und Geschichte einer Gattung,* ed. Jochen Vogt (München: Wilhelm Fink Verlag, 1971) 334.
[8] Richard Alewyn, "Anatomie des Detektivromans," *Der Kriminalroman: zur Theorie und Geschichte einer Gattung,* ed. Jochen Vogt. 372–404.

3 Curiosity and Entertainment—How Will the Story End?

Stories in this genre are the "pure crime" stories. These develop in a linear way, starting with the idea of the crime, describing the drama of its execution, and ending with its resolution.

A key feature of this genre is that the reader shares in all of the planning and execution of the crime and the encircling and conviction of the criminal. The criminal is known from the outset—but how will the story end? Suspense is created through the style and the narrative structure. While the protagonist in the detective story is the detective (or maybe his or her confidante—Dr. Watson, for example), the protagonist in the crime story is more often than not the criminal.

A good example of this type of story, included in this collection, is Walter Serner's "Der Sturm auf die Villa" ("The Invasion of the Mansion"). It is a somewhat ironic take on the genre, with the planning of the "crime" being promising but the execution—well . . . You will have to see for yourself!

A variation on this theme is the "thriller." This is more of a criminal adventure or action story, with the purpose being not to solve a crime, but to pursue a known villain and prevent him or her from committing more crimes. A thriller commonly includes a series of chases, arrests, releases, shoot-outs, and so forth, until the detective or investigator hunts the criminal down.

A deviation from the classic detective story is the "police story," which closely follows the pattern of the detective story, except that the civilian investigator as protagonist is replaced by a policeman or policewoman, who is able to draw on the resources of the law enforcement apparatus and enlist the help of fellow police officers in his or her efforts to solve a crime. A good example of this type of story is Karin Holz's "Der letzte Stich" ("The Last Trick"), in which a Bavarian chief police constable, characterized as both gruff and amiable, solves a crime with common sense and ingenuity.

4 Social Commentary: The Problem of Evil

However, not all crime mysteries follow the patterns described above. It is not always the intellectual challenge of solving the

crime or the tantalizing question of how the story ends that is the focus; rather, it may be the uniquely human circumstances that lead to a crime, such as the emotional motives or the psychopathology of the perpetrator, that is the focal point.[9] Such stories explore the evil that often underlies a serious crime—that is, the evil that motivates an individual to inflict pain, loss, and destruction. These stories pose the question: if the deed wasn't driven by the Devil personified, what was it in human nature or in human society that inspired it? And some stories, like those featuring Sherlock Holmes, remind us that even the righteous investigator of a crime may have a dark side.

The thesis that evil is not just some rare and random aberration that is "out there," but may be something latent in all of us, finds its most explicit depictions in stories about serial killers. This genre has roamed the literary landscapes with increasing frequency in recent years and is perhaps most prominently represented in the American writer Thomas Harris's novel *The Silence of the Lambs* (1988). Surely the serial murderer Hannibal Lecter, who personifies evil, is the perfect investigator of evil? After all, who better than the Evil One to unravel the inner workings of evil?

Much of German crime fiction promotes this idea—that evil lives in some, or even all, of us, and may be triggered at any moment—and so many of the stories represented in this collection emphasize a philosophical and psychological approach to understanding or solving crimes. For example, traces of a surprisingly modern and heavily psychological insight can be glimpsed in the account of Friedrich Schiller's villain ("The Criminal of Lost Honor"), who was launched on his path of crime by an injustice done to him. And from Willibald Alexis's thief ("The Pledge of the Three Thieves") we learn that he embarked on a path of evil behavior because of adverse social circumstances: his upbringing in a family that these days would be characterized as "dysfunctional."

---

[9] *Texte und Materialien für den Unterricht: Deutsche Kriminalgeschichten der Gegenwart*, ed. Günter Lange (Stuttgart: Philipp Reclam jun, 1990) 4f.

Similarly to Schiller's villain, Friedrich Hebbel's protagonist Anna ("Anna") becomes unhinged and thereby driven to commit a deed that ends in disaster, all because of a grave injustice she experienced, literally at the hand of her master. On the other hand, Christian Spieß's lovely Marianne ("Marianne L.") falls victim to a seemingly respectable, but as it turns out, evil duo, one of whom is driven by an indiscriminate appetite for wickedness, while the other is a spineless and selfish wimp who surrenders to temptation. Their combination turns into a lethal cocktail of evil that spells doom for the noble Marianne—the true heroine of the story.

The idea that the victim somehow "invites" evil and even incites crime is best illustrated in Iris Klockmann's contemporary story "Der Kuss des Todes" ("The Kiss of Death"). Although the setting is historical, the themes are hot-button, and the suspense runs deep.

The American and British vs. the German Tradition in Modern Crime Fiction

Like the classic short story, crime fiction is a "chameleon" among the literary genres; it adapts to the historical and social conditions of the era within which it is written, and can therefore be regarded as an "open form."[10] Consequently, an "avant garde" of mystery writers have been free to target the social problems of their time. This opportunity promoted the development of the "new German mystery story," which has broken out of the traditional mold of its American and British ancestors, much as crime stories by many Scandinavian writers have done, by combining entertainment with illustration and criticism of contemporary social issues.[11] Contemporary German crime writers have used the opportunity to enrich their stories with historical,

---

[10] Helmut Heissenbüttel, "Spielregeln des Kriminalromans," *Der Kriminalroman: zur Theorie und Geschichte einer Gattung,* ed. Jochen Vogt (München: Wilhelm Fink Verlag, 1971) 371.
[11] Peter Nusser, "Kritik des neuen deutschen Kriminalromans," *Der neue deutsche Kriminalroman,* ed. Jochen Vogt (München: Wilhelm Fink Verlag, 1971) 19.

romantic, fantasy, and science fiction elements, contributing to an explosive growth of the genre.

One of the latest developments is the rise of regional crime stories. As the term implies, the regional setting plays an important part in this crime-fiction genre. Such stories have become so popular that there has been a literary backlash. In 2011, for example, *Die Welt* journalist Joachim Feldmann asked the question, "Who still wants to read regional crime stories?"[12] A year later his colleague Axel Hacke, who writes for the prestigious German paper *Die Süddeutsche Zeitung*, mocked the proliferation of regional crime stories with the following words: "Only when the last German teacher and the last German journalist have written a regional crime story, will we notice that it can be overdone."[13]

However, the German regional crime story remains alive and well, and some of it is successful even in translation, as Anna Maria Schenkel's novel *Tannöd* (*The Murder Farm*, 2014) proves. Maybe regional crime fiction is so successful because, as Ms. Schenkel stated in an interview with the renowned newspaper *Der Tagesspiegel*, it gives readers an outlet for their desire to glimpse into the local abysses, "as did public executions in olden days."[14]

As an avid and passionate reader of mystery stories in both English and German, I have greatly enjoyed the opportunity for an in-depth reading survey of the breadth of stories that this

---

[12] "Wer will die Region-Krimis noch lesen?" (Joachim Feldmann, "Görlitz ist noch krimifrei," *Die Welt*, 5 March 2011, 21 July 2014 <http://www.welt.de/print/die_welt/vermischtes/article12705151/Goerlitz-ist-noch-krimifrei.html>.)

[13] "Erst wenn der letzte deutsche Lehrer und der letzte deutsche Journalist einen Regionalkrimi geschrieben haben werden, werdet ihr merken, dass man's auch übertreiben kann." (Alex Hacke, "Das Beste aus aller Welt," *Süddeutsche Zeitung Magazin*, Heft 34/201, 21 July 2014<http://sz-magazin.sueddeutsche.de/texte/anzeigen/38041/Das-Beste-aus-aller-Welt>.)

[14] "Andrea Maria Schenkel sagt, die Leute wollen in Abgründe sehen. Dafür brauche es ein Ventil, 'so wie früher die öffentlichen Hinrichtungen.'" (Verena Mayer, "Mord vor Ort," *Der Tagesspiegel*, 7 Oct. 2013, 22 July 2014 <http://www.tagesspiegel.de/kultur/erfolg-der-regionalkrimis-mord-vor-ort/8893314.html>.)

collection represents. I hope readers will find the same pleasure when indulging in this selection that spans more than 200 years, with most of the stories appearing in English translation for the first time.

M. Charlotte Wolf, Ph.D.
September 2014

ACKNOWLEDGMENTS

I owe thanks to Acquisitions Editor Katharine Maller at Dover Publications, Inc., whose enthusiasm for German literature encouraged my search for literary pieces that may appeal to American readers with a fondness for German fiction.

Also, I would like to thank my husband Martin who, as always, provided much appreciated and valuable feedback during my late hour and early morning translation sessions.

Thanks are owed also to my German high school and college teachers, who tried to instill a passion for stories in their students. In my case, their efforts were decidedly successful.

Last but not least, I would like to express my deepest appreciation to the legions of German-speaking writers who have created stories of suspense. I have devoured them with relish since the day I discovered that reading not only broadens my mind, but also makes my pulse race and my spine tingle.

M. Charlotte Wolf, Ph.D.
September 2014

German Stories
of Crime and
Evil from the
18th Century to
the Present

Deutsche Geschichten
von Verbrechen und
Bösem vom 18.
Jahrhundert bis
zur Gegenwart

AUGUST GOTTLIEB MEIβNER

August Gottlieb Meißner was born in Bautzen, Germany, on November 3, 1753. After graduating from secondary school, he enrolled at the University of Wittenberg and later at the University of Leipzig to study law. During this time he became interested in theater and poetry. He later joined the Freemasons in Dresden. In 1783, Meißner married; the couple had several children.

In 1785, he was offered a professorship in classical literature and aesthetics at the University of Prague in what then was Bohemia. Twenty years later, he became the university's director, a position which he held until his death in Fulda on February 18, 1807, at the age of fifty-three.

Meißner is considered the founder of the German detective story. Although there had been reports and depictions of crime in the form of sensational journalism and collections of legal cases—very popular at the time—Meißner's stories distinguished between legal and ethical responsibility for a crime. Accordingly, the titles of his stories, such as "Mord aus Schwärmerei" ("Murder of Passing Fancy") or "Unkeusche, Mörderin, Mordbrennerin, und doch blos ein unglückliches Mädchen" ("Unchaste, Murderess, Incendiary, and Still Only an Unhappy Girl"), already give the reader a clue as to the criminal's motives or the circumstances of the crime.

Through his work, Meißner was able to "humanize" legal proceedings by allowing social and psychological components of a crime to be introduced into legal judgments. The shift from the legal offense and the subsequent punishment to the

1

psychological and social circumstances of the crime was a revolutionary move, and it presented readers with an opportunity to look inside the mind of a criminal at the time the deed occurred. This tradition was continued by Friedrich Schiller in his story "The Criminal of Lost Honor," found later in this collection.

All in all, Meißner published more than fifty hugely popular crime and detective stories.[1]

The following story tells of the cunning stratagem a noblewoman employs when she is forced to deal with a gang of marauding bandits.

---

[1] Karl Heinrich Jördens, *Lexikon deutscher Dichter und Prosaisten,* vol. 3 (Leipzig: Weidmannische Buchhandlung, 1808) 473.

AUGUST GOTTLIEB MEIßNER

AUGUST GOTTLIEB MEIβNER

Die Edelfrau unter Mördern

Ein sehr schönes Landgut war es, in wahrhaft romantischer
Gegend, nur etwas fern von der Heerstraße gelegen, wo Baron
von R. den Sommer hinzubringen pflegte. Sein Schloss, auf
einem kleinen Hügel erbaut, war ganz seinem übrigen Reichtum
gemäß, geraum, schön von innen und außen, ausgeführt in
einem edlen Stil, getrennt vom übrigen Dorfe um ein paar hundert Schritte ungefähr.

Einst musste der Baron in Geschäften auf wenige Tage weg-
reisen. Seine Gemahlin, eine schöne junge Dame, kaum zwanzig
Jahre alt, blieb zurück. Sei es aus Laune oder aus Notwendigkeit,
kurz, sie blieb. Ein paar seiner besten Bedienten hatte er mit sich
genommen, ein paar andere blieben bei ihr zurück. Von
Unsicherheit hatte man nie noch in dieser Gegend etwas
gespürt. Die Baronin überhaupt gehörte nicht zum furchtsamen
Teil ihres Geschlechtes; Gedanken der Gefahr kamen daher
auch nicht im Traume ihr bei.

Jetzt, des zweiten Abends, wollte sie eben in ihr Bett einstei-
gen, als in dem Nebenzimmer ein schreckliches Getöse ent-
stand. Sie rief. Niemand antwortete ihr, aber immer stärker
ward das Lärmen, das Schreien, das Poltern. Sie begriff nicht
sogleich, was das sein könne, warf ein leichtes Gewand um sich
und ging nach der Tür, um nachzusehen. Ein schrecklicher
Anblick, der sich ihr darbot! Zwei ihrer Bedienten lagen in der
Mitte des Zimmers, halb nackt und mit zerschmettertem
Haupte; das ganze Gemach war voll fremder grässlicher

AUGUST GOTTLIEB MEIβNER

A Noblewoman Amongst Murderers

It was a fine estate—located in a truly romantic area only a short distance from the military road—where Baron R. used to spend his summers. His castle, built on a small hill, was—in accordance with the rest of his rich possessions—spacious, beautiful inside and out, done in an exquisite style, and separated from the rest of the village by about a few hundred paces.

Once the baron had to travel away on business for a few days. His wife, an attractive young lady, barely twenty years old, remained behind. It may have been because of a whim or out of necessity; but in short, she stayed. He had taken along some of his best servants, and a few others stayed behind with her. Nobody had ever felt any unease in these whereabouts. Least of all the baroness, as she did not belong to the timid section of her sex; therefore she did not have any notions of fear, not even in her dreams.

Now, on the second evening, she was about to enter her bed when a dreadful ruckus arose in the next room. She called out. Nobody answered, but the noise, the shouting, and the crashing about increased. She did not immediately understand what it could be, [so she] threw on a gossamer garment and went to the door to have a look. A terrible sight greeted her! Two of her servants were lying in the center of the room, half undressed and with their heads crushed; the entire chamber was full of

Menschen; vor einem derselben kniete so eben der Baronin
Kammerfrau und empfing, statt der gebetenen Gnade, den töd-
lichen Stoß. Auf die eröffnete Tür eilten sogleich mit gezogenem
Säbel zwei dieser Barbaren los. Welcher Mann, geschweige
welches Weib, hätte bei solch einem Auftritt nicht im namenlo-
sen Schrecken Leben und alles für verloren geachtet? Ein lauter
Schrei der Verzweiflung, eine Flucht von wenigen Schritten,
eine fruchtlose Bitte um Verschonung, das wären vermutlich die
letzten Rettungsversuche von vielen Tausenden gewesen. Doch
die Baronin handelte nicht also!

»Seid ihr da?« rief sie mit dem Tone der innigsten Freude aus
und stürzte selbst ihren zwei Angreifern mit einer Hast entgegen, die beide gleich stark befremdete, die das gezückte Gewehr
von beiden glücklich zurückhielt. »Seid ihr da?« rief sie noch
einmal. »Gäste wie euch habe ich mir längst gewünscht.«

»Gewünscht?« brüllte einer von diesen Mördern! »Wie
meinst du das? Warte, ich will –«

Er schwang den Hirschfänger bereits, sein eigener Kamerad
hielt ihn auf. »Halt noch einen Augenblick, Bruder!« sprach er,
»lass uns erst hören, was sie will!«

»Nichts anderes, als was auch euer Wille ist, brave
Spießgesellen! Ihr habt trefflich hier aufgeräumt, wie ich sehe.
Ihr seid Leute nach meinem Sinn, und gereuen wird es weder
euch noch mich, wenn ihr nur zwei Minuten lang mich anzuhö-
ren geruht.«

»Rede!« schrie der ganze Schwarm. »Rede!«

»Aber mach's kurz!« rief der Grässlichste von ihnen: »Denn
auch mit dir werden wir des Federlesens nicht allzu viel treiben!«

»Was ich doch hoffe, wenn ihr mir nur auszureden vergönnt.
Seht, ich bin zwar die Frau des reichsten Kavaliers im Lande.
Aber unglücklicher als ich kann selbst die Frau des niedrigsten
Bettlers nicht sein. Mein Mann ist der schäbigste, eifersüch-
tigste Filz, den je die Erde trug. Ich hasse ihn, wie man seine
Sünde hasst, und von ihm loszukommen, ihm auszuzahlen
zugleich, was er bisher mir lieh, das war längst mein innigster
Wunsch. Zwanzigmal wäre ich schon entwischt, nur das
Wegkommen galt Kunst. Alle meine Bediente waren seine

unfamiliar, hideous people; before one of them the baroness's chambermaid was kneeling and received, instead of the mercy for which she had asked, a fatal blow. Immediately, two of these barbarians hurried to the opening door with their swords drawn. What man, let alone woman, when faced with such a scene, would not have deemed life and everything else lost in a nameless horror? A loud cry of despair, an escape of a few paces, an inefficacious plea for pardon; presumably, they would have been the last attempts at rescue for thousands of people. However, the baroness did not act in this way!

"Are you here?" she cried out in a tone of innermost joy and rushed toward her two attackers in a hurry which struck them equally as strange and, fortunately, caused them both to hold back their brandished rifles. "Are you here?" she cried out again. "I have wished for guests just like you for the longest time."

"Wished for?" one of these murderers roared! "What do you mean by that? Wait, I will—"

He was already swinging his hunting knife, when his own comrade held him back. "Hold on a moment, brother!" he said, "Let us first hear what she wants!"

"Nothing else, but that which is also your desire, my brave accomplices! You have cleaned up splendidly here, as I can see. You are people after my own heart, and neither you nor I will regret it if you will deign to listen to me for just two minutes."

"Speak!" the entire horde shouted. "Speak!"

"But keep it short!" the most hideous of them called out: "Because we will also proceed with you without much ado!"

"Which I do hope [you will do], if you will only let me finish my speech. You see, I may be the wife of the richest nobleman in the land. However, not even the wife of the lowliest beggar can be unhappier than I am. My husband is the most sordid, jealous sleaze whom the earth has ever carried. I hate him like one hates one's own sins, and to get away from him, to pay him back what he has loaned me so far, that has been my deepest desire. I would have already fled twenty times before, only getting away requires real skill. All of my servants were his

Kundschafter, derjenige, dessen Hirnschale ihr dort so kräftig handhabt, war der Ärgste von allen. Selbst dass ich allein schlafe, ist ein Probestück von der Eifersucht meines Gemahls. Seht, ich bin erst zweiundzwanzig Jahre alt und bin, wie mich dünkt, wenigstens nicht ungestaltet. Trüge jemand von euch mich mit sich zu nehmen Belieben, ich schlüge ein, folgte ihm nach, die Reise möchte nun in den Busch oder zu einer Dorfschenke gehen. Auch sollte es euch alle nicht gereuen, das Leben mir geschenkt zu haben. Ihr seid in einem reich versehenen Schlosse; doch alle Schlupfwinkel desselben kennt ihr unmöglich. Ich will sie sämtlich euch zeigen, und tut mir dann, wie ihr meiner Kammerfrau tatet, wenn dies nicht wenigstens um sechstausend Taler euch reicher macht.«

Bösewichter sind Räuber dieser Art freilich, aber *Menschen* bleiben sie dennoch. Das gänzlich Unerwartete in der Baronin Rede, der unbefangene Ton, mit dem sie sprach, die nicht gemeine Schönheit einer jungen, halb entkleideten Frau – alles dies brachte bei Männern, deren Hände noch von eben vergossenem Blute rauchten, eine ganz sonderbare Wirkung hervor. Sie traten zusammen auf einen Haufen und besprachen sich halbleise einige Minuten durch. Ganz allein stand die Baronin jetzt, doch machte sie nicht den geringsten Versuch, zu entfliehen. Sie hörte gar wohl die Worte von zwei oder dreien: »Nieder mit ihr, und das Spiel hat ein Ende!« Aber sie veränderte ihre Farbe kaum, denn der Widerspruch der übrigen entging ihrem feinen spitzenden Ohre ebensowenig, und jetzt trat auch einer, der mutmaßlich Hauptmann der Bande sein mochte, zu ihr.

Er wiederholte zwei- bis dreimal die Frage: Ob man auch buchstäblich ihren Worten trauen dürfte? Ob sie wirklich von ihrem Manne weg- und mit ihnen durchzugehen entschlossen sei? Ob sie bereit wäre, sich einem von ihnen, und wenn er es selber wäre, zum Vergnügen für die wenigen ruhigbleibenden Nächte zu überlassen?

Und als sie dies alles bejaht, als sie den kräftigen Kuss des Räubers geduldet, ja selbst – denn was entschuldigt Not nicht? – erwidert hatte, erging endlich der Befehl an sie: »Nun so komm dann und führe uns herum! Der Teufel trau euch

spies; the one whose skull you worked on so vigorously there was the worst of all. Even the fact that I sleep by myself is a veritable illustration of my husband's jealousy. You see, I am only twenty-two years old and I am, as I think, at least not ungainly. Should one of you like to take me with him, I would agree to the deal, follow him, regardless if the journey should be into the forest or to a village tavern. In addition, you [all] shall not regret having spared my life. You are in a richly bedecked castle; however, it is impossible for you to know all its hiding places. I shall point them out to you in their entirety, and, if this will not make you richer by at least six thousand thalers, you shall do to me what you did unto my chambermaid."

Villains such robbers may be, but they still retain their *humanity*. The entirely unexpected [content] of the baroness's speech, the uninhibited tone with which she spoke, the unusual beauty of a young, half disrobed woman—all this had a decidedly strange effect on the men whose hands were still smoking with the blood which they had just shed. They all clustered together and, in a semi-muted tone, discussed for several minutes. The baroness stood alone by herself now, but she did not undertake the slightest attempt to escape. She was very well able to hear the words of two or three of them: "Let's finish her, and the charade will have an end!" However, she hardly changed color because her fine ears, pricked-up, also did not miss the objection of the rest of them, and just then one of them, presumably the gang's captain, approached her.

Two or three times, he repeated the questions to her: Whether they might be able to trust the literal meaning of her words? Whether she really were determined to leave her husband and run off with them? Whether she were ready to give herself over to one of them, even if it were to himself, for the purpose of enjoyment for the few remaining restful nights?

And when she affirmed all of this, had endured the robber's forceful kiss, even responded to it—for what does distress not excuse—then finally the order was given to her: "Well, then come along and show us around! The devil may trust you

Edelweibern zwar, doch wollen wir es wagen für dies Mal. Nur so viel wisse: bis zur Gurgel spaltet sich dein Kopf, und wenn er zehnmal hübscher noch wäre, in eben dem Augenblick, als wir eine Miene von Entfliehen oder Betrug an dir merken.«

»So wird er nie gespalten! So werde ich, wenn dies nur Bedingung meines Todes wäre, euch alle und selbst den ewig wandernden Juden überleben!«

Lächelnd sagte die Baronin dies, ergriff mit einer Hast, als sei ihr selbst an Plünderung und Entfliehen wer weiß wieviel gelegen, das nächste Licht, führte den ganzen Schwarm in allen Gemächern herum, schloss jede Tür, jeden Schrank und jede Kiste ungefordert auf, half ausleeren und einpacken, scherzte mit der heitersten Laune, sprang gleichgültig über die ermordeten Körper hinweg, sprach zu jedem dieses schändlichsten Gelichters wie zu einem alten Bekannten und bot willig, selbst zur mühsamsten Arbeit, ihr zartes Händchen an.

Silberwerk und Gerätschaften, bares Geld und Geldeswert, Kleinodien und Kleider waren nun zusammengerafft, und der Hauptmann der Bande gab schon zum Abmarsch Befehl, als seine neubestimmte Braut ihn hastig beim Arme ergriff.

»Sagte ich's nicht«, rief sie aus, »dass es euch keineswegs gereuen sollte, an mir eine Freundin gefunden und meines Lebens geschont zu haben? Ihr könnt zwar weidlich ausräumen, wo ihr etwas *offen* findet, aber schade nur, dass bei jedem etwas *verborgen* liegenden Schatze eure Wünschelruten nicht anschlagen!«

»Verborgen? Was? Wo ist noch etwas verborgen?«

»Wie, glaubt ihr denn, dass es in den Schränken, der kostbaren Güter so voll, gar keine heimlichen Fächer geben könne? Merkt auf hier, und ihr werdet dann anders urteilen!«

Sie zeigte auf eine verborgene Feder im Schreibpult ihres Gemahls. Man drückte, sie sprang auf, und sechs Rollen, jede von zweihundert Dukaten, fielen heraus.

»Wetter!« rief der Räuber-Anführer aus, »nun sehe ich, du bist ein braves Weib. Ich will dich halten dafür wie eine kleine Herzogin.«

»Und wohl gar höher noch«, fiel sie lachend ein, »wenn ich noch eines, obschon das letzte von allen, euch sage? Dass ihr

noblewomen, so we shall risk it this time. However, be reminded of this: your head will be split open down to your gut, even if it were ten times as pretty as it is, in the very moment we become aware of any sign of escape or deception."

"Therefore it will never be split! I shall, if this were the only condition for my death, outlive all of you and even the eternally wandering Jew!"

The baroness said this with a smile, then reached for the nearest candle with such haste as if she herself cared who knows how much about plundering and escaping, then led the whole swarm through each and every chamber, opened each door, cabinet and chest without being asked; helped emptying and packing them; cracked jokes in the most cheerful spirits; jumped indifferently over the murdered bodies; addressed each of this most disreputable riff-raff as if they were old acquaintances; and offered her soft little hands for even the most arduous work.

Silver objects and equipment, cash and precious items, jewels and clothes were then snatched up, and the gang's captain was just about to give the order to march out when his newly chosen bride quickly took his arm.

"Didn't I tell you," she called out, "that you shall not regret to have found a friend in me and to have spared my life? You are welcome to thoroughly clean [out] everything where you find something *in plain sight*; it is, however, a pity that your dowsing rods do not strike each time you come across a slightly *hidden* treasure!"

"Hidden? What? Where is there still something hidden?"

"What, do you really believe that these cabinets, so full of precious goods, do not have any secret compartments? Pay attention here, and then you may judge differently!"

She pointed to a hidden spring in her husband's writing desk. They pushed it, it sprang open, and six rolls, each of them containing two hundred ducats, fell out.

"Goodness!" the robber-ringleader called out. "Now I can see that you are a good woman. I shall keep you like a little duchess because of this!"

"And probably even higher," she chimed in, laughing, "when I tell you one more thing, even though it will be last? That you

Kundschafter gehabt, die meines Tyrannen Abwesenheit euch
steckten, das begreif ich wohl. Aber haben diese nicht auch von
den viertausend Gulden, die er vorgestern erst einnahm, ein
Wörtchen euch gesagt?«

»Nicht eine Silbe: Wo sind sie?«

»O gut verwahrt! Unter Schloss und Riegel siebenfach! Ihr
hättet sie und den eisernen Kasten, der sie einschließt, sicher
nicht gefunden, stände meine Wenigkeit nicht mit euch im
Bunde. Mit mir, Kameraden! *Über* der Erde sind wir fertig; nun
mag's auch *unter* dieselbe gehen. Mit mir, in den Keller, sage
ich!«

Die Räuber folgten, aber nicht ohne Vorsicht. An den
Eingang des Kellers, mit einer tüchtigen eisernen Falltür verse-
hen, ward ein Mann zur Schildwache gestellt. Die Baronin gab
auf alles das nicht acht. Immer voran führte sie den Schwarm in
des Kellers äußerste Vertiefung zu einem unterirdischen
Kämmerchen. Sie schloss auf, und der angegebene Kasten stand
in einem Winkel da.

»Hier!« sagte sie und bot dem Hauptmann einen Schlüsselbund
dar: »Hier! Schließ auf und nimm, was du findest, zum
Hochzeitsgeschenk an, wenn du deiner Gefährten Einwilligung
so leicht als die meinige erhältst!«

Der Räuber versuchte einen Schlüssel nach dem andern; keiner passte. Er ward ungeduldig; die Baronin war es noch weit
mehr.

»Weis her!« sprach sie. »Ich hoffe besser und schneller damit
umzugehen. Wahrlich, der Morgen könnte sonst – Ha, sieh da,
nun begreif ich sehr wohl, warum dir und mir es misslang.
Verzeiht! So lieb euer Besuch mir ist, so hat er mich doch, wie
ich gern gestehe, eben dieser Freude, eben dieses Unerwarteten
halber, ein wenig aus der Fassung gebracht. Ich habe den falschen Schlüsselbund vorhin ergriffen. Zwei Minuten Geduld,
und der Fehler soll gehoben sein.«

Sie lief die Treppe hinauf, und ehe jene zwei Minuten vorbei
waren, hörte man schon sie wieder kommen, doch ging sie lang-
samer, gleichsam atemlos von allzu großer bisheriger Eile.
»Gefunden! Gefunden!« rief sie schon von ferne. Jetzt war sie
ungefähr drei Schritte noch von der Schildwache an des Kellers

had spies who tipped you off about my tyrant's absence, I understand well. But did they not also tell a single word about the four thousand guilders, which he received only the day before yesterday?"

"Not a syllable: where are they?"

"Oh, they are stored away safely! Under lock and key, seven times over! You would surely have not found them and the iron chest which holds them, if yours truly were not in league with you. With me, comrades! We are done *above* ground; now we shall proceed *under* ground. With me to the cellar, I say!"

The robbers followed, but not without caution. At the entrance to the cellar, which was equipped with a well-built iron trapdoor, a man was posted to keep watch. The baroness did not pay attention to any of this. Always in the lead, she led the gang into the farthest recesses of the cellar to a little underground chamber. She unlocked it, and there in a corner stood the specified chest.

"Here!" she said and offered the captain a ring of keys: "Here! Unlock and take whatever you find as a wedding present, if you are able to receive your companions' approval as readily as mine!"

The robber tried one key after another: none of them fit. He became impatient; the baroness even more so.

"Give here!" she said. "I hope I can deal with it better and faster! Truly, otherwise the morning may—Huh, look here, now I understand very well why you and I both failed. My sincere apologies! As much as your visit is dear to me, I must readily admit that precisely this joy, precisely this unexpected [pleasure], have flustered me a bit. Earlier, I grabbed the wrong ring of keys. [Give me] two minutes of patience, and the mistake will be remedied."

She ran up the stairs, and before two minutes had passed, they heard her return already, but she went more slowly, breathless, as it were, from too much haste previously. "I found it, I found it!" she even called out from afar. Now she was approximately three steps from the sentry at the entrance to the

Eingang. Aber jetzt sprang sie auch mit einem Sprung auf diesen Elenden los, der eher des Himmels Einsturz als solch einen Überfall sich versah. Ein einziger Stoß aus allen Leibeskräften, und hui flog er die Kellertreppe hinab. In eben dem Nu schlug sie die Falltür zu, schob den Riegel vor und hatte die ganze Bande in den Keller versperrt. Alles dies das Werk eines Augenblicks! Im nächsten flog sie über den Hof des Schlosses und steckte mit dem Lichte in der Hand einen ganz einsam stehenden Schweinestall an. Er loderte auf wie eine Schütte Stroh. Im nahen Dorfe sah der Wächter die Flamme sogleich und machte Lärm. Binnen wenigen Minuten war alles aus den Betten, und eine Menge von Bauern und Knechten eilte aufs Schloss zu. An der Hoftür wartete die Baronin ihrer.

»Dies Geniste zu löschen oder zu verhüten bloß, daß die Flamme nicht weiter greife«, sprach sie, »sind wenige von euch schon genüglich. Aber bewaffnet euch jetzt mit Gewehr, welches ihr in der Rüstkammer meines Gemahls im Überfluss finden werdet, umsetzt die Zuglöcher des Kellers und lasst von dem hineingesperrten Mörder- und Räubergesindel keinen entfliehen!«

Man gehorchte, und es entkam kein einziger der Gefangenschaft und seiner Strafe.

cellar. However, she jumped in one leap at this miserable man, who would have rather expected the sky to collapse than such an ambush. [It only took] one push with all her might and whoosh, he shot down the staircase to the cellar. In just this instant, she slammed the trapdoor shut, pushed the bolt into place and had [thus] locked up the entire gang in the cellar.

All this [was] the work of a moment! In the next, she flew across the courtyard of the castle and, with the candle she held, set fire to a secluded pigsty. It burst into flames like a sheaf of straw. In the nearby village, the watchman right away noticed the flames and sounded the alarm. Within a few minutes, everybody had left their beds, and a crowd of farmers and servants hurried up to the castle. The baroness awaited them at the entrance to the castle.

"To extinguish the flames [at the source of fire] or simply to prevent them from spreading," she said, "a few of you shall suffice. But now arm yourself with the guns which you shall find in abundance in my husband's armory, man the ventilation shafts of the cellar, and do not allow any of the murderers and robbers, those vermin, locked up in the cellar to get away!"

They obeyed, and not a single one evaded his imprisonment and punishment.

FRIEDRICH SCHILLER

Friedrich von Schiller was born on November 10, 1759, in Marbach, Germany. After receiving a sound educational foundation from his father, a retired lieutenant, he was ordered to attend the despotic Duke of Württemberg's military school (infamous for its back-breaking regimentation), where he studied first law and then medicine. Later, he took up an appointment as an assistant medical officer in a nearby regiment.

Having spent his adolescence under the rule of that tyrannical duke, Schiller deeply resented the abuse of power, which became a recurring theme in his literary and dramatic work. His first play in particular, *Die Räuber (The Robbers, 1782)*, was a passionate protest against the rigid conventions of the time and corruption in high places. Schiller was forced to flee from Stuttgart after opening night. He decided first on Mannheim, then on Thuringia, and later returned to Mannheim for a brief period.

In 1787, Schiller set out for Weimar, renowned for its literary circles and the many writers who resided there, among them the famous poet and statesman Johann Wolfgang von Goethe. In 1789, Schiller was appointed professor of History and Philosophy at the nearby University of Jena. The year 1794 marked the beginning of the friendship between Schiller and Goethe, documented in an extensive exchange of letters between those two giants of German literature. Schiller died of tuberculosis at the age of 45 on May 9, 1805, in Weimar, Germany.

Schiller is generally considered the leading German dramatist, poet, and literary theorist, and the second most important

playwright in Europe after William Shakespeare. Among his best-known works are *Die Räuber*, the *Wallenstein* trilogy (1800–1801), and *Wilhelm Tell* (1804). In addition, he translated literary works from Greek, English, French, and Italian, and wrote prose pieces, poems, and histories. Ludwig van Beethoven set Schiller's poem "Ode to Joy" to music in his Ninth Symphony, and the Italian composer Giuseppe Verdi adapted several of Schiller's stage plays for his operas.

The University of Jena, where Schiller held a professorship, is named after him, and virtually every large city in Germany has a Schiller street. The city of Stuttgart holds a Schillerfest every year in the great playwright's memory. A literature prize of the State of Baden-Württemberg, the Schiller Memorial Prize, acknowledges outstanding work in the field of German literature or intellectual history, and is endowed with the impressive sum of 25,000 euros.

Nobel Prize winner Thomas Mann (1955) said about Schiller: "It is not easy to stop once one has begun to talk about Schiller's specific importance." ("Es ist nicht leicht, zu enden, wenn man von Schillers spezifischer Größe einmal zu reden begonnen hat.")

The story "The Criminal of Lost Honor" details how a poor and lazy youth degrades into a hardened criminal beyond redemption...

FRIEDRICH SCHILLER

FRIEDRICH SCHILLER

Der Verbrecher aus verlorener Ehre – Eine wahre Geschichte

In der ganzen Geschichte des Menschen ist kein Kapitel unterrichtender für Herz und Geist als die Annalen seiner Verirrungen. Bei jedem großen Verbrechen war eine verhältnismäßig große Kraft in Bewegung. Wenn sich das geheime Spiel der Begehrungskraft bei dem matteren Licht gewöhnlicher Affekte versteckt, so wird es im Zustand gewaltsamer Leidenschaft desto hervorspringender, kolossalischer, lauter; der feinere Menschenforscher, welcher weiß, wie viel man auf die Mechanik der gewöhnlichen Willensfreiheit eigentlich rechnen darf und wie weit es erlaubt ist, analogisch zu schließen, wird manche Erfahrung aus diesem Gebiet in seine Seelenlehre herübertragen und für das sittliche Leben verarbeiten.

Es ist etwas so Einförmiges und doch wieder so Zusammengesetztes, das menschliche Herz. Eine und eben dieselbe Fertigkeit oder Begierde kann in tausenderlei Formen und Richtungen spielen, kann tausend widersprechende Phänomene bewirken, kann in tausend Charakteren anders gemischt erscheinen, und tausend ungleiche Charaktere und Handlungen können wieder aus einerlei Neigung gesponnen sein, wenn auch der Mensch, von welchem die Rede ist, nichts weniger denn eine solche Verwandtschaft ahndet. Stünde einmal, wie für die

FRIEDRICH SCHILLER

The Criminal of Lost Honor: A True Story

In the entire history of humankind, no chapter has been more educational for the heart and spirit than the chronicles of its aberrations. In the instance of each great crime, a relatively large force was the motivating factor. If the mysterious play of the force of desire is [generally] concealed in the softer light of ordinary emotions, it will be all the more prominent, colossal, [and] perceptible in the state of violent passion; the more discriminating anthropologist, who knows how much we may actually reckon with the mechanism of the common free will and to what degree it is acceptable to deduce analogically, will transfer many an experience from this field into his doctrine of the soul and [then] work them into the doctrine of ethics.

The human heart is something so homogenous, and then again, so multifaceted. One and the same ability or aspiration may express itself in a thousand different styles and directions; it may result in a thousand contradicting phenomena; it may appear in a different combination in a thousand personalities, and then again, a thousand dissimilar personalities and actions may be shaped from one single inclination, even if the person whom we are discussing knows absolutely nothing about such an association. If only a man like Linnäus[1] spoke up for the

---

[1] Carl von Linné, 1707–1778, Swedish naturalist and explorer. (See also Staffan Müller-Wille, "Carolus Linnaeus," *Encyclopedia Brittanica*, 2013, 22 Aug. 2014 <http://www.britannica.com/EBchecked/topic/342526/Carolus-Linnaeus>.)

übrigen Reiche der Natur, auch für das Menschengeschlecht ein Linnäus auf, welcher nach Trieben und Neigungen klassifizierte, wie sehr würde man erstaunen, wenn man so manchen, dessen Laster in einer engen bürgerlichen Sphäre und in der schmalen Umzäunung der Gesetze jetzt ersticken muss, mit dem Ungeheuer Borgia in einer Ordnung beisammen fände. Von dieser Seite betrachtet, lässt sich manches gegen die gewöhnliche Behandlung der Geschichte einwenden, und hier, vermute ich, liegt auch die Schwierigkeit, warum das Studium derselben für das bürgerliche Leben noch immer so fruchtlos geblieben. Zwischen der heftigen Gemütsbewegung des handelnden Menschen und der ruhigen Stimmung des Lesers, welchem diese Handlung vorgelegt wird, herrscht ein so widriger Kontrast, liegt ein so breiter Zwischenraum, dass es dem letztern schwer, ja unmöglich wird, einen Zusammenhang nur zu ahnden. Es bleibt eine Lücke zwischen dem historischen Subjekt und dem Leser, die alle Möglichkeit einer Vergleichung oder Anwendung abschneidet und statt jenes heilsamen Schreckens, der die stolze Gesundheit warnet, ein Kopfschütteln der Befremdung erweckt. Wir sehen den Unglücklichen, der doch in eben der Stunde, wo er die Tat beging, so wie in der, wo er dafür büßet, Mensch war wie wir, für ein Geschöpf fremder Gattung an, dessen Blut anders umläuft als das unsrige, dessen Wille andern Regeln gehorcht als der unsrige; seine Schicksale rühren uns wenig, denn Rührung gründet sich ja nur auf ein dunkles Bewusstsein ähnlicher Gefahr, und wir sind weit entfernt, eine solche Ähnlichkeit auch nur zu träumen. Die Belehrung geht mit der Beziehung verloren, und die Geschichte, anstatt eine Schule der Bildung zu sein, muss sich mit einem armseligen Verdienste um unsre Neugier begnügen. Soll sie uns mehr sein und ihren großen Endzweck erreichen, so muss sie notwendig unter diesen beiden Methoden wählen – Entweder der Leser muss warm werden wie der Held, oder der Held wie der Leser erkalten.

Ich weiß, dass von den besten Geschichtschreibern neuerer Zeit und des Altertums manche sich an die erste Methode gehalten und das Herz ihres Lesers durch hinreißenden Vortrag bestochen haben. Aber diese Manier ist eine Usurpation des

human species as he had for the remaining kingdoms of nature, who would classify [humans] according to impulses and inclinations, we would be very surprised to see many a person, whose vices presently are bound to suffocate in the constricting, bourgeois sphere and the narrow enclosures of the law, to be placed in the same category as the monster Borgia.

Looking at it from this perspective, one may make an objection to the ordinary approach to this story, and I assume therein also lies the difficulty why its study has to this day remained without any consequence for the bourgeois life. Between the intense emotion of the acting individual and the tranquil disposition of the reader to whom this action is presented, there exists such an adverse contrast, there lies such a wide interval, that it is difficult, even impossible, for the latter to perceive a connection. There remains a hiatus between the historical subject and the reader which cuts off any and all opportunities for comparison or adaptation and, instead of that beneficial dismay which alarms the proud health, causes a head-shaking resulting from disconcertment. We regard the unfortunate person, who appeared just as human as we are in the moment when he committed the deed as he was in the moment when he atones for it, as a creature of an unfamiliar species, whose blood runs differently from ours, whose will is subjected to other rules than ours; his fates do not move us much, for the ability to be moved is based merely on the dim realization of comparable peril, and we are far away from even dreaming of such a comparison. The indoctrination gets lost with the [loss of] connection, and the story, instead of providing a forum for edification, has to be content with, as a trifling accomplishment, having earned our curiosity. If it wants to become more [than that] and arrive at its grand ultimate purpose, it necessarily must choose from these two methods—either the reader has to grow heated like the protagonist or the protagonist [must] become cold like the reader.

I recognize that some of the best storywriters of the recent times and [also] of antiquity kept with the first method and captivated their readers' hearts with an enrapturing delivery.

Schriftstellers und beleidigt die republikanische Freiheit des lesenden Publikums, dem es zukommt, selbst zu Gericht zu sitzen; sie ist zugleich eine Verletzung der Grenzengerechtigkeit, denn diese Methode gehört ausschließend und eigentümlich dem Redner und Dichter. Dem Geschichtschreiber bleibt nur die letztere übrig.

Der Held muss kalt werden wie der Leser, oder, was hier ebensoviel sagt, wir müssen mit ihm bekannt werden, ehe er handelt; wir müssen ihn seine Handlung nicht bloß vollbringen sondern auch wollen sehen. An seinen Gedanken liegt uns unendlich mehr als an seinen Taten, und noch weit mehr an den Quellen seiner Gedanken als an den Folgen jener Taten. Man hat das Erdreich des Vesuvs untersucht, sich die Entstehung seines Brandes zu erklären; warum schenkt man einer moralischen Erscheinung weniger Aufmerksamkeit als einer physischen? Warum achtet man nicht in eben dem Grade auf die Beschaffenheit und Stellung der Dinge, welche einen solchen Menschen umgaben, bis der gesammelte Zunder in seinem Inwendigen Feuer fing?

Den Träumer, der das Wunderbare liebt, reizt eben das Seltsame und Abenteuerliche einer solchen Erscheinung; der Freund der Wahrheit sucht eine Mutter zu diesen verlorenen Kindern. Er sucht sie in der unveränderlichen Struktur der menschlichen Seele und in den veränderlichen Bedingungen, welche sie von außen bestimmten, und in diesen beiden findet er sie gewiss. Ihn überrascht es nun nicht mehr, in dem nämlichen Beete, wo sonst überall heilsame Kräuter blühen, auch den giftigen Schierling gedeihen zu sehen, Weisheit und Torheit, Laster und Tugend in einer Wiege beisammen zu finden.

Wenn ich auch keinen der Vorteile hier in Anschlag bringe, welche die Seelenkunde aus einer solchen Behandlungsart der Geschichte zieht, so behält sie schon allein darum den Vorzug, weil sie den grausamen Hohn und die stolze Sicherheit ausrottet, womit gemeiniglich die ungeprüfte aufrechtstehende Tugend auf die gefallene herunterblickt; weil sie den sanften Geist der Duldung verbreitet, ohne welchen kein Flüchtling zurückkehrt, keine Aussöhnung des Gesetzes mit seinem

However, this method represents a usurpation by the writer and insults the republican freedom of the audience of readers, which deserve to render their own judgments; at the same time, it is a violation of equitable boundaries because this method belongs entirely and properly to the orator and poet. The storywriter has to contend with the latter.

The protagonist must become cold like the reader, or, which in the context here means the same, we must become acquainted with him before he acts; not merely do we have to see him perform his actions, but also see his intentions. We are far more interested in his thoughts than in his deeds, and even more on where his thoughts originate than on the consequences of those actions. They have examined the soil around Mount Vesuvius in order to explain how the fire was created; why do we give less attention to an ethical phenomenon than to a physical one? Why don't we pay attention to that same degree, to the quality and condition of objects to be found in the environment of such a human being, until the accumulated tinder inside of him catches fire?

As a matter of fact, the dreamer who loves the miraculous is enticed by the strange and adventurous [character] of such a phenomenon; the lover of truth is seeking for a mother for these lost children. He is looking for them in the changeless structure of the human soul and in the changeable conditions which have defined them externally, and he will certainly find them in both. Subsequently, he is no longer surprised to see, in the same plot of land where otherwise and in all places only healing herbs bloom, there also thrives the poisonous hemlock; [and to] find wisdom and foolishness, vice and virtue together in one cradle.

Even if I do not focus on any of the advantages, which the science of the soul may get from this type of treatment of a story, then I will give the science of soul preference for the simple reason that it has eradicated the malicious contempt and the self-righteous confidence with which the unconfirmed virtue, standing erect, more often than not looks down on the fallen one; because it has disseminated the tender spirit of tolerance, without whom no refugee returns [home], no reconciliation with his insulter can occur, [and] no member of

Beleidiger stattfindet, kein angestecktes Glied der Gesellschaft von dem gänzlichen Brande gerettet wird.

Ob der Verbrecher, von dem ich jetzt sprechen werde, auch noch ein Recht gehabt hätte, an jenen Geist der Duldung zu appellieren? Ob er wirklich ohne Rettung für den Körper des Staats verloren war? – Ich will dem Ausspruch des Lesers nicht vorgreifen. Unsere Gelindigkeit fruchtet ihm nichts mehr, denn er starb durch des Henkers Hand – aber die Leichenöffnung seines Lasters unterrichtet vielleicht die Menschheit und – es ist möglich, auch die Gerechtigkeit.

Christian Wolf war der Sohn eines Gastwirts in einer …schen Landstadt (deren Namen man aus Gründen, die sich in der Folge aufklären, verschweigen muss) und half seiner Mutter, denn der Vater war tot, bis in sein zwanzigstes Jahr die Wirtschaft besorgen. Die Wirtschaft war schlecht, und Wolf hatte müßige Stunden. Schon von der Schule her war er für einen losen Buben bekannt. Erwachsene Mädchen führten Klagen über seine Frechheit, und die Jungen des Städtchens huldigten seinem erfinderischem Kopfe. Die Natur hatte seinen Körper verabsäumt. Eine kleine unscheinbare Figur, krauses Haar von einer unangenehmen Schwärze, eine plattgedrückte Nase und eine geschwollene Oberlippe, welche noch überdies durch den Schlag eines Pferdes aus ihrer Richtung gewichen war, gab seinem Anblick eine Widrigkeit, welche alle Weiber von ihm zurückscheuchte und dem Witz seiner Kameraden eine reichliche Nahrung darbot.

Er wollte ertrotzen, was ihm verweigert war; weil er missfiel, setzte er sich vor zu gefallen. Er war sinnlich und beredete sich, dass er liebe. Das Mädchen, das er wählte, misshandelte ihn; er hatte Ursache, zu fürchten, dass seine Nebenbuhler glücklicher wären; doch das Mädchen war arm. Ein Herz, dass seinen Beteuerungen verschlossen blieb, öffnete sich vielleicht seinen Geschenken, aber ihn selbst drückte Mangel, und der eitle Versuch, seine Außenseite geltend zu machen, verschlang noch das Wenige, was er durch eine schlechte Wirtschaft erwarb. Zu bequem und zu unwissend, einem zerrütteten Hauswesen durch Spekulation aufzuhelfen, zu stolz, auch zu weichlich, den Herrn,

society who has been infected will be completely saved from the disease.

About whether the criminal of whom I am going to talk also would have had the right to appeal to that spirit of tolerance? About whether he was really lost to the body of the state without redemption?—I do not want to get ahead of the reader's verdict. Our gentleness will no longer be of avail to him, for he died by the executioner's hand—However, the postmortem of his vice may be educational to humankind and—possibly—also to justice.

Christian Wolf was the son of an tavern's landlord in a rural town in ... (whose name has to be kept secret for reasons which shall be revealed subsequently) and, because his father had passed away, helped his mother with running the tavern until he had reached twenty years of age. The tavern was going badly, and Wolf had time to be idle. Since the time he attended school, he had been known as a slacker. Grown-up girls complained about his brazenness, and the boys of the little town rendered homage to his ingenious mind. Nature had [sorely] neglected his body. A small, plain physique, wiry hair of an unpleasant blackness, a flattened nose, and a swollen upperlip, which, what is more, had abandoned its straightness as a result of a horse's kick; [these features] bestowed upon him an appearance so repulsive that it made all women recoil from him, and offered plenty of opportunities for his comrades to tease him.

He wanted to obtain by sheer obstinacy what was refused him; because he aroused displeasure, he decided to please. He was sensual and convinced himself that he loved. The girl whom he chose treated him badly; he had reason to believe that his rivals in love would be more fortunate; still, the girl was poor. A heart which may have remained closed to his assertions might open up to his presents; however, he very much lacked means, and the vain attempt to make his outward appearance more becoming ate up what little [means] he had acquired by running the tavern poorly. Too lethargic and too ignorant to put an end to the disorder of his domestic affairs through [business] adventure; too arrogant [and] also too timid to exchange

der er bisher gewesen war, mit dem Bauern zu vertauschen und seiner angebeteten Freiheit zu entsagen, sah er nur einen Ausweg vor sich – den Tausende vor ihm und nach ihm mit besserem Glücke ergriffen haben – den Ausweg, honett zu stehlen. Seine Vaterstadt grenzte an eine landesherrliche Waldung, er wurde Wilddieb, und der Ertrag seines Raubes wanderte treulich in die Hände seiner Geliebten.

Unter den Liebhabern Hannchens war Robert, ein Jägerbursche des Försters. Frühzeitig merkte dieser den Vorteil, den die Freigebigkeit seines Nebenbuhlers über ihn gewonnen hatte, und mit Scheelsucht forschte er nach den Quellen dieser Veränderung. Er zeigte sich fleißiger in der »Sonne« – dies war das Schild zu dem Wirtshaus –, sein lauerndes Auge, von Eifersucht und Neide geschärft, entdeckte ihm bald, woher dieses Geld floss. Nicht lange vorher war ein strenges Edikt gegen die Wildschützen erneuert worden, welches den Übertreter zum Zuchthaus verdammte.

Robert war unermüdet, die geheimen Gänge seines Feindes zu beschleichen; endlich gelang es ihm auch, den Unbesonnenen auf frischer Tat zu ergreifen. Wolf wurde eingezogen, und nur mit Aufopferung seines ganzen kleinen Vermögens brachte er es mühsam dahin, die zuerkannte Strafe durch eine Geldbuße abzuwenden. Robert triumphierte. Sein Nebenbuhler war aus dem Felde geschlagen und Hannchens Gunst für den Bettler verloren. Wolf kannte seinen Feind, und dieser Feind war der glückliche Besitzer seiner Johanna. Drückendes Gefühl des Mangels gesellte sich zu beleidigtem Stolze, Not und Eifersucht stürmen vereinigt auf seine Empfindlichkeit ein, der Hunger treibt ihn hinaus in die weite Welt, Rache und Leidenschaft halten ihn fest. Er wird zum zweitenmal Wilddieb; aber Roberts verdoppelte Wachsamkeit überlistet ihn zum zweitenmal wieder. Jetzt erfährt er die ganze Schärfe des Gesetzes: denn er hat nichts mehr zu geben, und in wenigen Wochen wird er in das Zuchthaus der Residenz abgeliefert.

Das Strafjahr war überstanden, seine Leidenschaft durch die Entfernung gewachsen und sein Trotz unter dem Gewicht des Unglücks gestiegen. Kaum erlangt er die Freiheit, so eilt er nach seinem Geburtsort, sich seiner Johanna zu zeigen. Er erscheint:

the [role of] landlord, which he had assumed up to that time, for [that of] a farmer and renouncing his cherished freedom, he only saw one way out—one which thousands both before him and after him had pursued with better luck—the alternative to steal honorably. His hometown bordered a land-owning lord's forest; he became a poacher, and the proceeds from his spoils wandered faithfully into the hands of his mistress.

Among Hannchen's suitors was Robert, one of the forest ranger's hunting assistants. At an early stage, he noticed the advantage which his rival's generosity had gained on him, and full of envy, he did research into the sources of this transformation. More frequently, he showed up at the "Sun"—this was what the [tavern's] sign said—[and] his furtive eye, sharpened by jealousy and envy, soon revealed to him from whence this stream of money came. Not long before, a strict edict against poachers had been renewed, condemning any transgressor to penal servitude.

Robert tried tirelessy to stalk his enemy when he was on one of his secret errands; finally, he managed to catch the imprudent man red-handed. Wolf was arrested, and only by sacrificing the entirety of his little fortune did he manage just barely to convert the mandated punishment into a monetary penalty. Robert triumphed. His rival in love had been driven from the field, and the beggar had lost Hannchen's affection. Wolf knew his adversary, and this adversary was [now] the cheerful possessor of his Johanna. A depressing feeling of dispossession joined his offended pride; the union of hardship and jealousy overwhelm his vulnerability; lack of food hurries him out into the wide world, revenge and passion hold him down. For a second time, he becomes a poacher; however, Robert's redoubled vigilance outfoxes him for a second time. He now experiences the full severity of the law because he has nothing more to give, and in a few weeks he will be delivered to the penitentiary in the sovereign's capital.

The year of that punishment had been endured; his passion had grown with the distance, and his defiance had increased under the burden of his misfortune. No sooner has he obtained his freedom, then he hurries to his hometown in order to show

man flieht ihn. Die dringende Not hat endlich seinen Hochmut gebeugt und seine Weichlichkeit überwunden – er bietet sich den Reichen des Orts an und will für den Taglohn dienen. Der Bauer zuckt über den schwachen Zärtling die Schultern; der derbe Knochenbau seines handfesten Mitbewerbers sticht ihn bei diesem fühllosen Gönner aus. Er wagt einen letzten Versuch. Ein Amt ist noch ledig, der äußerste verlorne Posten des ehrlichen Namens – er meldet sich zum Hirten des Städtchens, aber der Bauer will seine Schweine keinem Taugenichts anvertrauen. In allen Entwürfen getäuscht, an allen Orten zurückgewiesen, wird er zum drittenmal Wilddieb, und zum drittenmal trifft ihn das Unglück, seinem wachsamen Feind in die Hände zu fallen. Der doppelte Rückfall hat seine Verschuldung erschwert. Die Richter sahen in das Buch der Gesetze, aber nicht einer in die Gemütsverfassung des Beklagten. Das Mandat gegen die Wilddiebe bedurfte einer ernsten und exemplarischen Genugtuung, und Wolf ward verurteilt, das Zeichen des Galgens auf den Rücken gebrannt, drei Jahre auf der Festung zu arbeiten.

Auch diese Periode verlief, und er ging von der Festung – aber ganz anders, als er dahin gekommen war. Hier fängt eine neue Epoche in seinem Leben an; man höre ihn selbst, wie er nachher gegen seinen geistlichen Beistand und vor Gerichte bekannt hat.

»Ich betrat die Festung«, sagte er, »als ein Verirrter und verließ sie als ein Lotterbube. Ich hatte noch etwas in der Welt gehabt, das mir teuer war, und mein Stolz krümmte sich unter der Schande. Wie ich auf die Festung gebracht war, sperrte man mich zu dreiundzwanzig Gefangenen ein, unter denen zwei Mörder und die übrigen alle berüchtigte Diebe und Vagabunden waren. Man verhöhnte mich, wenn ich von Gott sprach, und setzte mir zu, schändliche Lästerungen gegen den Erlöser zu sagen. Man sang mir Hurenlieder vor, die ich, ein liederlicher Bube, nicht ohne Ekel und Entsetzen hörte; aber was ich ausüben sah, empörte meine Schamhaftigkeit noch mehr. Kein Tag verging, wo nicht irgendein schändlicher Lebenslauf wiederholt, irgendein schlimmer Anschlag geschmiedet ward. Anfangs floh ich dieses Volk und verkroch mich vor ihren Gesprächen, so gut mir's möglich war; aber ich brauchte

himself to his Johanna. He appears; everybody flees from him. Finally, the pressing need has dented his pride and triumphed over his wimpishness—he offers himself to the town's affluent and agrees to work as a day laborer. The farmer shrugs his shoulders at the sight of the weak and pampered man; the coarse bone structure of the latter's competitor makes the latter the loser in the eyes of this uncaring employer. He hazards a final attempt. One job is still open, the very last stand of an honorable name—he applies for the post of the town's swineherd, but the farmer does not want to entrust his pigs to the care of a wastrel. Disillusioned by all of his plans, rejected from all places, he becomes a poacher for the third time, and for the third time he meets with the misfortune of falling into the hands of his watchful adversary. The judges looked into the book of laws, but not a single one of them [looked] at the culprit's state of mind. The mandate against the poachers required a solemn and exemplary consequence, and so Wolf was sentenced to three years of working in fortress detention, with the sign of the gallows burned into his back.

This period also passed, and he left the fortress—although completely different from the way in which he had arrived there. Here a new era in his life begins; let us listen to what he confessed later to his spiritual adviser and before the court.

"I entered the fortress," he said, "as an errant, and left it as a scoundrel. I had still possessed something [out there] in the world, which was dear to me, and my pride cringed in the face of the disgrace. When I was brought to the fortress, they locked me up with twenty-three prisoners amongst whom were two murderers, and the rest were all notorious thieves and vagabonds. They ridiculed me when I spoke of God, and they pressed me to utter disgraceful blasphemies against the Savior. They sang to me songs about whores which I, [though] a wanton young man, heard with disgust and shock; however, what I saw them do offended my moral sensibilities even more. Not a day went by without some nefarious biography being recounted, or without a malevolent attack being planned. In the early days, I turned my back on this crowd and avoided their conversations as much as was possible for me; however, I

ein Geschöpf, und die Barbarei meiner Wächter hatte mir auch meinen Hund abgeschlagen. Die Arbeit war hart und tyrannisch, mein Körper kränklich; ich brauchte Beistand, und wenn ich's aufrichtig sagen soll, ich brauchte Bedauerung, und diese musste ich mit dem letzten Überrest meines Gewissens erkaufen. So gewöhnte ich mich endlich an das Abscheulichste, und im letzten Vierteljahr hatte ich meine Lehrmeister übertroffen. Von jetzt an lechzte ich nach dem Tag meiner Freiheit, wie ich nach Rache lechzte. Alle Menschen hatten mich beleidigt, denn alle waren besser und glücklicher als ich. Ich betrachtete mich als den Märtyrer des natürlichen Rechts und als ein Schlachtopfer der Gesetze. Zähneknirschend rieb ich meine Ketten, wenn die Sonne hinter meinem Festungsberg heraufkam; eine weite Aussicht ist zwiefache Hölle für einen Gefangenen. Der freie Zugwind, der durch die Luftlöcher meines Turmes pfeifte, und die Schwalbe, die sich auf dem eisernen Stab meines Gitters niederließ, schienen mich mit ihrer Freiheit zu necken und machten mir meine Gefangenschaft desto grässlicher. Damals gelobte ich unversöhnlichen, glühenden Hass allem, was dem Menschen gleicht, und was ich gelobte, hab' ich redlich gehalten.

»Mein erster Gedanke, sobald ich mich frei sah, war meine Vaterstadt. So wenig auch für meinen künftigen Unterhalt da zu hoffen war, so viel versprach sich mein Hunger nach Rache. Mein Herz klopfte wilder, als der Kirchturm von weitem aus dem Gehölze stieg. Es war nicht mehr das herzliche Wohlbehagen, wie ich's bei meiner ersten Wallfahrt empfunden hatte. – Das Andenken alles Ungemachs, aller Verfolgungen, die ich dort einst erlitten hatte, erwachte mit einemmal aus einem schrecklichen Todesschlaf, alle Wunden bluteten wieder, alle Narben gingen auf. Ich verdoppelte meine Schritte, denn es erquickte mich im voraus, meine Feinde durch meinen plötzlichen Anblick in Schrecken zu setzen, und ich dürstete jetzt ebenso sehr nach neuer Erniedrigung, als ich ehemals davor gezittert hatte.

»Die Glocken läuteten zur Vesper, als ich mitten auf dem Markt stand. Die Gemeinde wimmelte zur Kirche. Man erkannte mich schnell, jedermann, der mir aufstieß, trat scheu zurück. Ich hatte von jeher die kleinen Kinder sehr lieb gehabt,

needed human contact, and, besides, the barbarity of my guards had deprived me [even] of my dog. The labor was hard and tyrannical, [and] my body was in poor health; I needed support, and if I must be truthful, I was in need of compassion, and this I was forced to acquire by shedding the last remaining shred of my sense of right and wrong. Therefore in due course I got accustomed to [even] the most nauseating [acts], and by the last three months I had surpassed my mentors. From that time on I thirsted for revenge as much as I thirsted for the day of freedom. All of humankind had offended me, for all [of them] were better and happier than I. I regarded myself as a martyr of the natural order and a victim of the laws. Teeth clenching, I shook my chains when the sun was rising behind the mountain of my fortress; for a prisoner, a panoramic view is two times the hell. The draft of free air which whistled through the holes in my tower, and the swallow which came to rest on the iron rod of my barred window, seemed to be teasing me with their freedom and made my incarceration all the more dreadful. In those days I pledged unforgiving, incandescent hatred unto everything concerning humankind, and what I pledged I faithfully upheld.

"My first thought, as soon as I was free, was of my hometown. Though I had little hope of finding a livelihood there for the future, my hunger for revenge expected much prospect. My heart began to beat wilder when the church tower emerged from the forest afar. It was no longer the cordial and comfortable feeling that I had experienced on the occasion of my first pilgrimage.—The memory of all the adversities [and] all the persecution which I had once suffered there awoke from its horrible sleep of death; all my wounds began to bleed again [and] all my scars broke open. I redoubled my steps, for it revitalized me in anticipation of putting the fear of God into my adversaries by my sudden appearance, and I was thirsting as much for fresh humiliation as formerly I had shaken with fear in the face of it.

"The vesper bells rang out when I stood in the center of the marketplace. The community was swarming to church. Quickly, they recognized me [and] everyone who encountered me stepped back timidly. I had always felt a strong love for little

und auch jetzt übermannte mich's unwillkürlich, dass ich einem
Knaben, der neben mir vorbeihüpfte, einen Groschen bot. Der
Knabe sah mich einen Augenblick starr an und warf mir den
Groschen ins Gesicht. Wäre mein Blut nur etwas ruhiger gewesen, so hätte ich mich erinnert, dass der Bart, den ich noch von
der Festung mitbrachte, meine Gesichtszüge bis zum Grässlichen
entstellte – aber mein böses Herz hatte meine Vernunft ange-
steckt. Tränen, wie ich sie nie geweint hatte, liefen über meine
Backen.

»›Der Knabe weiß nicht, wer ich bin, noch woher ich
komme‹, sagte ich halblaut zu mir selbst, ›und doch meidet er
mich wie ein schändliches Tier. Bin ich denn irgendwo auf der
Stirn gezeichnet, oder habe ich aufgehört, einem Menschen
ähnlich zu sehen, weil ich fühle, dass ich keinen mehr lieben
kann?‹ – Die Verachtung dieses Knaben schmerzte mich bitterer
als dreijähriger Galliotendienst, denn ich hatte ihm Gutes getan
und konnte ihn keines persönlichen Hasses beschuldigen.

»Ich setzte mich auf einen Zimmerplatz, der Kirche gegenüber; was ich eigentlich wollte, weiß ich nicht; doch ich weiß
noch, dass ich mit Erbitterung aufstand, als von allen meinen
vorübergehenden Bekannten keiner mich nur eines Grußes
gewürdigt hatte, auch nicht einer. Unwillig verließ ich meinen
Standort, eine Herberge aufzusuchen; als ich an der Ecke einer
Gase umlenkte, rannte ich gegen meine Johanna. ›Sonnenwirt!‹
schrie sie laut auf und machte eine Bewegung, mich zu umarmen. ›Du wieder da, lieber Sonnenwirt! Gott sei Dank, dass du
wiederkommst!‹ Hunger und Elend sprach aus ihrer Bedeckung,
eine schändliche Krankheit aus ihrem Gesichte; ihr Anblick
verkündigte die verworfenste Kreatur, zu der sie erniedrigt war.
Ich ahndete schnell, was hier geschehen sein möchte; einige
fürstliche Dragoner, die mir eben begegnet waren, ließen mich
erraten, dass Garnison in dem Städtchen lag.

›Soldatendirne!‹ rief ich und drehte ihr lachend den Rücken
zu. Es tat mir wohl, dass noch ein Geschöpf unter mir war im
Rang der Lebendigen. Ich hatte sie niemals geliebt.

»Meine Mutter war tot. Mit meinem kleinen Hause hatten
sich meine Kreditoren bezahlt gemacht. Ich hatte niemand und
nichts mehr. Alle Welt floh mich wie einen Giftigen, aber ich

children, and even then I was so overwhelmed by it that I offered a penny to a boy who skipped by me. The boy looked at me with a frozen look on his face for a moment, and [then] threw the penny into my face. If my blood have been [running] only a little more calmly, I would have remembered that the beard which I still wore from my [time at the] fortress distorted my face most hideously—however, my evil heart had infected my rationality. Tears that I had never shed before, ran down my cheeks.

" 'The boy does not know who I am, nor where I come from,' I said to myself in a low voice, 'and still, he avoids me like a disgraceful animal. Do I wear a sign somewhere on my forehead, or have I ceased to look like a human being because I sense that I am no longer able to love anybody?' This little boy's contempt pained me more bitterly than the three years of compulsory labor, because I had given him a gift and could not accuse him of a personal hatred.

"I sat down on a place for the squaring of timber, opposite the church; I don't recall what I actually wanted; although, I do remember that I rose with bitterness after none of my acquaintances who had been passing by had given me a greeting; not a single one. Indignantly, I left my location in order to find an tavern; when I turned at the corner of an alley, I ran into my Johanna. 'The Sun's landlord!' she cried out loudly and made a motion to embrace me. 'You here again, dear Sun's landlord! Thank God that you have returned!' Her clothes bespoke hunger and hardship, [and] her face a shameful disease; her appearance announced the depravity of the creature to which she had been degraded. I quickly discerned what might have happened here; the few of the Prince's dragoons whom I had just encountered made me guess that a garrison was stationed in the little town.

'You soldiers' wench!' I called out and turned my back, laughing. It felt good that there was still a creature lower than me in the ranks of the living. I had never loved her.

"My mother had died. My debtors had repaid themselves with my little house. I had nobody and nothing anymore. The entire world shunned me like a poisonous man, but at last I had

hatte endlich verlernt, mich zu schämen. Vorher hatte ich mich dem Anblick der Menschen entzogen, weil Verachtung mir unerträglich war. Jetzt drang ich mich auf und ergötzte mich, sie zu verscheuchen. Es war mir wohl, weil ich nichts mehr zu verlieren und nichts mehr zu hüten hatte. Ich brauchte keine gute Eigenschaft mehr, weil man keine mehr bei mir vermutete.

»Die ganze Welt stand mir offen, ich hätte vielleicht in einer fremden Provinz für einen ehrlichen Mann gegolten, aber ich hatte den Mut verloren, es auch nur zu scheinen. Verzweiflung und Schande hatten mir endlich diese Sinnesart aufgezwungen. Es war die letzte Ausflucht, die mir übrig war, die Ehre entbehren zu lernen, weil ich an keine mehr Anspruch machen durfte. Hätten meine Eitelkeit und mein Stolz meine Erniedrigung erlebt, so hätte ich mich selber entleiben müssen.

»Was ich nunmehr eigentlich beschlossen hatte, war mir selber noch unbekannt. Ich wollte Böses tun, soviel erinnere ich mich noch dunkel. Ich wollte mein Schicksal verdienen. Die Gesetze, meinte ich, wären Wohltaten für die Welt, also fasste ich den Vorsatz, sie zu verletzen; ehemals hatte ich aus Notwendigkeit und Leichtsinn gesündigt, jetzt tat ich's aus freier Wahl zu meinem Vergnügen.

»Mein Erstes war, dass ich mein Wildschießen fortsetzte. Die Jagd überhaupt war mir nach und nach zur Leidenschaft geworden, und außerdem musste ich ja leben. Aber dies war es nicht allein; es kitzelte mich, das fürstliche Edikt zu verhöhnen und meinem Landesherrn nach allen Kräften zu schaden. Ergriffen zu werden, besorgte ich nicht mehr, denn jetzt hatte ich eine Kugel für meinen Entdecker bereit, und das wusste ich, dass mein Schuss seinen Mann nicht fehlte. Ich erlegte alles Wild, das mir aufstieß, nur weniges machte ich auf der Grenze zu Gelde, das meiste ließ ich verwesen. Ich lebte kümmerlich, um nur den Aufwand an Blei und Pulver zu bestreiten. Meine Verheerungen in der großen Jagd wurden ruchbar, aber mich drückte kein Verdacht mehr. Mein Anblick löschte ihn aus. Mein Name war vergessen.

»Diese Lebensart trieb ich mehrere Monate. Eines Morgens hatte ich nach meiner Gewohnheit das Holz durchstrichen, die Fährte eines Hirsches zu verfolgen. Zwei Stunden hatte ich

forgotten how to be ashamed. Until that time, I had kept out of the sight of other people because [their] contempt was unbearable to me. Now I forced myself upon them and delighted in scaring them away. It felt good because I had nothing to lose and nothing to guard anymore. No longer did I require good attributes, because they no longer assumed that I had any.

"The whole world was open to me; I might have been perceived as an honest man in a foreign province, but I had lost the courage even to appear as such. Desperation and dishonor finally had forced this point of view upon me. It was the last resort open to me; to learn how to live without honor, because I was no longer allowed to claim it. If my vanity and my pride had experienced my degradation, I would have had been forced to take my own life.

"What I had decided to do henceforth was still unknown to me. I wanted to perform wicked acts; that much I still dimly remember. I wanted to deserve my destiny. The laws, I thought, were intended to be a boon for the world, ergo I made a resolve to break them; in earlier days, I had sinned out of necessity and recklessness; now I did it out of free will, for my pleasure.

"The first thing I did was to continue with poaching. Little by little, I had become passionate about hunting in general and, after all, I had to live. However, it was not merely that; I was titillated by the thought of mocking the princely proclamation and doing harm to my sovereign with all my strength. I no longer cared about being captured, because now I had a bullet ready for my discoverer, and I was sure that my shot would not miss the man. I shot all the game which I hunted up; I turned only a little of it into money at the border, most of it I left to rot. I lived meagerly in order to pay the expenses for lead and gunpowder. My ravages in the big game hunt became known, but I was no longer touched by any suspicion. The sight of me obliterated it. My name had been forgotten.

"For several months, I pursued this lifestyle. One morning, I had been roaming the forest, as I usually did, following the tracks of a stag. I had tired myself out in vain for two hours and was already beginning to give up my prey as lost to me, when

mich vergeblich ermüdet, und schon fing ich an, meine Beute
verloren zu geben, als ich sie auf einmal in schussgerechter
Entfernung entdecke. Ich will anschlagen und abdrücken – aber
plötzlich erschreckt mich der Anblick eines Hutes, der wenige
Schritte vor mir auf der Erde liegt. Ich forsche genauer und
erkenne den Jäger Robert, der hinter dem dicken Stamm einer
Eiche auf eben das Wild anschlägt, dem ich den Schuss bestimmt
hatte. Eine tödliche Kälte fährt bei diesem Anblick durch meine
Gebeine. Just das war der Mensch, den ich unter allen lebendigen Dingen am grässlichsten hasste, und dieser Mensch war in
die Gewalt meiner Kugel gegeben. In diesem Augenblick dünkte
mich's, als ob die ganze Welt in meinem Flintenschuss läge und
der Hass meines ganzen Lebens in die einzige Fingerspitze sich
zusammendrängte, womit ich den mörderischen Druck tun
sollte. Eine unsichtbare fürchterliche Hand schwebte über mir,
der Stundenweiser meines Schicksals zeigte unwiderruflich auf
diese schwarze Minute. Der Arm zitterte mir, da ich meiner
Flinte die schreckliche Wahl erlaubte – meine Zähne schlugen
zusammen wie im Fieberfrost, und der Atem sperrte sich erstick-
end in meiner Lunge. Eine Minute lang blieb der Lauf meiner
Flinte ungewiss zwischen dem Menschen und dem Hirsch mitten inne schwanken – eine Minute – und noch eine – und wieder
eine. Rache und Gewissen rangen hartnäckig und zweifelhaft,
aber die Rache gewann's, und der Jäger lag tot am Boden.

»Mein Gewehr fiel mit dem Schusse ... ›Mörder‹ ...stammelte
ich langsam – der Wald war still wie ein Kirchhof – ich hörte
deutlich, dass ich ›Mörder‹ sagte. Als ich näher schlich, starb
der Mann. Lange stand ich sprachlos vor dem Toten, ein helles
Gelächter endlich machte mir Luft. ›Wirst du jetzt reinen Mund
halten, guter Freund!‹ sagte ich und trat keck hin, indem ich
zugleich das Gesicht des Ermordeten auswärts kehrte. Die
Augen standen ihm weit auf. Ich wurde ernsthaft und schwieg
plötzlich wieder stille. Es fing mir an, seltsam zu werden.

»Bis hierher hatte ich auf Rechnung meiner Schande gefre-
velt; jetzt war etwas geschehen, wofür ich noch nicht gebüßt
hatte. Eine Stunde vorher, glaube ich, hätte mich kein Mensch
überredet, dass es noch etwas Schlechteres als mich unter dem

suddenly I come upon it at a distance convenient for a shot. I get ready and am just about to shoot—but I am startled all of a sudden by the sight of a hat lying on the ground in front of me, only a few steps away. I take a closer look and recognize Robert, the huntsman who, behind the broad trunk of an oak tree, is aiming at precisely the quarry that I had elected for my shot. At this sight, a deathlike chill runs through my bones. There was exactly the man whom I hated most dreadfully amongst all living things, and this man was given into the control of my bullet. In this moment, it appeared to me as if the whole world were contained in my gunshot, and [as if] my entire life's hatred was concentrated in the single fingertip with which I was going to perform the murderous squeeze. An invisible, frightful hand was hanging over me, [and] the hour hand of my destiny once and for all pointed to this black moment. My arm was shaking because I had given my shotgun permission to carry out the horrifying choice—my teeth were chattering as if in a feverish chill and my breath was locked in my lungs, threatening to suffocate me. For a [whole] minute, the barrel of my shotgun was swinging back and forth indecisively between the man and the stag—one minute—and another one—and yet another one. Revenge and conscience were struggling unwaveringly and uncertainly, but revenge won out and the huntsman lay on the ground, dead.

"My shotgun sagged down at the same moment as the shot rang out... 'Murderer'... I stammered haltingly—the forest was silent as a churchyard—I clearly heard myself say 'Murderer'. As I crept closer, the man died. Speechless, I stood before the dead man for a long time; finally, ringing laughter enabled me to let off steam. 'Will you now keep your mouth shut, dear friend!' I said and, cheekily, I stepped closer, while I turned the murderered man's face away. His eyes were wide open. I became serious and fell silent again. I began to feel strange.

"Till then, I had poached in retaliation for my disgrace; now something had happened for which I had not yet atoned. An hour earlier, I had thought that nobody could persuade me that there was somebody under the sun more evil than I; now I was

Himmel gebe; jetzt fing ich an zu mutmaßen, dass ich vor einer Stunde wohl gar zu beneiden war.

»Gottes Gerichte fielen mir nicht ein – wohl aber eine, ich weiß nicht welche? verwirrte Erinnerung an Strang und Schwert und die Exekution einer Kindermörderin, die ich als Schuljunge mit angesehen hatte. Etwas ganz besonders Schreckbares lag für mich in dem Gedanken, dass von jetzt an mein Leben verwirkt sei. Auf mehreres besinne ich mich nicht mehr. Ich wünschte gleich darauf, dass er noch lebte. Ich tat mir Gewalt an, mich lebhaft an alles Böse zu erinnern, das mir der Tote im Leben zugefügt hatte, aber sonderbar! mein Gedächtnis war wie ausgestorben. Ich konnte nichts mehr von alledem hervorrufen, was mich vor einer Viertelstunde zum Rasen gebracht hatte. Ich begriff gar nicht, wie ich zu dieser Mordtat gekommen war.

»Noch stand ich vor der Leiche, noch immer. Das Knallen einiger Peitschen und das Geknarre von Frachtwagen, die durchs Holz fuhren, brachte mich zu mir selbst. Es war kaum eine Viertelmeile abseits der Heerstraße, wo die Tat geschehen war. Ich musste auf meine Sicherheit denken.

»Unwillkürlich verlor ich mich tiefer in den Wald. Auf dem Wege fiel mir ein, dass der Entleibte sonst eine Taschenuhr besessen hätte. Ich brauchte Geld, um die Grenze zu erreichen – und doch fehlte mir der Mut, nach dem Platz umzuwenden, wo der Tote lag. Hier erschreckte mich ein Gedanke an den Teufel und eine Allgegenwart Gottes. Ich raffte meine ganze Kühnheit zusammen; entschlossen, es mit der ganzen Hölle aufzunehmen, ging ich nach der Stelle zurück. Ich fand, was ich erwartet hatte, und in einer grünen Börse noch etwas weniges über einen Taler an Gelde. Eben da ich beides zu mir stecken wollte, hielt ich plötzlich ein und überlegte. Es war keine Anwandlung von Scham, auch nicht Furcht, mein Verbrechen durch Plünderung zu vergrößern – Trotz, glaube ich, war es, dass ich die Uhr wieder von mir warf und von dem Gelde nur die Hälfte behielt. Ich wollte für einen persönlichen Feind des Erschossenen, aber nicht für seinen Räuber gehalten sein.

»Jetzt floh ich waldeinwärts. Ich wusste, dass das Holz sich vier deutsche Meilen nordwärts erstreckte und dort an die Grenzen des Landes stieß. Bis zum hohen Mittage lief ich atemlos.

beginning to speculate that I might even have been the subject of envy an hour earlier.

"I could not recall any judgments of God—but a perhaps confusing memory, I don't know exactly which, of a death-cord and a sword, and of the execution of a child murderess, which I had witnessed as a schoolboy. The thought that my life might be forfeited from now on had an outrageously dreadful quality. I cannot recall anything else. Immediately after that, I wished that he was still alive. I strained terribly to remember in vivid detail all the evil things the dead man had inflicted upon me when still alive, but, strangely, my memory [of these] seemed to be wiped out. I was unable to recall anything which had driven me into a rage [only] a quarter of an hour ago. I could not understand at all how I had arrived at this murderous deed.

"I was still standing before the corpse. Several whip-cracks and the squeaking of freight wagons driving through the forest brought me back [to my senses]. The deed had happened hardly a quarter of a mile away from the military road. I had to consider my own safety.

"Instinctively I disappeared deeper into the forest. On my way, I remembered that the murdered man had habitually carried a pocket watch. I was in need of money to reach the border—nonetheless, I did not have the courage to turn back to the scene where the dead man lay. Considering this, I was frightened by the notion of the Devil and the omnipresence of God. I gathered all of my courage [and], determined to take on all of Hell, I returned to the place. I found what I had expected, and in a green purse [I discovered] a little over a thaler in currency. I was just about to pocket both, when suddenly I paused and deliberated. It was not [because of] an attack of shame, and neither was it fear to make my crime worse by spoliation—I believe it was out of defiance that I threw away the watch and kept only half of the money. I wanted to be regarded as the man's personal enemy, but not as his robber.

"Afterwards I fled into the woods. I knew that the forest stretched out for four German miles to the north, and there it touched the border of the state. Until high noon I ran without

Die Eilfertigkeit meiner Flucht hatte meine Gewissensangst zerstreut, aber sie kam schrecklicher zurück, wie meine Kräfte mehr und mehr ermatteten. Tausend grässliche Gestalten gingen an mir vorüber und schlugen wie schneidende Messer in meine Brust. Zwischen einem Leben voll rastloser Todesfurcht und einer gewaltsamen Entleibung war mir jetzt eine schreckliche Wahl gelassen, und ich musste wählen. Ich hatte das Herz nicht, durch Selbstmord aus der Welt zu gehen, und entsetzte mich vor der Aussicht, darin zu bleiben. Geklemmt zwischen die gewissen Qualen des Lebens und die ungewissen Schrecken der Ewigkeit, gleich unfähig zu leben und zu sterben, brachte ich die sechste Stunde meiner Flucht dahin, eine Stunde, vollgepresst von Qualen, wovon noch kein lebendiger Mensch zu erzählen weiß.

»In mich gekehrt und langsam, ohne mein Wissen den Hut tief ins Gesichte gedrückt, als ob mich dies vor dem Auge der leblosen Natur hätte unkenntlich machen können, hatte ich unvermerkt einen schmalen Fußsteig verfolgt, der mich durch das dunkelste Dickicht führte – als plötzlich eine rauhe befehlende Stimme vor mir her: ›Halt!‹ rufte. Die Stimme war ganz nahe, meine Zerstreuung und der heruntergedrückte Hut hatten mich verhindert, um mich herum zu schauen. Ich schlug die Augen auf und sah einen wilden Mann auf mich zukommen, der eine große knotigte Keule trug. Seine Figur ging ins Riesenmäßige – meine erste Bestürzung wenigstens hatte mich dies glauben gemacht – und die Farbe seiner Haut war von einer gelben Mulattenschwärze, woraus das Weiße eines schielenden Auges bis zum Grausen hervortrat. Er hatte statt eines Gurts ein dickes Seil zwiefach um einen grünen wollenen Rock geschlagen, worin ein breites Schlachtmesser bei einer Pistole stak. Der Ruf wurde wiederholt, und ein kräftiger Arm hielt mich fest. Der Laut eines Menschen hatte mich in Schrecken gejagt, aber der Anblick eines Bösewichts gab mir Herz. In der Lage, worin ich jetzt war, hatte ich Ursache, vor jedem redlichen Mann, aber keine mehr, vor einem Räuber zu zittern.

»›Wer da?‹ sagte diese Erscheinung.

»›Deinesgleichen‹, war meine Antwort, ›wenn du der wirklich bist, dem du gleich siehst!‹

»›Dahinaus geht der Weg nicht. Was hast du hier zu suchen?‹

pausing for breath. The hastiness of my escape had dissipated the agony of my conscience, but it returned more dreadfully as my strength waned more and more. A thousand frightful spectres rushed past me and, like razor-sharp daggers, plunged into my bosom. Caught between a life replete with a restless fear of dying and of a violent death by my own hand, I was left with a horrifying choice, and I was compelled to choose. I did not have the courage to leave this world by suicide, and was terrified at the prospect of having to stay in it. Trapped between the certain torments of life and the uncertain terrors of eternity, equally incapable of living or of dying, I passed the sixth hour of my escape, one hour, squeezed by agony of which no living man has been able to tell.

"My gaze turned inward and, with the hat pushed deeply [down] over my face without my knowing it, as if this had obliterated me before the eyes of inanimate nature, I was following a narrow footpath, unnoticed, which led me through the darkest undergrowth—when, suddenly, a rough and commanding voice from in front of me called 'Halt!' The voice was very close to me; my absentmindedness and the pulled down hat had prevented me from looking around. I looked up and saw a wild fellow with a big nobbly bludgeon advance toward me. His figure had a propensity toward the giant—at least I believed this in my initial consternation—and the color of his skin resembled a yellowish quadroon black from which the white of a lazy eye protruded, which filled me with horror. In place of a belt, around his green woolen jacket he had twice wound a thick rope, in which was stuck a butcher's knife with a broad blade, next to a pistol. The call was repeated, and a strong arm held me fast. The sound of a human being had frightened me, but the sight of a villain made me take heart. In my present situation I had reason to tremble before any honest man, but none before a robber.

" 'Who is there?' the apparition said.

" 'One of your kind,' I countered, 'if you are, in fact, whom you bear a resemblance to!'

" 'That is not the way out [of the woods]. What business have you got for being here?'

»›Was hast du hier zu fragen?‹ versetzte ich trotzig.

»Der Mann betrachtete mich zweimal vom Fuß bis zum Wirbel. Es schien, als ob er meine Figur gegen die seinige und meine Antwort gegen meine Figur halten wollte –

›Du sprichst brutal wie ein Bettler‹, sagte er endlich.

»›Das mag sein. Ich bin's noch gestern gewesen.‹

»Der Mann lachte. ›Man sollte darauf schwören‹, rief er, ›du wolltest auch noch jetzt für nichts Bessers gelten.‹

»›Für etwas Schlechteres also‹ – Ich wollte weiter.

»›Sachte Freund! Was jagt dich denn so? Was hast du für Zeit zu verlieren?‹

»Ich besann mich einen Augenblick. Ich weiß nicht, wie mir das Wort auf die Zunge kam: ›Das Leben ist kurz‹, sagte ich langsam, ›und die Hölle währt ewig.‹

»Er sah mich stier an. ›Ich will verdammt sein‹, sagte er endlich, ›oder du bist irgend an einem Galgen hart vorbeigestreift.‹

»›Das mag wohl noch kommen. Also auf Wiedersehen, Kamerad!‹

»›Topp, Kamerad!‹ schrie er, indem er eine zinnerne Flasche aus seiner Jagdtasche hervorlangte, einen kräftigen Schluck daraus tat und mir sie reichte. Flucht und Beängstigung hatten meine Kräfte aufgezehrt, und diesen ganzen entsetzlichen Tag war noch nichts über meine Lippen gekommen. Schon fürchtete ich, in dieser Waldgegend zu verschmachten, wo auf drei Meilen in der Runde kein Labsal für mich zu hoffen war. Man urteile, wie froh ich auf diese angebotene Gesundheit Bescheid tat. Neue Kraft floss mit diesem Erquicktrunk in meine Gebeine und frischer Mut in mein Herz, und Hoffnung und Liebe zum Leben. Ich fing an, zu glauben, dass ich doch wohl nicht ganz elend wäre; so viel konnte dieser willkommene Trank. Ja, ich bekenne es, mein Zustand grenzte wieder an einen glücklichen, denn endlich, nach tausend fehlgeschlagenen Hoffnungen, hatte ich eine Kreatur gefunden, die mir ähnlich schien. In dem Zustande, worein ich versunken war, hätte ich mit dem höllischen Geiste Kameradschaft getrunken, um einen Vertrauten zu haben.

»Der Mann hatte sich aufs Gras hingestreckt, ich tat ein gleiches.

" 'What business have you got for asking me?' I replied defiantly.

"The man looked at me from head to toe, twice. It appeared as if he wanted to compare my appearance with his, and my answer with my appearance—

" 'You are talking crudely, like a beggar,' he finally said.

" 'That may be so. Until yesterday, I still was one.'

"The man laughed. 'One could swear to it,' he called out, 'that you still don't want to be taken for anything better.'

" 'For something worse, then'—I was getting ready to move on.

" 'Slow down, my friend! What is haunting you? What have you got to lose?'

"I contemplated this for a moment. I don't know how the words found their way into my mouth: 'Life is short,' I said slowly, 'and Hell lasts for eternity.'

"He looked at me hard. 'I shall be damned,' he said finally, 'if you didn't miss the gallows by a hair somehow.'

" 'That may still be waiting in the wings. Well, good-bye then, comrade!'

" 'It's a go, comrade!' he hollered as he reached for a pewter bottle in his hunting bag, took a large gulp from it, and handed it to me. The escape and my trepidations had used up my strength completely, and nothing had passed my lips all day. I was beginning to fear that I would fade away in these woodlands where I could not hope for any refreshment within a three-mile radius. [You may] judge for yourself how happily I responded to the toast offered to me. With this refreshing drink, new vigor poured into my bones and fresh courage into my heart, and a love for life. I began to believe that I was probably not too miserable: this welcome drink was able to accomplish all of this. Yes, I confess to it—my situation was verging on a happy one again because finally, after a thousand dashed hopes, I had encountered a creature which appeared to bear a resemblance to me. In the condition to which I had sunk, I would have drunk to close friendship with the Infernal Spirit, [merely] to have a confidant.

"The man had stretched out on the grass, and I did likewise.

»›Dein Trunk hat mir wohlgetan!‹ sagte ich. ›Wir müssen bekannter werden.‹

»Er schlug Feuer, seine Pfeife zu zünden.

»›Treibst du das Handwerk schon lange?‹

»Er sah mich fest an. ›Was willst du damit sagen?‹

»›War das schon oft blutig?‹ Ich zog das Messer aus seinem Gürtel.

»›Wer bist du?‹ sagte er schrecklich und legte die Pfeife von sich.

»›Ein Mörder wie du – aber nur erst ein Anfänger.‹

»Der Mensch sah mich steif an und nahm seine Pfeife wieder.

»›Du bist nicht hier zu Hause?‹ sagte er endlich.

»›Drei Meilen von hier. Der Sonnenwirt in L..., wenn du von mir gehöret hast.‹

»Der Mann sprang auf wie ein Besessner. ›Der Wildschütze Wolf?‹ schrie er hastig.

»›Der nämliche.‹

»›Willkommen, Kamerad! Willkommen!‹ rief er und schüttelte mir kräftig die Hände. ›Das ist brav, dass ich dich endlich habe, Sonnenwirt. Jahr und Tag schon sinn' ich darauf, dich zu kriegen. Ich kenne dich recht gut. Ich weiß um alles. Ich habe lange auf dich gerechnet.‹

»›Auf mich gerechnet? Wozu denn?‹

»›Die ganze Gegend ist voll von dir. Du hast Feinde, ein Amtmann hat dich gedrückt, Wolf. Man hat dich zu Grund gerichtet, himmelschreiend ist man mit dir umgegangen.‹

»Der Mann wurde hitzig – ›Weil du ein paar Schweine geschossen hast, die der Fürst auf unsern Äckern und Feldern füttert, haben sie dich Jahre lang im Zuchthaus und auf der Festung herumgezogen, haben sie dich um Haus und Wirtschaft bestohlen, haben sie dich zum Bettler gemacht. Ist es dahin gekommen, Bruder, dass der Mensch nicht mehr gelten soll als ein Hase? Sind wir nicht besser als das Vieh auf dem Felde? – Und ein Kerl wie du konnte das dulden?‹

»›Konnt' ich's ändern?‹

»›Das werden wir ja wohl sehen. Aber sage mir doch, woher kömmst du denn jetzt, und was führst du im Schilde?‹

" 'Your libation has done me good!' I said to him. 'We must become better acquainted.'

"He struck a match to light his pipe.

" 'Have you been in this line of trade for a long time?'

"He looked at me closely. 'What are you inferring?'

" 'Has this been bloody many times?' I pulled the knife from his belt.

" 'Who are you?' he said in a frightening tone and put the pipe away.

" 'A murderer like you—but merely a beginner.'

"The man looked at me stiffly and picked up his pipe again.

" 'You are not from here?' he finally said.

" 'Three miles from here. The Sun's landlord in L... in case you have heard of me.'

"The man jumped up like one possessed. 'Wolf the Poacher?' he shouted abruptly.

" 'The same.'

" 'Welcome, comrade! Welcome!' he called out and shook my hands wildly. 'That is a good thing that I finally have got you, the Sun's landlord. For years and years I have pondered how to get you. I know you very well. I know about everything. I have counted on you for a long time.'

" 'Counted on me? What for, then?'

" 'The entire region is full [of talk] of you. You have enemies; a district magistrate has squeezed you, Wolf. They have ruined you; they have treated you scandalously.'

"The man became hot-tempered 'Because you shot a couple of boars which the prince feeds in our fields, they kept you in the penitentiary for years and moved you around in the fortress; they stole your house and your tavern from you, [and] made you a beggar. Has it come to this, my brother, that a human being is not worth more than a rabbit? Are we not better than the creatures in the field? And a tough guy like you allowed himself to suffer that?'

" 'Would I have been able to change it?'

" 'We shall see, indeed. But, tell me, where do you come from now, and what is your game?'

»Ich erzählte ihm meine ganze Geschichte. Der Mann, ohne abzuwarten, bis ich zu Ende war, sprang mit froher Ungeduld auf, und mich zog er nach. ›Komm, Bruder Sonnenwirt‹, sagte er, ›jetzt bist du reif, jetzt hab' ich dich, wo ich dich brauchte. Ich werde Ehre mit dir einlegen. Folge mir.‹

»›Wo willst du mich hinführen?‹

»›Frage nicht lange. Folge!‹ – Er schleppte mich mit Gewalt fort.

»Wir waren eine kleine Viertelmeile gegangen. Der Wald wurde immer abschüssiger, unwegsamer und wilder, keiner von uns sprach ein Wort, bis mich endlich die Pfeife meines Führers aus meinen Betrachtungen aufschreckte. Ich schlug die Augen auf, wir standen am schroffen Absturz eines Felsen, der sich in eine tiefe Kluft hinunterbückte. Eine zweite Pfeife antwortete aus dem innersten Bauche des Felsen, und eine Leiter kam, wie von sich selbst, langsam aus der Tiefe gestiegen. Mein Führer kletterte zuerst hinunter, mich hieß er warten, bis er wiederkäme. ›Erst muss ich den Hund an Ketten legen lassen‹, setzte er hinzu, ›du bist hier fremd, die Bestie würde dich zerreißen.‹ Damit ging er.

»Jetzt stand ich allein vor dem Abgrund, und ich wusste recht gut, dass ich allein war. Die Unvorsichtigkeit meines Führers entging meiner Aufmerksamkeit nicht. Es hätte mich nur einen beherzten Entschluss gekostet, die Leiter heraufzuziehen, so war ich frei, und meine Flucht war gesichert. Ich gestehe, dass ich das einsah. Ich sah in den Schlund hinab, der mich jetzt aufnehmen sollte; es erinnerte mich dunkel an den Abgrund der Hölle, woraus keine Erlösung mehr ist. Mir fing an, vor der Laufbahn zu schaudern, die ich nunmehr betreten wollte; nur eine schnelle Flucht konnte mich retten. Ich beschließe diese Flucht – schon strecke ich den Arm nach der Leiter aus – aber auf einmal donnert's in meinen Ohren, es umhallt mich wie Hohngelächter der Hölle: ›Was hat ein Mörder zu wagen?‹ – und mein Arm fällt gelähmt zurück. Meine Rechnung war völlig, die Zeit der Reue war dahin, mein begangener Mord lag hinter mir aufgetürmt wie ein Fels und sperrte meine Rückkehr auf ewig. Zugleich erschien auch mein

"I told him my story in its entirety. The man, without waiting for me to finish it, jumped up in cheerful impatience and then pulled me up [too]. 'Come, my brother, the Sun's landlord,' he said, 'you are ready for it now, where I needed to have you. You will do me proud. Follow me.'

" 'Where are you going to take me?'

" 'Don't waste time asking. Follow me!'—He dragged me away forcefully.

"We had walked a quarter of a mile. The forest became steeper and steeper, more and more impassable, [and] neither of us said a word until my guide's whistle jolted me out of my reflections. I opened my eyes; we were standing at the steep drop-off of a boulder which reached down into a deep ravine. A second whistle answered from the innermost belly of the rock, and slowly a ladder appeared from the deep, as if of its own accord. My guide climbed down first, asking me to wait until his return. 'I have to have the dog chained first,' he added, 'you are a foreigner here, and the beast would tear you apart.' With these words he left.

"I was now standing at the abyss all by myself, and I was well aware that I was alone. My guide's carelessness did not escape my attention. It would have taken merely a courageous decision on my part to pull up the ladder and I would have been free, and my escape would have been safe and sound. I acknowledge that I contemplated this. I looked down into the gorge which was going to receive me; it reminded me vaguely of the abyss of Hell, from which there is no more salvation. I began to shudder in the face of the career which I was about to enter; only a hurried escape would be able to save me. I resolved to resort to this escape—with my arm, I was already reaching for the ladder—when a thunderous voice rises in my ears; a derisive laughter is echoing around me: 'What does a murderer dare [to hope for]?' And my arm falls down, devoid of all strength. My calculation was complete; the moment for atonement had ended, [and] the murder I had committed lay behind me, towering like a large rock and preventing my return for all eternity. At the same moment, my guide reappeared and announced that I was

Führer wieder und kündigte mir an, dass ich kommen solle. Jetzt war ohnehin keine Wahl mehr. Ich kletterte hinunter.

»Wir waren wenige Schritte unter der Felsmauer weggegangen, so erweiterte sich der Grund, und einige Hütten wurden sichtbar. Mitten zwischen diesen öffnete sich ein runder Rasenplatz, auf welchem sich eine Anzahl von achtzehn bis zwanzig Menschen um ein Kohlfeuer gelagert hatte. ›Hier, Kameraden‹, sagte mein Führer und stellte mich mitten in den Kreis; ›unser Sonnenwirt! heißt ihn willkommen!‹

»›Sonnenwirt!‹ schrie alles zugleich, und alles fuhr auf und drängte sich um mich her, Männer und Weiber. Soll ich's gestehn? Die Freude war ungeheuchelt und herzlich, Vertrauen, Achtung sogar erschien auf jedem Gesicht, dieser drückte mir die Hand, jener schüttelte mich vertraulich am Kleide, der ganze Auftritt war wie das Wiedersehen eines alten Bekannten, der einem wert ist. Meine Ankunft hatte den Schmaus unterbrochen, der eben anfangen sollte. Man setzte ihn sogleich fort und nötigte mich, den Willkomm zu trinken. Wildbret aller Art war die Mahlzeit, und die Weinflasche wanderte unermüdet von Nachbar zu Nachbar. Wohlleben und Einigkeit schien die ganze Bande zu beseelen, und alles wetteiferte, seine Freude über mich zügelloser an den Tag zu legen.

»Man hatte mich zwischen zwei Frauen sitzen lassen, welches der Ehrenplatz an der Tafel war. Ich erwartete den Auswurf ihres Geschlechts, aber wie groß war meine Verwunderung, als ich unter dieser schändlichen Rotte die schönsten weiblichen Gestalten entdeckte, die mir jemals vor Augen gekommen. Margarete, die älteste und schönste von beiden, ließ sich Jungfer nennen und konnte kaum fünfundzwanzig sein. Sie sprach sehr frech, und ihre Gebärden sagten noch mehr. Marie, die jüngere, war verheiratet, aber einem Manne entlaufen, der sie misshandelt hatte. Sie war feiner gebildet, sah aber blass aus und schmächtig und fiel weniger ins Auge als ihre feurige Nachbarin. Beide Frauen eiferten aufeinander, meine Begierden zu entzünden; die schöne Margarete kam meiner Blödigkeit durch freche Scherze zuvor, aber das ganze Weib war mir zuwider, und mein Herz hatte die schüchterne Marie auf immer gefangen.

supposed to come along. At any rate, now I no longer had a choice. I climbed down.

"We had walked but a few steps underneath the rocky wall when the ground widened and a few cabins appeared. In their center a round area of grass came into sight on which were camped out around a coal fire about eighteen to twenty people. 'Here, comrades,' my guide said and placed me in the center of the circle; '[here is] our Sun's landlord! Bid him your welcome!'

" 'The Sun's landlord!' every one shouted at once, and they all started up and crowded around me, men and women. Should I confess to it? The happiness was unfeigned and cordial, trust, even respect, appeared on each face, this one pressed my hand, that one tugged on my clothes in a friendly way, the entire scene was like a reunion with an old acquaintance toward whom one is well-disposed. My arrival had interrupted the feast which had been just about to begin. They immediately commenced with it and urged me to drink to my welcome. The meal consisted of wild game of all kinds, and the wine bottle traveled tirelessly from neighbor to neighbor. Well-being and harmony seemed to animate the whole gang, and they all vied with each other to show their unrestrained joy at [my arrival].

"I had been placed between two women, which was the place of honor at the table. I had expected the scum of their gender, but how great was my amazement when I discovered the most beautiful female figures, which I had ever laid eyes upon, among this nefarious horde. Margarete, the older and more beautiful of the two, addressed herself as 'maiden,' and must have been barely twenty-five. She spoke very impudently, and her gestures were even more telling. Marie, the younger one, had been married, but ran away from a husband who treated her ill. She was built more delicately, but looked pale and slim, and was less eye-catching than her fiery neighbor. Both women competed to arouse my appetite; the beautiful Margarete preempted my diffidence with her cheeky banter, but I loathed the whole woman, and my heart had been captured evermore by the bashful Marie.

»›Du siehst, Bruder Sonnenwirt‹, fing der Mann jetzt an, der mich hergebracht hatte, ›du siehst, wie wir untereinander leben, und jeder Tag ist dem heutigen gleich. Nicht wahr, Kameraden?‹

»›Jeder Tag ist wie der heutige!‹ wiederholte die ganze Bande.

»›Kannst du dich also entschließen, an unserer Lebensart Gefallen zu finden, so schlag ein und sei unser Anführer. Bis jetzt bin ich es gewesen, aber dir will ich weichen. Seid ihr's zufrieden, Kameraden?‹

»Ein fröhliches ›Ja!‹ antwortete aus allen Kehlen.

»Mein Kopf glühte, mein Gehirne war betäubt, von Wein und Begierden siedete mein Blut. Die Welt hatte mich ausgeworfen wie einen Verpesteten – hier fand ich brüderliche Aufnahme, Wohlleben und Ehre. Welche Wahl ich auch treffen wollte, so erwartete mich Tod; hier aber konnte ich wenigstens mein Leben für einen höheren Preis verkaufen. Wollust war meine wütendste Neigung; das andere Geschlecht hatte mir bis jetzt nur Verachtung bewiesen, hier erwartete mich Gunst und zügellose Vergnügungen. Mein Entschluss kostete mich wenig. ›Ich bleibe bei euch, Kameraden‹, rief ich laut mit Entschlossenheit und trat mitten unter die Bande; ›ich bleibe bei euch‹, rief ich nochmals, ›wenn ihr mir‹ meine schöne Nachbarin abtretet!‹ – Alle kamen überein, mein Verlangen zu bewilligen, ich war erklärter Eigentümer einer H*** und das Haupt einer Diebesbande.«

Den folgenden Teil der Geschichte übergehe ich ganz; das bloß Abscheuliche hat nichts Unterrichtendes für den Leser. Ein Unglücklicher, der bis zu dieser Tiefe herunter sank, musste sich endlich alles erlauben, was die Menschheit empört – aber einen zweiten Mord beging er nicht mehr, wie er selbst auf der Folter bezeugte.

Der Ruf dieses Menschen verbreitete sich in kurzem durch die ganze Provinz. Die Landstraßen wurden unsicher, nächtliche Einbrüche beunruhigten den Bürger, der Name des Sonnenwirts wurde der Schrecken des Landvolks, die Gerechtigkeit suchte ihn auf, und eine Prämie wurde auf seinen Kopf gesetzt. Er war so glücklich, jeden Anschlag auf seine Freiheit zu vereiteln, und verschlagen genug, den Aberglauben des wundersüchtigen Bauern zu seiner Sicherheit zu benutzen. Seine Gehilfen mussten

" 'You see, my brother, the Sun's landlord,' the man who had brought me here began, 'you see how we live together, and how every day is like today. Isn't it, comrades?'

" 'Every day is like today!' the entire gang echoed.

" 'Thus, if you can make up your mind to take a fancy to our way of life, then shake hands on it and be our leader. Up till now, it was I [who was the leader], but I shall make way for you. Are you happy with that, comrades?'

"A cheerful 'Yes!' from every mouth was the reply.

"My head was glowing hot, my brain was dazed from the wine, and [carnal] desires made my blood boil. The world had cast me out like a pestilential man—here I found brotherly acceptance, well-being, and honor. Whatever choice I was going to make, death was awaiting me; here at any rate I was able to sell my life for a higher price. Lust was my fiercest proclivity; the other sex had bestowed only contempt upon me thus far; here I would be met with affection and unbridled pleasures. It did not cost me much [time] to make up my mind. 'I will stay with you, comrades,' I called out loudly and with resolve, and stepped amidst the gang; 'I will stay with you,' I called out again, 'if you will surrender to me my beautiful neighbor!' They all agreed to grant me my wish, [and] I became the acknowledged proprietor of a whore, and the head of a gang of thieves."

I will completely pass over the remainder of the story; the purely repugnant [passages] hold no educational significance for the reader. An unfortunate man who has sunk to such depths ultimately and unavoidably would resort to all of the liberties which disgust mankind—though he did not commit a second murder, which he testified during torture.

Before long, this man's reputation had spread throughout the whole province. The highways became unsafe, [and] nightly burglaries troubled the residents; the name of the Sun's landlord became the terror of the country people; the authorities began to look for him, and a bounty on his head was determined. He was lucky enough to thwart each and every attack on his freedom, and [he was] devious enough to use the superstition of the farmers who were eager for miracles for his safety. His adjutants had

ausstreuen, er habe einen Bund mit dem Teufel gemacht und könne hexen. Der Distrikt, auf welchem er seine Rolle spielte, gehörte damals noch weniger als jetzt zu den aufgeklärten Deutschlands; man glaubte diesem Gerüchte, und seine Person war gesichert. Niemand zeigte Lust, mit dem gefährlichen Kerl anzubinden, dem der Teufel zu Diensten stünde. Ein Jahr schon hatte er das traurige Handwerk getrieben, als es anfing, ihm unerträglich zu werden. Die Rotte, an deren Spitze er sich gestellt hatte, erfüllte seine glänzenden Erwartungen nicht. Eine verführerische Außenseite hatte ihn damals im Taumel des Weines geblendet; jetzt wurde er mit Schrecken gewahr, wie abscheulich er hintergangen worden. Hunger und Mangel traten an die Stelle des Überflusses, womit man ihn eingewiegt hatte; sehr oft musste er sein Leben um eine Mahlzeit wagen, die kaum hinreichte, ihn vor dem Verhungern zu schützen. Das Schattenbild jener brüderlichen Eintracht verschwand; Neid, Argwohn und Eifersucht wüteten im Innern dieser verworfenen Bande. Die Gerechtigkeit hatte demjenigen, der ihn lebendig ausliefern würde, Belohnung und, wenn es ein Mitschuldiger wäre, noch eine feierliche Begnadigung zugesagt – eine mächtige Versuchung für den Auswurf der Erde! Der Unglückliche kannte seine Gefahr. Die Redlichkeit derjenigen, die Menschen und Gott verrieten, war ein schlechtes Unterpfand seines Lebens. Sein Schlaf war von jetzt an dahin, ewige Todesangst zerfraß seine Ruhe, das grässliche Gespenst des Argwohns rasselte hinter ihm, wo er hinfloh, peinigte ihn, wenn er wachte, bettete sich neben ihm, wenn er schlafen ging, und schreckte ihn in entsetzlichen Träumen. Das verstummte Gewissen gewann zugleich seine Sprache wieder, und die schlafende Natter der Reue wachte bei diesem allgemeinen Sturm seines Busens auf. Sein ganzer Hass wandte sich jetzt von der Menschheit und kehrte seine schreckliche Schneide gegen ihn selber. Er vergab jetzt der ganzen Natur und fand niemand, als sich allein zu verfluchen.

Das Laster hatte seinen Unterricht an dem Unglücklichen vollendet, sein natürlich guter Verstand siegte endlich über die traurige Täuschung. Jetzt fühlte er, wie tief er gefallen war, ruhigere Schwermut trat an die Stelle knirschender Verzweiflung.

to spread the rumor that he had entered into a pact with the Devil and that he was capable of sorcery. The district in which he played his role was among the [less] enlightened ones in Germany in those days; the people believed these rumors and he was [thus] protected. Nobody had any inclination to take on a dangerous [and tough] guy with the Devil at his service.

He had practiced his sad trade for a year when it began to become unbearable to him. The horde, whose leader he had become, did not fulfill his glamorous expectations. Caught in the dizziness of the wine back then, he had been blinded by an alluring façade; now he began to realize with horror how outrageously he had been deceived. Hunger and deprivation had replaced the abundance with which he had been lured; many, many times he had to risk his life in exchange for a meal, which was hardly enough to protect him from starvation. The mirage of that brotherly harmony had disappeared; envy, suspicion, and jealousy ranted and raved within this nefarious gang. The authorities had promised a reward to the person who would deliver him alive and, if he were an accomplice, also an official pardon—a powerful enticement for the scum of the earth! The unfortunate man knew his risk. The integrity of those who would betray both men and God was a poor safeguard for his life. Sleep had fled him from that time on, an eternal fear of death eroded his tranquility, [and] the dreadful ghost of suspicion came rattling after him, no matter where he fled; it tormented him when he awoke, bedded down next to him when he went to sleep, and terrorized him with monstrous dreams. At the same time, his conscience, which had become silent, had recovered its voice and the dormant viper of remorse awoke during this all-embracing storm inside his bosom. His entire hatred then turned away from mankind and turned its horrifying edge toward himself. Subsequently, he forgave all of nature, and found nobody at all to curse but himself.

Vice had concluded its education of the unfortunate man; finally, his naturally bright mind triumphed over the miserable deception. He now felt how low he had fallen, [and] a calm melancholy replaced the jarring despondency. With tears, he

Er wünschte mit Tränen die Vergangenheit zurück; jetzt wusste er gewiss, dass er sie ganz anders wiederholen würde. Er fing an zu hoffen, dass er noch rechtschaffen werden dürfe, weil er bei sich empfand, dass er es könne. Auf dem höchsten Gipfel seiner Verschlimmerung war er dem Guten näher, als er vielleicht vor seinem ersten Fehltritt gewesen war.

Um eben diese Zeit war der siebenjährige Krieg ausgebrochen, und die Werbungen gingen stark. Der Unglückliche schöpfte Hoffnung von diesem Umstand und schrieb einen Brief an seinen Landesherrn, den ich auszugsweise hier einrücke:

»Wenn Ihre fürstliche Huld sich nicht ekelt, bis zu mir herunter zu steigen, wenn Verbrecher meiner Art nicht außerhalb Ihrer Erbarmung liegen, so gönnen Sie mir Gehör, durchlauchtigster Oberherr. Ich bin Mörder und Dieb, das Gesetz verdammt mich zum Tode, die Gerichte suchen mich auf – und ich biete mich an, mich freiwillig zu stellen. Aber ich bringe zugleich eine seltsame Bitte vor Ihren Thron. Ich verabscheue mein Leben und fürchte den Tod nicht, aber schrecklich ist mir's zu sterben, ohne gelebt zu haben. Ich möchte leben, um einen Teil des Vergangenen gutzumachen; ich möchte leben, um den Staat zu versöhnen, den ich beleidigt habe. Meine Hinrichtung wird ein Beispiel sein für die Welt, aber kein Ersatz meiner Taten. Ich hasse das Laster und sehne mich feurig nach Rechtschaffenheit und Tugend. Ich habe Fähigkeiten gezeigt, meinem Vaterlande furchtbar zu werden; ich hoffe, dass mir noch einige übriggeblieben sind, ihm zu nützen.

»Ich weiß, dass ich etwas Unerhörtes begehre. Mein Leben ist verwirkt, mir steht es nicht an, mit der Gerechtigkeit Unterhandlung zu pflegen. Aber ich erscheine nicht in Ketten und Banden vor Ihnen – noch bin ich frei – und meine Furcht hat den kleinsten Anteil an meiner Bitte.

»Es ist Gnade, um was ich flehe. Einen Anspruch auf Gerechtigkeit, wenn ich auch einen hätte, wage ich nicht mehr geltend zu machen. – Doch an etwas darf ich meinen Richter erinnern. Die Zeitrechnung meiner Verbrechen fängt mit dem Urteilspruch an, der mich auf immer um meine Ehre brachte. Wäre mir damals die Billigkeit minder versagt worden, so würde ich jetzt vielleicht keiner Gnade bedürfen.

wished for the past to return; he was now certain that he would repeat it completely differently. He began to hope that he might become honest after all, because deep down he sensed that he was capable of it. At the highest peak of his evilness he may have been closer to being good than he was before his first misstep.

Around that same time, the Seven Years' War had begun and recruitment had intensified. The unfortunate man drew hope from this circumstance and wrote a letter to his sovereign, from which I have included excerpts below:

"If your Grace does not feel disgusted by [the idea of] lowering yourself down to me; if criminals of my kind do not lie outside the scope of your mercy, then [graciously] lend me your ear, Your Most Serene Highness. I am a murderer and thief, the law has sentenced me to death, [and] the courts are searching for me—and here I am offering to give myself up voluntarily. However, at the same time I am bringing a strange request to your throne. I have become disgusted with my life and I don't fear death, but I feel terrible about dying without having lived. I would like to live in order to partially atone for what has happened in the past; I would like to live in order to reconcile with the state which I offended. My execution will be an example for the world, but not a compensation for my acts. I hate the vices and fervently long for honesty and virtue. I have shown skills to become a terror to my native land; I hope I shall have left some that will be helpful to it.

"I know that I am requesting something outrageous. My life is forfeited, [and] I have no right to negotiate for justice. However, I do not appear in chains and manacles before you— as of yet, I am free—and, in my request, my fear accounts for only the smallest part.

"What I beg of you is mercy. I no longer have the courage to claim justice, even if I had a right to do so.—However, I would like to remind my judge of something. The history of my crimes starts with the verdict that took my honor from me. If, at that time, fairness had been withheld from me to a lesser degree, perhaps [now] I might not be in need of mercy.

»Lassen Sie Gnade für Recht ergehen, mein Fürst! Wenn es in Ihrer fürstlichen Macht steht, das Gesetz für mich zu erbitten, so schenken Sie mir das Leben. Es soll Ihrem Dienste von nun an gewidmet sein. Wenn Sie es können, so lassen Sie mich Ihren gnädigsten Willen aus öffentlichen Blättern vernehmen, und ich werde mich auf Ihr fürstliches Wort in der Hauptstadt stellen. Haben Sie es anders mit mir beschlossen, so tue die Gerechtigkeit denn das Ihrige, ich muss das Meinige tun.«

Diese Bittschrift blieb ohne Antwort, wie auch eine zweite und dritte, worin der Supplikant um eine Reuterstelle im Dienste des Fürsten bat. Seine Hoffnung zu einem Pardon erlosch gänzlich, er fasste also den Entschluss, aus dem Land zu fliehen und im Dienste des Königs von Preußen als ein braver Soldat zu sterben. Er entwischte glücklich seiner Bande und trat diese Reise an. Der Weg führte ihn durch eine kleine Landstadt, wo er übernachten wollte. Kurze Zeit vorher waren durch das ganze Land geschärftere Mandate zu strenger Untersuchung der Reisenden ergangen, weil der Landesherr, ein Reichsfürst, im Kriege Partei genommen hatte. Einen solchen Befehlt hatte auch der Torschreiber dieses Städtchens, der auf einer Bank vor dem Schlage saß, als der Sonnenwirt geritten kam. Der Aufzug dieses Mannes hatte etwas Possierliches und zugleich etwas Schreckliches und Wildes. Der hagre Klepper, den er ritt, und die burleske Wahl seiner Kleidungsstücke, wobei wahrscheinlich weniger sein Geschmack als die Chronologie seiner Entwendungen zu Rat gezogen war, kontrastierte seltsam genug mit einem Gesicht, worauf so viele wütende Affekte, gleich den verstümmelten Leichen auf einem Schlachtfeld, verbreitet lagen. Der Torschreiber stutzte beim Anblick dieses seltsamen Wanderers. Er war am Schlagbaum grau geworden, und eine vierzigjährige Amtsführung hatte in ihm einen unfehlbaren Physiognomen aller Landstreicher erzogen. Der Falkenblick dieses Spürers verfehlte auch hier seinen Mann nicht. Er sperrte sogleich das Stadttor und forderte dem Reuter den Pass ab, indem er sich seines Zügels versicherte. Wolf war auf Fälle dieser Art vorbereitet und führte auch wirklich einen Pass bei sich, den er unlängst von einem geplünderten Kaufmann erbeutet hatte. Aber dieses einzelne Zeugnis war nicht genug, eine

"Temper justice with mercy, my Prince! If it is within your princely powers to appeal to the law on my behalf, then spare my life. It shall be dedicated to your service from this time on. If you can do this [for me], then have your serene will announced to me in the public papers, and I shall hand myself over in the capital, on your princely word. Should you have decided to proceed with me in a different manner, then let justice do its bidding, as I will have to do mine."

This letter of petition remained unanswered, as did a second and a third, in which the supplicant asked for a position as a horseman in the service of the prince. His hope for a pardon died completely, [and] he decided to flee the land and die as a good soldier in the service of the King of Prussia.

He effectively escaped from his gang and set out on this journey. His way led him through a little town in the country where he had planned to stay the night. As the sovereign, a prince of the Empire, had taken sides in the war, tougher mandates had been issued all over the land only a short time before, requiring a strict check of travelers. Such an order had been given to this little town's gatekeeper also, who sat on a bench before the toll bar, when the Sun's landlord was riding up. This man's getup had, all at the same time, something droll and terrible and wild about it. The scraggy nag which he rode, and the burlesque choice of his garments, for which probably not so much his taste but rather the chronology of their purloinment were responsible, stood in strange contrast to his face, on which were displayed a good many angry emotions, reminiscent of the mutilated corpses on a battlefield. The gatekeeper hesitated at the sight of this strange wanderer. He had grown gray [working] at the toll bar, and an administration of forty years had created inside him an unfailing recognition of all vagrants. The eagle eye of this examiner did not miss his mark this time either. Immediately he barred the town gate and demanded his travel documents from the horseman while grabbing his horse's reins. Wolf had been [was] prepared for such occasions [eventualities] and indeed carried travel documents with him, which he had recently obtained from a merchant whom he had robbed. However, this single certificate did not suffice to overturn forty

vierzigjährige Observanz umzustoßen und das Orakel am
Schlagbaum zu einem Widerruf zu bewegen. Der Torschreiber
glaubte seinen Augen mehr als diesem Papiere, und Wolf war
genötigt, ihm nach dem Amtshaus zu folgen.

Der Oberamtmann des Orts untersuchte den Pass und
erklärte ihn für richtig. Er war ein starker Anbeter der Neuigkeit
und liebte besonders, bei einer Bouteille über die Zeitung zu
plaudern. Der Pass sagte ihm, dass der Besitzer geradeswegs aus
den feindlichen Ländern käme, wo der Schauplatz des Krieges
war. Er hoffte, Privatnachrichten aus dem Fremden herauszulo-
cken, und schickte einen Sekretär mit dem Pass zurück, ihn auf
eine Flasche Wein einzuladen.

Unterdessen hält der Sonnenwirt vor dem Amtshaus; das
lächerliche Schauspiel hat den Pöbel des Städtchens scharen-
weise um ihn her versammelt. Man murmelt sich in die Ohren,
deutet wechselweise auf das Ross und den Reuter; der Mutwille
des Pöbels steigt endlich bis zu einem lauten Tumult.
Unglücklicherweise war das Pferd, worauf jetzt alles mit den
Fingern wies, ein geraubtes; er bildet sich ein, das Pferd sei in
Steckbriefen beschrieben und erkannt. Die unerwartete
Gastfreundlichkeit des Oberamtmanns vollendet seinen
Verdacht. Jetzt hält er's für ausgemacht, dass die Betrügerei
seines Passes verraten und die Einladung nur die Schlinge sei,
ihn lebendig und ohne Widersetzung zu fangen. Böses Gewissen
macht ihn zum Dummkopf, er gibt seinem Pferde die Sporen
und rennt davon, ohne Antwort zu geben.

Diese plötzliche Flucht ist die Losung zum Aufstand.
»Ein Spitzbube!« ruft alles, und alles stürzt hinter ihm her.
Dem Reuter gilt es um Leben und Tod, er hat schon den
Vorsprung, seine Verfolger keuchen atemlos nach, er ist seiner
Rettung nahe – aber eine schwere Hand drückt unsichtbar
gegen ihn, die Uhr seines Schicksals ist abgelaufen, die unerbitt-
liche Nemesis hält ihren Schuldner an. Die Gasse, der er sich
anvertraute, endigt in einem Sack, er muss rückwärts gegen
seine Verfolger umwenden.

Der Lärm dieser Begebenheit hat unterdessen das ganze
Städtchen in Aufruhr gebracht, Haufen sammeln sich zu
Haufen, alle Gassen sind gesperrt, ein Heer von Feinden kommt

years of observance and to motivate the sage at the toll bar to repeal [his arrest]. The gatekeeper believed his eyes more than [he believed] the papers, and Wolf was compelled to follow him to the town hall.

The town's chief bailiff examined the travel documents and declared them to be real. He enthusiastically adored news, and particularly loved chatting about the latest news over a bottle. The travel documents indicated that their owner came directly from enemy territory, where the theater of war was located. He hoped to be able to tease out private news from the stranger and sent his secretary back with the travel documents to invite the [traveler] to [share] a bottle of wine.

Meanwhile, the Sun's landlord comes to a stop before the town office [hall]; the ridiculous pageant has prompted the little town's riffraff to crowd around. They murmur in each other's ears, pointing alternately at the horse and at the rider; finally, the riffraff's disorder increases to a noisy commotion. Unfortunately, the horse at which everybody was pointing with their fingers at this moment was a stolen one; he imagined that the horse had been described in Warrants of Capture and had been recognized. The chief bailiff's unexpected hospitality arouses his suspicion. Now he thinks it a foregone conclusion that the deceit with his travel documents is discovered, and the invitation is no more than the noose in which to catch him alive and without a fight. His bad conscience makes a fool of him; he spurs his horse and runs away without a word.

This sudden escape is the motto for the revolt.

"A rogue!" everybody calls out, and rushes after him. For the horseman, it is now about life and death; already he has a head-start, his pursuers are breathlessly panting after him, [and] he is close to his deliverance—however, a heavy hand pushes invisibly against him; the clock of his destiny has halted, [and] relentless Nemesis has stopped her debtor. The alley to which he has entrusted himself is a dead-end; he is forced to turn around to face his pursuers.

Meanwhile, the commotion of this incident has brought the entire little town up in arms; crowds gather together, all alleys are barred, [and] an army of enemies is marching toward him.

im Anmarsch gegen ihn her. Er zeigt eine Pistole, das Volk weicht, er will sich mit Macht einen Weg durchs Gedränge bahnen. »Dieser Schuss«, ruft er, »soll dem Tollkühnen, der mich halten will« – Die Furcht gebietet eine allgemeine Pause – ein beherzter Schlossergeselle endlich fällt ihm von hinten her in den Arm und fasst den Finger, womit der Rasende eben losdrücken will, und drückt ihn aus dem Gelenke. Die Pistole fällt, der wehrlose Mann wird vom Pferde herabgerissen und im Triumph nach dem Amthaus zurückgeschleppt.

»Wer seid Ihr?« frägt der Richter mit ziemlich brutalem Ton.

»Ein Mann, der entschlossen ist, auf keine Frage zu antworten, bis man sie höflicher einrichtet.«

»Wer sind Sie?«

»Für was ich mich ausgab. Ich habe ganz Deutschland durchreist und die Unverschämtheit nirgends als hier zu Hause gefunden.«

»Ihre schnelle Flucht macht Sie sehr verdächtig. Warum flohen Sie?«

»Weil ich's müde war, der Spott Ihres Pöbels zu sein.«

»Sie drohten, Feuer zu geben.«

»Meine Pistole war nicht geladen.« Man untersuchte das Gewehr, es war keine Kugel darin.

»Warum führen Sie heimliche Waffen bei sich?«

»Weil ich Sachen von Wert bei mir trage, und weil man mich vor einem gewissen Sonnenwirt gewarnt hat, der in diesen Gegenden streifen soll.«

»Ihre Antworten beweisen sehr viel für Ihre Dreistigkeit, aber nichts für Ihre gute Sache. Ich gebe Ihnen Zeit bis morgen, ob Sie mir die Wahrheit entdecken wollen.«

»Ich werde bei meiner Aussage bleiben.«

»Man führe ihn nach dem Turm.«

»Nach dem Turm? – Herr Oberamtmann, ich hoffe, es gibt noch Gerechtigkeit in diesem Lande. Ich werde Genugtuung fordern.«

»Ich werde sie Ihnen geben, sobald Sie gerechtfertigt sind.«

Den Morgen darauf überlegte der Oberamtmann, der Fremde möchte doch wohl unschuldig sein; die befehlshaberische Sprache würde nichts über seinen Starrsinn vermögen, es wäre

He holds up a pistol, the mob draws back, [and] he is set to make his way through the throng forcibly. "This shot," he calls out, "is intended for the fool who wants to detain me."—fear demands a general pause—finally, a courageous locksmith apprentice enfolds him in his arms from behind and gets a hold of the finger with which the furious man is just about to pull the trigger and dislocates it. The pistol drops, the defenseless man is being pulled from his horse and dragged back to the town hall in triumph.

"Who are you?" the magistrate asks, rather brutally.

"A man who is determined not to answer any question unless it is asked more politely."

"Who are you?"

"[I am] who I said I was. I have traveled throughout Germany and have not found disrespect to be at home anywhere but here."

"Your hurried escape makes you very suspicious. Why did you flee?"

"Because I was tired of being the butt of your riffraff's mockery."

"You threatened to fire."

"My pistol was not loaded." They examined the pistol; there was no bullet in the barrel.

"Why do you carry a concealed weapon?."

"Because I carry with me items of value, and because I was warned of a certain Sun's landlord who is said to roam these parts."

"Your answers give much proof of your presumption, but nothing for your good cause. I shall give you time until tomorrow to enlighten me with the truth."

"I shall abide by my statement."

"Take him to the tower."

"To the tower?—Chief Bailiff, sir, I do hope there is still justice in this land. I shall demand satisfaction."

"I shall give it to you as soon as you are vindicated."

On the next morning, the chief bailiff pondered that the stranger might well be innocent; the authoritative tone would not be able to conquer his mulishness; it might well be better

vielleicht besser getan, ihm mit Anstand und Mäßigung zu begegnen. Er versammelte die Geschwornen des Orts und ließ den Gefangenen vorführen.

»Verzeihen Sie es der ersten Aufwallung, mein Herr, wenn ich Sie gestern etwas hart anließ.«

»Sehr gern, wenn Sie mich so fassen.«

»Unsere Gesetze sind streng, und Ihre Begebenheit machte Lärm. Ich kann Sie nicht freigeben, ohne meine Pflicht zu verletzen. Der Schein ist gegen Sie. Ich wünschte, Sie sagten mir etwas, wodurch er widerlegt werden könnte.«

»Wenn ich nun nichts wüsste?«

»So muss ich den Vorfall an die Regierung berichten, und Sie bleiben so lang' in fester Verwahrung.«

»Und dann?«

»Dann laufen Sie Gefahr, als ein Landstreicher über die Grenze gepeitscht zu werden oder, wenn's gnädig geht, unter die Werber zu fallen.«

Er schwieg einige Minuten und schien einen heftigen Kampf zu kämpfen; dann drehte er sich rasch zu dem Richter.

»Kann ich auf eine Viertelstunde mit Ihnen allein sein?«

Die Geschwornen sahen sich zweideutig an, entfernten sich aber auf einen gebietenden Wink ihres Herrn.

»Nun, was verlangen Sie?«

»Ihr gestriges Betragen, Herr Oberamtmann, hätte mich nimmermehr zu einem Geständnis gebracht, denn ich trotze der Gewalt. Die Bescheidenheit, womit Sie mich heute behandeln, hat mir Vertrauen und Achtung gegen Sie gegeben. Ich glaube, dass Sie ein edler Mann sind.«

»Was haben Sie mir zu sagen?«

»Ich sehe, dass Sie ein edler Mann sind. Ich habe mir längst einen Mann gewünscht wie Sie. Erlauben Sie mir Ihre rechte Hand.«

»Worauf will das hinaus?«

»Dieser Kopf ist grau und ehrwürdig. Sie sind lang' in der Welt gewesen – haben der Leiden wohl viele gehabt – Nicht wahr? und sind menschlicher geworden?«

»Mein Herr – wozu soll das?«

to meet him with good grace and moderation. He assembled the jurors of the place and had the detainee brought before them.

"You must excuse my treating you somewhat harshly yesterday in the first heat of the moment, dear sir."

"With great pleasure, if you put it that way."

"Our laws are strict, and the incident which you created caused a lot of noise. I am unable to set you free without violating my duties. All appearances speak against you. I wish you told me something which would belie them."

"[And] if I didn't know of anything?"

"Then I will have to inform the government, and you will have to remain in custody until then."

"And then?"

"Then you run the risk of being whipped across the border as a vagabond, or, if fortune smiles on you, you will end up with the conscriptors."

He was silent for several minutes and seemed to fight a mighty struggle; then quickly he turned around to the magistrate.

"Can I see you alone for a quarter of an hour?"

The jurors looked at each other ambiguously, but then they departed when their master beckoned imperiously.

"Well, what is your request?"

"The attitude you demonstrated [toward me] yesterday, Chief Bailiff, sir, would never have encouraged me to a confession because I disregard authority. The moderation with which you treat me today has given me trust and respect for you. I believe that you are a noble man."

"What do you have to tell me?"

"I can see that you are an honest man. I have long since wished to meet a man such as you. Please give me your right hand."

"What is the purpose of this?"

"This head is gray and dignified. You have been in this world for a long time; you may have met with many hurts; have you not? And thereby have become kinder?"

"My dear sir—what is the purpose of this?"

»Sie stehen noch einen Schritt von der Ewigkeit, bald – bald brauchen Sie Barmherzigkeit bei Gott. Sie werden sie Menschen nicht versagen – – Ahnen Sie nichts? Mit wem glauben Sie, dass Sie reden?«

»Was ist das? Sie erschrecken mich.«

»Ahnen Sie noch nicht? – Schreiben Sie es Ihrem Fürsten, wie Sie mich fanden und dass ich selbst aus freier Wahl mein Verräter war – dass ihm Gott einmal gnädig sein werde, wie er jetzt mir es sein wird – bitten Sie für mich, alter Mann, und lassen Sie dann auf Ihren Bericht eine Träne fallen: Ich bin der Sonnenwirt.«

"You are still a step away from eternity; soon—soon, you will require God's mercy. You are not going to deny it to others—Can't you guess? With whom do you think you are talking?"

"What is this? You are giving me a fright."

"Can't you still guess it?—Write to your prince how you found me and that I delivered myself, of my own free will—may God have mercy on him one day, such as he may have mercy on me now—ask for my pardon, old man, and then let a tear fall on your report: I am the Sun's landlord."

CHRISTIAN HEINRICH SPIEβ

Born April 4, 1755, in Freiberg (Saxony), the son of a pastor, Spieβ completed secondary school and then attended the University of Prague, where he enrolled in lectures on German writing and style (*Vorlesungen über die deutsche Schreibart*). He went on to join a traveling theater troop, his favorite role being that of the old Moor in Friedrich Schiller's *Die Räuber* (*The Robbers*, 1782).

In 1783, Spieβ published his tragedy *Maria Stuart*. However, he was better known for his "Knight, Robber, and Ghost Novels," among them the drama *Klara von Hoheneichen* (1792), which became the blueprint for all knightly dramas in Germany. The play was so highly regarded that it appeared in theaters throughout the country; the great Johann Wolfgang von Goethe staged ten performances at the ducal theater in Weimar.

By that time, Spieβ had assumed the position of manager of Count Künigl's estate in Bohemia, which allowed him the time and leisure to become one of the most productive novel writers of his era. Most notably, his ghost story *Das Petermännchen*, about a ghost who haunts the castle of Schwerin, became a bestseller and was translated into English and French.

Spieβ had been accompanied to Count Künigl's estate by his mistress, the actress Sophie Körner. When Spieβ's mother and the highly revered Countess Künigl died within a short time of each other, Spieβ became afflicted by insane rages and soon died in Klattau, Southern Bohemia (now the Czech Republic),

on August 17, 1799. In an ironic twist of fate, his mistress became the new Countess of Künigl shortly thereafter.

Because of his highly popular stories about ghosts and insane and suicidal protagonists, Spieß is viewed as one of the cofounders of the gothic novel in German literature.[1]

The following story reveals how a meticulous investigation, aided by chance discoveries, eventually leads to the conviction of the criminal.

---

[1] Johann Wilhelm Appell, *Die Ritter-, Räuber- und Schauerromantik: Zur Geschichte der deutschen Unterhaltungsliteratur* (Leipzig: Engelmann, 1859 35–41).

CHRISTIAN HEINRICH SPIEβ

CHRISTIAN HEINRICH SPIEβ

Marianne L — Eine wahre Begebenheit vom Jahre 1788

Am Morgen nach einer höchst stürmischen Herbstnacht verbreitete sich in dem Städtchen V. das Gerücht, dass eine halbe Stunde unterhalb dieser Stadt ein totes Mädchen liege, welches die Maas diese Nacht ausgeworfen habe. – »Gott, wenn das unsere Marianne wäre«, jammerte die Witwe L., indem sie vier verkrüppelte menschliche Gestalten übersah, die bereits verzweifelt die Hände rangen. »Was würde aus diesen Armen werden?« Und schon erzählte ein vorübergehender Bauer, der vom nächsten Ort kam, den Nachbarn, dass der vom Fluss ausgeworfene Leichnam mit Blut und Wunden bedeckt sei. Einer fragte nach der Kleidung der Unglücklichen und die Unruhe der Witwe stieg zur Höllenangst, als diese Beschreibung, die der Bauer von dieser machte, der Kleidung ähnelte, die ihre Tochter den Tag zuvor getragen hatte. Trotz ihrer Lähmung und Kränklichkeit eilte nun die Arme nach dem Platz, wo der Leichnam lag. Eben bemächtigte sich das Gericht desselben. Besinnungslos stürzte die Alte neben diesem nieder, denn sie erkannte in diesem Augenblick ihre Tochter.

Das unglückliche Mädchen war die Tochter eines sehr rechtschaffenen und wohlhabenden Bandwirkers. Ihre Geburt hatte auf ihre Mutter so übel gewirkt, dass dieselbe gelähmt wurde und mehrere Jahre in einem völlig hilflosen Zustand zu Bett zubringen musste. In der Folge war sie insoweit geheilt, dass sie das Bett verlassen konnte, sie blieb aber doch auf der einen Seite ganz und auf der anderen zum Teil gelähmt. In diesem Zustand

CHRISTIAN HEINRICH SPIEß

Marianne L: A True Incident from the Year 1788

In the morning after a most tempestuous autumn storm, the rumor spread in the little town of V. that half an hour downstream from the town there lay a dead girl, which the River Maas had cast out the previous night.—"Oh God, what if this were our Marianne," the Widow L. lamented, looking over four crippled human forms who were already wringing their hands in despair. "What should become of these poor things?" And already a farmer, passing by from the next village, told the neighbors that the corpse, cast out by the river, was covered in blood and wounds. One of them asked about the clothes of the unfortunate [girl], and the widow's anxiety increased to terrible fear when the description the farmer gave of them resembled those her daughter had worn the day before. In spite of her paralysis and her sickliness, the poor woman hurried to the place where the corpse lay. Just then, the tribunal took charge of it. Senseless, the old woman fell down beside it because in that instant she had recognized her daughter.

The unfortunate girl had been the daughter of an exceedingly upright and well-to-do inkle weaver. Her birth had affected her mother so badly that the latter became paralyzed and had to spend several years in bed in a completely helpless condition. In the years following, she was cured to such a degree that she was able to leave her bed; however, she remained completely paralyzed on one side and partially on the other. In this condition,

gebar sie noch 4 Kinder, die sämtlich der Abdruck des elenden Zustandes der Mutter waren. Unter dieser traurigen Familienlast schwand das Vermögen und der unglückliche Vater erlag dem Jammer seiner Lage.

Marianne war 13 Jahre alt, als ihr Vater starb. Die Natur schien an ihr verschwendet zu haben, was sie ihren Geschwistern entzogen hatte. Sie galt für das schönste Mädchen in der Stadt. Dabei hatte die Erziehung, die sie durch die Freigebigkeit einer Pate erhielt, ihren Geist und ihr Herz gleich gut ausgebildet. Nach des Vaters Tod fing Marianne, die sich für die obleich unschuldige Ursache des Unglücks der Familie hielt, an, Tag und Nacht zu arbeiten, um ihrer Mutter und Geschwister, die schlechterdings außer Stande waren zu arbeiten, durch den Verdienst ihrer Handarbeit zu ernähren. Dies gelang ihr über alle Erwartung. Die Familie litt nie Not, obgleich die nötige Pflege der unglücklichen verkrüppelten Geschöpfe manche schweren Ausgaben nötig machte. So hatte es sechs Jahre gedauert und die Aussichten schienen sich für die unglückliche Familie zu verbessern, da Mariannes jüngere Geschwister nun insoweit herangewachsen waren, dass sie gleichfalls etwas verdienen konnten, als Marianne an einem Sonntag gegen Abend ausging um, wie sie sagte, einen Spaziergang in der Allee vor dem Städtchen zu machen. Es war Nacht und Marianne kam noch nicht nach Hause, die Familie suchte sie in der ganzen Stadt und auf allen Spaziergängen; da sie sie nicht fanden, beruhigten sie sich damit, dass Marianne, wie sie sonst öfters zu tun pflegte, zu einem zwei Stunden vor dem Städtchen auf dem Land wohnenden Verwandten gegangen sei, der dort ein Pachtgrundstück hatte und die Familie ansehnlich unterstützte. Nur die zweite Schwester meinte ängstlich, dass Marianne, wenn sie zu dem Vetter gegangen, es ihr gesagt haben würde. Aber auch diese beruhigte sich, als eine Nachbarin die Nachricht brachte, dass ihre Söhne Marianne gegen Abend in der Allee gesehen hätten, die nach dem Wohnort des Vetters führte, und dass S., welchen die Familie als Mariannes begünstigten Liebhaber kannte, nebst dessen Bruder, der Chorherr des dortigen Stifts ist, sie begleitet hätten. – Man schickte nun sogleich in das S–sche Haus um sich zu erkundigen, ob Marianne

she gave birth to four more children who all shared the miserable condition of their mother. Under this unhappy familial burden their fortunes declined, and the sorrowful father succumbed to the misery of his situation.

Marianne had been thirteen when her father died. Nature seemed to have lavished on her what it had withheld from her siblings. She was widely regarded as the most beautiful girl in the town. At the same time, the education which she had received on account of the generosity of a godmother had educated her mind and heart equally well. After her father's death, Marianne, because she felt that she had been—although innocent—the cause of the family's misfortunate, began to work day and night in order to support her mother and her siblings, who were absolutely unable to work, with the income she derived from manual labor. This she managed despite all expectations to the contrary. The family never lacked anything, even though the necessary caregiving required great expense. In this way six years passed, and prospects seemed to improve for the unfortunate family, since Marianne's siblings had now grown to the extent that they also were able to earn money, when Marianne went out one Sunday around evening in order to, as she put it, take a walk on the tree-lined road just outside the little town. Then it was night and Marianne still had not returned home; the family searched the entire town and all the promenades for her. When they were unable to find her, they reassured each other [by] saying Marianne, as she used to do once in a while, had gone to visit a relative in the country who lived in a little town two hours away, and who had a leased property there, and who supported the family handsomely. Only the second sister said anxiously that Marianne would have told her if she had gone to see the cousin. But she also was reassured when one of their neighbors, a woman, brought word that her sons had seen Marianne on the tree-lined road which led to the cousin's town of residence around evening, and that S., who was known to the family as Marianne's favored admirerer, had accompanied her together with his brother, the canon of the local monastery.—Immediately, they dispatched a messenger to S.'s family, in order to inquire if

wirklich nach O. gegangen sei, und die Verlegenheit der Familie vermehrte sich wieder, als der dahin geschickte Bote mit der Nachricht zurückkam, dass der junge S. Marianne nicht gesehen, dessen Mutter aber auf diese, als die Verführerin ihres Sohnes, heftig geschimpft habe.

Diese Erzählung teilte die unglückliche Mutter dem Gericht bei der Leiche ihrer Tochter mit, so wie sie sich nur von ihrer Ohnmacht erholt hatte. – Ein junger Mensch, der dies mit anhörte, trat bedenklich aus dem Kreise der Umstehenden, die alle gleiches Mitleid mit der Unglücklichen und gleicher Abscheu gegen die Tat beseelte, und bat den Richter um ein geheimes Gehör, indem er sich zugleich auf einige ebenfalls anwesende junge Leute berief, die der Richter ebenfalls auf der Stelle anhörte und dann den anwesenden Gerichtsdienern strenge Befehle erteilte, die die neugierige Menge umsonst sich zu erforschen bemühte.

Der Körper der unglücklichen Marianne war nun gerichtlich untersucht, man fand ihn mit siebzehn Stichen durchbohrt, wovon jedoch nur einer tödlich war. Übrigens fand man Beweise einer von ihr gegen den Mörder geleisteten wütenden Gegenwehr. Fest hielt sie in der einen Hand einen Büschel blonder Haare, in der anderen einen Rockknopf. – Die Unglückliche wurde schwanger befunden.

Die Gerichte fingen sogleich die Untersuchung an. Die Söhne der Nachbarn, die wir oben erwähnten, hatten die Aussage, dass sie am Abend zuvor Marianne mit dem jungen S. und dessen Bruder gesehen hätten, vor Gericht wiederholt und die Gerichtsdiener, welchen der Richter den Befehl gegeben hatte, auf die beiden S. in der Stille und ohne Aufsehen zu erregen, aufmerksam zu sein und sie nicht entfliehen zu lassen, brachten die Nachricht, dass der Kanonikus S. bei dem ersten entstandenen Lärmen aus V. abgereist sei. Hierauf ließ nun der Richter den zurückgebliebenen jungen S. arretieren, dieser behauptete aber in dem ersten Verhör, das man sogleich mit ihm vornahm, er habe Marianne des Tags zuvor gar nicht gesehen.

Die drei Jünglinge, die bei der Leiche den Richter im Geheimen zu sprechen verlangt hatten, wurden nun noch mal förmlich vernommen. Sie konnten aber weiter nichts aussagen,

Marianne had actually gone to O., and the family's worry grew greater when the courier, whom they had sent, returned with the message that the young S. had not seen Marianne; his mother, however, had vehemently railed against the latter, declaring her [to be] her son's seductress.

This account was given to the tribunal by the unhappy mother at the side of her daughter's corpse, as soon as she had recovered from her faint.—A young man who had overheard the account deliberately stepped forward from the circle of those who had gathered, all similarly inspired by sympathy for the unfortunate woman and disgust for the deed, and asked for a private audience with the judge invoking the precedent that the judge had also heard on the spot several of the [other] young people who were also present; the judge then gave strict orders [of secrecy] to the bailiffs, which the curious crowd endeavored in vain to uncover.

The body of the unfortunate Marianne was then subject to an inquest; they found it pierced by seventeen stabs, of which however only one was fatal. Incidentally, there was proof that she had fiercely resisted her murderer. In the one hand, she held a tuft of blond hair, in the other a jacket button.—The unhappy woman was found to have been pregnant.

The tribunal immediately began the investigation. The sons of the neighbor woman, whom we mentioned above, had repeated before the tribunal their statements that they had seen Marianne the previous evening with the young S. and his brother, and the bailiffs, who had been given the order to keep an eye on the two brothers S., quietly and without drawing attention, and to not let them escape, furnished the information that the canon S. had departed the monastery of V. after the first clamor arose. Thereupon the judge had the young S. arrested; however, he maintained during the first interrogation, which they conducted immediately, that he had not seen Marianne at all on the previous day.

The three young men who had asked to speak with the judge in secret at the [place where the] body [had been found] were questioned again, this time formally. However, they could not provide anything besides that they had both seen the two

als dass sie am vorhergehenden Tage ebenfalls die beiden S. mit Marianne gegen das Ende der Allee nach O. zu gehen gesehen und dass nach einer Stunde die beiden S. hastig in die Stadt zurückgeeilt seien. Da diese zugleich ausgesagt hatten, dass der jüngere S. sogleich in ein Kaffeehaus, das am Ende der Vorstadt lag, gegangen sei, so wurde nun auch der Kaffeehauswirt und die dort damals zugegen gewesenen Personen vernommen.

Diese gaben an: Als S. in das Kaffeehaus gekommen, habe er im Vorhaus seine Hände und einige Stellen seiner Kleidung gereinigt, auch glaubten sie bemerkt zu haben, dass Hände und Kleidung mit Blut befleckt gewesen seien.

Da der junge S. auf die Frage des Richters, wo er am Nachmittag und Abend der vollbrachten Tat gewesen, verschiedene Orte angegeben hatte, wo er, wie die deshalb eingezogene Erkundigung bewies, nicht gewesen war, so war derselbe allerdings mit schwerem Verdacht belastet. Er wurde daher verhaftet und es fing ein Kriminalprozess an, an welchem die ganze Gegend Anteil nahm, da dieser junge Mensch ihr Liebling gewesen war.

Wilhelm S. war der Sohn eines der reichsten und angesehensten Kaufleute im Land. Er hatte bei seinem Vater den Handel erlernt und eine Erziehung genossen, bei welcher man nichts gespart hatte. Einige Reisen in Frankreich und England hatten dazu gedient, seinen Geist auszubilden und ihn zu einem der angenehmsten Jünglinge zu machen, so wie der ohne Zweifel einer der schönsten war. – Eine Menge einzelner wohltätiger Züge sprachen für sein Herz und man hatte ihn bisher allgemein für einen sehr edlen Jüngling gehalten. Zudem war es bekannt, dass die Entleibte seine Geliebte gewesen, an der er, des Zornes seiner Eltern ungeachtet, mit der leidenschaftlichsten Wärme hing. Bei der gerichtlichen Obduktion des Leichnams der Ermordeten hatte sich gezeigt, dass diese schwanger war; und Wilhelm leugnete nicht, dass er der Vater dieser unglücklichen Frucht sei.

Um desto standhafter leugnete er, an dem Mord des Mädchens einigen Anteil zu haben. Zwar gestand er, als sein Arrest bereits ein Jahr lang gedauert hatte und seine Richter stärker in ihn drangen, weil alle Anzeigen gegen ihn waren, dass er zugegen

brothers S. walk toward the far end of the tree-lined road to O. with Marianne, and that after an hour the two brothers S. had hurried back to town in great haste. Since they had both also stated that the younger S. had immediately entered a coffee house located at the far end of the outskirts, the coffee house keeper and the people who had been present at the time were therefore also questioned.

They stated the following: When S. arrived at the coffee house, he cleaned his hands and some places on his clothes; also, they believed to have noticed blood on his hands and clothes.

Because the young S. [in response] to the judge's question of where had he spent the afternoon and evening of the uncovered deed, had named several different places where, according to the investigations conducted thereupon, [it seemed] he had not been, the [young S.] was therefore under much suspicion. As a consequence, he was arrested, and a criminal trial commenced in which the entire region took a strong interest, because this young man had been their favorite.

Wilhelm S. was the son of one of the richest and most distinguished merchants in the country. He had learned the trade business from his father and enjoyed an education where no cost had been spared. Several journeys to France and England had served to educate his mind and turned him into one of the most pleasant young men, just as he was doubtless one of the most attractive.—A multitude of generous traits spoke in favor of his heart and hitherto he had been generally considered to be a very noble young man. Furthermore, it was general knowledge that the deceased had been his lover, to whom, his parent's wrath notwithstanding, he had been attached with the most passionate warmth. During the forensic postmortem of the body of the murdered woman, it had become apparent that she had been pregnant, and Wilhelm did not deny that he was the father of this unfortunate unborn child.

All the more steadfastly, he denied he had any part in the girl's murder. However, after his arrest had already lasted for a year and his judges pressed him even harder because all evidence pointed against him, he admitted to having been present

gewesen, als Marianne ermordet wurde; er schob aber die ganze
Schuld auf seinen entwichenen Bruder, dessen Flucht ihm
bekannt geworden war, und gab an, er habe sich diesem,
solange es seine Kräfte vermocht hätten, widersetzt. Nichts vermochte ihn, einen Teil der Tat auf sich zu nehmen, so wenig er
auch im Stande war, alle die vielfachen Wiedersprüche zu ent-
kräften, die in seinen Aussagen lagen und welche der Richter
unablässig ihm vorhielt.

So hatte der Prozess bereits fast drei Jahre gedauert, ohne
dass die Richter Klarheit in der Sache erhalten hätten, und
schon wollte man Wilhelm S., welchem für sein Geld die geüb-
testen und fähigsten Verteidiger zu Gebote standen, loslassen,
als ein an sich äußerst unbedeutend scheinender Umstand die
Wahrheit endlich in das hellste und klarste Licht setzte.

Der Angestellte des Gerichts, vor welchem die Untersuchung
geführt wurde, kommt nach L., der ungefähr zehn Stunden von
dem Ort der Untersuchung entfernten Hauptstadt. Dort geht
der zufällig mit einem seiner Freunde, der ihn hierher begleitet
hatte, an einer Trödelbude vorbei, in welcher eine Menge getra-
gener Kleidungsstücke dem Verkauf angesetzt und zum
Beschauen aufgehängt waren. »Siehe da, der ganze Wilhelm S.
wie ausgeplündert!« rief der muntere Begleiter des
Gerichtsangestellten, indem er auf ein graugelbes Kleidungsstück,
eine genähte Weste und ein paar hellgrüne Beinkleider deutete,
welche etwas seitwärts in der Trödlbude hingen. Man scherzte
über den Einfall und ging endlich aus Mutwillen in die Bude,
wo man die Kleidungsstücke und vorzüglich jene, welche die
Neugier der beiden Freunde gereizt hatte, betrachtete, und ver-
gisst die Sache, so wie man sich aus der Bude entfernte.

Mehrere Wochen nachher kam der Gerichtsangestellte ebenso
zufällig im Aktenraum des Gerichts [Asservatenkammer] an ein
Fach, in welches man nichts bedeutende Kleinigkeiten, um sie
aus dem Wege zu schaffen, durcheinander zu werfen pflegte.
Ein kleines zusammengerolltes Papier fällt ihm entgegen; er
entfaltete es, um zu sehen, was es enthalte; der Knopf und jener
Büschel Haare, welche die unglückliche Marianne in den
Händen gehalten, als der Fluss ihren Leichnam ausgespieen
hatte, waren darin eingewickelt. Das Gericht hatte es bisher,

when Marianne had been murdered; [but] he laid the entire blame on his runaway brother, whose escape had been made known to him, and stated he had resisted his brother as long as his strength had allowed him. Nothing could move him to take upon himself the consequences for a part in the deed, while he was also so little able to refute the numerous contradictions inherent in his statements, for which the judge challenged him unrelentingly.

In this way, the trial had proceeded for almost three years without the judges obtaining clarity in the matter, and they were about to discharge Wilhelm S., whose money had made available the most experienced and capable defense attorneys, when a circumstance, appearing extremely insignificant in itself, finally presented the truth in the brightest and plainest light.

The clerk of the court, before whom the investigation had been conducted, arrives in the capital L., which is located approximately ten hours from the place where the investigation [is conducted]. With one of his friends who had accompanied him here, he happens to pass a junk shop where there were hung up for sale and examination a lot of [previously] worn clothes. "Look here, the entire Wilhelm S., as if [he had been] robbed!" called out the clerk's spirited companion, pointing to a grayish green piece of clothing, a stitched vest, and a pair of light green trousers which were hanging off to one side of the junk shop. They joked about the idea and finally, from wantonness, they entered the shop where they inspected the articles of clothing, in particular those which had piqued the two friends' curiosity, and then forget about the affair as soon as they had left the shop.

Several weeks thereafter, the court clerk, again accidentally, happened to come across a compartment in the court's file room [evidence room], wherein they used to haphazardly throw articles of clothing which held no significance in order to get them out of the way. A little rolled up paper falls toward him; he unfolds it to see what it contains; the button and that tuft of hair which the unfortunate Marianne had held [clutched] in her hands, when the river had cast out her body, were enveloped in it. Until that moment, because of the large size to which the

über der Fülle, zu welcher die Untersuchungsakten herangewachsen waren, übersehen, dass dieser Knopf und Haarbüschel
zu etwas mehr als zur Verstärkung des Beweises, dass die
Unglückliche gewaltsam ermordet worden war, dienen können,
und so waren sie in Vergessenheit geraten.

Als der Gerichtsdiener den Knopf sah, glaubte er sich dunkel
zu erinnern, diese Garnitur Knöpfe irgendwo gesehen zu haben.
Der Knopf war von der ausgezeichneten Art, wie man sie am
Anfang der 1790er Jahre auf Männerkleidung trug, wo
Gemälde und Figuren von Stroh, Moos und dergleichen hinter
Glas, welches die äußere Knopfform festhielt, befestigt waren
und also schon deswegen sehr kenntlich waren, weil jede
Garnitur dieser teuren Knöpfe andere Darstellungen enthielt.
Nach langem Hin- und Hersinnen schien es dem
Gerichtsangestellten, als habe er diese Knöpfe auf der Kleidung
bemerkt, welche er in L. in der Trödelbude gesehen hatte und
von welcher damals sein Begleiter behauptet hatte, dass sie einst
Wilhelm gehört habe.

Der Gerichtsdiener eilte, diese Beobachtungen dem Gericht
vorzulegen. Sein Begleiter war vorgeladen, welcher angab, dass
es zwar durchaus ebenso vorkomme, als wenn dieser Knopf zu
der Garnitur jener Knöpfe gehöre, mit denen das betreffende
Kleidungsstück besetzt gewesen sei, dass er aber hierin sich einer
genaueren Bestimmung enthalten wolle, weil ein Irrtum in einer
so bedeutenden Sache von zu wichtigen Folgen sein würde.

Es war nun sogleich an das Gericht in L. geschrieben, von
welchem der Trödler, der das Kleidungsstück gekauft hatte,
vernommen war. Dieser gab an, er habe es von einem Fremden
gekauft, den er aber weder zu nennen noch genau zu beschrei-
ben wisse. Die Zeit, zu welcher er dasselbe gekauft zu haben
angab, war etwa ein halbes Jahr nach dem unglücklichen Mord.
Das Kleidungsstück war inzwischen an einen Friseur verkauft
worden, der kurz zuvor aus L. hinweg, und nach Angaben seiner Verwandten zufolge nach Brüssel gereist war. Man schrieb
nun auch nach Brüssel, aber der Friseur, der mit vieler Mühe
von den dortigen Gerichten ausfindig gemacht worden war,
hatte das Kleid wieder an den Kammerdiener des Grafen D.
verkauft, der mit seinem Herrn nach Ungarn gereist war.

investigation files had grown, the court had overlooked that this button and tuft of hair might serve as something more than just a [simple] strengthening of the evidence that the unfortunate woman had been violently murdered, and so they had faded into obscurity.

When the court clerk saw the button, he seemed to vaguely remember that he had seen this set of buttons somewhere before. The button was of an exquisite kind such as were worn on men's fashion at the beginning of the 1790s, with paintings and characters of straw, moss, and similar [materials], framed by the shape of the button and attached behind glass and fixed to it, and thus were very conspicuous precisely because each set of these expensive buttons contained different images. After pondering back and forth for a long time, it appeared to the court clerk that he had noticed these buttons on the piece of clothing he had seen in the junk shop, and which his companion had suggested had once belonged to Wilhelm.

The court clerk rushed to present these observations to the court. His companion was summoned and stated that it had definitely occurred [to him] as well as though this button belonged to the set of buttons with which the piece of clothing in question had been adorned; but he would like to refrain from making a more certain determination because an error in such an important matter would have serious consequences.

Right away, a letter was sent to the court in L. which questioned the junk dealer who had acquired the piece of clothing. This man stated that he had bought it from an unfamiliar person whom he was, however, able neither to name nor describe in detail. The time he gave for when he had bought the piece of clothing was about half a year after the unfortunate murder. Meanwhile, the piece of clothing had been sold to a hairdresser who had just recently moved away from L. to Brussels, according to information from his relatives. A letter was then also sent to Brussels; however, the hairdresser, who had been tracked down with much difficulty by the local courts, had in turn sold the piece of clothing to the valet of the Count of D., who had traveled to Hungary with his master.

Nach einer Menge Hindernisse und unbeschreiblicher Arbeit kam endlich das Kleidungsstück, auf welches jetzt so viel anzukommen schien, an die Gerichte nach V. zurück. Glücklicherweise war es bisher wenig getragen worden, da der Kammerdiener des Grafen D. es dem Friseur weniger aus Bedürfnis, als um seinem Landsmann aus einer Geldnot zu helfen, abgekauft hatte. Der Trödler beschwor nun zuerst, dass solches eben das Kleidungsstück sei, welches er an den Friseur verkauft habe, und der Freund des Gerichtsdieners, der solches zuerst in L. in der Trödelbude entdeckt hatte, und noch zwei andere, welche den jungen S. gleichfalls genau kannten, erkannten ohne Mühe dasselbe als ihm zugehörig und beschwörten ihre Aussagen. Dies beschworen auch noch jene Zeugen, welche an dem Tag des Mordes diesen mit Marianne in der Allee gesehen hatten, sowie jene, welche ihn an jenem Abend im Kaffeehaus gesehen hatten, dass Wilhelm an jenem Abend dieses Kleidungsstück getragen habe. – Man verglich nun den Knopf, welchen die tote Marianne in der Hand gehabt hatte, mit jenen, welche sich noch auf dem Kleidungsstück befanden, und nicht nur überzeugte die Ähnlichkeit auf den ersten Blick, dass derselbe zu dieser Garnitur gehörte, sondern es fehlte auch diesem Kleidungsstück genau vor der Brust ein Knopf und die Spuren des Abrisses zeigten, dass solcher mit heftiger Gewalt abgerissen worden sein müsse.

Nun wurde der Verhaftete darüber vernommen, wie er an dem Tag des unglücklichen Vorgangs gekleidet gewesen ware, und sorgfältiger hat sich noch keine Dame um das Ankleiden ihrer Feindin erkundigt, als es hier in der ernsthaftesten Sache von der Welt geschah. Zwar wollte Wilhelm hiervon anfangs nichts wissen und fand die deshalb an ihn gestellen Fragen höchst lustig; als aber endlich der Richter ihm das Kleidungsstück und den abgerissenen Knopf vorlegte; als man den Büschel Haare, welchen die Ermordete in den Händen gehabt hatte, mit den Kopfhaaren des Angeklagten verglich und in Farbe und Konsistenz ähnlich fand, da verlor der Elende die Fassung, welche bis jetzt noch keinen Augenblick ihn verlassen hatte; da fiel er vor dem Gericht nieder und gestand den ganzen Umfang seiner Schuld.

After a multitude of obstacles and indescribably hard work, the piece of clothing, to which so much seemed to come down, finally arrived back at the courts in V. Fortunately, it had been worn little up to then because the valet of the Count of D. had purchased it from the hairdresser less out of necessity than to help his fellow countryman in a financial crisis. First the junk dealer swore to it that this was precisely the piece of clothing which he had sold to the hairdresser, and then the court clerk's friend, who had first discovered it in the junk shop in L., and then two other men who both knew the young S. very well, all recognized it without any trouble as belonging to him and took their statements under oath. This—that Wilhelm had worn the piece of clothing on that evening—was also affirmed under oath by those witnesses who had seen him with Marianne in the tree-lined road on the day of the murder and also by those who had seen him in the coffee house that evening.—They compared the button, which the dead Marianne had had in her hands, with those which were still affixed to the piece of clothing; not only was the similarity at first glance convincing that it belonged to this set [of buttons], but also there was a button missing from this piece of clothing exactly at the chest, and the traces of the torn-off part showed that it must have been ripped off with great force.

The arrested [individual] was subsequently questioned about this—how he had been dressed on the day of the unfortunate event—and no lady had inquired more thoroughly about her enemy's dressing than happened here as if it were the most serious affair in the world. It must be said that at first Wilhelm did not want to hear about this and found the questions that were asked of him exceedingly funny; however, when the judge presented to him the piece of clothing and the torn-off button, and when the tuft of hair which the murdered woman had held in her hands was compared to the hair on the head of the accused and found to be similar in color and consistency, the miserable man lost the composure which had not left him for a single moment until then; he fell down before the judge and confessed the full extent of his culpability.

Schon war der Elende, nachdem die arme Marianne sich ganz seiner Liebe geopfert, vom Genuss übersättigt, als diese ihm anzeigte, dass sie Mutter sein würde. – Ein wütender, ihm selbst unbegreiflicher Hass, sagte der Bösewicht, habe sich seiner gegen die Arme bemächtigt, als sie ihm diese Nachricht mit all der Unschuld ihres reinen Herzens, vertrauend ohne Arg auf seine Redlichkeit und begeistert von dem jüngsten aller Gefühle, dem Muttergefühl, freudig mitgeteilt habe. Wilhelms Eltern hatten eben zum Unglück für diesen, der ihr Liebling war, eine Heirat mit einem der schönsten und reichsten Mädchen in einer benachbarten Stadt geplant und grösstenteils in Richtigkeit gebracht. Da derselbe zuvor mit aller Wärme der Liebe an Marianne gehangen habe und die Eltern diese Liebe als ein Hindernis ihres Lieblingsplanes ansahen, so scheuten sie nichts, um diesen ihren Sohn von seiner Liebschaft abzubringen, welches freilich bei dessen eingetretener Sinnesänderung überflüssig war. Indessen gossen doch die Beleidigungen und Verleumdungen, welche sich Wilhelms Mutter zu diesem Zweck gegen die unglückliche Marianne erlaubte, gleichwohl Öl in die Flamme und versetzte diesen in jenen Zustand der Raserei, in der es allein möglich war, eine so unnatürliche und schändliche Tat zu begehen. Hierzu kam noch, dass Wilhelm Marianne, um sie seiner Wollust zu opfern, in Gegenwart mehrer Zeugen die Ehe versprochen hatte. Dieses unglückliche Mädchen war also an sich schon ein Hindernis der Heirat Wilhelms, und das umso mehr, da der Gegenstand seiner Liebe, die er jetzt noch heißer liebte als ehedem Marianne, erklärt hatte, dass sie, wenn sich das gehörte Gerücht bestätigte, nie den Verführer eines unglücklichen Mädchens heiraten werde. So vereinigte sich alles dahin zu wirken, dass der Hass des jungen Menschen gegen das ebenso unglückliche als unschuldige Hindernis seiner Wünsche zur Raserei anwuchs.

In dieser peinlichen Lage wandte sich Wilhelm an seinen älteren Bruder, einen Klostergeistlichen, der das Orakel des Hauses machte. Dieser niederträchtige Pfaffe war seiner Unsittlichkeit wegen überall als Ungeheuer gehasst und geflohen. Seine Schlauheit war ebenso bekannt als sein kühner Unternehmungsgeist und er war wegen beiden der Gegenstand

The miserable man had already been sated by pleasure when poor Marianne, after she had sacrificed herself entirely to his love, indicated to him that she was going to be a mother. A fierce hatred against the poor woman, inexplicable to him, the wicked man said, had taken hold of him when she joyously told him the news with all the innocence of a pure heart, relying without malice on his integrity and delighted by the latest of all of her feelings, the feeling of motherhood. To the misfortune of him who was their favorite [child], Wilhelm's parents had planned, and for the most part already set in motion, his marriage to one of the most beautiful and richest girls of the neighboring town. Since he, Wilhelm, had previously been attached to Marianne with all the warmth of love, and the parents had seen this love as an obstacle to their cherished plan, they spared nothing to dissuade this son of theirs of his amour, which had of course already become superfluous because of the change of mind that had occurred [in him]. However, the insults and defamations that Wilhelm's mother permitted herself against the unfortunate Marianne for this very purpose added fuel to the flames and put him into a rage, which was the sole reason that made it possible for him to commit such an unnatural and reprehensible act. To this was added that Wilhelm, in order to sacrifice her to his lechery, had promised marriage to Marianne in the presence of several witnesses. Thus, the unfortunate girl was already an obstacle to Wilhelm's marriage, and even more so since the [new] object of his love, whom he now loved even more than Marianne previously, had declared that, should the rumor she had heard be confirmed, she would never marry the seducer of an unfortunate girl. All of this united to work to the point that the hatred of the young man toward the obstacle to his desires, as unfortunate as she was innocent, grew into rage.

In this distressing situation Wilhelm had turned to his elder brother, a priest in a monastery, who acted as the decision maker for the family. This malicious cleric was detested and shunned everywhere as a monster on account of his immorality. His cunning was as well known as his audacious initiative, and he was the object of widespread fear because of both. This

allgemeiner Furcht. Dieser Unmensch hauchte den Gedanken von Mord in Wilhelms Seele, für welchen dieser in der Stimmung, in welcher er sich befand, nur zu empfänglich war. Für die Summe von 200 Dukaten, welche Wilhelm von seinem Taschengeld zurückgelegt hatte, erbot er sich sogleich den Mord vollführen zu helfen, und er war es, der die Anstalten hierzu leitete. Nach diesem musste Wilhelm die bedauernswürdige Marianne zu dem unglücklichen Spaziergang einladen. Man heuchelte Heiterkeit, als das harmlose Geschöpf erschien, sprach viel davon, dass durch die Vermittlung eben dieses boshaften Pfaffens Wilhelms Eltern nachgiebiger gegen dessen Heirate mit Marianne zu werden anfingen, und lockte das arglose Mädchen an einen etwas abgelegenen und weniger besuchten Platz an dem Gestade des Flusses. Dort stieß das Ungeheuer von Priester von hinten zu mit einem Dolch nach der Unglücklichen, der aber, weil er nur die Schulter traf, zerbrach. In dem Augenblick, als Marianne sich schreiend umdrehte, zieht Wilhelm ein großes Taschenmesser, das er eigens zu diesem Gebrauch zuvor geschärft hatte, und gibt damit derselben mehrere Stiche. Diese flieht, ruft um Hilfe, beschwört ihre Mörder um Gnade, erinnert die Bösewichter an das schuldlose Geschöpf, das sich in ihrem Innern bilde, kämpfte gegen die Buben, bis sie endlich ermattet von der Anstrengung und dem Blutverlust unter der Menge von Wunden, welche die Barbaren mit kaltem Blut immer tiefer bohren, um, wies sie mit teuflischen Spott sagen, das Lebendige zu treffen, zu Boden sinkt. Noch war sie nicht ganz tot und die Mörder bereits eine Strecke weit weggegangen, als es Wilhelm einfällt, dass es doch sicherer sei, den Leichnam in den Fluss zu werfen. Er kehrte daher um und findet, dass die Arme ihre letzten Kräfte zusammengefasst und sich wieder aufgerafft hatte. – Mit dem empörenden Spotte, dass sie sich von der gehabten Erhitzung abkühlen müsse, schleppt er die Halbentseelte zum Ufer und wirft sie in den Fluss. – Hier war es, wo Marianne die Verzweiflung und Todesangst neue Kräfte lieh; sie fasst mit der einen Hand den Rockknopf des Mörders, der nachher dessen Verräter und ihr Rächer war, mit der anderen wühlte sie in dessen Haaren.

monster breathed the thought of murder into Wilhelm's soul, to which the latter was only too susceptible while in the mental state in which he found himself. For the sum of 200 ducats, which Wilhelm had set aside from his allowance, [the priest] offered without further ado to help execute the murder, and it was he who made the preparations for it. On his instruction, Wilhelm had to invite the unfortunate woman to the ill-fated promenade. They pretended merriment when the innocent creature appeared, and spoke much of the fact that because of the wicked cleric's mediation, Wilhelm's parents had begun to become accepting about the thought of his marriage to Marianne, and they lured the unsuspecting girl to a somewhat remote and less frequented place on the shores of the river. There the monster of a priest stabbed the unfortunate woman from behind with a dagger, which shattered however, because it hit only the shoulder. In the instant when Marianne turned around, screaming, Wilhelm pulls out a large pocket knife, which he had sharpened earlier for this very purpose, and with it he stabs her several times. She flees, calls for help, implores her murderers to show her mercy, reminds the evildoers of the innocent creature which was growing inside her, fought against the two men, until finally, weakened by the exertion and the loss of blood from the multitude of wounds which the cold-blooded barbarians are drilling deeper and deeper in order to, as they say in diabolical mockery, hit the lifeforce, she sinks to the ground. She was still not completely dead and the murderers had already gone away a [long] distance, when Wilhelm has the thought that it might be safer after all to throw the body into the river. He therefore turns around and finds that the poor woman had summoned her last strength and picked herself up.—With the outrageous sarcasm that she needed to cool off from the sweating from her exertion, he drags the half lifeless woman to the bank of the shore and throws her into the river.—It was here where despair and the fear of dying had given Marianne new strength; with one hand she gets a hold of the jacket button of the murderer, which was to become his traitor and her avenger, [and] with the other she dug in his hair.

Am anderen Morgen hörte der Pfaffe ein dunkles Gerücht, er geht, von Gewissensangst getrieben, das Ufer des Flusses hinab, er findet Mariannes Körper vom Wasser ausgespieen und schon von Leuten umgeben und flieht. – Man hat nachdem nichts weiter von ihm gehört, als dass er als Pfaffe in einer französischen Gemeinde bei Lyons angestellt war, und glaubt, dass er bei massenweise standrechtlichen Erschießungen unter einem französischen Revolutionär und Richter dort sein Ende gefunden habe. Wilhelm war verwegen genug gewesen zu bleiben, besonders weil er glaubte, im äußersten Fall alle Schuld auf seinen entflohenen Bruder schieben zu können.

Wilhelms Vater, durch einen Brief des entwichenen Pfaffen von dem ganzen Hergang unterrichtet und aufmerksamer als die Gerichte, hatte das fatale Kleid selbst nach L. gebracht und dort verkauft, um alles zu entfernen, was gegen seinen Sohn zeugen könne. Als er erfuhr, dass gerade diese Vorsicht dem Unglücklichen verderblich geworden war, starb er nach einem Schlaganfall, ehe noch dessen Urteil erschien. Wilhelm S. erhielt bald darauf sein Urteil. An dem Ort, wo er Marianne ermordet hatte, wurde er mit glühenden Zangen gezwickt und dann lebendig gerädert. – Einfache Kreuze, in die dort stehenden Obstbäume gekerbt, bezeugen dem Wanderer den Ort, wo sich die schauerliche Geschichte zugetragen hat.

On the following morning, the cleric heard a vague rumor; driven by a guilty conscience, he walks down the embankment of the river, he finds Marianne's body, cast out by the water and already surrounded by people, and he flees. Nothing was heard of him thereafter, other than that he was employed as a cleric in a French church community near Lyons, and it is believed that he met his Maker there during a mass shooting according to martial law [conducted] by a French revolutionary and judge. Wilhelm had been audacious enough to hang about, especially because he believed that he would be able to shift the blame onto his escaped brother, if worse came to worst.

Wilhelm's father had been informed of the complete course of events via a letter from the escaped cleric and, more attentive than the courts, had taken the damaging piece of clothing to L. in person and sold it there, in order to remove anything which might bear witness against his son. When he learned that it was precisely this precaution that had become the unfortunate man's downfall, he died from a stroke even before the latter's verdict was rendered. Wilhelm S. received his verdict soon thereafter. At the place where he murdered Marianne, he was pinched with red hot tongs and then broken alive on the wheel.—Simple crosses, cut into the fruit-bearing trees there, testify to the passerby the site where the gruesome story was acted out.

WILLIBALD ALEXIS

Georg Wilhelm Heinrich Häring was born on June 29, 1798, in Breslau, Poland (which then belonged to the Kingdom of Prussia). After Napoleon's army conquered the city in 1806, young Georg and his mother relocated to Berlin, where they lived with his mother's relatives. In 1815, the youth joined the wars of liberation against the French as a volunteer.

In 1817, he began to study law and history in Berlin and Breslau, and later worked as a legal clerk at the Superior Court of Justice in Breslau. After his first novel (*Walladmor*, 1824) became a success, he abandoned his legal career. Supposedly, he assumed the pen name Willibald Alexis in order to avoid puns on his real last name, which is German for "herring."

From 1827 on, Alexis lived in Berlin, where he worked as the editor-in-chief of the *Berliner Konversationsblatt* (*Berlin Conversational Paper*), from which he resigned in 1835 in protest against increasing censorship by the authorities. He became a freelance and feature writer for various newspapers, and also he continued to write novels. From 1842 until 1860, he co-published with great success *Der neue Pitaval* (*The New Pitaval*), a collection of notorious criminal cases.

In the years following, besides completing a number of hugely successful novels, Alexis also founded a series of reading societies, managed bookstores, bought and sold real estate, and traveled extensively through France, Scandinavia, and East Prussia. During this time, he developed close friendships with other famous writers such as Joseph von Eichendorff, Ludwig Tieck, and Wilhelm Hauff.

After he had supported the unsuccessful revolutionaries in the political struggles of the 1848 revolution, he left Berlin for Rome and later settled in Arnstadt, a picturesque town in Thuringia, where he spent almost the rest of his life. He died in Arnstadt in 1871.

Alexis is commonly regarded as the creator of the realistic historical novel in German literature. In addition to his novels, he wrote shorter narratives and stories, poems and ballads, travelogues, and biographies.

In a format reminiscent of Schiller's story, "The Criminal of Lost Honor," Alexis's story tells us about the villain's downfall in his own words.

WILLIBALD ALEXIS

WILLIBALD ALEXIS

Das Gelöbnis der drei Diebe

Der Diener einer vornehmen Familie in Berlin trat am Abend des 2. Dezember 1843 in einen Branntweinladen und forderte ein Glas Likör. Der Wirt, bei dem er ein alter Kunde war, befragte ihn, warum er sich so lange nicht eingefunden habe. Der Diener, in reicher Jägerlivree, klagte über das Jammerleben, das er zu führen habe, tagaus, tagein im Frondienste, seine Fräuleins, die Herrschaft, von morgens bis abends in Putzläden, zum Juwelier, zu Besuch begleiten zu müssen, dann nach dem Dienst im Hause ins Konzert, ins Theater. Er wisse gar nicht, wo ihm von dem vielen Laufen und Rennen, Bestellen und Befehlen der Kopf stünde. Heute sei es aber kaum auszuhalten, denn das älteste gnädige Fräulein mache Hochzeit. Alles Silberzeug habe hervorgeholt und geputzt werden müssen. Eben jetzt müsse er noch zum Goldarbeiter, um einen Armleuchter zu holen, der dort in Arbeit sei. Der Jäger ging, nachdem er die Hoffnung aussprach, dass, wenn der schwere Tag vorbei sei, wohl wieder etwas Ruhe eintreten werde.

Ein Mensch in abgetragener Kleidung im Winkel der Stube, aber ein Stammkunde, fragte den Wirt, wer der Jäger sei. Der Wirt nannte den Namen und die Herrschaft, bei welcher der Jäger diente, und setzte hinzu, dass sie ungeheuer reich und freigebig sei; der Dienstbote habe es da gut. Der Fragende stieß einen Fluch aus: »Ja, wer hat, bei dem liegt's in Haufen!« Er brummte über die ungerechte Verteilung der Güter und zog sich

WILLIBALD ALEXIS

The Pledge of the Three Thieves

The servant of a noble family entered a store serving liquor on the evening of December 2, 1843, and asked for a glass of brandy. The host, whose establishment he had frequented often, asked him why he had not come to visit for such a long time. The servant, in rich hunter's livery, lamented the miserable life which he had to lead; day in, day out, he was in compulsory service, forced to accompany his young ladies, who employed him, to the finery stores from morning till evening, [then] to the jeweler, and then, after his service inside the house, to concerts [and] to the theater. He said he didn't know whether he was coming or going, from all the walking and running, the ordering of items and being ordered around. Today especially it was hardly manageable, because the oldest young miss was getting married. All of the silverware had to be dragged out and polished. Just now he had to go to the goldsmith's to fetch a candelabra which was being worked on there. The hunter left, after having expressed his hope that after the end of this difficult day, a little tranquility might be restored.

A man in threadbare clothes [who sat] in the corner of the room but was a regular customer, asked the host who the hunter was. The host mentioned the name and that of the young ladies in whose service the hunter was, and added that they were incredibly rich and openhanded; the servant had it good there. The inquirer uttered a curse: "Yes, those who have, have it in heaps!" He muttered about the unfair distribution of

auf eine Bank im Hintergrunde zurück, wo er mit noch zwei anderen Gästen ein leises Gespräch führte. Dann bezahlten alle drei und verließen zugleich den Schenkladen.

Im Dunkel der Straße setzten sie ihr Gespräch fort. Der eine sagte leise:»Ich will des Teufels sein, komme ich nicht.« Der zweite:»Bruder, verlass dich auf mich, wenn ich nicht das Bein breche, so komme ich.« Der dritte sagte:»Und soll mich's zehn Jahr kosten, ich bin dabei.«

»Schlag zwei Uhr, wenn der Wächter vorbei!« war das Losungswort, mit dem sie sich trennten.

Das Haus, in dem die Herrschaft des Jägers wohnte, stieß mit seinem Hintergebäude auf eine Gasse, von der aus die Diebe ihren Einbruch bewerkstelligten. Kein Wächter störte sie, als sie mit dem Schlage zwei nach Mitternacht eine mitgebrachte Leiter an ein Fenster der oberen Etage setzten. Der Vorderste drückte ohne Geräusch die Scheibe ein und öffnete das Fenster, durch das alle drei mit Äxten, Nachschlüsseln und Säcken stiegen. Der letzte zog die Leiter noch herein und lehnte sie auf dem Gange, wo sie sich befanden, an die Wand.

Mit der Lokalität des Hauses vertraut, schlichen sie über den Gang bis zu einer Treppe, die nach dem Hofe führte, und gingen von da ins Vorderhaus. Die Hoftür war nur angelehnt. Erst die Glastür des Vorsaals fanden sie verschlossen. Mit einem Dietrich wurde sie leicht geöffnet. Nicht mehr Schwierigkeit stellte ihnen die Flügeltür entgegen, die zu dem großen Saale führte, wo das Hochzeitsmahl gefeiert worden war.

Alles war still, als sie ihre Diebeslaterne anzündeten, bei deren mattem Schein sie auf der noch unabgeräumten langen Tafel den ganzen Reichtum an Silbergeschirr entdeckten. Freudig erstaunt, griffen sie hastig, doch ohne den geringsten Lärm zu machen, zu, warfen und stopften in die Säcke, was ihnen wertvoll schien und darin Platz hatte. Auch dies Werk war vollkommen gelungen, und mit leisen Schritten machten sie sich auf den Rückweg.

Der Jäger, der unbewusst der Verräter seiner Herrschaft geworden war, erwachte nicht durch das Geräusch, sondern durch einen kalten Luftzug, der über sein Gesicht strich. Er schlief im Hinterhause; seine Kammer ging auf den Gang. Der

possessions and moved back to a bench in the back where he had a quiet conversation with two other patrons. After that they paid and all left the tavern at the same time.

In the darkness of the street they continued their conversation. One of them said quietly: "I shall be the Devil's if I don't come!" The second one [said]: "Brother, you can rely on me; if I don't break a leg, I shall come." The third one said: "And if it will get me ten years, I am in it."

"At the stroke of two o'clock, when the guardsman has passed!" was the watchword on which they parted.

The house where the hunter's employers lived bordered with its rear building onto an alley from which the thieves carried out their burglary. No watchman disturbed them when at the stroke of two after midnight, they put a ladder which they had brought with them to a window at the upper level. The one at the front pushed the glass in without a sound and opened the window, through which all three of them entered with axes, picklocks, and sacks. Then the last one pulled up the ladder and leaned it against the wall of the hallway in which they were.

Familiar with the layout of the house, they crept along the hallway to a staircase which led to the courtyard, and from there they entered the building in the front. The gate to the court stood ajar. The glass door to the foyer, though, they found locked. With a picklock it was easily unlocked. The double door to the large hall, where the wedding feast had been celebrated, did not present any more difficulties.

Everything was quiet when they lit their thief's lantern [and], by the faint light of it, discovered the complete wealth of the silver dishware on the long table which had not yet been cleared. Pleasantly surprised, but without making even the smallest sound, they quickly reached for it and stuffed into their sacks what appeared precious to them and they had room for. This task also was completed perfectly, and with quiet steps they set out on their way back.

The hunter, who had unknowingly become a traitor to his employer, did not awake because of a sound, but because of the cold draft which brushed over his face. He slept in the rear building extension; his chamber opened to the hallway. The

Luftzug kam aus der zerbrochenen Scheibe. In der Meinung, dass er oder ein anderer ein Fenster aufgelassen hätte, sprang er auf, um es zu schließen. In der Dunkelheit stieß er an eine Leiter, die nie hier gestanden hatte. Seine bloßen Füße traten auf Glasscherben, und beim nächsten Blick bemerkte er die eingeschlagene Scheibe.

Schnell bewusst und rasch entschlossen, sprang er in die Kammer zurück, riss den Hirschfänger aus der Scheide und war schon auf dem Gange, als er die Diebe die Treppe heraufkommen hörte. Mutig stürzte er ihnen entgegen, »Diebe! Diebe!« schreiend. Sie warfen ihre Säcke fort. Der eine schwang seine Axt und wollte auf den Jäger losgehen. Bevor dieser seine schwere Waffe benutzen konnte, gab er ihm mit der Klinge einen Hieb über den Kopf, so dass er bewusstlos niederstürzte. Der zweite war währenddessen rasch durch das offene Fenster auf die Straße gesprungen. Der dritte, vor Angst und Furcht regungslos, wagte weder zu fliehen noch Widerstand zu leisten.

Der Jäger hielt ihn gepackt, während auf sein Schreien die anderen Hausbewohner erwachten und herbeieilten. Von draußen war auch der Nachtwächter herbeigekommen und schrie hinauf, was es denn gäbe; auf dem Steinpflaster läge ein Kerl, der jämmerlich ächze. Die Polizei war bald herbeigerufen und verhaftete die Diebe. Zwei von ihnen wurden in das Gefängnislazarett gebracht.

Derjenige, den der Hirschfänger des Jägers getroffen hatte, konnte nicht mehr bekennen und nicht mehr vernommen werden. Der Hieb des Jägers war tief ins Gehirn gedrungen. Nach elfstündigem Todeskampfe verschied er am Tage darauf. Man erkannte in ihm einen mehrmals verurteilten Dieb und Betrüger.

Der zweite Verwundete hatte den rechten Schenkel durch den Sprung aus dem Fenster an zwei Stellen gebrochen. Auch hatte er eine starke Gehirnerschütterung und Prellungen der Brust erlitten und konnte nur wenig sprechen. Auch in ihm erkannte man einen schon mehrmals verurteilten Dieb, der sich längere Zeit als Vagabund in Berlin herumgetrieben hatte.

Der Brand kam in das rechte Bein, und es musste ihm abgenommen werden. Er legte vor Gericht ein vollständiges

draft came from the broken glass. Assuming that he or someone else had left the window open, he jumped up to close it. In the darkness he bumped against a ladder which had never been there before. His naked feet stepped on broken pieces of glass, and with his next glance he noticed the glass pane that had been smashed in.

Rapidly gaining consciousness and quickly determined, he jumped back into his chamber, ripped the hunting knife from its scabbard, and was already in the hallway when he heard the thieves come up the stairs. Bravely he rushed at them, calling out, "Thieves! Thieves!" They threw away their sacks. One of them swung his axe and was about to attack the hunter. Before he was able to use his heavy weapon, [the hunter] hit him on the head with the blade so that he fell to the ground, unconscious. Meanwhile, the second one had jumped through the open window into the street. The third one, paralyzed with fear and terror, dared neither to flee nor to resist.

The hunter held him tightly while the other residents of the house awoke from his shouts and came running. From the outside, the night watchman had arrived and shouted up to them what was going on; there was a chap lying on the cobblestones, moaning miserably. Soon the police were called forth and the thieves arrested. Two of them were brought to the prison's sick bay.

The one hit by the hunter's knife was no longer able to make a statement and could never be questioned again. The blow from the hunter had entered deeply into the brain. After a death struggle of eleven hours, he passed away next day. They recognized him as a thief and crook who had been sentenced several times [before].

The second wounded [man] had broken his right thigh in two places when jumping out of the window. Also, he suffered a severe concussion and contusions on his chest, and he was able to talk only sparingly. They recognized him also as a thief who had been sentenced several times [before], and who had roved about Berlin as a vagabond for some time.

His right leg turned gangrenous and they had to amputate it. He made a full confession before the court, and an even fuller

Bekenntnis ab, noch vollständiger vor dem Arzt. Es ist eine Lebensgeschichte, die sich tausendmal wiederholt, und doch erinnern wir uns nicht, sie so schon aus dem Munde eines Verbrechers von seiner Bildungsstufe gehört zu haben.

»Ich bin zu Brandenburg im Jahre 1807 geboren, wo mein Vater Maurergeselle war. Er hatte Arbeit genug, und meine Mutter verdiente als Wäscherin schönes Geld. In meiner Jugend bis zum achten Jahre ging mir nichts ab, ich war gesund und wurde zu kleinen häuslichen Verrichtungen, zum Warten und Wiegen meiner jüngeren Geschwister angehalten, aber zur Schule schickte man mich nicht. Von der Mutter lernte ich das Vaterunser und die Zehn Gebote, die ich alle Morgen und Abende beten musste, vor die Tür zu andern Jungen durfte ich nicht.

»Da es in den damaligen Kriegsjahren an Durchmärschen und Gelegenheit zum Verdienst nicht fehlte, hatte mein Vater einen kleinen Schnapsladen angelegt; seitdem sah und hörte ich viel Böses, das ich leider schnell genug lernte. Das Fluchen, Schwören und Lästern der Gäste, zumal der, die täglich kamen, und ihre Reden träuften Gift in meine Seele, und der Branntwein, den mir der eine oder der andere gab, verwilderte mich vollends. Ich wurde trotzig gegen die Mutter, stahl dem Vater heimlich Geld aus der Lade, ging ihm über die Flaschen; als er mich einige Male ertappte, züchtigte und zur Strafe in die Schule schickte, hielt ich es dort kaum ein Jahr aus. Ich lernte notdürftig lesen, und da meine Beihilfe in der Schenke erforderlich wurde, behielt mich der Vater wieder ganz zu Hause.

»Ich habe seitdem viele Bücher gelesen. Räuber- und Diebesgeschichten verschlang ich gleichsam. Ein Gast, der eine Leihbibliothek hatte, erlaubte mir, sie zu benutzen, und ehe ich fünfzehn Jahre alt wurde, hatte ich sie durchlesen. Das verdarb mich vollends, ich wollte auch ein berühmter Räuber werden, und alles, was ich von dem freien Leben dieser Menschen las, reizte mich außerordentlich. Eine Bibel war in unserem Hause nicht zu finden, nur ein alter Katechismus, und meine Mutter besaß ein Gesangbuch, worin sie zuweilen las. Zur Kirche ging keiner von uns, denn des Sonntags und Feiertags war die ganze Zeit bei uns Gastverkehr.

one before the doctor. It is a life story which repeats itself a thousand times, and yet, we do not recall having heard it before from the mouth of a criminal of his educational level.

"I was born in the year 1807 in Brandenburg, where my father was a journeyman bricklayer. He had enough work, and my mother earned good money as a laundress. In my childhood, until I was eight, I lacked nothing; I was healthy and was encouraged to do smaller domestic chores, [and] tending to and rocking my younger siblings; however, I was not sent to school. From my mother I learned the Our Father and the Ten Commandments, which I had to recite each morning and evening; I was not allowed outside with the other boys.

"Because there was no lack of soldiers marching through and opportunities for earning money in the years of war in those days, my father started up a small liquor store; since then I have seen and heard much evil, which I, sadly, learned quickly enough. The swearwords, cursing, and backbiting of the guests, particularly those who came daily, and their discourse, dribbled poison into my soul, and the brandy which one or the other gave me made me into a complete savage. I became defiant toward my mother, stole money from my father, [and] drank from his bottles; when he caught me a few times, he beat me with a cane and, as a punishment, sent me to school, [and] I was hardly able to bear it for a year. I learned how to read [only] poorly and, because my support in the store was required, my father kept me home again entirely.

"Since then, I read many books; I virtually devoured stories of robbers and thieves. A patron who owned a lending library allowed me to use it, and before I had reached the age of fifteen, I had finished reading [all of] it. That spoiled me completely; I too wanted to become a notorious robber, and everything I read about the independent life of these people tantalized me extraordinarily. There was no Bible to be found in our house, only an old catechism, and my mother owned a hymnbook in which she occasionally read. None of us went to church, because on Sundays and holidays there was customer traffic the entire time.

»Erst als ich eingesegnet werden sollte, bekam ich eine Bibel. Ich wurde sechs Wochen von einem Geistlichen unterrichtet, was mir sehr langweilig vorkam. Nach meiner Einsegnung, wobei ich viel Tränen vergoss, weil auch die anderen Kinder weinten, ging ich mit meiner Mutter zum Abendmahl. Seitdem habe ich es nur im Gefängnis wieder genossen.

»Inzwischen war in unserem Hause eine traurige Veränderung vorgegangen. Mein Vater fand beim Schank seine Rechnung nicht mehr. Es ging rückwärts, und war er früher schon gerade kein Säufer, aber doch ein Liebhaber des Branntweins, so trank er jetzt immer stärker, misshandelte die Mutter und uns Kinder, zerschlug in der Besoffenheit alles, was er ergriff, und wollte sich von der Mutter, die ihm zu still war und auf die er alle Schuld warf, scheiden lassen. Der Tod der Mutter, die sich abzehrte, kam dazwischen.

»Dieser Tod brachte in unser Hauswesen die größte Zerrüttung, mit dem Vater war es nicht mehr auszuhalten, er lebte mit der Magd, die uns Kinder ganz vernachlässigte, so dass wir vom Ungeziefer fast aufgerieben waren, viel Schläge, aber keine regelmäßige Mahlzeiten bekamen und in zerrissenen Kleidern gingen.

»Was man mir nicht gab, das suchte ich zu nehmen. Aus Schlägen und Scheltworten machte ich mir nichts. Ich wuchs dem Vater über den Kopf.

»Um mich loszuwerden, gab er mich als Handlanger unter die Maurer seiner Bekanntschaft. Hier bekam ich die weitere Ausbildung im Fluchen, Saufen und rohen Wesen. Des Winters, wo es keine Arbeit gab, kam ich wohl zum Vater zurück und half in der Wirtschaft. Öfter besoff ich mich und prügelte mich mit ihm, denn ich ließ mir nichts sagen. Er warf mich auf die Straße, und ich geriet nun mit den verworfensten Menschen in Gemeinschaft. Noch hatte ich nicht fremde Leute bestohlen, jetzt nahmen mich die Kameraden mit, lehrten mich alle Schliche und Listen, und ich wurde nicht nur ihnen gleich, sondern tat es ihnen bald zuvor.

»Mein Gewissen, wenn es mich mahnen wollte, erstickte ich in Branntwein und Ausschweifungen. Aber es war doch ein jämmerliches Leben. Keine Ruhe im Herzen, Blöße und Hunger

"Only when the time of my confirmation drew nearer was I given a Bible. I received instructions by a cleric for six weeks, which I found exceedingly monotonous. After my confirmation, on which occasion I shed a lot of tears because the other children also shed tears, I partook in the Lord's Supper. Since that time, I have enjoyed it again only in prison.

"Meanwhile, in our home a heartbreaking change had occurred. My father was unable to make his business meet ends. It declined, and while he had never been an outright drunkard but unquestionably a brandy enthusiast, he now drank more and more habitually, physically abused our mother and us children, smashed everything he touched in his drunkenness, and intended to get divorced from our mother, who was too quiet for him and on whom he put the blame for everything. Our mother's death, [after] she grew weak, prevented this.

"This death created the greatest disintegration in our household; my father became insufferable; he lived with the maidservant who neglected us children entirely so that we were almost worn down by the vermin, received many beatings but no regular meals, and went around in torn clothes.

"What I was not given, I tried to take. I did not care about beatings and cusswords. I outgrew my father.

"In order to dispose of me, he handed me off to the bricklayers amongst his acquaintances as an unskilled laborer. Here I received more education in swearing, heavy drinking, and crude manners. During the winter, when there was no work, I did return to my father and helped him with the [rundown] inn. I frequently got drunk, and we came to blows with each other because I did not want to listen to him. He threw me out, and then I came into the company of the most depraved people. Until then, I had not stolen from strangers, [but] now my comrades took me along, taught me all the ruses and tricks, and not only did I become like them, but soon I surpassed them.

"I drowned my conscience, when it tried to admonish me, in brandy and debauchery. And yet, it was a miserable life. No peace at heart, [and] nakedness and hunger in the winter.

im Winter. Oft wusste ich nicht, wo ich nachts Herberge finden würde; war ein Sündengeld durch Betrug und Diebstahl erworben, wurde es, wie im Sommer der Wochenlohn, verjubelt.

»Ich habe manchmal vor Gericht gestanden, aber ich log frech und befreite mich. Das machte mich nur noch dreister im Stehlen. Einmal aber wurde ich doch ertappt und kam auf fünf Monate in das Untersuchungsgefängnis. Hatte ich zuvor noch nicht ausgelernt, so erhielt ich hier erst die rechte Einweihung in die Diebsgenossenschaft.

»Ich kam viel schlechter heraus, als ich hineingekommen war, und wusste nun meine Diebereien schlauer und durch Mitwirkung Bekannter erfolgreicher zu betreiben.

»Jetzt fand ich Unterkommen, jetzt kannte ich die Hehler, jetzt war ich unterrichtet, wie man sich aus den Schlingen ziehen und den Richter auslachen kann. Auch die Strafe fürchtete ich nicht mehr, denn es ging mir im Gefängnis gar nichts ab. Wir waren da in Gesellschaft beieinander, erzählten uns, waren lustig und guter Dinge und zeigten unter uns ganz andere Gesichter als vor den Aufsehern und Richtern. Auch standen wir mit unseren Leuten draußen in fortwährendem Verkehr, und es bedurfte nicht eben großer Schlauheit, um durch Entlassene unsere gemeinschaftlich ausgesonnenen Diebespläne auszuführen.

»An Essen und Trinken, Kleidern und Wäsche fehlte es nicht, die Arbeit war ein Kinderspiel; und wurde man entlassen, bekam man noch ein paar Hemden, Schuhe, ja selbst noch etwas Geld. Da hatte man wieder etwas zu vertun und zu verkaufen. War's alle, ging die Dieberei wieder los, und wurde man erwischt, was konnte einem Arges passieren? Denn wenn es auch im Zuchthaus etwas strenger war und die Schläge weh taten, wenn man da auch zum Geistlichen in den Unterricht und in die Kirche musste, so ging's ja immer noch sorgenlos und lustig genug zu, und wenn man gut heucheln konnte, wie ich's aus dem Grunde lernte, und seine Arbeit verrichtete, die immer leichter war, als sie jeder Arme draußen tun muss, da war's ein prächtiges Leben, besonders wenn's nicht gar zu lange dauerte.

»So hab ich's Jahre lang getrieben. Zu den Soldaten mochten sie mich nicht nehmen, ich wäre auch ausgerissen, denn nichts

Often, I did not know where to stay the night; if I acquired wages of sin by means of skullduggery and theft, it was squandered, just like the weekly earnings in the summer.

"At times I was put on trial, but I lied insolently and was set free. That made me even more audacious when stealing. On one occasion, however, I was caught and came to spend five months in a detention center. If my training was not complete by then, now I received the final induction into the thieves' collective.

"I left much more iniquitous than when I had entered, and now was able to perform my pilferage more shrewdly and, with the aid of my acquaintances, more successfully.

"Now I found work; now I knew the dealer in stolen goods; now I knew how to cheat the gallows and laugh at the judges. Also, I was no longer afraid of being sentenced, because in prison I did not lack anything. We were in the company of friends there, told each other stories, were merry and in cheerful spirits, and we assumed entirely different airs amongst ourselves than when before the prison wardens and the judges. Also, we were in constant communication with our comrades on the outside, and really it did not take a lot of astuteness to have our collectively contrived plans for theft carried out by released prisoners.

"There was no shortage of food and drink, of clothes and underwear, [and] work was a walk in the park; and if one was released, he received a couple of shirts [and] shoes into the bargain and, what's more, even a little money. When that was spent, then the thieveries started anew, and if one was caught, what dreadful thing could happen to one? Inasmuch as it was a bit stricter in the penitentiary and the beating gave pain, [and] even if also one had to attend lessons and church services given by a cleric, there was still a sufficient amount of carefreeness and gaiety, and if one was able to feign as profoundly as I had learned to do and did his work, which was at all times easier than what every poor man had to do on the outside, then it was a splendid life, particularly if it did not all last too long.

"I practiced this [way of life] for years. The army did not accept me; also, I would have deserted because nothing was

war mir unausstehlicher als Zwang, dem ich mich im Gefängnis doch leicht fügte. Da mich zuletzt auch keiner mehr in Arbeit haben wollte, zog ich in die große Stadt Berlin, wo ich viele Bekannte aus den Zuchthäusern her hatte.

»Mein Vater war inzwischen verstorben, und auf jedes Kind kamen 12 Taler Erbteil. Ich mietete mit dem Geld einen Keller und legte einen kleinen Holzhandel an, wobei mir eine geschiedene Frau, zu der ich mich hielt, behilflich wurde; aber das war nur der Deckmantel vor der Polizei. Es glückte mir auch lange genug. Ich wurde aber doch zuletzt entlarvt; mir wurde alles genommen und ich selbst nach sechswöchigem Arrest in meine Heimat gewiesen.

»Mein ältester Bruder diente als Kutscher, die anderen Geschwister waren im Elend verkommen, niemand nahm mich auf, und ich fing an, zu vagabundieren und von Bettelei und Diebstahl zu leben. Sperrte man mich ein, so fütterte ich mich im Gefängnis wieder auf, bekam Kleider, wurde dann an Gesellschaften gewiesen, welche entlassene Sträflinge unterstützten, und habe so manchen Taler bekommen, der durch die Gurgel ging. Arbeiten wollte ich durchaus nicht mehr; Arbeit war mir im freien Zustande das Schrecklichste.

»So bin ich wieder nach Berlin zurückgekommen und wurde Bote in einer Buchhandlung, wo ich Zeitschriften an die Abnehmer in der Stadt umhertragen musste. Weil ich nun bei diesem Geschäft viele Gelegenheiten in den Häusern abpassen konnte, kamen meine alten Kameraden, von denen ich mich eine Zeitlang getrennt sah, wieder an mich.

»›Kerl, du wirst uns doch nicht untreu werden, du wirst dich hier um ein Lumpengeld schinden und plagen, du kannst es besser haben; komm mit in die Schenke, wir müssen dir etwas sagen!‹ Ich ging wieder zu ihnen, und das ganze Lasterleben fing von neuem an.

»Meine Herren jagten mich aus dem Botendienste, nun war ich wieder ganz in der Gewalt derjenigen, die mich freihielten und mit denen ich nun auf Betrug, Dieberei und Raub ausging.«

Die drei Diebe, die sich in der Branntweinschenke getroffen hatten, schworen feierlich, sich in der Nacht wieder zu treffen.

more intolerable to me than commands, which I still complied with so easily in prison. Since nobody wanted to give me work any longer, I moved to the big city of Berlin where I had many acquaintances from [my time in] the penitentiaries.

"Meanwhile my father had died, and each child received 12 thalers as their share of an inheritance. With the money I rented a cellar, and started a small timber business in which I received help from a divorced woman with whom I kept company; however, this was only a pretext for the police. It was successful long enough. However, eventually I was unmasked; everything was taken from me and, after a six-week arrest, I was deported to my hometown.

"My eldest brother was in service as a coachman; my other siblings had gone to rack and ruin in dejection; nobody took me in and I began to rove around and make a living by begging and stealing. When I was incarcerated, I fattened up again in the penitentiary, received clothes, was subsequently referred to agencies which supported released prisoners, and received many a thaler which then ran down my throat. I no longer wanted to work at all; when I was free, I perceived work was the most terrible thing.

"So I returned to Berlin again and took a post as a messenger in a bookstore, where my job consisted of having to deliver newspapers to subscribers around the city. Because I was now able to spy out numerous opportunities in these homes, my former comrades, from whom I was separated for a while, approached me again.

" 'Old chap, you aren't going to desert us; you have to sweat and toil for the most meager wages here; you can have it much better; come to the tavern with us, we have to tell you something!' I took up with them again, and the whole dissolute life started anew.

"My employers drove me out of my messenger service job, [and] now I was entirely in the power of those who paid for me and with whom I embarked on skullduggery, thievery, and robbery."

The three thieves who had met in the brandy tavern solemnly swore to meet again at night. The carpenter declared this with

Der Tischler beteuerte es mit den Worten: »Ich will des Teufels sein!« Er war es, dem der Hirschfänger des Jägers den Schädel spaltete. Der Maurerhandlanger mit den Worten: »Ich will das Bein brechen!« Er sprang aus dem Fenster und brach das Bein. Der dritte, der Jüngste unter ihnen, mit den Worten: »Und soll mich's zehn Jahre kosten!«

Er wurde wegen gewaltsamen Einbruchs zu zehn Jahren Zuchthaus verurteilt.

the words: "I shall be the Devil's!" His was the skull that the hunter's knife had split. The bricklayer's assistant [declared this] with the words: "I shall break a leg!" He jumped out of the window and broke a leg. The third one, the youngest among them, [declared this] with the words: "And even if it costs me ten years!"

He was sentenced to ten years of penal servitude for violent burglary.

FRIEDRICH HEBBEL

Friedrich Hebbel was born on March 18, 1813, in Wesselburen, Schleswig-Holstein, which belonged to Denmark at the time.

The son of a poor mason, he grew up in poverty. After his father died in 1827, he worked for a tyrannical parish bailiff until 1834. During that time, he founded a literary circle and began to publish poems in local and regional newspapers. At the invitation of the editor of a Hamburg fashion magazine, he moved to Hamburg to attend college there. He lived with Elise Lensing, a seamstress, who supported him financially. After brief stints at the University of Heidelberg, where he studied law, and at the Ludwig Maximilian Unversity in Munich, where he pursued studies in philosophy, history, and literature, he was penniless and ill and returned to Hamburg, where he was nursed back to health by Elise.

Finally he achieved fame, if not fortune, with his play *Judith* in 1840 and was able to obtain support from the Danish king for an extended stay in Paris, where he wrote the tragedy *Maria Magdalena*. In this play, he perfected his skill of portraying the middle class, which was a new concept at the time.

In 1845, Hebbel moved to Vienna and subsequently married the much younger Christine Enghaus, a famous and well-off actress. Here he continued his literary work. The play *Gyges und sein Ring* (*Gyges and His Ring*, 1854) is considered his most mature work and clearly shows his penchant for depicting complex psychological problems.

On his fiftieth birthday and only nine months before his death, Hebbel was the first recipient of the prestigious Schiller

Prize. The Prussian King Wilhelm had created the prize in 1859, on the occasion of the 100th anniversary of Schiller's birthday, with the stipulation that it be awarded to a playwright who had produced an outstanding dramatic piece. Hebbel died on December 13, 1863, in Vienna, Austria.

Hebbel left behind a large legacy of written works, among them diaries, novellas, plays, and poems. In his works, he often describes the tragic and fateful concatenation of events and addresses the social problems of his era—social change and injustice due to the industrial revolution, the pauperization of farmers and factory workers, and the exploitation of women and children.

In 1903, his widow founded the Friedrich Hebbel Foundation, which annually awards a prize of 5000 euros to outstanding northern German writers.

The story "Anna" describes the humiliation of a nobleman's servant and its outcome. In addition to being a gripping narrative, it is a brilliant and precise study of human behavior.

FRIEDRICH HEBBEL

FRIEDRICH HEBBEL

Anna

»Himmel blau und milde die Luft,
Blumen voll von Tau und Duft,
Und am Abend Tanz und Spiel,
Das ist mehr als allzuviel!«

Lustig sang dies an einem hellen Sonntagmorgen Anna, die
junge Magd, während sie zugleich aufs fleißigste mit Reinigung
der Küchen- und Milchgeschirre beschäftigt war. Da ging im
grün-damastenen Schlafrock der Freiherr von Eichenthal, in
dessen Diensten sie seit einem halben Jahre stand, an ihr vorüber, ein junger verlebter Mann, voll Hypochondrie und Grillen.
»Was soll das Gejohle?« herrschte er, indem er vor ihr stehen
blieb, ihr zu. »Sie weiß, dass ich keine Leichtfertigkeiten leiden
kann!« Anna erglühte über und über, sie erinnerte sich, dass der
gestrenge Herr sie vor einigen Abenden in der Gartenlaube gern
leichtfertig gefunden hätte, sie hatte ein scharfes Wort auf der
Zunge, griff aber, es mit Gewalt unterdrückend, nach einer
weißporzellänenen Suppenterrine, und ließ diese, in heftigem
Kampf mit der ihr eigenen Unerschrockenheit begriffen, zu
Boden fallen. Das kostbare Geschirr zerbrach, der Freiherr, der
bereits einige Schritte vorwärts getan hatte, kehrte zornglühen-
den Gesichts um. »Was?« rief er laut aus und trat dicht vor das
Mädchen hin. »Will Sie Tückmäuserin an meiner Mutter
Küchengerätschaften Ihr Mütchen kühlen, weil Ihre
Verstocktheit es Ihr nicht erlaubt, einen wohl verdienten

116

FRIEDRICH HEBBEL

Anna

"Skies blue and mild the air,
Flowers filled with dew and scent,
And in the evening dance and play,
That is more than overmuch!"

Anna, the young maid, sang this happily on a bright Sunday
morning, while at the same time occupied with cleaning, most
industriously, the kitchen crockery and milking equipment. At
that moment, the Baron Eichenthal, a young, dissipated man,
full of hypochondria and fancies, with whom she had been in
service for half a year, walked by in his greenish damask dressing gown. "What's up with this howling?" he shouted, stopping in front of her. "She knows that I cannot abide frivolities!"
Anna turned crimson red all over; she remembered that the
strict master would have liked very much to find her frivolous
several evenings ago in the gazebo; she had a sharp word on
the tip of her tongue, but, suppressing it with all her might, she
reached instead for the white porcelain soup tureen and, while
struggling mightily with her own boldness, let it drop to the
floor. The expensive dishware broke; the baron, who had
already taken several steps away, turned around, his face red
with anger. "What?" he shouted and stepped closely up to the
girl. "Is she, this underhanded person, trying to take out her
anger on my mother's kitchenware because her impenitence
does not allow her to accept a well-deserved reproach with

Vorwurf ruhig hinzunehmen, wie sichs geziemt?« Und damit gab er ihr rechts und links, scheltend und tobend, Ohrfeigen, während sie ihn, erstarrend, wie ein Kind, der Sprache, ja fast der Sinne beraubt, in der einen Hand noch den Henkel der Terrine haltend, die andere unwillkürlich gegen die Brust drückend, ansah. Aus diesem, an Ohnmacht grenzenden Zustand wurde sie erst durch das spöttische Gelächter des Kammermädchens Friederike erweckt, die, gefälliger, wie sie, es sich gern gefallen ließ, dass der Freiherr, lüstern tändelnd, sie in die Wangen kniff und mit ihren Locken spielte. Höhnisch schaute die freche Dirne zu ihr hinüber und rief ihr zu: »Das gibt guten Appetit für die Kirmes, Jungfer Männerscheu.« Der Freiherr aber stemmte, laut lachend, die Arme in die Seite und sagte: »Lass Sie sich das Gelüste nach Tanz und Spiel nur vergehen; ich nehme die von meiner Mutter erteilte Erlaubnis zurück, Sie soll das Haus hüten.«

»Gibts denn heute nichts für sie zu tun?« fuhr er, mit sich selbst ratschlagend, fort. Friederike flüsterte einiges. »Richtig«, rief er überlaut, »sie soll Flachs hecheln, bis spät in die Nacht, hört sie's?« Anna, in gänzlicher Verwirrung, nickte mit dem Kopf und sank dann kraftlos auf die Kniee, ergriff aber zugleich, instinktartig, ein messingenes Gefäß und begann, während ihr die Tränen heiß und unaufhaltsam aus den Augen drangen, es blank zu scheuern.

Da ging der Gärtner, der ihr, frisch und blühend, wie sie war, längst, aber vergebens, nachgestellt, und den vorigen Auftritt von ferne angesehen hatte, an ihr vorbei, grüßte sie und fragte hämisch, wie's ihr gehe. »Oh, oh!« stöhnte sie, krampfhaft zusammenzuckend, sprang auf und packte den hohnsprechenden Buben bei Brust und Gesicht. »Rasende!« rief er erschreckend und stieß sie, sich ihrer mit aller Manneskraft erwehrend, zurück. Sie, als wüsste sie selbst nicht, was sie getan, starrte ihm nach mit weit aufgerissenen Augen; dann, wie sich besinnend, ging sie wieder an ihre Arbeit, die sie ununterbrochen, nur zuweilen unbewusst laut aufseufzend, fortsetzte, bis man sie mittags zum Essen in die Küche rief. Hier sah sie sich empfangen von lauter schadenfrohen Gesichtern, und von mehr oder minder unterdrücktem Gelächter und Gekicher, welches, da sie

acquiescence, as is appropriate?" And with that, he slapped her on the face, left and right, reprimanding her and raving, while she looked at him, paralyzed, as if she were a child robbed of speech, and almost of her senses, still holding the handle of the tureen in the one hand and instinctively pressing the other one against her chest. From this state, which bordered on a trance, she was awakened only by the scornful laughter of the chambermaid, Friederike, who, more acquiescent than she, readily put up with the baron [when he was] lecherously teasing, pinching her cheeks and playing with her locks. Scornful, the brazen lass looked over to her and called out: "That will give [you] a good appetite for the fun fair, haughty spinster maiden." The baron, bracing his arms against his side and laughing loudly, said: "Just let the desire for dance and play pass away; I'll revoke the permission my mother gave; she shall stay at home."

"Isn't there anything to do for her today?" he continued, deliberating with himself. Friederike whispered something. "Right" he called out, too loud, "she shall heckle flax, until late at night, does she hear that?" Anna, in utter confusion, nodded her head and then sank to her knees, powerless; at the same time, however, she reached for a brass container and began to rub it until it shined, while the tears, hot and unceasingly, were streaming from her eyes.

At that moment, the gardener—who had been vainly and for a long time chasing after her, fresh and blossoming as she was—had witnessed the earlier scene from afar, walked by her, greeted her, and maliciously asked how she was doing. "Oh, oh!" she moaned, flinching convulsively; [then she] jumped up and grabbed the deriding young man by the chest and by the face. "Madwoman!" He shouted, terrified, and pushed her away, warding her off with all of his masculine strength. She, as if she did not know herself what she had done, stared after him, eyes wide open; then, as if coming to her senses, she continued with her interrupted work, only sighing loudly and unconsciously from time to time, until she was called to lunch in the kitchen at mid-day. Here she found herself received by nothing but gleeful faces, and by more-or-less suppressed

mit brennenden Wangen auf ihren Teller niederblickte und zu allen reichlich vorgebrachten Anspielungen kein Wort sagte, immer stärker und rücksichtsloser ward. Die Mägde, teilweise schon im Putz, neckten sich in unverkennbarem Bezug auf sie gegenseitig mit den Liebhabern, die sie gefunden hatten oder zu finden hofften, und der breitnasigte Küchenjunge, durch Großknecht und Kutscher mit Augenzwinkern zu dieser Frechheit aufgemuntert, fragte Anna, ob er nicht ihre rotgeblümte Schürze, sowie den bunt bebänderten Hut, den des Majors Bedienter Friedrich ihr zur Weihnacht geschenkt, leihen dürfe; sie werde ja in der Flachskammer diese Sachen entbehren können, und er hoffe, sich ein Mädchen, dem es an Putz fehle, dadurch geneigt zu machen.»Bube«, rief sie aus mit blassen, bebenden Lippen,»ich will dir, wenn du krank liegst und von niemanden beachtet wirst, keine Milchsuppen wieder kochen«; schob ihren Teller zurück, und ging, die leeren Wassereimer ergreifend, um sie, wie es ihr zukam, frisch aus dem Brunnen zu füllen, hinaus.»Pfui«, sagte Johann, ein alter Diener, der, im Dienst seines Vaters grau geworden, bei dem Freiherrn von Eichenthal das Gnadenbrot genoss,»es ist Unrecht, der Dirne Essen und Trinken durch gallige Reden zu verderben!«»Ei«, versetzte der Gärtner,»der schadts nicht, sie ist so hochmütig, seit der Friedrich, der dünnleibigte Speichellecker, hinter ihr herläuft, als ob ein Edelmann angebissen hätte!«»Hochmut kommt vor dem Falle!« sagte Liese, die kleine dralle Köchin, mit einem zärtlichen Blick auf den phlegmatischen Großknecht, »wisst Ihr, dass sie sich schnürt?«»Warum auch nicht hochmütig«, sagte der Kutscher,»ist sie doch des Schulmeisters Tochter!«

Friederike, das Kammermädchen, trat mit erhitztem Gesicht in die Küche.»Ist die Anna nicht hier?«, fragte sie, sich die Stirn mit dem seidenen Taschentuche trocknend,»der gnädige Herr hat sich eben zu Bett gelegt, er war sehr spaßhaft«, hier hustete sie, weil die anderen sich mit bedeutenden Blicken ansahen und lachten,»und ich soll ihr sagen, dass sie gleich mit dem Flachshecheln beginnen und«, dies setzte sie eigenmächtig hinzu,»vor zehn Uhr nicht Feierabend machen soll!«»Ich wills ihr schon ausrichten, Rike!« versetzte Liese. Friederike tänzelte

giggling which, because she looked down on her plate with burning cheeks and made no answer to any of the abundantly presented innuendo, grew stronger and more unkind. The maids, some of them already dressed up, teased each other about the lovers they had found or hoped to find with unmistakable reference to her, and the broad-nosed kitchen boy, encouraged to this insolence by winks from the chief farmhand and the coachman, asked Anna if he might borrow her apron adorned with a red flower design, as well as the hat with colorful ribbons which the major's valet, Friedrich, had given her for Christmas; after all, she would not wear these items in the flax chamber, and he hoped thereby to make a girl, who was lacking a fanciful dress, gracious toward him. "Boy," she called out with pale, trembling lips, "I shall never again make you milk soup when you are lying down sick and nobody pays attention to you." [She] pushed her plate back and went away, reaching for the empty water buckets, in order to fill them with fresh water from the well, as was her duty. "Fie," said Johann, an old servant who enjoyed the Baron of Eichenthal's charity, having grown gray in the father's service, "it is wrong to spoil the girl's eating and drinking with ill-tempered speech!" "Well," replied the gardener, "it does not distress her; she is so high and mighty, as if a nobleman had risen to the bait since Friederich, the scrawny brown noser has been chasing her!" "Pride goes before a fall," Liese, the short, plump cook said, with a tender look at the phlegmatic chief farm hand, "don't you know that she is wearing a laced-up corset?" "Why not be proud," said the coachman, "after all, she is the schoolmaster's daughter!"

Friederike, the chambermaid, entered the kitchen, her face flushed. "Is Anna not here?" she asked, drying her forehead with the silk handkerchief, "Milord has just laid down, he was in a very funny mood," here she coughed while the others gave each other meaningful looks and laughed, "and I am supposed to tell her to start right away with heckling the flax, and," this she added on her own authority, "she is not supposed to call it a day before ten!" "I shall certainly tell her that, Rike!" Liese replied. Friederike sashayed away again. "I wonder if she also

wieder fort. »Ob die sich nicht auch schnürt?« fragte der
Großknecht. »Pst! Pst!« wisperte Johann und klimperte verlegen mit seiner Gabel auf dem Teller. Anna trat mit ihrer Tracht
Wasser in die Küche. »Anna«, begann Liese geschäftig, »ich soll
dir sagen…«»Ich weiß schon Bescheid«, erwiderte Anna trock-
en in festem Ton. »Ich bin dem Boten begegnet. Wo hängt der
Schlüssel zur Flachskammer?« »Drüben am Nagel!« versetzte
die Köchin und zeigte mit dem Finger auf die Stelle. Anna,
gelassen, weil im Innersten zerschlagen, nahm den Schlüssel
und ging, während die übrigen sich zu ihren Koffern begaben,
um dort vor einem Drei-Groschen-Spiegel den Anzug zu vollenden, hastig in die Flachskammer, deren Fenster auf Schlosshof
und Landstraße hinausgingen. Sie setzte sich, das Gesicht gegen
die Fenster gewendet, so, dass sie alle Fröhlichen, die aus dem
Dorfe auf die Kirmse zogen, sehen und ihre muntern Gespräche
hören konnte, an die Arbeit, die sie in dumpfer Emsigkeit
begann, und, wenn sie auch zuweilen in unbewusstes Hinbrüten
versank, doch sogleich aus diesem, wie vor Schlangen- und
Tarantelstich, schreckhaft auffahrend, mit verstärktem, ja
unnatürlichem, Eifer fortsetzte. Nur einmal während des ganzen langen Nachmittags stand sie von ihrem niedrigen, harten
Blockstuhl auf, und zwar, als ihr Mitgesinde, auf bequemem,
von raschen Pferden gezogenen Leiterwagen den Schlosshof
hinunterjagte, aber laut auflachend, wie zu eigener Verspottung,
setzte sie sich wieder nieder und trank, obwohl sie in all der
Hitze und all dem Staub durstig ward, dass ihr die Zunge am
Gaumen klebte, nicht einmal den Kaffee, den ihr um vier oder
fünf Uhr die alte Brigitte, die bei einer Gelegenheit, wie die heutige, für die Mägde das Haus zu hüten pflegte, mitleidig
gebracht hatte. Als die Nacht allmählich hereinbrach, ging sie,
ohne sich die wild ums Gesicht herunterhängenden Locken
zurückzustreichen, in die Küche, wo sie, auf Brigittes freundli-
che Einladung, dort zu bleiben und eine leckere Pfanne voll
gebratener Kartoffeln mit ihr zu verzehren, nichts erwidernd,
ein Licht aus dem Lichtkasten nahm, und sich dann mit diesem,
es mit darübergehaltener Hand vor dem Zugwind schützend, in
die Flachskammer zurückbegab. Nicht lange dauerte es, so
klopfte es bei ihr ans Fenster, und als sie die Tür öffnete, trat

wears a laced-up corset," the chief farm hand asked. "Shush,
shush," Johann whispered and, embarrassed, clinked his fork
on his plate. Anna entered the kitchen with her load of water.
"Anna," Liese began importantly, "I am supposed to tell
you..." "I already know," Anna said drily, in a determined
voice. "I met the messenger. Where is the key to the flax chamber?" "Over there, on the nail," replied the cook and pointed
with her finger to the place. Anna, calm because she was shattered inside, took the key and left hastily for the flax chamber,
whose windows faced the courtyard and the country road,
while the rest of them went to their trunks to complete their
outfits before a threepenny mirror. She sat down, her face
turned toward the windows, so that she was able to see all the
merry people from the village who went to the fun fair, and to
hear their animated conversations; with dull diligence she began
her work, even though from time to time she sank into unconscious brooding, then immediately snapped out of this with a
frightened start, as if bitten by a snake or tarantula, and resumed
with renewed and even unnatural vigor. Only once during the
whole long afternoon did she get up from her low, hard chair
made from a block of wood—exactly when her fellow servants
were racing down the courtyard in comfortable rack wagons
drawn by fast horses; they were laughing out loud as if mocking
her. She sat down again, without even drinking the coffee which
old Brigitte, who used to house-sit for the maids on occasions
such as the one today, had brought out for her, out of compassion, around four or five o' clock, even though she had become
thirsty in all this heat and dust, so that her tongue was stuck to
the roof of her mouth. As night was falling gradually, [and]
without brushing back her locks which were tumbling wildly
around her face, she went into the kitchen; there she did not
respond to Brigitte's cordial invitation to stay and share with
her a mouth-watering pan full of fried potatoes, [but] took a
candle from the candle cabinet and then returned with it to the
flax chamber, protecting it from the drafty air by holding her
hand over it. Not long after that there was a knock at her window, and when she opened the door, Friedrich entered, sweating all over from rushing about. "After all, I have to see," he

Friedrich, über und über schwitzend, mit Hast herein. »Ich muss doch sehen«, sagte er, fast außer Atem und sich die Weste aufreißend, »sie flüstern allerlei!« »Du siehst!« erwiderte Anna schnell, dann aber stockend und steckte ihren Busenlatz, der sich etwas verschoben hatte, fest. »Dein Herr ist ein Hundsfott!« brauste Friedrich auf und knirschte mit den Zähnen. »Ja, ja!« sagte Anna. »Ich mögt ihm begegnen, drüben am Abhang«, rief Friedrich, »o, es ist entsetzlich!« »Wie heiß bist du«, sagte Anna, indem sie sanft seine Hand fasste, »hast du schon getanzt?« »Wein hab ich getrunken, fünf, sechs Gläser«, versetzte Friedrich, »komm, Anna, zieh dich an, du sollst mit, jedem Teufel zum Trotz, der sich drein legen will.« »Nein, nein, nein!« sagte Anna. »Ja doch«, fuhr Friedrich auf und legte seinen Arm um ihren Leib, »Doch!« »Ganz gewiss nicht!« erwiderte Anna leise, ihn innig umschlingend. »Du sollst, ich wills«, rief Friedrich und ließ sie los. Anna ergriff, ohne etwas zu antworten, die Hechel und sah vor sich nieder. »Willst du oder nicht?« drängte Friedrich und trat dicht vor sie hin. »Wie könnt ich?« entgegnete Anna, indem sie, ihm vertrauensvoll in die Augen sehend, ihre Hand aufs Herz legte. »Gut, gut«, rief Friedrich, »du willst nicht? Gott verdamme mich, wo ich dich wieder seh!« Wie rasend stürzte er fort. »Friedrich«, schrie Anna ihm nach, »bleib doch, bleib einen Augenblick, horch, wie der Wind braust!« Sie wollte ihm nacheilen, da streifte ihr Kleid das niedrig auf einen Eichenklotz gestellte Licht; es fiel herunter und entzündete den schnell in mächtiger Flamme auflodernden Flachs. Friedrich, von Wein und Zorn berauscht, zwang sich, wie dies in solchen Augenblicken wohl geschieht, ein Lied zu singen, während er in die sehr unfreundlich gewordene Nacht hinausschritt; in wilder Lustigkeit drangen die wohlbekannten Töne zu Anna hinüber. »Ach! Ach!« seufzte sie aus tiefster Brust. Da erst bemerkte sie, dass die Kammer schon halb in Feuer stand. Mit Händen und Füßen schlagend und tretend, warf sie sich in die gefräßigen Flammen, die ihr heiß und brennend entgegenschlugen und sie selbst verletzten. Dann rief sie – Friedrichs Stimme verklang eben in weiter Ferne in einem letzten Halloh – »Ei, was lösch ich, lass! lass!« und eilte, die Tür mit Macht hinter sich zuwerfend, mit einem grässlichen Lachen

said, and, almost out of breath, he tore open his vest. "They are whispering all sorts of things!" "You see... [now]," Anna replied quickly but then haltingly, and fastened her kerchief which had shifted a bit over her bosom. "Your master is a scoundrel!" Friedrich replied, flying into a rage and grinding his teeth. "Yes, yes!" Anna said. "I would like to encounter him, over there, by the side of the hill!" Friedrich said loudly. "Oh, it is abominable!" "How hot you are," Anna said, at the same time grasping his hand softly. "Have you danced already?" "I have had wine; five, six glasses," Friedrich replied. "Come on, Anna, get dressed up, you shall come along, in defiance of every devil who wants to prevent this." "No, no, no!" Anna said. "Yes, indeed," Friedrich flying into a rage and put his arm around her. "Yes, indeed!" "Most certainly not!" Anna replied quietly, giving him a heartfelt embrace. "You shall [come along]; I want it," Friedrich called out, and let her go. Anna reached for the heckle and, without giving a reply, lowered her gaze. "Do you want to or not?"

Friedrich urged and stepped up close to her. "How could I?" Anna replied, putting her hand on her heart as she looked trustingly into his eyes. "All right, all right," Friedrich said, "you don't want to? God damn me when I see you again!" As if berserk, he rushed away. "Friedrich!" Anna called after him. "Please stay, stay a moment; listen, how the wind is blustering!" She was about to hurry after him when her dress brushed the candle which was sitting low on an oak block; it fell and ignited the flax, which quickly blazed up into an energetic flame. Friedrich, intoxicated by wine and anger, forced himself to sing a song, as sometimes happens in such moments, as he strode into the night which had become very unfriendly; the familiar sounds, wildly cheerful, carried over to Anna. "Oh, dear! Oh dear!" she sighed from the bottom of her heart. Only then did she notice that already half of the chamber was on fire. Beating and trampling it down with hands and feet, she threw herself into the hungry flames, which greeted her, burning and hot, and injured her. Then she called out, [but] Friedrich's voice was dying out far away in a last halloo. "Aye, why am I extinguishing them; stop it! Stop it!" And she

hinaus, unwillkürlich den nämlichen Weg durch den Garten
einschlagend, den Friedrich gegangen war. Bald aber, auf einer
Wiese, die zunächst an den Garten stieß, sank sie kraftlos, fast
ohnmächtig, zusammen und drückte, laut stöhnend, ihr Gesicht
ins kalte, nasse Gras. So lag sie lange Zeit. Da ertönten dumpf
und schrecklich von nah und von fern die Not- und Feuerglocken.
Sie richtete sich halb auf, doch sah sie sich nicht um; aber über
ihr war der Himmel blutrot und voll von Funken; eine unnatürliche Wärme verbreitete sich, von Minute zu Minute zuneh-
mend; Geheul und Gebrause des Windes, Geprassel der
Flammen, Wehklage und Geschrei. Sie legte sich wieder der
Länge nach am Boden nieder, ihr war, als ob sie schlafen könne,
doch schreckte sie im nächsten Augenblick aus diesem, dem
Tode ähnlichen Zustand die Rede zweier Vorübereilenden wieder auf, von denen einer ausrief: »Herr Jesus, es brennt schon
im Dorf!« Jetzt, mit Riesenkraft, raffte sie sich zusammen und
eilte mit fliegenden Haaren in das hart an die brennende Seite
des Schlosses stoßende Dorf hinunter, wo die leicht Feuer fan-
genden Strohdächer bereits an mehr als einer Stelle in lichten
Flammen aufschlugen. Immer gewaltiger erhob sich der Wind,
die meisten Einwohner, Kinder und alte, schwächliche Personen
ausgenommen, waren über vier Meilen entfernt auf der Kirmse;
die elenden Feueranstalten hätten den zwei verbündeten furcht-
baren Elementen ohnehin, auch wenn die nötige Mannschaft
zur Stelle gewesen wäre, nur eitlen Widerstand leisten können,
es fehlte sogar, denn der Sommer war ungewöhnlich trocken, an
Wasser. Unglück, Gefahr, Verwirrung wuchs mit jeder Minute;
ein kleiner Knabe rannte umher und schrie: »Ach Gott, ach
Gott! mein Schwesterlein!« und wenn man ihn fragte: wo ist
deine Schwester? so begann er, als ob er, jedes klaren Gedankens
unfähig, die Frage nicht verstanden hätte, von neuem sein
Entsetzen erregendes Geschrei. Eine alte Frau musste mit Gewalt
gezwungen werden, ihr Haus zu verlassen; sie jammerte: »Meine
Henne, meine arme kleine Henne«, und in der Tat war es rüh-
rend anzusehen, wie das Tierchen in dem erstickenden Rauche
ängstlich von einer Ecke in die andere flatterte, und sich dennoch, weil es in bessern Zeiten gewöhnt sein mochte, die
Schwelle nicht zu überschreiten, von seiner Herrin selbst nicht

hurried outside with a dreadful laugh, slamming the door hard behind her; instinctively, she followed the very same path through the garden that Friedrich had taken. Soon, however, in a meadow which bordered the garden, she sank down feebly, almost fainting, and pressed her face into the cold, wet grass, moaning loudly. Thus she lay for a long time. Then the disaster and fire bells began to ring out, hollow and terrible, from nearby and afar. She sat up halfway, yet did not look around; but the sky above her was blood-red and full of sparks; unnatural warmth spread, growing with every minute; the wind howling and roaring, the flames crackling, wailing and crying. She stretched out again on the ground; it seemed to her as if she might be able to sleep, but the next moment she was awoken from this state, which resembled death, by two passers-by talking, one of them calling out, "Lord Jesus, the village is burning!" Now, with enormous strength, she pulled herself together and, with her hair flying, hurried to the part of the village right next to the burning castle, where the thatched rooves, prone to catching fire, had already gone up in bright flames in more than one place. More and more fiercely, the wind rose; most of the residents, except the children and old, feeble people, were attending the fun fair more than four miles away; the undersized fire brigades would have been able only to put up unsuccessful resistance to the two allied [and] frightening elements anyway, even if the required crew had been on the scene, because the summer had been unusually dry; even water was lacking. The desolation, danger, and disorientation grew with every minute; a little boy was running around, screaming: "Oh, God, oh, God! My little sister!" And when they asked him: where is your little sister?, he began his horrifying screaming all over again, as if he were incapable of any clear thinking, [and] therefore had not been able to comprehend the question. An old woman had to be coerced to leave her house; she wailed: "My chicken, my poor little chicken!" And, without a doubt, it was heartbreaking to watch the little animal fluttering anxiously from one corner to the other in the suffocating smoke, and even then, because it may have been used to not crossing the threshold in better

durch die offne Tür ins Freie hinausscheuchen ließ. Anna, mit der Tollkühnheit der Verzweiflung, weinend, schreiend, sich die Brust zerschlagend, dann wieder lachend, stürzte sich in jede Gefahr, rettete, löschte, und war allen anderen zugleich Gegenstand des Erstaunens, der Bewunderung und unheimliches Rätsel. Zuletzt, als man in allgemeiner Kleinmütigkeit selbst die Hoffnung aufgab, dem Feuer, das immer weiter um sich griff und das ganze Dorf mit der Einäscherung bedrohte, Einhalt tun zu können, sah man sie in einem brennenden Hause auf die Knie sinken und mit gerungenen Händen zum Himmel emporstarren. Da rief der Pfarrer: »Um Gottes willen, rettet das heldenmütige, brave Mädchen, das Dach schießt herunter!« Anna, seine Worte hörend, bleckte ihm, noch immer auf den Knien liegend, mit einer Gebärde des heftigsten Abscheus die Zunge entgegen und lachte ihn wahnsinnig an. In diesem Augenblick erschien Friedrich, der sie nur kaum in der entsetzlichen Todesgefahr erblickte, als er, bleich werdend, wie eine Wand, auf das den Einsturz drohende Haus zustürzte. Sie aber, ihn sogleich gewahrend, sprang erschreckt auf und rief: »Lass! Lass! Friedrich! ich, ich bin schuld, dort – dort –.« Und mit der Hand auf die Gegend zeigend, wo das Schloss lag, eilte sie, um jegliche Rettung unmöglich zu machen, die schon brennende Leiter, welche zum Boden des Hauses führte, hinauf. Die Leiter, bereits zu stark vom Feuer versehrt, brach unter ihr, zugleich aber schoss, eine Flammenmauer bildend, das Strohdach herunter; man hörte noch einen durch Mark und Bein dringenden Schrei, dann ward's still.

Der Freiherr von Eichenthal kam. Sowie Friedrich ihn erblickte, eilte er auf ihn zu und stieß ihn, bevor der Freiherr sich seiner er wehren konnte, mit dem Fuß vor den Leib, dass er rücklings zu Boden schlug; dann ließ er die Bauern, die sich auf Befehl des Schulzen seiner Person zu bemächtigen suchten, ruhig gewähren.

Als der Freiherr am andern Morgen erfuhr, was sich mit Anna begeben hatte, befahl er, ihre Gebeine aus dem Schutt hervor zusuchen und sie auf dem Schindanger zu verscharren. Dies geschah.

times, even its owner was unable to shoo it out outside through the open door. Anna, crying with the foolhardiness of despair, screaming, beating her chest, then laughing again, plunged into every peril, saved [lives], put out [fires], and was to all of the others the subject of, at the same time, amazement, admiration, and eerie mystery. Finally, when in universal despondency, they had abandoned any hope of stopping the fire, which kept on spreading and threatened to incinerate the entire village, she was seen in a burning house, having sunk to her knees, wringing her hands, and staring up at the heavens. [That was] when the minister called out: "For the love of God, save the courageous, treasured girl; the roof is coming down!" Anna, hearing his words [and] still kneeling, stuck out her tongue at him in a gesture of the most vehement repugnance and laughed at him maniacally. In this instant, Friedrich appeared; noticing the dire mortal danger which threatened her [and] turning pale like a wall, [he] rushed toward the house which was threatening to collapse. She, however, noticing him at once, jumped up, terrified and called out: "Don't! Don't Friedrich! It is my fault; there, there ..." And pointing with one hand in the direction of the castle, she hurried up the already burning ladder which led to the upper floor of the house, in order to forestall any attempts to save her. The ladder, already severely damaged by the fire, collapsed under her; at the same time the thatched roof dropped down, thus creating a wall of flames; they heard one heart-piercing scream, [and] then there was silence.

Baron Eichenthal appeared. As soon as Friedrich caught sight of him, he rushed at him and, before the baron could defend himself, gave him a kick to the belly, causing [the baron] to fall on his back on the ground; then he allowed the farmers who tried to arrest him on the bailiff's order to proceed, without any resistance.

Next morning, when the baron learned what had come to pass with Anna, he ordered her bones to be retrieved from the rubble, and that she be buried in the knacker's yard. This was done.

BALDUIN GROLLER

Austrian writer Balduin Groller was born Adalbert Goldschneider on September 5, 1848, in Arad, Hungary, which was then a part of the Austrian Empire. His family, who were Jewish and members of the Banat Swabian ethnic group, moved to Dresden because of political pressure exerted by the nationalistic Hungarian State. Groller finished secondary school in Dresden.

He moved to Vienna to study philosophy, law, and aesthetics. As a freelance journalist during his college years, he began to write for various newspapers about art and also joined the Freemasons. At the age of twenty-three, he founded the *Allgemeine Kunstzeitung (General Art Magazine)* in 1871, which folded only a year later. He then worked as an editor at the *Deutsche Schriftstellerzeitung (German Writers Magazine)* and various other print publications. Later, he turned to fiction, producing a mix of both long and short stories while continuing his journalistic endeavors. Groller also became vice president of Concordia, the association of Viennese authors and journalists. In 1890, Groller turned to writing crime stories.

Besides his career as a writer and journalist, Groller was passionate about sports. In 1906, he became a co-founder and vice president of the *Allgemeiner Sportausschuss für Österreich* (General Sports Committee for Austria), a forerunner of the Austrian Olympic Committee. Two years later, he was also elected president of the newly founded *Zentral-Verband für gemeinsame Sportinteressen* (Central Association for Common Sports Interests). Among his friends were Nobel Peace Prize

winner and fellow Austrian Bertha von Suttner, with whom he shared a strong interest in pacifism and social justice.

Groller died in Vienna on March 22, 1916.

Although his achievements as a writer are nearly forgotten, Groller is still remembered for creating the character of Dagobert Trostler, widely regarded as an Austrian version of the famous Sherlock Holmes.[1]

"The Great Embezzlement" begins with a bank director receiving a visit from private investigator Trostler in his resplendent office at the powerful ABB Bank.

---

[1] *Handbuch österreichischer Autorinnen und Autoren jüdischer Herkunft 18. bis 20. Jahrhundert,* ed. Österreichische Nationalbibliothek, vol. 1, (Vienna & Munich: K. G. Saur, 2002) 457f.

BALDUIN GROLLER

BALDUIN GROLLER

Der große Unterschleif

Das schönste Zimmer im Palast der A. B. B. – man sagte immer und überall nur A. B. B., und doch wusste jeder sofort, dass damit die Allgemeine Bauunternehmungs-Bank gemeint sei – war das Bureau des Generaldirektors. Dieser, ein verhältnismäßig noch junger Mann von gewinnender Erscheinung, saß vor seinem mächtigen Schreibtisch und ordnete mit seinen wohlgepflegten und ringgeschmückten Händen die vor ihm aufgehäuften Briefe und sonstigen Schriftstücke.

Da öffnete sich, ohne dass vorher angeklopft worden wäre, die nach dem Vorzimmer führende Tür. Er hob den Kopf. Ein hübscher Kopf. Die ob der wohl nicht ungewohnten, in dieser Form aber ungebührlichen Störung erstaunt blickenden Augen waren blau, und selbst durch den augenblicklichen Unmut hindurch, der nun gerade aus ihnen sprach, hätte ein Menschenkenner und Beobachter einen Strahl von Güte und einer gewissen, beinahe künstlerischen Schwärmerei erkennen müssen. Das glänzende braune Haupthaar war gescheitelt, und zu diesem bildete der erheblich lichtere, ja entschieden blonde Vollbart einen ganz bemerkenswerten Kontrast.

Der Kopf, der nun zunächst bei der Tür hereingesteckt wurde, war auch wohl geeignet, Aufmerksamkeit zu erregen. Es war ein Charakterkopf, der so die Mitte hielt zwischen faunischer und biblischer Erscheinung. Das von einem schwarzen Bart umrahmte volle Gesicht sprühte ordentlich von Freude am Lebensgenuss, während das Petrusschöpfchen auf dem

BALDUIN GROLLER

The Great Embezzlement

The most striking room in the ABB palace—it was called, always and everywhere, only the ABB, even though everybody knew at once that the Allgemeine Bauunternehmungs-Bank [General Building Companies Bank] was meant—was the General Director's office. Still a relatively young man with a winsome appearance and well-manicured hands adorned with rings, he sat at his massive desk and sorted the letters and other documents lying in a heap before him.

Just at that moment the door leading to the outer office opened, without a preceding knock. He lifted his head. A good-looking head. The eyes, looking surprised at the disruption—not unusual, yet in this manner improper—were blue, and [in them], even in their current displeasure which they bespoke, an expert observer of human nature would have been compelled to recognize a beam of benevolence along with a certain, almost artistic, reverie. The lustrous brown hair was parted and the substantially lighter, most definitely blonde, full beard created an entirely remarkable contrast.

The head that now appeared in the doorway also was well qualified to arouse attention. It was a head of character that achieved a balance between a faun-like and a biblical look. The full face, framed by a black beard, sparkled very much with pleasure of the enjoyment of life, while the little thatch of hair,

gelichteten Scheitel beinahe anlockte, genauer hinzusehen, ob nicht etwa der dazu gehörige Heiligenschein zu entdecken sei.

»Haben Sie ein halbes Stündchen für mich Zeit, Herr Ringhoff?« fragte der Mann mit dem fehlenden Heiligenschein.

»Ah, Herr Dagobert Trostler!« rief der Generaldirektor sich erhebend. Jede Spur des Unmuts war aus seinem offenen Gesicht geschwunden. »Ob ich Zeit habe? Für Sie immer, auch wenn Sie nicht mein gestrenger Verwaltungsrat wären. Welche Freude! Sie waren verreist, Herr Trostler?«

»Jawohl, mehrere Wochen, weit weg – sogar in Amerika!«

»Was Sie nicht sagen! Eine Vergnügungsreise, Herr Trostler?«

»Ja, es war recht vergnüglich, Herr Generaldirektor. Ich habe vieles gesehen.«

»Haben Sie sich auch den Yellowstone-Park angesehen? Der soll ja hochinteressant sein.«

»Natürlich habe ich den auch besucht.«

»Da müssen Sie aber erzählen, Herr Trostler.«

»Dazu bin ich ja zu Ihnen gekommen, Herr Generaldirektor!«

Man richtete sich ein. Dagobert setzte sich an die Seite des Schreibtisches mit dem Rücken zum Fenster. Der Generaldirektor rückte ihm ein Zigarrenkistchen zurecht, aber Dagobert lehnte ab. Er habe als Raucher seine Eigenheiten. Er sei einmal auf eine Sorte eingeschossen und von dieser gehe er nicht ab. Darum rauche er immer nur seine eigenen Zigarren. Tatsächlich habe er auch noch keine bessere Havanna-Marke angetroffen. Der Generaldirektor möge nur versuchen und sich selbst überzeugen. Ringhoff bediente sich und forderte seinen Besuch neuerdings auf, zu erzählen.

»Es ist ein ganzer Roman, den ich Ihnen zu erzählen habe, und ich muss ein bisschen weit ausholen, aber die Geschichte wird Sie interessieren.«

»Mich interessiert alles, was Sie betrifft, Herr Trostler.«

»Danke schön. Sagen Sie mal, lieber Generaldirektor, haben Sie sich niemals darüber gewundert, wie ich eigentlich in die A. B. B. hereingekommen bin!«

»Warum soll ich mich nun darüber gewundert haben, Herr Trostler?«

reminiscent of St. Peter, almost invited a closer look [to see] whether the requisite halo might not also be discerned.

"Have you got a half hour or so for me, Mr. Ringhoff?" the man with the missing halo asked.

"Ah, Mr. Dagobert Trostler!" the General Director called out as he rose. Any trace of displeasure had disappeared from his open face. "Have I got time? For you: always, even if you weren't my stern board director! What a pleasure! You have been out of town, Mr. Trostler?"

"Yes, for several weeks, far away—even in America!"

"You don't say! A pleasure trip, Mr. Trostler?

"Yes, it was quite amusing, General Director! I have seen many things."

"Have you also been to Yellowstone Park? That is supposed to be most interesting."

"Of course I visited that one, too."

"You've got to tell me about it, Mr. Trostler."

"That is why I came to [see] you, General Director!"

They settled down. Dagobert sat down at the side of the desk, with his back to the window. The General Director moved a little cigar box near him, but Dagobert declined. As a smoker, he had his idiosyncracies [he said]. In any case, he had homed in on a brand and did not veer away from it. For that reason, he would only ever smoke his own cigarettes. Indeed, he had never found a better Cuban brand. The General Director might like to try it and see for himself. Ringhoff availed himself of one, and again invited his visitor to recount.

"I have an entire novel to relate to you, and I have to go somewhat far afield, but you will find the story interesting."

"I am interested in everything which concerns you, Mr. Trostler."

"Thank you very much. Pray tell me, dear General Director, have you never asked yourself how I joined the ABB?"

"Why should I have asked myself that, Mr. Trostler?"

»Aber ich verstehe doch nichts vom Bankwesen, das heißt – ich verstand nichts davon, hatte nicht die blasseste Ahnung. Jetzt natürlich, nach mehr als einem Jahre, habe ich mich ordentlich eingearbeitet.«

»Sie kamen zu uns wie die übrigen Herrn Verwaltungsräte. Sie sind ein sehr vermögender Mann, Herr Trostler, und was das Sachverständnis betrifft, so haben Sie sehr bald alle übrigen Herren überflügelt. Zur Verwunderung lag für mich durchaus kein Anlass vor. Aber Sie wollten ja von Ihrer Amerikareise erzählen –«

»Ich bin dabei, das gehört mit dazu. Sie sollen erst erfahren, wie und warum ich zur A. B. B. kam. Ich war immer der Meinung, dass jeder irgendeinen Sport betreiben solle, und nun gar ein Mensch wie ich, der vollkommen frei und unabhängig ist, und nicht Kind und nicht Kegel hat. Ich habe also gleich zwei große Passionen. Die eine ist die Musik. Ich weiß nicht, ob Sie von meinen Leistungen auf diesem Gebiete schon gehört haben – «

»Gewiss habe ich davon schon gehört,« log der Generaldirektor verbindlich, »und – die andere?«

»Ja die andere – das ist ein ganz absonderlicher Fall. Ich bin Amateurdetektiv. Sie machen große Augen? Ich versichere Sie, – wenn man Passion für die Sache hat und etwas Vokation – es gibt nichts Interessanteres.«

»Mit der ersten Liebhaberei war bei uns nicht viel zu machen.«

»Wohl aber mit der zweiten! Sie erinnern sich ja der Geschichte, – wie sollten Sie nicht! Man hatte die A. B. B. gegründet und sich dazu als Präsidenten meinen Freund Grumbach geholt, der zugleich Präsident des Klubs der Industriellen ist. Das ging nun ein Jahr lang ganz gut, und dann, Sie wissen ja, verschwand der Kassier und mit ihm drei Millionen Kronen.«

»Es war ein furchtbarer Schlag!«

»Mein Freund Grumbach, er ist mein intimster Freund, hat in gewissen Dingen Pech. Er hatte, kaum warm geworden als Klubpräsident, auch so eine unangenehme Geschichte. Damals kam er zu mir und ich habe ihm herausgeholfen. Das könnte ich

"But I don't have any idea about banking; that is to say—I did not have any idea, did not have the slightest idea. Naturally now, after more than a year, I have learned the ropes reasonably [well]."

"You came to us like the other board directors. You are a remarkably wealthy man, Mr. Trostler, and regarding expert knowledge, you will soon have gained an edge over all the other gentlemen. There was no reason at all for me to be surprised. But you wanted to talk about your trip to America..."

"I am doing just that; that is part of it. I wanted to inform you first, how and why I came to join the ABB. It has always been my opinion that everybody should pursue some sort of sport, and particularly a person such as myself who is entirely free and independent, and has neither kith nor kin. Actually, I even have two great passions. One is music. I don't know if you have already heard of my accomplishment in this field..."

"Of course I have heard about it," the General Director lied obligingly, "and—the other?"

"Well, the other one—that is quite a peculiar matter. I am an amateur detective. You are surprised? I assure you—if one has passion for this subject and any calling—there is nothing more interesting."

"Regarding your first passion, there is not much that can be done here."

"But with the second, to be sure. You do remember the story—how could you not! The ABB had been founded and my friend Grumbach, who was the president of the Club of the Captains of Industry at that time, had been appointed as president. That went quite well for a year and then, as you know, the cashier disappeared, and with him three million korunas."

"It was a terrible blow!"

"My friend Grumbach—he is my most intimate friend—is unlucky in some ways. Hardly had he settled in as the Club's president when he experienced another unpleasant affair. He came to me at that time and I helped him get out of it. Actually, I could tell you about it. It was a truly exquisite caper; but, if

Ihnen eigentlich auch erzählen. Es war eine ganz feine Gaunerei; aber das würde uns doch zu weit führen. Dieses Mal kam er also auch wieder. Wenn einer helfen könnte, so sei ich es. Ich ließ mir den Fall genau auseinandersetzen, aber es gab nicht viel zu erzählen. Die Bücher waren scheinbar in der größten Ordnung, aber der Kassier und das Geld verschwunden. Zudem hatte der Kassier bereits einen Vorsprung von reichlich zwei Wochen.«

»Ich erinnere mich leider nur zu genau.«

»Er hatte unbehelligt seinen vertragsmäßigen Urlaub angetreten, und als dann der große Unterschleif aufkam, war jede Spur seines Erdenwallens verwischt. Nun sollte ich ihn suchen.«

»Das war allerdings viel verlangt!«

»Grumbach hat in solchen Dingen einen harten Schädel. Von einer Anzeige bei den Behörden wollte er durchaus nichts wissen, und ich konnte ihm in diesem Falle nicht einmal Unrecht geben. Drei Millionen – das ist allerdings ein kolossaler Betrag, aber der Diebstahl musste eine Bank mit sechzig Millionen eingezahltem Kapital nicht gleich zugrunde richten. Wohl aber hätte das schwindende Vertrauen sie zugrunde richten müssen, wenn es ruchbar geworden wäre, dass schon nach kurzem Bestande derlei möglich gewesen sei.«

»Das war auch meine Meinung, Herr Trostler.«

»Ich weiß. Auf Antrag des Präsidenten beschloss also der Verwaltungsrat, die fatale Geschichte vollkommen geheim zu halten, den Fehlbetrag auf die Verwaltungsräte zu repartieren und aus Eigenem zu ersetzen.«

»Es war schließlich doch der beste Ausweg.«

»Jawohl. Also nun sollte ich helfen. Ich überlegte. Zunächst musste ich einen vollkommen klaren Einblick in das Getriebe der A. B. B. gewinnen. Ich dachte daran, mich zu diesem Zwecke als Beamten anstellen zu lassen, verwarf aber die Idee sehr bald. Dazu konnte und wusste ich zu wenig, und das hätte mich sehr schnell auffällig oder verdächtig gemacht. Ich ließ mich also als Verwaltungsrat kooptieren. Der macht sich nicht auffällig, wenn er nichts weiß und nichts kann.«

Der Generaldirektor schmunzelte diskret zu dieser satirischen Bemerkung und äußerte leichthin: »Dann waren Sie ja eigent-

truth be told, that would be going too far. So this time, he came to me again. If anyone could help him, it would be me [he said]. I had him explain the case in detail, but there was not much to tell. Apparently, the books were in perfect order, but both the cashier and the money had disappeared. In addition, the cashier already had had a head start of more than two weeks."

"Unfortunately, I remember it only too well."

"He had taken his contractual vacation unchallenged, and when the great embezzlement was revealed, every trace of his earthly existence had been wiped out. It was my turn then to track him down."

"Indeed, that had been asking a lot!"

"Grumbach is a bullhead in such matters. He did not want to hear anything about pressing charges with the authorities, and in this case I could not disagree with him. Three million— that is indeed a colossal amount, but the theft did not necessarily mean financial ruin for a bank with a paid-in capital of sixty million [korunas]. However, the loss of confidence would have unavoidably bankrupted it, if it had become public knowledge that a thing such as this was possible after only a short existence."

"That was my opinion as well, Mr. Trostler."

"I know. Upon the president's suggestion, the board of directors decided to keep the fatal story entirely secret, re-allot the missing amount to the board directors, and [thereby] replace it with their own money."

"That was the best solution, after all."

"Exactly. So, now I was supposed to help. I mused. Firstly, I had to acquire a completely clear picture of the inner workings of the ABB. I thought of becoming employed as a bank clerk, to that end, but I abandoned this idea very early on. I did not have enough skills and knowledge to do that, and that could have aroused negative attention or suspicion about me very quickly. So I was coopted as a board director. If such a person has no knowledge or skills, he does not arouse negative attention."

The General Director chuckled discreetly upon hearing this sardonic comment, and remarked airily, "Then you were

lich nicht sowohl als Verwaltungsrat, denn als Detektiv bei uns tätig?«

»Natürlich!«

»Sie werden es begreiflich finden, Herr Trostler, dass es mich einigermaßen verstimmen muss, dass man mir davon nicht ein Sterbenswörtchen gesagt hat!«

»Mein lieber Herr Generaldirektor, wenn die Katze darauf ausgeht, Mäuse zu fangen, da wird sie sich nicht erst eine Schelle um den Hals binden. Kein Mensch außer dem Präsidenten hat davon gewusst, und Sie sind nun der erste, dem ich die offenherzigen Mitteilungen mache – wenn Sie's überhaupt interessiert, was ich ja nicht wissen kann.«

»Es interessiert mich sehr!«

»Dann will ich also weiter erzählen von meiner – Amerikareise. Ich musste mich also erst ordentlich einarbeiten bei uns. Das hat sich gemacht, nicht schlecht gemacht, wie Sie zu bezeugen die Güte gehabt haben, Herr Generaldirektor.«

»Ich kann nur sagen, dass Sie die Seele unserer Verwaltung geworden sind, Herr Trostler.«

»Besten Dank, Herr Generaldirektor. Ein solches Urteil von so kompetenter Seite muss mich stolz machen. Meine erste Sorge musste also darauf gerichtet sein, die Wiederholung solcher Ereignisse unmöglich zu machen. Sie begreifen, dass solche Wiederholungen auf die Dauer doch ein wenig ermüdend wirken müssten.«

»Ich begreife vollkommen.«

»Das ist gelungen. Ich darf sagen, dass die Kontrolleinrichtungen der A. B. B. jetzt geradezu mustergültige und schulbildende geworden sind.«

»Sie sind es und werden überall anerkannt und nachgeahmt.«

»Meine weitere Sorge war dann die Nachforschung nach dem verschwundenen Kassier, und was eigentlich noch wichtiger war, nach dem verschwundenen Gelde. Keine leichte Sache. Der Mann war spurlos verschwunden und dann – der Vorsprung! Alle Bemühung schien von Haus aus aussichtslos.«

»Und haben Sie wirklich einen Erfolg gehabt?«

»Mein Gott, ich bin zufrieden. Man konnte mir auf meinen Wunsch eine Photographie des Verschwundenen und mehrere

not actually active as a board director, but [rather] as a detective?"

"Of course!"

"You may understand, Herr Trostler, that I am somewhat bent out of shape that nobody breathed a word to me about this."

"My dear General Director, when the cat is about to catch mice, she won't first tie a bell around her neck. Nobody except for the president knew about this, and you are the first to whom I communicate this so candidly—if you are interested in any way, which I do not know, after all."

"This interests me greatly!"

"Then I shall continue the account of my—journey to America. So, first I had to properly learn the ropes here. That worked out well, not badly at all, as you have had the kindness to attest to, General Director."

"All I can say is that you have become the heart and soul of our administration, Mr. Trostler."

"Many thanks, General Director. Such an assessment from someone so competent inevitably makes me proud. Therefore, my first concern must be to make a reoccurrence of this kind of event impossible. You understand that in the long run, reoccurrences of this type [of event] might become tiresome."

"I understand perfectly."

"That has been successful. I may say that now the ABB security devices have become nothing less than exemplary and educational."

"They are, and they have been widely recognized and imitated."

"After that, the investigation into the vanished cashier was of further concern to me, and, actually even more important, the search for the missing money. Not an easy matter. The man had disappeared without a trace, and then—the head start! All effort appeared inherently hopeless."

"And were you actually successful?"

"By God, I am content. At my request, I was provided with a photo of the vanished man and several specimens of his

Schriftproben zur Verfügung stellen. Das war nicht viel, nicht wahr? Aber was will man machen, wenn man nicht mehr hat?! Dann – Sie dürfen mich aber nicht auslachen, Herr Generaldirektor! – wandte ich mich an eine Auskunftei um eine Information über den abgängigen Herrn Josef Benk.«

»Da war allerdings für den vorliegenden Fall voraussichtlich wenig zu holen.«

»Ich gebe es zu und habe es auch im voraus gewusst, aber ich erfuhr doch einige Einzelheiten, mit deren Erhebung ich mich sonst selbst hätte beschäftigen und aufhalten müssen und die doch notwendig waren zu meinen weiteren Erhebungen. Die Auskunft war eine glänzende: Josef Benk Ritter von Brenneberg – von seinem Adelstitel hatte er keinen Gebrauch gemacht und in der Bank hatte man nichts davon gewusst – gewesener Offizier, höchst ehrenhafter Charakter, unbedingt verlässlich –«

»Dafür hatte er auch bei uns immer gegolten bis –«

»Ich weiß. Damit war also nicht viel anzufangen, immerhin gab es doch einige Details, an welche ich weitere Nachforschungen anknüpfen konnte. Nun dachte ich an Isouards kriminalistische Grundregel: Cherchez la femme. Sie dürfen mich wieder nicht auslachen, Herr Generaldirektor. Das ist ja wirklich ein Gemeinplatz, und jeder Laie würde sich seiner erinnern, aber das spricht doch nicht gegen seine Stichhaltigkeit. Tatsächlich ist es für kriminalistische Untersuchungen sehr häufig von Belang, nach den Beziehungen zum Ewigweiblichen zu forschen. Glauben Sie mir, Herr Generaldirektor. Ich bin zwar nur Amateurdetektiv, nehme aber für mich die Erfahrungen eines Professionellen in Anspruch. Ich meine nicht, dass immer die Frau die Anstifterin des Verbrechens sein müsste oder dass gerade um des Weibes willen die meisten Verbrechen begangen werden, ich vertrete nur die Ansicht, dass das weibliche Element für viele Verbrecher das Siegfriedsche Lindenblatt bedeutet. Sie verstehen mich doch, Herr Generaldirektor. So etwas wie die Achillesferse oder den Kürassfehler, es weist auf die Stelle hin, wo sie sterblich sind. Es ist Ihnen doch klar?«

»Vollkommen.«

handwriting. That was not much, was it? But, what can you do if you haven't gotten more?! Then—you must not laugh at me, General Director!—I turned to a credit agency for information about the missing Mr. Josef Benk."

"However, there was little to be gotten for the case at hand."

"I admit that, and I already knew this, but still I found out some details which otherwise I would have had to spend time uncovering by myself and [because] they were needed for my further investigation. The information was excellent: Josef Benk, Baronet of Brennerberg—he did not make use of his title of nobility and nobody in the bank knew about it—was a former officer with a most honorable charcter, absolutely reliable—"

"We too had always regarded him as that, until—"

"I know. So, that was not much to work with, but even so there were some details to which I was able to link additional investigations. Next, I thought of Isouard's ground rule of criminology: Cherchez la femme [find the woman]. Again, you must not laugh at me, General Director. Without a doubt this is such a commonplace that every amateur would [be expected to] remember it, but that does not contradict its validity. In fact, it is very often relevant for criminological investigations to search for associations with the eternal feminine. Believe me, General Director. Even though I am merely an amateur detective, I do claim [to have] the experiences of a professional one. I don't believe that a woman always serves as the instigator of a crime, or that most crimes are committed for a woman; I am simply of the opinion that for many criminals the feminine element represents Siegfried's linden leaf. You do understand what I am saying, don't you, General Director. Something like an Achilles' heel or a flaw in the body armor; it points to the place where they are mortal. Have I made that clear to you?"

"Completely."

»Ich glaube da entschieden im Rechte zu sein. Samson wäre nie zu bändigen gewesen, wenn er sein Haupt nicht in Delilas Schoß gebettet hätte.«

»Und haben Sie, Herr Trostler, jene so wichtigen weiblichen Beziehungen auch in diesem Falle aufgespürt?«

»Aber natürlich! Der Flüchtige hatte eine Braut zurückgelassen – alle Achtung! Eine Bürgerschullehrerin – das reizendste Persönchen, das Sie sich vorstellen können; die verkörperte Anmut, Klugheit und Ehrenhaftigkeit. Kein Mensch auf der Welt hätte besser wählen können.«

»Und die hat er schnöde im Stiche gelassen?«

»Nicht doch! Es war abgemacht, dass sie nachkommen solle, sowie er sich drüben eine geregelte Existenz eingerichtet haben werde.«

»Und hat man von ihm wieder etwas gehört?«

»Er hat sich eine vollständig geordnete Existenz ausgebaut. Diese Angelegenheit ist vollkommen glatt erledigt. Mir war es vergönnt, ihm die reizende Braut zuzuführen – es ging doch nicht an, sie die weite Reise über das Meer allein machen zu lassen –, und ich hatte die Ehre, bei ihrer Vermählung als Beistand zu fungieren.«

Der Generaldirektor erhob sich.

»Verzeihen Sie, Herr Trostler,« sagte er lächelnd, »wenn ich Ihre Erzählung einen Augenblick unterbreche. Ich will nur rasch in der Buchhaltung einen Auftrag geben um dann ganz ungestört Ihrem interessanten Bericht folgen zu können.«

»Sie bemühen sich umsonst, Herr Generaldirektor,« erwiderte Dagobert ruhig sitzenbleibend. »Dort kommen Sie nicht durch. Im Nebenzimmer sitzen nämlich auch zwei Detektive, und zwar wirkliche Detektive der Polizei und nicht armselige Amateure wie ich. Unnötig zu sagen, dass auch auf der anderen Seite – im Vorzimmer – ebenfalls zwei sitzen. Die sorgen schon dafür, dass wir völlig ungestört bleiben. Sie haben strikten Auftrag, niemanden hereinzulassen. Es kann aber auch – außer mir – niemand dieses Zimmer verlassen, ohne sofort festgenommen zu werden. Wollen Sie es darauf ankommen lassen, Herr Generaldirektor?«

»Nein. Was wollen Sie von mir?«

"I believe I am entirely correct here. Samson could never have been subdued if he had not put his head down in Delilah's lap."

"And have you, Mr. Trostler, also unearthed such a significant feminine relation in this case?"

"But naturally! The fugitive had left behind his bride—I take my hat off! A public school teacher—the most charming little woman you can imagine; loveliness personified, intelligence, and integrity. No man in the world could have made a better choice."

"And he abandoned such a woman disdainfully?"

"Of course not! They had agreed that she was going to follow as soon as he had been able to begin a regular life."

"And has he ever been heard of again?"

"He has created a fully ordered life. This matter is completely and neatly finished. I had the pleasure of bringing his charming bride to him—it would not have been acceptable to let her make the long journey across the ocean by herself—and I had the honor of acting as the best man at her wedding."

The General Director stood up.

"Excuse me, Mr. Trostler," he said, smiling, "for interrupting your account for a moment. I shall merely give a quick assignment in the accounting department, so that I may be able to follow your interesting report entirely unimpeded."

"You're trying in vain, General Director," Dagobert replied calmly, remaining seated. "You won't be able to get through to there. To tell the truth, in the next office there are also two detectives, in fact real police detectives and not paltry amateurs such as I. Unnecessary to mention that on the other side—in the outer office—there are sitting two more [detectives]. They will surely take care that we will remain entirely undisturbed. They have strict orders to let nobody in. Indeed, except for me, nobody is able to leave this room without being arrested on the spot. Do you want to take the chance, General Director?"

"No. What do you want from me?"

»Ich will vor allen Dingen Ihnen gegenüber volle Aufrichtigkeit
walten lassen. Nicht um mir dadurch auch Ihre Aufrichtigkeit
zu erschleichen. Meine Position wäre eine sehr schlechte, wenn
ich auf sie angewiesen wäre. Ich brauche sie nicht. Was ich will,
ist nur, Ihnen die Überzeugung beizubringen, dass ich Sie mit
eisernen Klammern festhalte, so fest, als stäken Sie in einem
Schraubstock. Erst wenn Sie davon völlig überzeugt sind, kann
ich auf jene Entschließung Ihrerseits rechnen, die meines
Erachtens noch einzig möglich und vernünftig ist, und die ich
noch brauche.«

»Welche Entschließung?«

»Darauf kommen wir gleich, erst muss ich Sie noch besser
überzeugen. Sie gestatten mir ja, mich kurz zu fassen. Ich habe
mich bei Frau von Benk als Zimmerherr einquartiert. Das ist die
Mutter   unseres   gewesenen   Kassiers,   die   Witwe   eines
Oberstleutnants. Sie lebt in engen Verhältnissen, aber es ist ein
durchaus ehrenhaftes, moralisch reinliches Milieu. Wie kein
Meister, so fällt auch kein Verbrecher vom Himmel. Ich war
ordentlich aus der Kontenance gebracht, und meine Hoffnung,
da den Schlüssel zu einer verbrecherischen Tat zu finden, ward
stark heruntergedrückt. Ich hatte mich für einen Klavierlehrer
ausgegeben und führte ein sehr solides und häusliches Leben, um
mir das Vertrauen der Damen zu erwerben. Der Damen; denn
Benks Braut, Fräulein Ehlbeck, kam täglich zu Besuch und
gehörte sozusagen zum Hause. Das gelang mir denn auch ohne
besondere Schwierigkeit. Ich hatte die Vorsicht gebraucht, gleich
bei meinem Einzug die Bemerkung fallen zu lassen, dass ich nur
einige Monate zu bleiben gedenke, bis ich mir genug zusammen-
gespart hätte, um meinen Plan der Übersiedlung nach Amerika
ausführen zu können. Diese harmlose Andeutung traf ihr Ziel.
Sowohl Fräulein Ehlbeck, mit dem ich sehr viel vierhändig
spielte, wie die Mutter kamen immer wieder auf das Thema
Amerika zurück. Ich ging systematisch vor. Ich sandte von Zeit
zu Zeit durch Postanweisung verschiedene bescheidene Beträge
an meine Adresse, angeblich Honorar für meine Lektionen, und
bat Frau von Benk sie für mich aufzuheben. Das Geld sei bei ihr
besser aufgehoben als bei mir, und ich wolle es zusammenhalten
für die Reise. Von dem flüchtigen Sohne war nie die Rede, aber

"I want to be completely truthful, particularly with you. Not because I want to trick you into being sincere. My position would be a very bad one if I had to depend on that. I don't need it. What I want is to convince you that I am gripping you with iron clamps, as tightly as if you were in a vice. Only when you are completely convinced of it can I count on that decision on your part, which in my opinion is the only possible and reasonable one that remains, and which I still require."

"What decision?"

"We will discuss that in a moment; first I have to convince you more thoroughly. Allow me to make it short. I have quartered myself as a lodger with Ms. von Benk. That was the mother of our former cashier, the widow of a lieutenant-colonel. She has been living in straitened circumstances, but it is an entirely honorable, morally clean milieu. Just as no masterpiece falls from heaven, so also falls no criminal. I had quite lost my composure and I had little hope left of finding the key to the criminal act. I pretended to be a piano teacher and led a very solid and domestic life in order to gain the ladies' trust. [I say] the ladies' because Benk's bride, Miss Ehlbeck, visited daily, and for all practical purposes was regarded as belonging to the household. I succeeded even without much difficulty. I had been careful, when I moved in, to let drop the comment that I intended to stay only a few months, until I had saved enough money to carry out my plan of emigrating to America. This harmless intimation hit the bull's eye. Both Miss Ehlbeck, with whom I played a lot of four-handed [piano], and also the mother, went back again and again to the topic of America. I proceeded systematically. From time to time I sent a variety of modest sums of money to my address via postal order—ostensibly professional fees for my lessons—and I asked Frau von Benk to keep them for me. The money would be safer in her hands than in mine, and I wanted to keep it all together for the journey. The fugitive son was never talked about, but at no time was there any sign of fear or secrecy. Possible pangs of conscience were definitely not there, and it was clear that their

es war auch nie ein Symptom von Angst oder Heimlichkeit wahrzunehmen. Etwaige Gewissensqualen waren da entschieden nicht vorhanden, und es war klar, von einer Mitwissenschaft oder gar Mitschuld konnte da nicht die Rede sein. Aber es scheint, Herr Generaldirektor, dass meine Rede Sie angreift. Soll ich Ihnen vielleicht ein Glas Wasser einschenken?«

»Ich danke Ihnen, Herr Trostler, vollenden Sie, und bitte machen Sie's kurz!«

»Ich werde es kurz machen. Endlich traf ein, worauf ich lange gewartet hatte, – ein Brief aus Amerika. Sie können sich's denken, dass ich ein scharfes Auge auf die Briefträger hatte. Ich sah den Umschlag und erkannte die Schrift. Den Brief hätte ich leicht stehlen oder heimlich lesen können. Derlei tue ich nicht. Man hat seine Grundsätze. Fremde Briefe waren mir immer ein Heiligtum. Ich erbat nur die Briefmarke für meine Sammlung. Natürlich war es mir nur um den Poststempel zu tun, und da fand ich bestätigt, was ich ohnedies schon wusste. Ich hatte ja längst schon die Adresse, die auch Sie sehr genau kennen, Herr Generaldirektor: Mr. Brenneberg, 1400 Second Avenue South, Minneapolis, Minnesota, U. S. A.«

Der Generaldirektor wurde bei diesen Worten noch blässer. Mit einer plötzlichen verzweifelten Aufraffung steckte er den Schlüssel in seine Schreibtischlade, um sie aufzureißen.

»Nur keine Unbesonnenheit, Herr Generaldirektor!« rief ihm Dagobert zu. »Lassen Sie die Lade ruhig geschlossen; sie kann Ihnen nichts helfen. Sie haben dort einen Revolver, und ich habe die Hand in der Tasche und in der Hand auch einen Revolver. Ich würde entschieden geschwinder sein, und außerdem – Ihr Revolver war geladen, meiner ist es. Ich hatte mir nämlich erlaubt, bei meiner Inspektion die Kammern für alle Fälle zu entleeren und die Patronen zu mir zu stecken.«

»Sie haben mit Nachschlüsseln gearbeitet!«

»Natürlich! Sogar zu Ihrer großen Kasse habe ich mir die Duplikate der Schlüssel verschafft.«

»Wissen Sie, dass das infam ist! Und das hat Grundsätze und rührt keine fremden Briefe an!«

»Regen wir uns nicht auf, Herr Generaldirektor. Die Aufregung kann nur schaden, und ich bin kein Freund von

complicity or even having knowledge [of the crime] were out of the question. However, it appears as if my account is distressing you, General Director. Would you perhaps like me to pour you a glass of water?"

"Thank you, Mr. Trostler; finish, and, I beg of you, keep it short!"

"I shall keep it short. At last, something for which I had waited a long time, arrived—a letter from America. You can imagine that I watched the mailman very closely. I saw the envelope and recognized the handwriting. I could have stolen or secretly read the letter without any difficulty. I don't do this kind of thing. I have my principles. Someone else's letters have always been sacrosanct to me. I merely asked for the stamp, for my collection. Naturally, I was interested only in the postmark, and what I found confirmed what I already knew. I had already long known the address, which you also know very well, Mr. General Director: Mr. Brenneberg, 1400 Second Avenue South, Minneapolis, Minnesota, USA."

Upon hearing these words, the General Director turned even paler. In an unexpected and desperate surge of energy, he inserted the key into the lock in his desk drawer in order to pull it open.

"Now don't be rash, General Director!" Dagobert called out to him. "You may leave the drawer shut; it cannot help you at all. You have a revolver there, and I have my hand in my pocket, and in my hand there is also a revolver. I would definitely be much faster, and what's more—your revolver was loaded, but mine [still] is. You see, I took the liberty of emptying the chamber during my inspection and took the bullets with me, just in case."

"You worked with duplicate keys!"

"As you would expect! Indeed, I even managed to acquire duplicate keys to your main cash box."

"You know that this is infamous! And someone like you has principles and does not touch other people's letters!"

"Let's not get upset, General Director. All this excitement can only be detrimental to your health, and I am no friend of

dramatischen Szenen außerhalb der Bühne. Sie müssen doch selbst sehen, wie Sie sich damit schaden. Diese Aufwallung, mit der Sie da nach dem Revolver greifen wollten, war doch eine Anwandlung von Schwäche, die Ihrer entschieden nicht würdig war. Verlieren Sie doch nur die Ruhe nicht. Sie gehören ja zu den großen Dieben, die man laufen lässt, laufen lassen muss, – leider! Sie glauben mir doch, dass ich das ehrlich bedauere?«

»Weiter, kommen wir zum Schluss!«

»Ich bin schon dabei. Erst wollte ich Ihnen nur noch zweierlei sagen: Erstlich, dass Sie infolge meiner freundlichen Bemühungen schon längst hinter Schloss und Riegel säßen, wenn es nicht das Interesse der A. B. B. erforderte, dass Ihre Gaunerei – Sie haben doch nichts dagegen, dass ich mir in diesem Stadium kein Blatt mehr vor den Mund nehme? – nicht an die große Glocke gehängt werde. Aber ausgeschlossen ist natürlich auch das nicht, wenn unsere Unterhandlungen hier nicht zu dem gewünschten Ziele führen sollten. Und zweitens: man hat allerdings seine Grundsätze, und ich werde tatsächlich nie etwas Ungesetzliches oder auch nur Ungehöriges tun. Es ist aber weder ungesetzlich noch ungehörig, dass der Herr die Sachen eines ungetreuen Dieners durchsucht, mein Herr Generaldirektor! Der Präsident war bei der Durchsuchung zugegen.«

»Vollenden Sie!«

»Viel habe ich nicht gefunden. Dass Sie die Zeugnisse Ihrer unreinlichen galanten Abenteuer lieber in Ihrem Bureau aufheben als im Bereiche Ihrer Frau, das begreift sich, das geht uns nicht an. Also nicht viel, aber doch zwei wertvolle Fingerzeige. Erstens die bereits erwähnte Adresse, und zweitens der Nachweis Ihrer Verbindung mit der Nationalbank unter dem Decknamen Ihrer Frau Schwiegermama.«

»Das ist kein Deckname. Das Geld gehört tatsächlich ihr!«

»Es wäre schlimm für uns, wenn es so wäre, aber es ist nicht so. Sehen Sie, Herr Generaldirektor, ohne es zu wollen, haben Sie mir zu einer von mir selbst nicht gewollten Karriere verholfen. Erst musste ich Verwaltungsrat werden, und dann wurde es unbedingt nötig, dass ich Zensor der Nationalbank wurde. Mit der mächtigen Hilfe unseres Präsidenten ging auch das. Ich musste es werden, um ganz genauen Einblick zu gewinnen. Mir

dramatic scenes off the stage. Surely you realize how you hurt yourself with this. This impulse which made you want to reach for the revolver was but an impulse of weakness, and that was decidedly not worthy of you. Simply don't lose your calm. You rank among the great thieves that one turns loose, has to turn loose—unfortunately! You do believe that I honestly regret this, don't you?"

"Carry on, let's get to the end [of this]!"

"I am already in the process of doing that. Before I do that, I would like to put you in the picture about two additional fine points: First of all, you would already have been under lock and key due to my friendly efforts, if the interests of the ABB did not require that your deception—you won't take exception if I don't mince words any more at this stage?—be kept from being shouted from the rooftops. However, that is not yet off the table, should our negotiations not lead to the desired outcome. And second: I do have principles, and, if truth be told, I will never do anything illegal or merely indecent. It is, on the other hand, neither illegal nor indecent for an employer to search the personal effects of a disloyal servant, my dear General Director! The president was present during the search."

"Come to an end!"

"I did not find much. That you prefer to keep evidence of your sinful gallant adventures in your office rather than in the vicinity of your wife, that is understandable; that is none of our business. So, not much, but nevertheless two valuable clues. First, the aforementioned address and second, evidence of your connection with the National Bank under the pseudonym of your mother-in-law."

"That is not a pseudonym. The money really belongs to her!"

"It would be bad for us if that were so, but it isn't. You see, General Director, without intending it, you have helped provide a career for me which I had not wanted for myself. First I had to become a board director, and then it became absolutely necessary for me to become an auditor at the National Bank. With the powerful backing of our president, that also came to pass. I had to get in there in order to get a complete

können Sie also jetzt keine Romane über Ihre Frau Schwiegermama erzählen. Schließlich werde ich, und zwar heute noch, sogar Generaldirektor werden, aber nur für so lange, bis wir einen geeigneten Ersatz für Sie gefunden haben werden.«

»Sie tun immer, als wenn ich defraudiert hätte. Das werden Sie mir doch erst beweisen müssen!«

»Aber, lieber Generaldirektor – es ist wahrscheinlich das letztemal, dass ich Sie so nennen darf –, begreifen Sie denn Ihre Situation noch immer nicht? Ich kann Ihnen mit wenigen Worten verraten, wie Sie es angestellt haben. Sie kannten Benk von früher her und wussten, dass es die Sehnsucht seines Lebens war, sich in Amerika, in der Atmosphäre der Freiheit, einen Wirkungskreis zu schaffen. Als er seine Bücher abgeschlossen hatte und seinen Urlaub antreten wollte, boten sie ihm sechzigtausend Kronen dafür, dass er spurlos verschwinde. Ein Makel könne auf seinen Namen nicht fallen, da er doch die Kasse in voller Ordnung übergeben und sein Absolutorium in der Tasche habe. Sein Verschwinden werde zwar Bestürzung aber sonst keinerlei Nachteil hervorrufen. Für Sie würde die Bestürzung von unermesslichem Vorteil zur Befestigung Ihrer Stellung sein. Denn Sie seien dann der einzige, der für den weiteren ungestörten Gang der Maschine sorgen könne, und damit sei Ihre Unentbehrlichkeit eklatant dokumentiert. Das sei Ihnen das Opfer wert. Benk ließ sich überreden, umso eher, als Sie ihn schon von der Schule her kannten. Sie duzten sich ja auch, nur freilich auf Ihren Wunsch in der Bank nicht.«

»Es ging einfach nicht – der anderen Beamten wegen.«

»Ich begreife. Nun konnte also der große Coup von Ihnen gewagt werden. Sie fühlten sich sicher. Der Verdacht würde doch auf den verschwundenen Kassier fallen. Sie konnten wissen oder doch mit gutem Grund annehmen, dass man aus Scheu vor dem öffentlichen Skandal von der gerichtlichen Anzeige absehen werde. Übrigens hatten Sie auch für diesen Fall Ihre Maßnahmen getroffen. Soll ich Sie Ihnen rekapitulieren?«

»Ich danke, ich verzichte.«

and detailed understanding. Therefore, you can't tell me any stories about your mother-in-law [which I would believe]. Finally, I shall even become the General Director, and that as of today, but only until we have found a suitable replacement for you."

"You behave as if I had defrauded [the bank]. Nevertheless, you will have to prove that first!"

"But my dear General Director—it is probably the last time that I may call you that—don't you understand the situation yet? I am able to reveal to you in a few words how you managed this. You knew Benk from times past and were aware that it was his life's desire to create a life for himself in America in an environment of freedom. When he had closed his books and was about to go on vacation, you offered him sixty thousand korunas in exchange for his vanishing without a trace. [He assumed that] there would never be a stigma resting on him because, after all, he had delivered the cash box in perfect order, and he had corroboration of this in his pocket. To be sure, his disappearance might create bewilderment, but otherwise have no adverse consequences at all. This bewilderment would be of immeasurable advantage for you in fortifying your position. Because you would have been the only one who could arrange for the continual operation of the system, and for this reason your indispensability would have been proven spectacularly. That would have been worth the sacrifice for you. Benk let himself be persuaded, all the more so since you already knew him from school. Also you were on a first name basis, but certainly not at the bank, at your request."

"It was simply not possible—because of the other bank officers."

"I understand. Now the time had come to venture to carry out your grand coup. You felt safe. After all, suspicion would fall on the cashier who had disappeared. You could be sure, or at least assume with good reason, that because of an aversion to public scandal, any legal action would be disregarded. For that matter you had taken steps as well. Would you like me to recapitulate?"

"No thanks, I shall pass."

»Gut, so will ich nur andeuten, dass ich unter anderen auch bei der H. A. P. A. G. – das ist die Hamburg-Amerikanische Paketboot-Aktiengesellschaft – einiges erhoben habe. Ich habe mir die Nummer der Kajüte notiert, die Sie auf der ›Kolumbia‹ gemietet hatten. Die Urlaubsverhältnisse hätten Ihnen hinlänglich Zeit zu dem wünschenswerten Vorsprung gewährt.«

»Was wollen Sie nun von mir?«

»Eine Kleinigkeit, Ihre Unterschrift. Sie haben das durch Vollmacht ausgewiesene Verfügungsrecht über das Depot Ihrer ›Schwiegermama‹ bei der Nationalbank. Das Depot reicht gerade aus, um den Schaden der A. B. B. zu decken. Diese Vollmacht werden Sie auf mich übertragen. Hier ist das vollständig adjustierte Schriftstück, Sie brauchen nur Ihren werten Namen darunter zu setzen.«

»Das werde ich nicht tun!«

»Wie Sie glauben, – genötigt wird nicht. Ich wollte Ihr Bestes, und nur wenn Sie sich selbst davon überzeugt haben, sollen Sie unterschreiben, sonst nicht. Die Verhältnisse haben sich nämlich zu Ihren Ungunsten verschoben, geehrter Herr. Alle Vorkehrungen zur Sicherung jenes Depots sind getroffen, falls Sie sich wirklich weigern sollten. Sie müssten sich nämlich klar machen, dass die A. B. B. jetzt keine Ursache mehr hat, die gerichtliche Anzeige zu scheuen. Der etwaige üble Eindruck der Nachricht von dem großen Unterschleif würde durch die Tatsache paralysiert werden, dass man nicht nur deren Urheber prompt erwischt, sondern auch für die sofortige Schadensgutmachung prompt gesorgt hat. Nun – was meinen Sie?«

Der Generaldirektor unterschrieb. Dagobert fertigte einen im Vorzimmer des Auftrages harrenden Vertrauensmann mit dem Schriftstück ab.

»Nur noch zwei Minuten,« nahm er dann wieder das Wort. »Die Nationalbank ist ja gleich daneben. Inzwischen kann ich Ihnen ja sagen, dass es eine sinnige Überraschung für unseren Herrn Präsidenten sein wird, eine unschuldige Freude, die er nicht erwartet hat. Denn ich habe weder ihm, noch sonst jemandem von dem Fortgange meiner Bemühungen berichtet.

"Well, in this case I shall merely let you know that, among other things, I also dug up information at the HAPAG—which is the Hamburg American Line[2]. I took down the number of the cabin which you had rented on the 'Columbia'. The vacation set-up would have given you sufficient time for an advantageous headstart."

"So what do you want from me?"

"A trifle—your signature. You possess the right of disposal for your 'mother-in-law's' deposit at the National Bank, established by a power of attorney. The deposit is just enough to cover the ABB's damages. You will transfer this power of attorney to me. Here is the fully adjusted document; all you have to do is put your precious signature at the bottom."

"I shall not do that!"

"As you wish—there won't be any coercion. I wanted your best, and only after you have convinced yourself of this, you shall sign; otherwise, don't. You see, the circumstances have shifted to your disadvantage, dear sir. We have taken all measures to secure that deposit, in case you should in fact refuse. That is to say, you should have realized that the ABB no longer has any reason to draw back from legal action. The potentially negative impression of the news about the great embezzlement would be rendered invalid by the information that not only has its originator been swiftly caught, but also that amends for the damages sustained have already been promply arranged. Well—what do you say?"

The General Director signed. Dagobert dispatched a representative, who was awaiting orders in the outer office, with the document.

"Merely two more minutes," he began to speak again. "Indeed, the National Bank is practically next door. In the meantime, I may as well tell you that it will be an appropriate surprise for our [cherished] president, an innocent pleasure which he did not expect. The reason is that I have told neither him nor anybody else of the advancement of my efforts.

---

[2] HAPAG, English: *Hamburg American Packet-shipping Joint-stock company*, founded in 1912.

Ich liebe es, mit fertigen Tatsachen zu kommen. Man hat so seine Eigenheiten!«

Nach wenigen Minuten ertönte wirklich ein Signal vom Telephonapparat am Schreibtisch her. Der Generaldirektor legte die Hörmuschel ans Ohr.

»Die Nationalbank,« meldete er, »ich verstehe aber nicht –, der Mohr kann gehen – Schluss!«

»Ganz richtig!« rief Dagobert. »Das ist das Schlagwort, das ich mir bestellt habe zur Bestätigung, dass alles in Ordnung sei. Und jetzt, Herr Ringhoff, sind Sie Generaldirektor – gewesen! Erlauben Sie nur, dass ich die Türen öffne. Damit ist die Überwachung aufgehoben.«

Ringhoff nahm seinen Hut, verneigte sich und verließ die A. B. B., um sie nie wieder zu betreten.

I love to present completed facts. In any case, I have my idiosyncracies!"

After a few minutes, a ringing actually sounded from the telephone on the desk. The General Director put the receiver to his ear.

"The National Bank," he announced, "but I don't understand—'the Moor may go'—that's it!"

"Quite so!" Dagobert called out. "That is the password I commissioned to authenticate that everything is all right. And now, Mr. Ringhoff, you are the—former—General Director. Allow me to open the doors. The surveillance is hereby revoked."

Ringhoff took his hat, bowed, and left the ABB, never to enter it again.

HANS HYAN

Hans Hyan was born in Berlin on June 2, 1868. Little is known about his early life.

A court reporter, cabaret artist, and a prolific writer, he wrote more than fifty novels in as many years as well as a large number of shorter narratives and plays. Hyan also ran into trouble with the law at times. His liberal and socially critical leanings are reflected in his crime stories, which are often humorous and have ironic undertones.

His crime stories benefited from his thorough knowledge of crimes and criminals. Fellow writer and reporter Kurt Tucholsky, in a review of Hyan's *Sexualmörder in Düsseldorf* (*Sex Murderers in Dusseldorf*, Berlin-Hesselwinkel: Verlag der Neuen Gesellschaft, 1930), called him "an authority on criminal practice," and someone who possessed "excellent knowledge of [police] staff."[1]

Hyan had served time in prison and was pushing the legal boundaries of what was considered prim and proper in German society. Although Berlin, much like Munich, had begun to develop into a modern metropolis during the last decades of the German monarchy, the Wilhelmine police state exercised its power with an iron fist through censorship and oppression. The authorities were not happy about the performances staged at Hyan's famous cabaret Silberne Punschterrine (Silver Punchbowl) where he, as early as 1901, not only "sang songs about criminals and the poor, and insulted the people

---

[1] Kurt Tucholsky [Peter Panther], *Die Weltbühne*, 11 Feb 1930, No. 7: 248.

who came to his cabaret,"[2] but also performed works that were "very risqué." This inspired police reports that described his works as concerned "not so much with the cultivation of art, as with stimulating and tickling the senses" (**Berlin Cabaret,** footnote 2.)

Besides his accomplishments as a cabaret artist and crime story writer, Hyan was also a productive contributor of movie scripts, more than twenty-five in all. His gumshoe, Tom Shark, was the hero of a number of (silent) movies in 1916 and 1917.[3] Hyan even assumed acting parts in a handful of movies, and directed a movie, released in 1915, titled *Der Onkel aus Amerika (The Uncle from America)*.[4] Not surprisingly, when the Nazis assumed power in January 1933, Hyan's works landed on the infamous lists of banned (and burned) books which emerged as early as April of that year.

Hyan died in Berlin on January 6, 1944.

The story "In the Name of the Law," published in 1916, begins with a police raid on a disreputable establishment in Berlin, in the dead of night.

---

[2] Peter Jelavich, *Berlin Cabaret* (Harvard University Press, 1993).
[3] "Hans Hyan Filmografie,"10 June 2014 < http://www.filmportal.de/person/hans-hyan_3177d1026bd94dcc8e6b1cfc100e37a1>.4
[4] "Hans Hyan Filmography," 10 June 2014 <http://www.imdb.com/name/nm1330620>.

HANS HYAN

HANS HYAN

Im Namen des Gesetzes

Die kleine Maus im ersten Zimmer neben der Korridortür des Hotels erwachte von dem starken Klingeln und es wurde ihr gar nicht leicht, ihren Begleiter aufzuwecken, der am Abend vorher zuviel Sekt getrunken hatte.

»Um Gotteswillen, das ist die Polizei,« sagte sie, die schon im Unterrock und Korsett auf dem Bettrand saß und eilig die Strümpfe über ihre schlanken Beine streifte, »nun hab ich mich so lange gehalten, und nun komm ich doch ran! .... Aber nicht wahr, du sagst, wir haben ein festes?!«

Indem klingelte es von Neuem schrill und andauernd.

Der Mann, der ein starkes Phlegma besitzen musste, richtete seinen dicken Oberkörper in den weißen Decken und Kissen auf und stierte mit verschlafenen und trüben Augen in das elektrische Licht der Lampe, das die Kleine angedreht hatte.

»Das soll ja der Teufel holen!« sagte er, während der blonde, wirre Schnurrbart in dem pausbäckigen Gesicht sich vor Entrüstung sträubte, »nicht mal schlafen lassen sie einen?!« Er sah auf die Uhr: »Erst ein Viertel vier!... was will denn das Gesindel?«

»Es ist die Polizei... die revidiert!« sagte die Kleine, die schon dabei war, mit allen möglichen Verrenkungen ihres rundlichen Oberleibes die hinten zu schließende Bluse zuzuhaken.

»Mach mal, du!... Mach mal!... Wir müssen aufmachen!«

HANS HYAN

In the Name of the Law

The little sweetheart in the first room, [in the corridor] past the hallway door of the hotel, was awakened by the fierce ringing, and it was not an easy task for her to wake up her companion who had drunk too much sparkling wine the previous evening.

"For God's sake, that is the police," she said, already sitting on the edge of the bed in her underskirt and corset, and quickly pulling the stockings up her slim legs, "I have been able to hang on for so long, and now it's going to be my turn!... But you will say that we are going steady, won't you?!"

Meanwhile, the ringing had started anew, piercing and constant.

The man, who apparently was ruled by strong apathy, raised up his portly upper body amongst the white covers and pillows, and stared with sleepy and bleary eyes into the electric light of the lamp which the little woman had switched on.

"To hell with it!" he said, the blond, wiry moustache on his chubby-cheeked face bristling with indignation, "they don't even allow us to sleep?!" He looked at his watch. "Only a quarter after four!... What do the riffraff want?"

"It is the police... they are checking!" said the little woman, who was already busily contorting her plump upper body in all possible directions while closing the hooks on the back of her blouse.

"Come on, you!... Come on! We have to open [the door]!"

»Ih, fällt mir gar nicht ein!... Ich habe das Zimmer für die Nacht bezahlt, und ich möchte den mal sehen, der mich hier rausbringen wird!«

Dabei stellte aber der Gute seine dicken Beine doch auf den Bettvorleger hinaus und begann, fortwährend schimpfend, seine Unterhose anzuziehen.

Inzwischen war es in den Nachbarräumen auch lebendig geworden, man hörte das leise Öffnen der Zimmertüren und gedämpftes Sprechen auf dem Korridor. Vor der Eingangstür war es eine kurze Zeit still geworden, jetzt hörte man deutlich die Worte:

»Aufgemacht!... Im Namen des Gesetzes!... oder ich lasse die Tür öffnen!«

Von den Bewohnern dieser, der mehr oder weniger erlaubten Liebe geweihten, Gemäche schien keiner sich zum Amte des Pförtners berufen zu fühlen. Man vernahm ein Klirren am Schloss, und dann ging, für die kleine, ängstlich lauschende Maus deutlich vernehmbar, die Korridortür auf.

Der dicke Herr hatte sich aufgerichtet und stand, mit dem schwachen Versuch, seine Haltung zu bewahren, in der Nähe der Tür, an die eben stark gepocht wurde.

»Soll ich aufmachen?« flüsterte er der Kleinen zu.

Die zuckte mit furchtsamer Miene die Schultern.

Da öffnete er und fragte kläglich: »Was wünschen Sie denn?«

Von den beiden großen, einfach gekleideten Männern trat einer in die Stube. Der andere hatte das Gas im Eingang angezündet und blieb draußen, wahrscheinlich um die übrigen Bewohner dieser »Pension für Tage, Wochen und Monate« zu bewachen.

Der Eingetretene hielt die bekannte Blechmarke in die Höhe und sagte mit amtsmäßig kalter Stimme:

»Sie sind beide verhaftet!«

»Beide?« Der Dicke warf den Kopf zurück und sah den Beamten von der Seite an, »die da meinetwegen!...« er zeigte mit dem Daumen über die Schulter auf das Mädchen, »aber ich doch nicht etwa!«

Die Maus fing sofort an zu heulen:

"Eh, I don't think so!... I paid for the room for the night, and I would like to see who's going to get me out of here!"

At the same time, however, he put his heavy legs down on the bedside carpet and began pulling on his underpants, grumbling all the while.

Meanwhile, there were signs of life in the neighboring rooms as well; one could hear the quiet opening of doors and subdued talking in the hallway. Outside the hallway door it had become quiet for a short time; now they heard the words clearly:

"Open up!... In the name of the law!... or I shall have the door opened!"

None of the inhabitants of this establishment, which was dedicated to [acts of] more or less legitimate love, seemed to feel a calling for the office of doorman. They heard rattling, and then the hallway door opened, clearly audible to the little sweetheart, who was listening anxiously.

The portly gentleman had straightened up and, trying weakly to keep his composure, stood close to the door, on which now there was fierce knocking.

"Should I open it?" he whispered to the little woman.

The latter shrugged her shoulders, looking fearful.

Thereupon he opened [the door] and asked ruefully: "What is it that you want?"

One of the two tall men in plainclothes entered the room. The other had lit the gas[lights] in the hallway and stayed there, probably in order to watch the other inhabitants of this 'Pension for Days, Weeks, and Months.'

The one who had entered held up the familiar pewter badge and said in a government-style, cold voice:

"You are both under arrest!"

"Both?" The portly man threw his head back and looked at the officer sideways, "her maybe!..." [as], with his thumb, he pointed over his shoulder at the young woman, "but certainly not me!"

The sweetheart immediately started to cry:

»Ach, der gemeine Kerl, Herr Kommissar!... Ich bin ein anständiges Mädchen und wohne bei meine Eltern... ich wollte ja durchaus nicht mit... aber er hat mich betrunken gemacht!«

»Das Frauenzimmer!... na, das sehn Sie doch selbst, Herr Kommissar, da brauch' ich Ihnen doch nichts sagen!... Rauchen Sie vielleicht eine Zigarre, Herr Kommissar?

«Das Mädchen schluchzte und schimpfte dazwischen, der Beamte antwortete gar nicht, ging zur Tür und rief hinaus: »Die andern sämtlich hier reinbringen, Müller!«

Das geschah langsam.

Zuerst kam ein Alter, dürr, klapprig, wie ein verfallenes Gebäude, in dem aber die Fenster noch glühen und leuchten. Mit diesen schwarzen, unruhvollen Augen suchte er instinktive zuerst die kleine Brünette, als ihn der zweite Kriminalbeamte ins Zimmer schob. Hinter ihm her ging eine üppige Frau von vielleicht vierzig Jahren, mit Mänteln und Hüten auf dem Arm. Ihre Taille war vorn noch nicht geschlossen, man sah über dem Hemd den gelben, schon runzligen Hals. Sie weinte, während ihr Liebhaber unverständliche Worte der Empörung in seinen weißen Bartstummeln zerquetschte.

Nun erschien im Türrahmen eine hübsche, ritterliche Gestalt, ein junger Herr in den Dreißigern, der seiner Begleitung artig den Vortritt ließ und sich den ihm nachdrängenden Beamten vom Leib zu halten verstand.

Im Zimmer verneigte er sich flüchtig vor den Anwesenden und trat dann mit raschem Schritt dem Beamten näher: »Wer sind Sie?«

»Danach haben Sie nicht zu fragen, sondern ich!" schnauzte der Polizist.

»Einen Augenblick, bitte!" Der junge, elegante Herr ging etwas zur Seite und der Polizist folgte ihm unwillkürlich in die Zimmerecke.

»Hören Sie mal, indem Sie mir hier diese Unannehmlichkeiten machen, bereiten Sie sich selber welche! Ich bin Offizier, mein Name ist ...« Der junge Herr dämpfte seine Stimme noch mehr zum Flüstern.

Der andere machte eine fast höhnische Gebärde: »Das bedauere ich sehr... haben Sie einen Ausweis?«

"Oh, the louse, Inspector!... I am a reputable young woman, and I live with my parents... I really didn't want to come along... but he got me drunk!"

"That wench!... Well, you can see for yourself, Inspector, I don't have to tell you what's going on here... Would you perhaps like a cigar, Inspector?"

The young woman cursed between bouts of sobbing; the officer gave no reply at all, walked to the door and called: "Bring the other ones in here, all of them, Müller!"

Gradually, that happened.

An old man was first to appear; scrawny, frail, like a dilapidated building in which, however, the windows still glow and shine. With these black, restless eyes he instinctively looked first at the small brunette when the second detective pushed him into the room. Behind him walked a voluptuous woman of perhaps forty years with coats and hats over her arm. Her garment had not been closed completely at the waist; above the shirt one could see her yellow throat, already wrinkled. She cried while her lover muttered incomprehensible words of indignation into his white stubbly beard.

Next appeared in the door frame a handsome, gallant figure, a young gentleman in his thirties who yielded politely to his companion, and who knew how to keep the officer who was pressing him from behind at arm's length.

Once in the room, he bowed briefly to all present and then quickly stepped closer to the officer: "Who are you?"

"You have nothing to ask here, but I do!" snapped the policeman.

"One moment, please!" The young, elegant gentleman stepped slightly aside, and the policeman automatically followed him into the corner of the room.

"Listen, by creating trouble for me, you are also creating some for you! I am an army officer, my name is..." The young gentleman softened his voice even more, to a whisper.

The other made an almost mocking gesture: "I am very sorry about this... do you have ID?"

»Meine Karte dürfte Ihnen wohl genügen!« Er hielt dem Kriminalbeamten das Kartonblättchen entgegen.

Der trat zurück und sagte so laut, dass alle es hörten: »Visitenkarten kann sich jeder drucken lassen!... Wir suchen hier—damit Sie's übrigens wissen—ein Hochstaplerpaar; und gerade Sie, mein Verehrtester, haben eine verteufelte Ähnlichkeit mit dem Herrn!«

Die Dame des jungen Kavaliers, die nicht jünger war als er, aber unzweifelhaft den ersten Kreisen angehörte, nahm den breiten Hermelintaschenmuff, mit dem sie das sowieso verschleierte Gesicht bisher bedeckt hatte, herab und sagte ungeniert: »Eine solche Frechheit ist mir noch nicht vorgekommen!«

»Halten Sie den Mund!« schnaubte der Beamte, »oder ich lasse Sie krummschließen!«

Die Dame lachte hell auf, dann meinte Sie zu ihrem Geliebten: »Verzeih mir, Herbert, dass ich dich durch meinen Einfall, auch mal ein solches Heim kennen zu lernen, in Ungelegenheiten gebracht habe... wir sind nämlich richtige Eheleute,« wandte sie sich nachlässig an den Beamten, was diesem jedoch nur ein brutales Hohngelächter entlockte.

»Ich glaube im Übrigen nicht daran,« fuhr die Dame fort, »ich glaube nicht an die Beamteneigenschaft dieser Herren!... Das sind Schwindler!«

»Um Gotteswillen, Lo!... keine Beleidigung! Das sind Beamte! Du machst dich strafbar!«

Der junge Mann legte seiner Freundin die schlanke Hand auf den Schleier und redete leise auf sie ein. Doch der Polizist hatte die letzte Äußerung der Dame kaum gehört. Ein Lärm draußen auf dem Korridor ließ ihn rasch hinauseilen.

Da widersetzte sich jemand, eine Frau, und nur den vereinten Anstrengungen beider Polizisten gelang es, sie hereinzubringen.

»Seit sechs Jahren geh ich hier anschaffen!... Und noch nie nicht hat mich die Polizei besucht!... Was heißt das denn, ich zahle doch meine Steuern!... Wollen Sie mir ins Gewerbe pfuschen, Sie lackierter Affe, Sie!«

Der Beamte trat auf sie zu.

»Schweigen Sie... Sie sollen schweigen!«

"My card should be adequate!" He held out the little card-board card to the detective.

The latter stepped back and said so loud that all of them could hear it: "Everybody can have businesscards printed!... We are looking for—just so that you know it—an impostor couple; and you in particular, my dear sir, have a devilish likeness to the gentleman!"

The lady of the young cavalier, who was not younger than he but unquestionably belonged to the first circles [of society], took down the wide ermine pocket muff with which she had shielded her face, which was veiled anyway, and said unasham-edly: "Such an impertinence has never happened to me before!"

"Keep your mouth shut!" the officer grunted, "otherwise I will have you handcuffed!"

The lady gave a loud laugh, then she said to her lover: "Please forgive me, Herbert, that I got you into trouble with my pro-posal to get to know such a home... as a matter of fact, we really are a married couple," she said, turning to the officer in a casual manner which, however, elicited from the latter only savage, contemptuous laughter.

"Besides, I don't believe it," the lady continued, "I don't believe in the official status of these gentlemen!... They are swindlers!"

"For God's sake, Lo!... no insults! These are officers! You are liable to prosecution!"

The young man put his slim hand on his girlfriend's veil and talked quietly to her. The policeman, however, had hardly heard the lady's latest remark. A noise in the hallway outside made him quickly hurry out.

Someone was resisting out there, a woman, and only the com-bined efforts of both policemen managed to get her inside [the room].

"For six years I have been turning tricks here!... And never before have the police visited me!... What's that supposed to mean; after all, I pay my taxes!... Meddle in my business, would you, you painted ape, you!"

The officer stepped up to her.

"You be quiet... Be quiet, I tell you!"

»Ich rede, wenn ich will! Und ich will immer! Und von Ihnen nehm' ich keine Belehrung nicht an, Sie oller Polizeifatzke! Verstehen Sie?... Ihnen spuck ich auf die Stiefel, dass sie blank werden!... Wofür habe ich denn mein Bäckerbuch, was? Etwa damit Sie nachher kommen, Sie Affenarm, und vermasseln mir die Fahrt!... So ein Kujawe!... So ein Polizeipopel, so ein beschissener! Will mir hier mein Geschäft stören, wo das schon sowieso nicht mehr geht heutzutage! Wollen Sie etwa meine Schulden bezahlen, Sie olle Salatstaude, Sie...«

»Halten Sie jetzt endlich Ihr Maul,« donnerte der Kriminalbeamte, »Sie kommen ran wegen Beamtenbeleidigung!«

»Ach, Sie!... Sie... Sie...« Die Dirne sagte ein Schimpfwort von so empörender Unanständigkeit, dass der junge Offizier sich einmischte und sie bat, dieses Gespräch doch draußen, wenn sie mit »dem Herrn da« allein wäre, fortzusetzen.

Sofort wandte sich die offensichtlich berauschte Person dem jungen Mann zu und nickte ihm lachend zu.

»Recht haste, Kleiner, die Kerls sin des ja nicht wert, dass man sich mit ihnen abgibt!... Aber du bist ein netter Bursche!... Dir werd ich mal meine Adresse geben, ja?...«

Sie wurde von dem Polizisten unterbrochen, der mit einem »Ruhig!« sich an ihren Kavalier wandte.

»Sie da, mein Herr!... was krauchen Sie denn in den Ecken herum?! Lassen Sie sich doch mal ansehn! Hierher, bitte, unters Licht, wenn's gefällig ist!«

Nur widerstrebend gehorchte der Angeredete dem Befehl. Es war ein mittelgroßer Mann, sicher über fünfzig Jahre alt, dessen glattrasiertes Gesicht mit den großen Tränensäcken unter den verdächtig niedergeschlagenen Augen seinen Beruf verriet.

»Wie heißen Sie?«

»Kohlert.«

"I talk whenever I want! And I always want to [talk]! And I'm not gonna take any lecture from you, you stuffed-shirt policeman! Do you hear me?... I'll spit on your boots until they shine!... What do I have my baker's book [customer book] for, huh? So that you can show up afterwards, you monkey-butt, and mess up my ride!... Such a Kujawe[5] [originally: a hilltop amusement grove]!... Such a police booger, such a shitter! Wants to interfere in my business, when it's not going anywhere anyway these days! Do you want to pay my debts, you ol' let-tuce-head, you..."

"Once and for all, shut your mouth," the detective thundered, "you will be turned in for insulting an official!"

"Oh, you!... you... you..." The prostitute uttered a cussword of such outrageous impropriety that the young military officer intervened and asked her to continue this conversation outside, when she was alone with "the gentleman there."

Immediately, the apparently inebriated person turned to the young man and nodded at him, laughing.

"Right you are, my little one, these guys don't d'serve at all that one wastes time on them!... Although, you are one pleasant fella!... I'm gonna give you my address, okay?..."

She was interrupted by the policeman, who said, "Quiet!" and then turned to her cavalier.

"You over there, sir!... What are you creeping around in this corner for? Let us take a closer look at you! Come over here, please, under the light, if you don't mind!"

The [so] addressed obeyed the order only reluctantly. He was a man of medium height, surely past fifty years old, whose clean-shaven face with the large pouches under his suspiciously downcast eyes let on about his profession.

"What's your name?"

"Kohlert."

---

[5] Kujawe: "eine reizende bewaldete Anhöhe, die Kujawe oder die Buchenhöhe genannt, welche als Vergnügungsort für die Städter dient. (F.W.F. Schmidt, "Land und Leute in Westpreußen," 1870: 47b. In: Klaus-Dieter Kreplin, *Über Kaschuben: Ein Reader: Teil GQ: Geschichte - Quellen* 8 Aug. 2014 <http://www.studienstelleog.de/download/GQ2. PDF)

»Was sind sie [von Beruf]?«

»Das möchte ich Ihnen lieber allein sagen!«

»Ach was, wir haben hier keine Geheimnisse! Man raus damit, was sind Sie [von Beruf]?«

Dem Mann, der den weißen Umlegekragen und den schwarzen schmalen Bindeschlips noch in der Hand trug, standen die Schweißperlen auf der Stirn, er blieb stumm.

»Also, wenn Sie Ihren Beruf nicht angeben,« sagte der Beamte streng, »habe ich auch keine Veranlassung zu glauben, dass der mir angegebene Name stimmt, besonders da ich Sie in einer derartigen Gesellschaft angetroffen habe!«

Er wies mit der Kopfbewegung auf die Prostituierte hin, die sich ihrerseits an die Stirn tippte und grinsend von Neuem losschimpfte.

»Sind das alle, Müller?« fragte der Kommandierende jetzt den andern Beamten.

»Ja, die anderen Zimmer sind leer, Herr Wachtmeister.«

»Schön, dann nehmen Sie den Leuten sämtlich die Papiere und Wertsachen ab... damit sie sich auf dem Weg ins Präsidium nicht etwa der wichtigsten Beweisstücke entledigen!«

»Sehr wohl, Herr Wachtmeister... Sie!« er tippte dem Dicken auf den Bauch, »machen Sie mal Ihre Taschen leer!«

Der Mann tat es widerspruchslos. Die Dirne sagte: »Zähl man deinen Kies nach, Dicker, sonst fehlen nachher noch ein paar seltene Münzen! Das ist schon oft vorgekommen bei den Faulen! Die Brüder wissen nachher von gar nichts!«

Der mit ›Wachtmeister‹ Titulierte sah die Frau einige Sekunden an, dann sagte er zu dem anderen Polizisten: »Sie sind Zeuge, Müller, was die da eben sagt...! Das kostet sie sechs Monate!«

Die Dame, die mit ihrem Kavalier ans Fenster getreten war, wurde vielleicht nur durch diese Worte davon abgehalten, laut etwas Ähnliches zu äußern. Flüsternd sagt sie zu dem schlanken Blonden fortwährend: »Ich sage dir, Herbert, es sind Schwindler, so benehmen sich keine richtigen Beamten!«

Aber der Herr bat sie inständig, doch zu schweigen und sich nicht noch größeren Unannehmlichkeiten auszusetzen. Auch er gab, ohne zu murren, seine Börse, die Ringe, Uhr und Brieftasche ab.

"What is your occupation?"

"I would prefer to tell you in private!"

"Gobbledygook, we don't have any secrets here! Out with it, what is your occupation?"

The man, who still carried the white turn-down collar and the small, black necktie in his hand, had beads of perspiration on his forehead; he remained silent.

"Well, if you don't tell us your occupation," the officer said severely, "I have no reason to believe that the name you told us is accurate, particularly since I came across you in such company!"

He pointed with his head to the prostitute, who for her part tapped her forehead and began to complain anew, grinning.

"Are these all, Müller?" the commanding officer asked the other officer.

"Yes, the other rooms are empty, Sergeant."

"Very well, then take away all documents and valuables from these people... so that they won't rid themselves of the key pieces of evidence on the way to the police department!"

"Very good, Sergeant... You!" he tapped the portly man on the belly. "Empty out your pockets!"

The man did so without objection. The prostitute said: "You better count your money, fat man, otherwise you'll be missing a couple of rare coins! That has happened quite frequently with the lazy ones! Later on the brothers don't know anything!"

The one titled "Sergeant" looked at the woman for several seconds, then he said to the other policeman: "You are a witness, Müller, to what she just said...! That will cost her six months!"

The lady who had stepped to the window with her cavalier may have been prevented by these words only from uttering only something similar aloud. Whispering, she said to the slim blond man over and and over: "I am telling you, Herbert, these are tricksters; no real police officers behave this way!"

But the gentleman implored her to be quiet nevertheless, and not to to expose herself to greater unpleasantness. He also gave his purse, his rings, his watch, and his wallet, without complaining.

Dann kam der alte Herr daran, der sich als pensionierter Geheimer Rechnungsrat entpuppte. Und die Damen mussten ebenfalls ihre Taschen leeren, nur die Straßendirne weigerte sich entschieden und erklärte: »Wer seine Augen im Kopf behalten will, der soll mir ja vom Leib bleiben!«

Der Herr mit dem glatten Gesicht drückte sich bis zuletzt. Nun half ihm nichts, er musste auch seine Siebensachen hergeben. Während der zweite Kriminalbeamte ein Verzeichnis der Gegenstände in seinem Notizbuch anfertigte, blätterte der Wachtmeister in der Brieftasche des wie ein armer Sünder vor ihm Stehenden herum; er lächelte spöttisch: »Ach, Sie sind Geistlicher!...Und obendrein, wie ich sehe, Reichstagsabgeordneter!... Nun, da rat ich Ihnen, vergessen Sie in Ihrer nächsten Rede gegen die wachsende Unmoral der großen Städte nicht, diese Szene hier recht anschaulich zu schildern!... Müller, sind die Droschken da?«

»Jawohl, Herr Wachtmeister!«

»Dann holen Sie die Wirtin zur Befragung!«

Müller marschierte ab. Die Verhafteten standen schweigsam in dem hellen Licht, in diesem von einem eigentümlichen Geruch durchwehten Alkoven, alle von dem peinigenden Gefühl der Besorgnis durchwühlt vor dem, was ihnen auf der Polizeiwache bevorstand. Nur die Prostituierte schien frei von Angst. Sie hatte ein Kästchen mit Datteln aus dem Handtäschchen geholt, aß und spuckte die Kerne weit von sich.

Indes verging die Zeit.

»Er scheint Schwierigkeiten da unten zu finden!« murmelte der Wachtmeister. Und wie in plötzlichem Entschluss: »Dass mir hier keiner den Versuch macht, sich zu befreien!... Ich bin sofort wieder da!«

Damit war er schon bei der Tür, deren Schlüssel er von außen zweimal herumdrehte. Die Verhafteten warteten. Nach einiger Zeit sagte die Dirne: »Die kommen ja nicht! Das wird doch keine Falle sein?«

Und die Dame mit dem Hermelinmuff lachte leise und meinte:

»Wie ich es vorausgesagt habe, es sind Schwindler!«

Then it was the old gentleman's turn, who turned out to be a retired privy councilor in the ministry of finance. And the ladies also had to empty their purses; only the streetwalker refused resolutely and declared: "If you want to keep your eyes in your head, stay away from me!"

The gentleman with the clean-shaven face managed to cop out until the last moment. However, it was to no avail; he also had to part with his belongings. While the second detective created a list of the items in his notebook, the sergeant thumbed through the wallet of the man who was standing before him like a poor sinner; he smiled derisively: "Ah, you are a cleric!...And on top of that, as I can see, a member of the imperial parliament!... Well, I recommend you don't forget to describe these scenes very vividly in your next speech against the growing immorality in the big cities!... Müller, are the cabs here?"

"Yessir, Sergeant!"

"Then pick the landlady up for questioning!"

Müller marched off. The suspects stood silently in the bright light, in this alcove through which wafted a strange odor, all of them troubled by the gnawing sense of apprehension in anticipation of what might be in store for them at the police station. Only the prostitute seemed free of anxiety. She had produced a little box with dates from her little purse, ate them, and spat the pits far away from her.

Meanwhile, time passed.

"He seems to have met with trouble!" the sergeant murmured. And then, as if with a sudden resolve: "[I strongly suggest] that nobody tries to break free!... I will be right back!"

With that, he was already at the door, whose key he turned twice from the outside. The suspects waited. After a while, the prostitute said: "They are not coming back!.. Could this be a trap?"

And the lady with the ermine muff laughed quietly and said: "As I predicted, they are swindlers!"

Schließlich, als noch eine Viertelstunde vergangen war, mussten es die anderen auch glauben. Man rückte den Schrank fort, der vor der Tür zum Nebenzimmer stand, und fand diese offen.

»Na, ich bleibe hier,« sagte der Dicke, »soll ich etwa noch mal Hotelgeld bezahlen?«

Die andern gingen alle. Der kleinen Maus, die keinen Blick für ihren Kavalier übrig hatte, bot der pensionierte Geheime Rechnungsrat an, sich ihm anzuschließen.

Finally, when another quarter of an hour had passed, the others had to think so too. They pushed away the cabinet which had been standing in front of the door to the adjacent room, and they found the door was unlocked.

"Well, I'll stay here," the portly man said, "or am I supposed to pay for another hotel?"

The others all left. The retired privy counselor invited the little sweetheart, who had no eyes left for her cavalier, to accompany him.

WALTER SERNER

Walter Eduard Serner was born January 15, 1889, in Carlsbad, Bohemia. Raised in a Jewish family, he converted to Catholicism in 1909 and changed his last name from Seligmann to Serner. Although he completed a course of study in law with a doctoral degree, he soon turned away from the law to writing and political activism.

Serner began his writing career as an essayist and a writer in the Dadaist avant-garde art movement from the early twentieth century, born out of a negative reaction to the horrors of World War I.[1] Art professor Dona Budd's comment, "Dada rejected reason and logic, prizing nonsense, irrationality and intuition,"[2] accurately summarizes the hallmarks of this widely misunderstood movement. Only in recent decades has interest in the works of Dada artists and writers been renewed.

After separating himself from the Dadaist movement, Serner began to write crime stories. His novel *Die Tigerin* (*The Tigress*), published in 1925, caused a scandal. Only the intervention of his then-famous and influential colleague Alfred Döblin, who wrote the best-selling Depression-era novel *Berlin Alexanderplatz*, prevented Serner's book from falling prey to censorship. Serner wrote over one hundred stories, many of them with comical titles, such as "Zum blauen Affen" ("The

---

[1] Jörg Drews, "Sprich nicht zu oft zynisch, sei wie immer! Zum 100. Geburtstag Walter Serners," *Süddeutsche Zeitung*, 14 Jan 1989: 11.
[2] Dona Budd, *The Language of Art Knowledge* (Pomegranate Communications, Incorporated, 2005).

Blue Monkey," 1921) and "Der elfte Finger" ("The Eleventh Finger," 1923).

In August 1942, Serner was deported first to the Theresienstadt [Terezin] concentration camp, then to Riga, Latvia. It is thought that there, together with the other 999 people on the transport train, he was murdered in a forest near Riga, on August 23, 1942, but the details of his death remain unknown.

In his honor and memory, the city of Berlin created the Walter Serner Award. *The Tigress* was made into a movie with an international cast in 1992, and in 2012 the Walter Serner Society was founded.[3]

Although Serner had drifted away from Dadaism by the time he wrote "Der Sturm auf die Villa" ("The Invasion of the Mansion"), the story nevertheless displays a number of Dada characteristics—it is elliptic, enigmatic, ironic, and may even appear nonsensical in parts. Even the characters' names are true to the Dada tradition—"Schicketan" could be loosely translated as "someone acting and talking smoothly," which hints strongly at the protagonist's background as a metropolitan womanizer, con artist, and dandy; "Fidikuk" may indicate a "spotter," and "Klipprich" alludes to prosperity. Thus, keeping Serner's artistic roots in mind may help readers make sense of this amusing, albeit occasionally confusing account of a marriage scam that... well, read on!

[3] *Lexikon deutsch-jüdischer Autoren,* ed. by Archiv Bibliographia Judaica e.V., vol. 19 (Berlin: de Gruyter, 2012).

WALTER SERNER

WALTER SERNER

Der Sturm auf die Villa

Schicketan war mit der immer noch banalen, aber zweifellos oft vernünftigen Absicht in Berlin geblieben, sich reich zu verheiraten. Er hatte sich allerdings nicht freiwillig dazu entschlossen, sondern teils einem wohlgemeinten Rat seines Freundes Fidikuk folgend, teils unter dem Einfluss einer gewissen Müdigkeit, die wiederum verursachte, dass er nicht mit der ihm eigenen Energie Ausschau hielt, vielmehr tagelang in Berlin umherbummelte, als würde die reiche Braut ihm von selber vor die Füße stolpern.

Da begab es sich, dass Schicketan eines Nachmittags, als er den Kurfürstendamm überquerte, einer eleganten hübschen Dame begegnete, deren Bekanntschaft er vor Jahren gemacht hatte. Er eilte auf sie zu, kam aber zu spät. Denn plötzlich war ein junger Mann neben sie getreten, der allem Anschein nach sie hier erwartet hatte.

Schicketan ging schnell an dem Paar vorbei, da er die Situation für unbrauchbar hielt, legte aber Wert darauf, gesehen zu werden. Er erstaunte darüber, in dem jungen Mann einen äußerlich höchst unscheinbaren Spengler-Epigonen namens Hungel zu agnoszieren, den er persönlich kannte, und gleichwohl nicht gegrüßt zu werden. Der Zufall wollte es, dass Schicketan drei Tage später Hungel im Café Schilling an das Schienbein stieß. Man begrüßte einander lachend, tauschte kleine Erinnerungen

WALTER SERNER

The Invasion of the Mansion

Schicketan had stayed in Berlin with the still trivial, but no doubt reasonable, intention to marry rich. Albeit, he had not come to this conclusion voluntarily, but partly by the well-meaning advice of his friend Fidikuk, and partly under the influence of a certain fatigue, which in turn caused him to no longer be on the lookout with his innate energy, but rather to saunter around in Berlin for days, as if a rich bride would land at his feet by herself.

It happened that Schicketan, when he crossed the Kurfürstendamm one afternoon, met an elegant, pretty lady whose acquaintance he had made years earlier. He rushed toward her, but he was too late. For suddenly, a young man had stepped next to her who, by all appearances, had waited for her here.

Schicketan passed the couple fast because he regarded the situation as unusable, yet made a point of being noticed. Surprised, he recognized in the young man, who was outwardly most unremarkable, a Spengler[4] epigone named Hungel, whom he knew personally, and, at the same time, [was] not being greeted [by him]. As chance would have it, three days later, in the Café Schilling, Schicketan kicked Hungel in the shin. They greeted each other, laughing, exchanged tidbits of memories

---

[4] Oswald Spengler (1880–1936) was a German historical philosopher, cultural historian, and antidemocratic political writer.

aus und kam, nicht ohne Schicketans geschicktes Dirigieren, auch auf Frau Klipprich zu sprechen.

Als Schicketan sich von Hungel verabschiedete, war er über die gegenwärtigen Lebensumstände Frau Klipprichs im allgemeinen orientiert: sie war inzwischen von ihrem Gatten schuldfrei geschieden worden und in Zehlendorf-West Besitzerin einer schlossähnlichen Renaissance-Villa, die sie allein und infolge ihrer trüben Eheerfahrungen sehr zurückgezogen bewohnte. Da Schicketan sich erinnerte, dass Frau Klipprichs Vater ein sehr reicher Gummi-Fabrikant sein sollte, war sein Interesse so sehr gestiegen, dass er den taktischen Fehler beging, den Wunsch auszusprechen, Frau Klipprich wiederzusehen. Zu seinem Erstaunen war Hungel verlegen geworden und hatte, als hätte er es vergessen, rasch hingeworfen, Frau Klipprich habe ihn sogar gebeten, wenn er Schicketan begegnen sollte, ihm zu sagen, dass sie ihn gerne einmal bei sich sehen würde; und zum Überfluss hierauf dem Gespräch so unvermittelt eine andere Wendung gegeben, dass Schicketan nicht im Zweifel darüber war, was ihn dazu bestimmt hatte. Dies umsomehr, als Schicketan weder die Adresse Frau Klipprichs kannte noch die Zeit, zu der sie Besuche zu empfangen pflegte, weder die Fahrtverbindung noch die Telefonnummer, welche er auch nach wiederholtem Suchen nicht zu finden vermochte.

Schicketans Müdigkeit war wie fortgelächelt. Seine alte Energie kehrte wieder, wie stets, wenn lukrativen Zielen der Ehrgeiz sich verband, einen Gegner matt zu setzen. In wenigen Minuten wusste er die Wohnung Hungels und anderntags durch wohlüberlegte telefonische Anfragen mit mehrfach verstellter Stimme es zu erreichen, Hungels Wege für den folgenden Tag zu erfahren. Er lief ihm in der Tauentzienstraße in die Hände, zeigte sich über die Maßen erfreut über dieses schnelle Wiedersehen und war abermals sehr erstaunt, von Hungel zu hören, dass Frau Klipprich ihm aufgetragen habe, Schicketan für Sonntag zum Tee einzuladen und ihn zu diesem Zweck im Café Schilling zu suchen. Schicketan dankte, versprach zu kommen und lächelte

and, not without Schicketan's experienced maneuvering, also got on to Mrs. Klipprich.[5]

When Schicketan said good-bye to Hungel, he was generally familiar with Mrs. Klipprich's current personal status: she had by now been divorced from her husband, no fault, and acquired a castle-like Renaissance villa in Zehlendorf West (Berlin), where she lived alone and, due to her sad marital experiences, was very reclusive. Because Schicketan remembered that Mrs. Klipprich's father was an extremely wealthy rubber manufacturer, his interest had increased to such a degree that he made the tactical mistake of expressing his wish to see Mrs. Klipprich again. To his amazement, Hungel became embarrassed and added quickly, as if he had forgotten, that Mrs. Klipprich had even asked him to tell Schicketan, should he encounter him, that she would like to see the latter at her place some time; and then, quite superfluously and all of a sudden, [Hungel] gave the conversation a completely different direction, so that Schicketan did not have any doubts about what had compelled Hungel to do so. This was all the more amazing, since Schicketan neither knew Mrs. Klipprich's address nor the time at which she received visitors, and also neither the traffic connection nor the telephone number, the latter of which he was unable to produce even after searching repeatedly.

Schicketan's fatigue had vanished as if smiled away. His former energy returned as it always did when a lucrative goal joined up with his ambition to defeat an opponent. Within a few minutes he knew Hungel's residence, and the next day he was able to obtain information about Hungel's plans for the following day, through well thought out phone inquiries in multiple disguised voices. He crossed Hungel's path in the Tauentzienstrasse, expressed joy beyond measure over this quick reunion, and was again surprised to hear from Hungel that Mrs. Klipprich had told him to invite Schicketan for tea on Sunday, and to look for him in the Café Schilling for this purpose. Schicketan thanked him and promised to come, and did

---

[5] Mrs. Klipprich is the earlier mentioned elegant, pretty lady.

nicht einmal darüber, dass Hungel auch jetzt noch sich darauf beschränkte, ihm mitzuteilen, die Fahrtverbindung und der Weg zur Villa seien überaus kompliziert, er werde jedoch halb vor fünf im Café Schilling auf ihn warten und ihn persönlich hinausbegleiten.

Schicketan, davon überzeugt, dass Hungel zu diesem Rendezvous nicht erscheinen würde, machte sich Sonntag bereits um drei Uhr nachmittags auf den Weg zum Vorort-Bahnhof, der linker Hand hinter dem Potsdamer liegt. Da die Abgangszeit der Züge seit einer Woche mit dem Fahrplan divergierte, verlor Schicketan drei Viertelstunden, so dass es bereits ein Viertel nach vier war, als er Zehlendorf-West erreichte. Daselbst begab er sich unverzüglich zum Gemeinde-Amt, wo er nach langem Warten Frau Klipprichs Adresse erfuhr und auch den Weg gewiesen erhielt. Dieser stellte sich alsbald als wirklich kompliziert heraus. Und als, nach fortwährendem Fragen, es Schicketan endlich gelungen war, die Villa zu finden, zeigte seine Uhr fünf Uhr fünfzehn.

Die alte Frau, die ihm öffnete, teilte ihm verwundert mit, Frau Klipprich befinde sich in Berlin, und wackelte noch schneller mit dem Kopf, als sie hörte, dass es sich um eine persönliche Einladung handle. Sie ließ Schicketan nur ungern eintreten und konnte sich nicht entbrechen, grinsend zu äußern, es werde wohl sehr lange dauern.

Es dauerte auch wirklich lange. Und zwar bis sechs ein halb. Um welche Zeit Hungel erschien, der sich ausführlich darüber ärgerte, solch Pech gehabt zu haben: er habe während der letzten Tage Frau Klipprich wegen Zeitmangels nicht gesehen und ihr die Mitteilung von der Bestellung ihrer Einladung erst vor zwei Stunden telefonisch machen können, und zwar leider nur ihren Eltern, zu denen aber, wie er bestimmt wisse, Frau Klipprich heute sich begeben werde, so dass sie unter allen Umständen von seiner, Schicketans, Anwesenheit in ihrer Villa noch erführe, obwohl freilich doch nicht abzusehen sei, wann sie und ob überhaupt...

Schicketan weidete sich an Hungels Eifer und Ungeschick und versicherte geruhsamster Miene, er habe Zeit und werde

not even smile when Hungel limited himself to saying that the traffic connections and the route to the villa were exceedingly complicated; however, he would wait at the Café Schilling at 4:30 pm, and accompany him there in person.

Schicketan, convinced that Hungel would not show up to this rendezvous, set out for the suburb train station, which was located behind the Potsdam train station, at three o'clock in the afternoon. Since the departure time of the trains had differed from the [time given in the] railway schedule for a week now, Schicketan was three quarters of an hour late, so that it was already a quarter after four when he arrived in Zehlendorf West. There he immediately went to the town hall where, after a long wait, he learned Mrs. Klipprich's address and also was given directions. These soon turned out to be complicated. And when, after repeatedly asking [for the way], Schicketan finally managed to find the villa, his watch showed fifteen minutes after five o'clock.

The old woman who opened the door informed him with surprise that Mrs. Klipprich was in Berlin, and shook her head even faster when she heard that it was a personal invitation. Only reluctantly did she allow Schicketan to enter, and could not help saying with a grin that it may well be a very long wait.

And it really did take long. Until six-thirty, to be exact. At which time Hungel appeared, who at length expressed his anger over having had such misfortune: he hadn't seen Mrs. Klippirch during the last [couple of] days because of lack of time; he had only been able two hours ago to inform her by phone about having delivered her invitation, and this, admittedly, only to her parents, to whom, as he definitely knew, Mrs. Klipprich was going to visit today; so, come what may, she would learn of his, Schicketan's, presence at the villa, although it could certainly not be foreseen if and when at all she would...

Schicketan gloated over Hungel's eagerness and clumsiness and assured him with the most unhurried expression that he

warten, möge es auch bis zehn Uhr nachts dauern; schließlich werde Frau Klipprich ja doch einmal heimkehren.

Hungel kämpfte, wenn auch nicht mit vollem Erfolg, seine Wut nieder und musste es sich gefallen lassen, dass Schicketan ihn zu einem Gespräch zwang, das jener, um nicht zu zeigen, dass er ihn durchschaue, so heiter zu gestalten wusste, dass Hungel trotz seinem tristen Zustand einige Male lachen musste.

Frau Klipprich kam halb vor zehn nach Hause. Hungel war ihr, sobald er den Wagen hatte vorfahren hören, auf die Treppe entgegengeeilt, von wo aus Schicketan aufgeregte und unwillige Stimmen vernahm. Nachdem er eine halbe Stunde allein geblieben war, kam Hungel mit der Nachricht, Frau Klipprich bitte um Entschuldigung, sie mache Toilette.

Endlich, nach einer weiteren Stunde, die unter feixenden Konversationsversuchen verronnen war, erschien Frau Klipprich in einer allerliebsten Abendrobe. Es war nicht zu verkennen, dass sie ihrer Toilette höchste Gewissenhaftigkeit hatte angedeihen lassen. Sie erschöpfte sich in Entschuldigungen; es müsse wie verhext gewesen sein, dass Hungel... und sie könne es einfach nicht begreifen...

Schicketan begriff umso besser. Und ließ, während man selbdritt vorzüglichen Tee trank und unzählige Sandwichs verschlang, keine Gelegenheit vorüber, seine liebenswürdigsten Seiten vorzuweisen und Hungel vorsichtig zu ironisieren. Dies bewirkte, dass Frau Klipprich bereits um elf Uhr ihrem Hungel allerlei Schmollendes verabreichte, ja sogar zu kleinen Verweisen sich verstieg. Was Hungel, ziemlich deutlich desequilibriert, damit quittierte, dass er schon nach einer Stunde zum Aufbruch drängte.

Frau Klipprich wehrte sich heldenhaft. Hungel aber ließ nicht locker, und da Schicketan seinen ersten Besuch nicht zu einem nächtlichen Tête-à-tête missbrauchen, andererseits Frau Klipprich ihn auch nicht dazu auffordern durfte, blieb Hungel Sieger.

Nicht lange. Denn am übernächsten Tag rief Schicketan, der inzwischen mit den Geheimnissen der Gesellschafts-Anschlüsse sich vertraut gemacht hatte, telefonisch an und wurde für den folgenden Tag zum Tee gebeten.

had time and would wait, even if it should take until ten o'clock at night; after all, Mrs. Klipprich had to return home at some point.

Hungel suppressed his fury, even if not with complete success, and had to put up with Schicketan forcing him into a conversation which Schicketan, not letting on that he had seen through Hungel, was able to devise so cheerfully that Hungel, despite his somber mood, had to laugh several times.

Mrs. Klipprich arrived at home before nine-thirty. As soon as he heard the car drive up, Hungel hurried toward her on the stairs, from where Schicketan could hear excited and indignant voices. After he had been by himself for half an hour, Hungel arrived with the information that Mrs. Klipprich was asking his apologies; she was grooming herself.

Finally, after another hour, which passed with attempts at simpering conversation, Mrs. Klipprich appeared in the loveliest evening gown. There was no denying that she had dressed with the greatest care. She exhausted herself in apologies; it must have been jinxed that Hungel... she simply could not understand...

Schicketan understood all the better. And he did not let pass an opportunity to show his most amiable side and to carefully make fun of Hungel, while the three of them drank exquisite tea and devoured countless sandwiches. This had the effect that Mrs. Klipprich had already by eleven o'clock presented Hungel with a number of huffy remarks [and] even had the presumption to give little rebukes. Which Hungel, quite distinctly thrown off balance, answered by already urging for departure after only an hour [had passed].

Mrs. Klipprich resisted heroically. Yet, Hungel stuck to his guns, and since Schicketan did not mean to abuse his first visit to a nightly tête-à-tête, [and] conversely Mrs. Klipprich was not justified to encourage him to it, Hungel remained victorious.

Not for long. Because two days later Schicketan, who had meanwhile become familiar with the intricacies of social telephone connections, had called and been invited to tea for the following day.

Als er nurmehr wenige Schritte von der Gartentür der Villa entfernt war, tauchte miteins Hungel vor ihm auf, der ohne Zweifel irgendwo auf der Lauer gelegen war, um die Ankunft seines Gegners abzupassen. Obwohl Schicketan dieses Vorgehen nur damit sich zu erklären vermochte, dass Hungel ihn mit Frau Klipprich nicht allein lassen wollte, glaubte er an einem gewissen Plus von Heiterkeit zu erkennen, dass Hungel etwas plane. Glücklicherweise. Denn andernfalls hätte Schicketan vielleicht doch geglaubt, was Hungel ihm, als sie gemeinsam Frau Klipprichs Erscheinen erwarteten, wie nebenbei mitteilte: dass Frau Klipprich sich so lange nicht blicken lasse, weil sie indisponiert sei, unwohl... ein Zustand, der bei ihr stets langwierig und sehr schmerzhaft sich äußere, so dass sie in jeder Hinsicht dringend der Schonung bedürfe.

Schicketan, der Hungels Manöver, ihn zu veranlassen, seinen Besuch abzukürzen und etwaige Angriffspläne vorderhand zu begraben, sofort durchschaute, tat, als Frau Klipprich, wiederum in einer entzückenden Robe, eintrat, als wäre er zerstreut, und beschränkte sich darauf, die banalste Konversation zu machen.

Hungel war überzeugt, ihn unschädlich gemacht zu haben. Er zögerte deshalb nicht länger, seine Scharte vom letzten Mal dadurch auszuwetzen, dass er sich plötzlich mit der Behauptung erhob, eine wichtige Verabredung zu haben und sehr zu bedauern, die beiden allein lassen zu müssen.

Als dies geschehen war, arrangierte Schicketan sich weitläufig in ein Fauteuil und holte, mit Hilfe einer Zigarette, eines seidenen Taschentuchs und eines kleinen Flacons, auch szenisch weit aus.

Frau Klipprich saß ihm gegenüber auf dem Sofa, die schönen Hände lieblich in den Schoß gebettet, und harrte mit harmonischer Wohlerzogenheit und geschmackvollen kleinen Koketterien dessen, was so außergewöhnliche Vorbereitungen mit Recht versprachen.

»Man muss den zurückgebliebenen Dampf eines Weggegangenen sich verziehen lassen.« Schicketan sah erst jetzt auf. »Wenn man nicht in getrübter Atmosphäre sich beeinträchtigt wissen will.«

As he was standing only a few steps away from the villa's garden gate, all of a sudden Hungel, who had no doubt had been lying in ambush of his rival, appeared in front of him. Although Schicketan could explain this approach only by thinking that Hungel did not want to leave him alone with Mrs. Klipprich, he reckoned from a certain surplus of cheerfulness that Hungel was up to something. That was fortunate. Because otherwise Schicketan might have believed, in spite of everything, what Hungel communicated to him as if in passing as they were waiting for Mrs. Klipprich to emerge: that Mrs. Klipprich had not appeared for such a long time because she was indisposed, unwell... a condition that had always been long-drawn-out and very painful in her case, such that she was badly in need of rest, in every regard.

Schicketan, who immediately saw through Hungel's maneuver to make him shorten his visit and nip any attack plans in the bud, pretended to be absent-minded when Mrs. Klipprich entered, again in a lovely gown, and restricted himself to conversing in the most mundane way.

Hungel was convinced he had defanged him. Thus, he no longer hesitated to make amends for his behavior the previous evening by getting up suddenly, claiming that he had an important appointment, and saying that he was exceedingly sorry to have to leave their company.

After this had taken place, Schicketan stretched out in an armchair and also staged himself with the assistance of a cigarette, a silk handkerchief, and a little flacon.

Mrs. Klipprich was sitting on the sofa opposite him, with her fine-looking hands resting beautifully in her lap, and waiting with pleasant-sounding mannerliness and sophisticated little flirtations for what such extraordinary preparations justifiably promised.

"One has to wait until the residual steam of one who has left has faded away." Only now Schicketan looked up. "If one does not want to feel impaired, in a tarnished atmosphere."

Frau Klipprich drückte ihre schmalen rosigen Fingernägel noch schmaler, während sie mit hell läutender Stimme sich verwahrte: »Ich schätze Hungel sehr. Er ist ein absolut zuverlässiger Mensch.«

»Das ist vor allem bequem.« Schicketan steckte den Hals des Flacons sich in die Nase und schnupfte geräuschvoll an ihm. »Alle Eigenschaften, die man an anderen schätzt, müssen diesen Vorzug haben, wenn sie nicht entwertet werden wollen.«

Frau Klipprich, welche die Richtigkeit dieser Behauptung dumpf bezweifelte, widersprach unsicher: »Es gibt auch unbequeme Vorzüge.«

»Sie irren.« Schicketan trocknete sich mit dem Taschentuch die trockenen Mundwinkel. »Ein Vorzug, der anfängt, unbequem zu werden, ist nurmehr eine Eigenschaft, die man bestenfalls nachsichtig duldet.«

Frau Klipprich hielt es für einfacher, direkt zu antworten: »Sie mögen Hungel nicht.«

»Wie alle Leute, die überaus philosophisch parlieren, privatim aber, wenn ihre Interessen in Gefahr sind, nicht weniger schieben als alle anderen.«

»Und ich wiederhole Ihnen, Herr Schicketan, dass Sie Hungel eben nicht mögen. Ich habe wohl auch bemerkt, dass er... Das ist verzeihlich.«

Das Zimmermädchen trat ein, um den Tisch abzuräumen.

Nachher war es schwierig, geschickt auf das vorhergegangene Gespräch zurückzukommen. Schicketan überlegte nicht lange, sondern zog es vor, es kurzerhand wiederaufzunehmen. »Was macht Hungel eigentlich? Wenn er bloß wie Spengler dichten würde, das ginge noch an. Aber ich fürchte, er hat eine – Lebensaufgabe.«

Frau Klipprich steifte sich ein wenig. »Gewiss.«

»Ach«, stöhnte Schicketan spöttisch und ließ seine Zigarette wie gelangweilt fallen. »Lebensaufgaben sind die primitivste Form der Hysterie.«

Frau Klipprich ärgerte sich, als hätte es ihr selber gegolten. »Hungel ist nicht hysterisch.«

Mrs. Klipprich pressed her narrow rosy fingernails until [they were] still smaller, while she objected with a bright, ringing voice: "I appreciate Hungel very much. He is an absolutely reliable person."

"First and foremost, that is convenient." Schicketan inserted the narrow part of the flacon in his nose and noisily took a snuff from it. "All character traits which we appreciate in others must have this benefit, if they don't want to run the risk of losing importance."

Mrs. Klipprich, who vaguely doubted the validity of this pronouncement, objected insecurely: "There are also inconvenient benefits."

"You are wrong." Schicketan dried the dry corners of his mouth with his handkerchief. "A benefit which begins to become inconvenient is merely a character trait which is at best indulgently tolerated."

Mrs. Klipprich found it easier to reply in a direct manner: "You don't like Hungel."

"Like all people who drone on philosopically, but in private, when their interests are in danger, they don't hustle less than anybody else."

"And I repeat to you, Mr. Schicketan, that you don't like Hungel. I also noticed, to be sure, that he... That is forgivable."

The maid came to clear the table.

Afterwards it was difficult to get back to the earlier conversation. Schicketan did not reflect on this long, but preferred to resume it without further ado. "So, what is Hungel doing actually? If he merely wrote poetry like Spengler does, that would be alright. However, I am afraid that he has a—mission in life."

Mrs. Kipprich stiffened a bit. "Certainly."

"Oh," Schicketan moaned mockingly and let his cigarette fall down, as if bored. "Missions in life are the most primitive form of hysteria."

Mrs. Klipprich became annoyed as if it had been meant for her. "Hungel is not hysterical."

»Da ich beobachtet habe, dass er nicht Ihr Geliebter ist, ja Sie nicht einmal nachhaltig beeinflusst hat, dürfte meine Auffassung die richtigere sein.«

Frau Klipprich erboste sich beinahe, weil sie dieses versteckte Lob sich bereits als Manko deutete. »Ist man hysterisch, wenn man ein bisschen eifersüchtig ist?«

»Das wohl nicht. Aber wenn man es sich zur Aufgabe gemacht hat, dort den Wächter zu spielen, wo man nie Besitzrechte hatte.«

In dieser Art, bald amüsant bald médisant, sprach Schicketan noch lange Zeit, bis Frau Klipprich, immer mehr in Laune gebracht, ihn zum Abendessen zu bleiben bat. Beim Dessert spiralte das Gespräch nurmehr um sehr lockere Dinge, Frau Klipprichs Finger erregt um das Obstbesteck und Schicketans Gehirn sich vor den Sprung.

Er erhob sich plötzlich, nahm Frau Klipprich an der Hand, wies, als sie neugierig aufgestanden war, mit ausgestrecktem Arm auf den gestirnten Nachthimmel und führte sie so zu der auf dem Wege zum Fenster befindlichen Chaiselongue, auf die er sie blitzschnell niederwarf und sich auf sie... Der Sturm war unternommen. (Unblutig.)

Und bereits nach zehn Minuten verziehen. Denn Frau Klipprich hauchte hold: »Karl, wirst du... werden Sie...« – »Ja.«

»Hier bei mir?«

»Hier bei dir.«

»Immer?«

»Immer.«

»Aber Hungel?« Sie errötete lustig.

»Der hat doch seine Lebensaufgabe.«

»Und du...« Ihre Augen sprühten lachend auf. »Du hast – Druckknöpfe.«

»Bereit sein ist alles, süße Lissy.«

Nach etwa einer Stunde, die heißeste Lust und verrücktes Geplauder zugleich erfüllt hatten, vernahm Schicketans feines Ohr von der Straße her einen ihm nur zu bekannten Pfiff.

Weshalb Schicketan, nachdem er sich, mühselig genug, frei gemacht hatte, eine halbe Stunde später aus dem Garten trat,

"Since I observed that he is not your lover, indeed, has not even had a lasting effect upon you, I believe my judgment would be the more correct one."

Mrs. Klipprich was becoming almost furious because she already interpreted this hidden praise as a flaw. "Is one hysterical because one is a little bit jealous?"

"Perhaps not. But [one certainly is] when one has taken on the task of playing watchdog where one never had proprietary rights."

Thus, at times amusingly, at times slanderously, Schicketan talked at length until Mrs. Klipprich, ever more put into a [good] mood, asked him to stay for dinner. During dessert, the conversation only spiraled around very loose topics, Mrs. Klipprich's finger [spiraled] excitedly around the fruit utensils, and Schicketan's brain [spiraled] before the pounce.

He suddenly rose [from his chair], took Mrs. Klipprich's hand after she had risen curiously; pointed with his outstretched arm to the starry night sky, and in this way led her to the chaise lounge which was on the way to the window, and on which he threw her down with lightning speed and he himself onto her... The invasion was undertaken.

(Bloodless.)

And already forgiven after ten minutes. Then Mrs. Klipprich breathed meekly: "Karl, will you... will you..." – "Yes."

"Here in my place?"

"Here in your place."

"Always?"

"Always."

"But what about Hungel?" She blushed, amused.

"He has got his mission of life, after all."

"And you..." Her eyes glistened with laughter. "You have—push buttons."

"Being prepared is everything, sweet Lissy."

After perhaps an hour, which was filled with both the hottest passion and silly repartee, Schicketan's excellent ear heard from the street a whistle with which he was all too familiar.

Whereupon Schicketan, after he had freed himself with enough difficulty, half an hour later exited from the garden

wo Fidikuk, bereits ungeduldig wartend, ihm überstürzt mitteilte, die Polizei habe nun doch Wind bekommen und die Heirat würde also an der unvermeidlich schlechten Auskunft scheitern.

Schicketan tobte. »Und deshalb musstest du mich jetzt stören? Ausgerechnet jetzt?«

Fidikuk grinste gemein. »Nee, deswejen nich jerade. Aber ik rate dia, verschwinde noch bevor der Morjen jraut. Wat biste auch ganze Tage lang rumjeschweddert for nischt und wieda nischt? Mit so viel Margarine auffm Kopp jeht nur ein Verrückter in de Sonne.«

»Warum also?« Schicketan pfitschte wütend mit dem Stock. »Warum?«

»Et is wejen…« Fidikuk zögerte teilnahmsvoll.

»Die Sache mit Amanda am Ende gar?«

Fidikuk nickte still.

»Verflucht und angespien! Und ich bin so müde!«

Der Sturm auf die Villa war wie gewonnen so zerronnen.

where Fidikuk, already waiting impatiently, hastily informed him that the police had gotten wind [of the scheme] in spite of everything, and therefore the marriage was doomed to fail because of the inevitably bad information.

Schicketan raged. "And for this you have to interrupt me? Now, of all times?"

Fidikuk gave him a dirty smile. "Nah, not just 'cause of tha'. But, I s'ggest that'ye disappear ev'n before dawn breaks. Why did'ye have to swagger about entire days fo' nuttin'? With so much grease on the head, only a foolish person steps out into the sun."

"So, why then?" Schicketan furiously swished the air with his walking stick. "Why?"

"It's 'cause..." Fidikuk hesitated sympathetically.

"Is it the situation with Amanda then?"

Fidikuk nodded quietly.

"Damn it to hell! And I am so tired!"

The invasion of the mansion had been easy come, easy go.

KARIN HOLZ

Karin Holz is a native of the picturesque city of Regensburg, on the river Danube; the capital of the province of Upper Palatinate in southeast Germany.

She has worked at the University of Regensburg for sixteen years and is a member of the East Bavarian Writers Association and the Friends of the Bavarian Language and Dialects. Karin writes crime stories, poetry, fantasy stories (or, as she calls them, "fantasy journeys"), meditation texts, texts for anthologies, and audiobooks for a local publisher, Lohrbär Verlag.

Karin began writing poems in her native dialect, Upper Palatinian, and also short stories, at the age of twelve. She published the crime novel *Russenmädchen (Russian Girls)* in 2002; her second novel, *Phasmida*, followed in 2008. She has also made regular contributions to prose and poetry anthologies as well as to collections written in dialect. In 2013 and 2014, she was co-publisher of two volumes of vignettes written in the local dialect about growing up in Regensburg during the 1930s: *Wia i no da Wiggerl vom Arnunlfsplatz war... (When I Was Still the Little Ludwig from the Arnulfsplatz...)*. Karin is co-founder of the Regensburger Literaturbrettl (Little Literature Stage Regensburg), which she runs with fellow writer Marita Panzer. She is also a member of the Verband deutscher Schriftsteller (Association of German Writers).

Karin says about herself," I love Bavaria, the Bavarian Forest, nature, and people... In the Bavarian Forest, I find the leisure,

peace, and silence which I need because one of my basic traits is to require, temporarily, isolation from everyday life."[1]

Her story "Der letzte Stich" ("The Last Trick") appeared in a collection of crime and detective stories about Regensburg.[2] Word has it that the story is somewhat loosely based on the real-life experiences of members of the Regensburg police force.

The story begins with police officer Ewald Kröninger suffering from a bout of sciatica. To add insult to injury, it is his day off, and so his wife Roswitha has ample opportunity to subject him to an unpleasant and restrictive course of therapy.

---

[1] Karin Holz, "Vita," 12 June 2014 <www.karin-holz.de>.
[2] *Regensburger Requiem,* ed. Barbara Krohn (Hillesheim, Germany: KBV Verlags- und Mediengesellschaft, 2013).

KARIN HOLZ

KARIN HOLZ

Der letzte Stich

Hauptwachtmeister Ewald Kröninger lag im Bett und schwitzte. Sein Ischiasleiden machte ihm mal wieder zu schaffen, und deshalb hatte ihm seine Frau Roswitha energisch einen heißen Heilschlammwickel um Bauch und Rücken geschlungen.

Kröninger stöhnte und schimpfte ungeduldig vor sich hin. Roswitha war eine leidenschaftliche Amateur-Krankenschwester. Im Allgemeinen vermied es Kröninger sogar, mehrmals hintereinander zu niesen. Denn das hatte unweigerlich zur Folge, dass Roswitha eine Flut von mütterlichen Ratschlägen über ihn ergoss, ihn tagelang mit Medikamenten und Fieberthermometer verfolgte und mit Kräutertee traktierte.

Diesmal war es Kröninger nicht gelungen, das wachsame Auge seiner Frau zu täuschen. Sobald er eine unüberlegte Bewegung machte schoss ihm die Hexe in den Rücken, so dass er Mühe hatte, aufrecht zu stehen.Und da lag er nun, in heißen Schlamm gewickelt und ganz der krankhaften Fürsorge seiner Roswitha ausgeliefert.

In solchen Augenblicken fand der Hauptwachtmeister Kröninger die Welt gar nicht in Ordnung. Missmutig wischte er den Schweiß von der Stirn und blickte sich beinahe verzweifelt in dem kleinem Schlafzimmer um, indem er sich heute wie ein Gefangener fühlte. Und dabei hatte er dienstfrei.

»Saubere Freizeitgestaltung«, brummte er halblaut.

KARIN HOLZ

The Last Trick

Chief Sergeant Ewald Kröninger lay in bed, sweating. His sciatic condition bothered him once again, and therefore his wife Roswitha had resolutely slung a hot medicinal clay wrap around his belly and back.

Kröninger moaned and muttered to himself impatiently. Roswitha was a fanatical amateur nurse. More often than not, Kröninger even avoided sneezing several times in a row, because this inevitably resulted in Roswitha inundating him with a barrage of motherly advice, chasing him for days with medication and the fever thermometer, and plying him with herbal teas.

This time, Kröninger had failed to deceive the watchful eye of his wife. As soon as he made a careless movement, he experienced a sudden stabbing pain in his back as if cursed by a witch, such that he had difficulty standing upright. And now he lay there, wrapped in hot mud and entirely at the mercy of Roswitha's morbid ministration.

In such moments, the world was not all right at all for Chief Sergeant Kröninger. Annoyed, he wiped the sweat off his forehead and, almost desperately, looked around the little bedroom in which he felt like a prisoner today. And yet, it was his day off.

"Nice organization of my leisure time," he muttered in a low voice.

Im Flur klingelte das Telefon. Mit einem Ruck fuhr Kröninger im Bett hoch, sank aber sogleich wieder mit einem Schmerzenslaut zurück.

»Roswitha!« rief er laut, »Ros-wi-thaaaa!!! Te-le-fon!«

Die Schlafzimmertür öffnete sich, Roswitha steckte den Kopf herein: »Was schreist denn so? Ich hab den Hörer doch schon in der Hand.«

Sie ließ die Schlafzimmertür einen Spalt offen. Kröninger spitzte die Ohren.

»Nein, mein Mann kann nicht kommen«, hörte er die resolute Stimme seiner Frau. »Er hat einen Hexenschuss und schläft gerade... Ja, ich sag's ihm, sobald er wach ist... Wiederhören!«

Kurz darauf steckte sie noch einmal den Kopf durch die Tür. »Ich bringe Dir noch eine Tasse Tee.«

»Du weißt doch, ich mag's nicht, dass du schwindelst, wenn die Arbeit anruft«, brummte Kröninger. »Wer war es denn?«

Roswitha trat ganz ins Zimmer und machte eine wegwerfende Handbewegung. »Dein Herr Ebenhöh.«

»Und was hat er gewollt?« forschte Kröninger vorsichtig.

»Nichts Besonderes. Er faselte was von einem Zugriff. Du sollst dich melden, wenn es dir wieder besser geht.«

Wie der Blitz führ Ewald Kröninger in seinem Bett in die Höhe. Ächzend fasste er sich an den Rücken. Zum Entsetzen seiner Roswitha begann er heftig an seinem Schlammwickel zu zerren.

»Runter mit dem nassen Dreck!« sagte Kröninger entschlossen. »Der hilft mir doch eh nicht.«

Roswitha schnaubte beleidigt, aber Kröninger ließ seine Frau gar nicht erst zu Wort kommen.

»Ich muss schleunigst aufs *Einser*. Ich muss wissen, was da los ist. Schnell hilf mir aus dem Drecksglump!«

Widerwillig schälte Roswitha Ewalds Körper aus dem dampfenden Schlammwickel und zitierte dabei aus ihrem Gesundheitsbuch. »... die Heilerde, bereitet aus heimatlichen Schlamm, war schon bei den Römern ein bevorzugtes Mittel gegen Ischias und Verrenkungen...«

In the hallway, the telephone rang. Kröninger sat up in bed with a start, but immediately sank back again with a cry of pain.

"Roswitha!" he shouted. "Ros-wi-thaaaa!!! Te-le-phone!"

The bedroom door opened, Roswitha stuck her head in [and asked]: "Why are you shouting so? I've already got the receiver in my hand."

She left the bedroom door ajar. Kröninger pricked up his ears.

"No, my husband is unable to come," he heard the resolute voice of his wife. "He's had a bout of sciatica and he is sleeping now... Yes, I'll tell him as soon as he is awake... Good-bye!"

Shortly thereafter she stuck her head again through the doorway. "I'll bring you another cup of tea."

"You know, I don't like your fibbing when someone from work calls!" Kröninger muttered. "So, who was it?"

Roswitha stepped into the room fully and made a dismissive gesture with her hand. "Your Mr. Ebenhöh."

"And what did he want?" Kröninger inquired cautiously.

"Nothing in particular. He rambled on about a seizure. You're supposed to get in touch when you feel better again."

Lightning fast, Ewald Kröninger shot up in his bed. Moaning, he touched his back. To his [wife] Roswitha's shock, he began to tug furiously on his medicinal clay wrap. "Off with this wet crap!" Kröninger said firmly. "That's not going to help anyway."

Roswitha snorted sulkily, but Kröninger did not even give his wife a chance to speak.

"I have to get to [police station] *One* immediately. I have to know what's going on there. Quick, help me out of these filthy rags!"

Reluctantly, Roswitha peeled Ewald's body out of the steaming clay wrap, while quoting from her medical book. "... medicinal clay, prepared from native clay, was a favored remedy against sciatic pain and sprains already since Roman times..."

»Das kann schon sein«, knurrte Kröninger mit zwiderner
Miene, »aber die Römer hatten es auch besser als wir. Sie hatten keine schnellen polizeilichen Zugriffe.«

»Meiner Tante Anni hätte der Wickel auch beinahe
geholfen...«

Kröninger setzte sich behutsam auf die Bettkannte. »Wieso
beinahe?«

»Sie ist vorher an der Schwindsucht gestorben.«

»Aha!« versetzte Kröninger trocken. »Dann mache mir jetzt
bitte einen Kaffee, damit mein Kreislauf wieder in Schwung
kommt.«

»Dein Kräutertee ist doch schon fertig. Ich bringe ihn dir
sofort.«

Angeekelt verzog Kröninger sein Gesicht. »Den kannst Du
selber trinken. Ich brauche jetzt eine Schale mit starkem
Kaffee.«

Kröninger schlüpfte mit langsamen Bewegungen in seine
Dienstkleidung und ging auf den Flur zum Telefon. Er nahm
den Hörer ab und wählte.

»Du sollst jetzt nicht telefonieren, sondern dir den Dreck
vom Rücken runter waschen. Du kannst doch nicht das
Diensthemd...«

Nun wurde Kröninger ärgerlich. »Ros-wi-tha... ich bin im
Dienst! Und ich te-le-fo-nie-reeee!« Er betonte jede Silbe.
Sobald er diesen Ton anschlug, war jeder Widerspruch zweck-
los, das wussten sie beide.

»Was liegt an, Chef?« fragte Kröninger, als Ebenhöh sich
meldete.

Kröninger mochte seinen jungen, strebsamen Vorgesetzten
aus Oberbayern, dem er eine erfolgreiche Karriere prophezeite.
»Ich habe mir gedacht, es wird sie interessieren«, antwortete
Ebenhöh. »Wir haben einen anonymen Hinweis bekommen.
Stichwort ›Zigarettenschmuggel.‹ Am Schlachthof soll heute die
Übergabe erfolgen. Die Ware soll mehrere Tausend D-Mark
wert sein. Wir müssen das Gelände observieren und ich dachte
Sie übernehmen das, weil sie sich dort auskennen. Sie sind doch
gewissermaßen, äh, öfter in der Schlachthofgaststätte?« fügte er
hinzu.

"That may be the case," growled Kröninger, making an unpleasant face, "but the Romans had it also better than we do. They did not have quick police seizures."

"My aunt Anni almost benefited from the wrap too..."

Kröninger sat down cautiously on the edge of the bed. "Why almost?"

"She died from consumption before then."

"Aha!" Kröninger replied drily. "Then make me a cup of coffee now, please, so that my circulation can get up and running again."

"But your herbal tea is already done. I'll bring it right away."

Disgusted, Kröninger grimaced. "You can drink that yourself. I need a mug of strong coffee now."

Kröninger slipped into his uniform with slow movements and went into the hallway to the phone. He picked up the receiver and dialed.

"You are not supposed to call now, but [you are supposed to] wash the crud off your back. You cannot... the uniform shirt...."

Now Kröninger grew annoyed. "Ros-wi-tha... I am on duty! And, I am ma-king a te-le-phone call!" He emphasized every syllable. As soon as he adopted this tone, any objection was futile; they both knew that.

"What's the matter, chief?" Kröninger asked when Ebenhöh answered.

Kröninger liked his young, hard-working supervisor from Upper Bavaria, for whom he predicted a successful career. "I thought you might be interested," Ebenhöh replied. "We received an anonymous tip. Secret code 'Cigarette Smuggling.' The transfer is supposed to take place at the slaughterhouse. The goods are believed to have a value of several thousand Deutschmarks. We have to keep watch on the area and I thought you may want to take it on because you know the area. After all, you are, ahem, occasionally at the Slaughterhouse Tavern, aren't you?" he added.

»Interessant«, Kröninger räusperte sich. Das weiß er also auch schon, der Chef, dass ich mir dort hin und wieder, mit dem Schlegl Franze, während der Streife, einen oder zwei Schoppen Bier genehmige.

»Ich bin in einer Viertelstunde da.«

»Aber Sie sind doch krank. Sie brauchen wirklich nicht sofort kommen«, versicherte ihm Ebenhöh scheinheilig, der selbstverständlich hoffte, dass Kröninger und auch Schlegl mit von der Partie wären.

Hauptwachtmeister Kröninger galt als zuverlässiger Mann für die schwierigen Fälle. Oft zeigte er sich zwar bewusst in einer Rolle, die ihn als naiv, einfach und etwas schwer von Begriff erscheinen ließ, doch hinter dieser Fassade steckte ein Mann, dem man so leicht nichts vormachen konnte. Ebenhöh hielt schützend die Hand über den um zwanzig Jahre älteren Hauptwachtmeister, vor allem, wenn Kröninger wieder einmal während des Dienstes in der Gaststätte zum Schlachthof einkehrte.

Kröninger schleppte sich trotz Hexenschuss zum *Einser*. Im Zimmer des Polizeichefs fand die Lagebesprechung statt. In dem zweckmäßig eingerichteten Raum waren sechs uniformierte Polizisten des Überfallkommandos versammelt. Darunter auch der Schlegl Franze, wie Kröninger erleichtert feststellte.

Ebenhöh thronte hinter seinem Schreibtisch und rührte in seinem Kaffee. Sie besprachen die letzten Maßnahmen im Fall »Zigarettenschmuggel.«

Kröninger zupfte nervös an seiner Krawatte. Er folgte den Anweisungen Ebenhöhs schon lange nicht mehr.

Um mit einem Hexenschuss Zigarettenschmuggler dingfest zu machen, dazu brauchte er seine eigene Strategie, grübelte er.

Er deutete dem Schlegl Franze mit einem Wink an, ihm zu folgen. Sie gingen drei Türen weiter in ihr gemeinsames Dienstzimmer. Die Dielenbretter knarrten unter seinen schweren Tritten. Schlegl Franze hatte schon vorgesorgt. Lächelnd deutete er auf eine dampfende Tasse Kaffee, die auf Kröningers Schreibtisch stand.

"Interesting," Kröninger cleared his throat. So the boss already knows that as well; that off and on I indulge in a half pint of beer or two with Franz Schlegl[3] while we are on patrol.

"I'll be there in fifteen minutes."

"But you are sick, are you not? You really do not need to come right away," Ebenhöh assured him sanctimoniously, taking for granted that both Kröninger and Schlegl would take part in the seizure.

Chief Sergeant Kröninger had a reputation for being a reliable man for difficult cases. Though he often consciously played the role of someone who was naïve, simple-minded, and a bit slow on the uptake, behind this façade was a man who was not easily deceived. Ebenhöh held his hand protectively over the twenty-years-older chief sergeant, particularly when Kröninger had yet again stopped off at the Slaughterhouse Tavern during a shift.

Lower back pain notwithstanding, Kröninger dragged himself to the *One*. The review meeting was held in the police chief's office. In the functionally equipped room, six uniformed policemen from the riot squad had gathered. Franz Schlegl was among them, as Kröninger noticed with relief.

Ebenhöh sat enthroned behind his desk and stirred his coffee. They discussed the final steps in the "Cigarette Smuggling" case.

Kröninger tugged nervously on his necktie. He had given up following Ebenhöh's directives a long time ago.

In order to apprehend cigarette smugglers while suffering from sciatic pain, he needed his own strategy, he mused.

With a wink he signaled Franz Schlegl to follow him. They went three doors down to their shared office. The floorboards creaked under his heavy footfalls. Franz Schlegl had already made provisions. Smiling, he pointed at a steaming cup of coffee, which stood on Kröninger's desk.

---

[3] Actually: Franz Schlegl; "Franz" is the first name and "Schlegl" the last name. In Bavarian dialect, it is a well-observed custom to invert first name and last name when referring to someone. Also, "Franze" is a familiar form of "Franz," much like "Frankie" is for "Frank" in English.

»Du bist einfach der beste«, sagte Kröninger. Sie waren ein eingespieltes Team. Ewald Kröninger und Schlegl Franze ermittelten seit 1976 gemeinsam für das Regensburger Einser-Revier im Minoritenweg. Die Palette der Straftaten war breit: Betrug, Gewalt in der Ehe, Einbruch, Erpressung, Diebstahl oder gar Nackerte auf der Jahninsel. Mit menschlichem Einfühlungsvermögen und urbayerischem Humor fuhren Kröninger und Schlegl seit zehn Jahren gemeinsam Streife und waren auch privat eng befreundet.

Auf dem Schreibtisch lag eine Kopie des anonymen Hinweises der Schmuggelware. Kröninger ließ sich beim Lesen des Blattes Zeit.

»Sehr aufschlussreich«, murmelte er, während er genussvoll den Kaffee trank.

Franze rieb sich die Hände. »Heute um drei soll die Übergabe sein.« Er warf einen Blick auf die Uhr, sah Kröninger dann aufmunternd an. »Du, es ist gleich Mittag.«

Kröninger erhob sich eine Spur zu schnell und rieb sich das Kreuz an der Stelle, wo der Schmerz am schlimmsten war. »Gehen wir also, oder besser wir fahren zum Schlachthof, um uns vor Ort ein genaues Bild zu machen.«

Franze nickte. Genauso hatte er es gemeint.

Die Schlachthalle glich einem eilig hergestellten Heerlager. Beamte des Überfallkommandos und uniformierte Polizisten überwachten die Räumung der Halle. Nur die Kadaverhälften baumelten in aller Seelenruhe an ihren Haken.

»So habe ich es mir vorgestellt. Ein Wahnsinns-Remmidemmi zwengs ein paar kleinen Schmugglern.« Kröninger kratzte sich am Rücken. Die getrocknete Heilerde begann zu jucken und bröselte unter dem Hemd in den Hosenbund.

»Komm Franze, wir gönnen uns derweil eine Halbe in der Schlachthof Gaststätte. Hier ist mir zuviel Trubel.« Schlegl ließ sich das nicht zweimal sagen.

"You are simply the best," Kröninger said. They were a well-practiced team. Ewald Kröninger and Franz Schlegl had been investigating for the Regensburg police station One at the Minoritenweg[4] since 1976. The range of criminal offences had been wide: fraud, domestic violence, burglary, blackmail, larceny, even the nudists on the Jahn Island [in the river Danube]. With human empathy and archaic Bavarian humor, Kröninger and Schlegl had been patrolling together for ten years and also they were close personal friends.

On the desk lay a copy of the anonymous tip regarding the smuggled goods. Kröninger took his time reading the sheet of paper.

"Very enlightening," he muttered while drinking his coffee with relish.

Franz rubbed his hands. "The transfer is supposed to go down at three today." He glanced at his watch, then looked at Kröninger cheerily. "Hey, it's almost noon."

Kröninger rose a tad too quickly and rubbed his back in the place where the pain was worst. "Let's go, or rather, let's drive to the slaughterhouse, so we can get a more precise picture on location."

Franz nodded. That's exactly what he had thought.

The hall at the slaughterhouse resembled a hastily constructed military camp. Officers of the riot squad and uniformed policemen supervised the clearance of the hall. Only the half-carcasses were calmly dangling on their hooks.

"That's how I imagined it. A mind-blowing racket because of a few little smugglers." Kröninger scratched his back. The dried medicinal clay began to itch and crumbled into the waistband beneath his shirt.

"Come along, Franz, let's have a half pint in the Slaughterhouse Tavern. Too much excitement here." Schlegl didn't need to be told twice.

---

[4] Minoritenweg; former location of the Regensburg inner city police headquarters. ("Weg" = lane, alley; "Minoriten" = Order of Friars Minor Conventual)

»Von dort aus kann man das Gelände besser überblicken.« Die Gaststätte Schlachthof in der Prinz-Ludwig-Straße existierte seit über hundert Jahren. Sie war der Treffpunkt aller Metzger und Viehhändler aus dem Landkreis. Seit Polizeihauptwachtmeister Kröninger bei der Regensburger Polizei war, trafen sich hier auch gern die Kollegen nach der Nachtschicht. Oft blieben sie bis zum Mittag, bevor sie nach Hause gingen.

So auch heute. Ein paar Kollegen von der letzten Nachtschicht saßen noch am Stammtisch. Die Gaststätte war um diese Zeit voll besetzt. In einem seiner Nebenräume fand eine Feier statt, mitten unter der Woche. Kröninger schob vorsichtig seine breite Gestalt durch die Tischreihen und grüßte freundlich nach allen Seiten. Der Schlegl Franze folgte ihm und lächelte leutselig.

»Das ist ja der reinste Betriebsausflug«, sagte Kröninger, als er am Stammtisch der Polizisten angekommen war.

Polizeimeister Schnabel grinste. »Ich denke, du hast heute frei?«

Kröninger grinste zurück. »Ich hab mich daheim gelangweilt, und da hab ich gedacht, ihr könnt mich vielleicht brauchen.«

»Und ob!« meinte Schnabel. »Wir brauchen einen vierten Mann zum Schafkopfen, der Hampel muss nach Hause zu seiner Alten.«

Kröninger nickte zustimmend und zwängte sich vorsichtig auf den frei gewordenen Stuhl. Von hier aus hatte er das gesamte Areal des Schlachthofes im Blick. Er winkte einer vorübereilenden Serviererin. »Ich möchte ein Weißbier und der Franze auch.«

Kollege Hampel verabschiedete sich, und Kröninger sortierte seine Schafkopfkarten. Er hatte einen Eichel-Trumpf in der Hand und legte die erste Karte auf den Tisch. Reihum wurden die Spielkarten dazu gelegt und Schnabel gewann die erste Runde.

Schnabel legte wiederum den Schellen-König in die Mitte des Tisches und gerade als Kröninger die Schellen-Sau zücken wollte, schoss der Schlegl Franze, der nur Zuschauer beim Kartenspiel war und aus dem Fenster gestarrt hatte, in die Höhe und stürzte wie ein Wilder aus der Gaststätte. Kröninger

"From there, we will have a better view of the area." The Slaughterhouse Tavern in Prinz Ludwig Strasse had been there for over a hundred years. It was the gathering place for all the county butchers and cattle dealers. Since Chief Sergeant Kröninger had been with the Regensburg police force, his colleagues also liked meeting here after their night shift. Often, they stayed until lunchtime before they went home.

That's how it was today, too. A few colleagues from the recent night shift were still sitting at the regulars' reserved table. The tavern was crowded at this time of day. In one of the additional rooms, a midweek celebration was taking place. Carefully, Kröninger pushed his large frame through the rows of tables and said hello to all whom he passed. Franz Schlegl followed him, smiling affably.

"That is indeed a veritable staff outing," Kröninger said, when he had arrived at the regulars' reserved table.

Police officer Schnabel grinned. "I thought you were off duty today?"

Kröninger grinned back. "I was bored at home, and I thought you might need me."

"Yes, indeed!" Schnabel said. "We need a fourth man for our Sheepshead card game; Hampel has to go home to his missus."

Kröninger nodded his approval and squeezed carefully into the freed-up chair. From here he was able to look out over the entire slaughterhouse area. He waved to a waitress who was hurrying past him. "I would like a wheat beer, and so would Franz."

Their colleague Hampel said his good-byes, and Kröninger sorted his Sheepshead cards. He held an acorn [clubs] trump in his hand and put the first card down on the table. Going around the table, playing cards were added, and Schnabel won the first round.

In turn, Schnabel placed the king of bells [diamonds] in the center of the table, and just when Kröninger was about to whip out the ace of bells [diamonds], Franz Schlegl, who had been only an onlooker during the card game and had been staring out of the window, shot up and bolted from the tavern like a madman. Kröninger watched him, a little perplexed, then

schaute ihm ein wenig ratlos nach, ließ dann die Karten sinken und folgte ihm schnell, beziehungsweise langsam, halt wie er konnte. Er entdeckte Schlegl bei einem roten VW, der auf dem Hof des Schlachthofes ein wenig abseits stand.

Das Autokennzeichen CHA für Cham registrierte der Hauptwachtmeister sofort, und dass der Fahrer seine dunkelbraune Pudelmütze tief über die Augen gezogen hatte. Das war verdächtig! Kröninger humpelte mehr als dass er lief, zu dem roten VW hinüber. Typisch, dachte er, überall Bereitschaftspolizei, aber keiner hatte den VW bemerkt.

»Hier können Sie nicht durch!« sagte Schlegl Franze gerade und zeigte dem jungen Bürscherl am Steuer seinen Dienstausweis. Der Fahrer warf einen flüchtigen Blick auf den Ausweis.

»Darf ich Ihre Papiere sehen?!«

Kröninger war in der Zwischenzeit um das Auto herumgehumpelt, öffnete die Beifahrertür und hievte sich überraschend schnell auf den Sitz. Im selben Augenblick trat der junge Mützenträger auf das Gaspedal und raste mitsamt dem Hauptwachtmeiser über das Schlachthofgelände davon. Kröninger sah noch im Seitenspiegel, dass Franze blitzschnell reagierte, zu einem Streifenwagen stürzte, sich hinter das Steuer klemmte und ihnen folgte.

»Hat doch keinen Sinn«, meinte Kröninger, aber der junge Mann saß verbissen am Lenkrad, jagte die Straubinger Straße stadtauswärts und sah immer wieder genervt in den Rückspiegel. Der Streifenwagen folgte ihnen mit Blaulicht und Martinshorn.

»Jetzt gib doch auf«, sagte Kröninger. »Du willst dich doch nicht unglücklich machen.«

»Halts Maul«, schnauzte der junge Mann, trat das Gaspedal bis zum Anschlag durch und fluchte laut, weil der Motor nur 34 PS stark war. Das blaue Blinklicht kam näher und näher. Das Martinshorn gellte selbst in Kröningers Ohren. Sein Rücken schmerzte immer mehr, aber das durfte er jetzt auf keinen Fall zeigen. An der nächsten Kreuzung schaltete die Ampel auf Rot.

Das Bürscherl machte keinerlei Anstalten zu bremsen. Kröninger brach der kalte Schweiß aus und dann brach es wie

dropped his cards and followed him quickly or rather, slowly, to the best of his ability. He saw Schlegl next to a red VW which stood in the slaughterhouse yard, somewhat off to the side.

The chief sergeant immediately noticed the license plate letters CHA for Cham [a nearby district], and also that the driver had pulled his dark brown bobble hat deep down into his forehead. That was suspicious! Kröninger hobbled, more than ran, to the red VW. Typical, he thought, riot police everywhere, but none of them had noticed the VW.

"You cannot drive across here!" Franz Schlegl was saying at that moment, and showed his police identification to the young man at the wheel. The driver took a quick glance at the identification.

"May I see your papers?!"

Meanwhile, Kröninger had hobbled around the car and, surprisingly quickly, opened the door on the passenger side and hefted himself onto the seat. In this very moment, the young hat wearer pushed down the gas pedal and raced away across the slaughterhouse yard, along with the chief sergeant. Kröninger could see in his side view mirror that Franz had reacted with lightning speed by rushing to a patrol car, squeezing behind the wheel, and pursuing them.

"There's no point, you know," Kröninger said, but the young man sat stubbornly at the wheel, racing down the Straubinger Straße in the outbound lane and nervously looking into the rear view mirror again and again. The patrol car was in pursuit, blue light flashing and siren wailing.

"Now give it up," Kröninger said. "You really don't want to make yourself miserable."

"Keep your trap shut," the young man snapped, pushed the gas pedal to the floor, and cursed loudly because the engine had only 34 HP. The blue flashing light came closer and closer. Even to Kröninger's ears, the siren sounded shrill. His back hurt more and more, but he was certainly not allowed to show that. At the next intersection, the traffic lights turned red.

The young man did not show any inclination to hit the brakes. Kröninger broke out in a cold sweat, and then he

ein Vulkan aus ihm heraus: »Himmelherrgottsakrament, Zefix no amol, willst Du uns beide umbringen?!« brüllte er, und die Hexe in seinem Rücken steuerte ihren Teil dazu bei.

Das hatte der junge Mann am Steuer anscheinend nicht erwartet. Für einen Bruchteil der Sekunde blickte er zu Kröninger, und sah deshalb nicht den Hänger voller Zuckerrüben, der mit Tempo 20 direkt vor ihm auf der rechten Spur kroch. Er stieg im letzten Moment auf die Bremse, riss das Steuer scharf herum, der Wagen schlingerte, dann überholte Schlegl von links und stellte sich quer vor den VW. Kröninger riss die Handbremse hoch. Der junge Mann zerrte eine Pistole unter dem Sitz hervor. Aber Kröninger war schneller. Er schlug ihm die Waffe aus der Hand und brüllte: »Jetzt reicht's mir aber!!!«

Der Schlegl Franze riss die Fahrertür auf und zerrte den jungen Mann aus dem Auto und drehte ihm unsanft den Arm auf den Rücken. Sekunden später schnappten die Handschellen zu.

Während Kröninger sich langsam aus dem VW-Sitz quälte, drückte Franze den Verdächtigen gegen das Auto, tastet ihn nach weiteren Waffen ab und riss ihm wütend die Mütze vom Kopf. Und zischte an sein Ohr: »So Bürscherl, raus mit der Sprache, wo sind die Zigaretten?«

»Ich habe keine Zigaretten. Ich weiß gar nicht was ihr von mir wollt. Ich werde euch anzeigen...«

»Grundlos abhauen, fast meinen Kollegen dabei umbringen und auch noch frech werden. Bürscherl, überlege dir was du sagst.«

In dem Moment kickte der junge Mann Schlegl Franze ins rechte Bein, so wie eine Kuh die ausschlägt, wenn sie geärgert wird. Schlegl, am Schienbein getroffen, stöhnte auf und schwankte. Der junge Mann wollte trotz Handschellen davonstürzten. Doch Kröninger hatte es in diesem Moment um das Heck herum geschafft, streckte ein Bein vor und der Mützenträger stürzte der Länge nach hin.

Der Franze war gleich zur Stelle und ein ganzes Stück weniger höflich als zuvor. Endlich gab der Schmuggler auf.

»Ich habe keine Zigaretten«, ächzte er, »vorne im Kofferraum!«

erupted like a volcano: "Dear God in Heaven, dammit again, I say, do you want to kill us both?!" he roared, and the witch in his back contributed her part.

Apparently, the young man at the wheel had not expected that. For a split second he glanced at Kröninger and so did not see the trailer full of sugar beets, which was trundling at 12 miles an hour in the right lane, directly ahead of him. He slammed on the brakes at the last moment [and] violently yanked the wheel; the car swerved, then Schlegl passed on the left and jackknifed [the patrol car] in front of the VW. Kröninger pulled the emergency brake. The young man dragged a pistol out from under the seat. However, Kröninger was faster; he knocked the weapon out of his hand and roared: "I have had just about enough!!!"

Franz Schlegl wrenched the driver's door open and dragged the young man out of the car; then he twisted his arms roughly behind his back. Seconds later, the handcuffs snapped shut.

While Kröninger slowly peeled himself out of the VW seat, Franz pushed the suspect against the car, patted him down for more weapons, and angrily wrenched the hat off his head. And hissed at his ear: "All right son, out with it, where are the cigarettes?"

"I don't have any cigarettes. I have no idea what you want from me. I'll show you... I am going to press charges..."

"Running away without any reason, almost killing my colleague in the process, and then getting cheeky on top of it all. Son, think about what you're saying."

At this moment, the young man kicked Franz Schlegl in his right leg as a cow kicks when it is provoked. Schlegl, hit on the shin, gave a loud groan and staggered. Handcuffs notwithstanding, the young man was about to bolt. Kröninger, however, had managed to make it round the back of the car, thrust out his leg, and the young man fell flat on his face.

Franz was [back] on the scene right away, and a whole lot less polite than before. Finally, the smuggler relented.

"I don't have any cigarettes," he grunted, "up front in the trunk!"

»Schau du nach, Ewald!« rief Franze dem Kollegen zu. Als Kröninger den Deckel des Kofferraums öffnete, hielt er die Luft an. Vor ihm lagen unzählige Geldbündel, die aus einem geplatzten Karton herausgefallen waren. Das wurde ja immer wilder. Und immer wilder schmerzte auch sein Rücken.

»Welche Bank hast du überfallen?« rief er dem Gefangenen zu.

»Das ist Falschgeld«, presste der junge Mann hervor. »Sie haben mich gezwugen, das Falschgeld unter den Viehhändlern zu verteilen.«

»Da schau her, so einer bist du!« sagte Schelgl. »Und wer ist *sie*?«

»Das kann ich nicht ... Sie bringen mich um...«

»Das erzählst du uns auf dem Revier!« sagte Kröninger.

Der Streifenwagen, den Schlegl zur Verstärkung angefordert hatte, war inzwischen eingetroffen. Die Beamten verfrachteten den Schmuggler unsanft ins Auto. Aus einem zweiten Wagen stieg Ebenhöh.

»Jetzt sagen Sie mir bitte, was Sie hier machen, Kröninger und Schlegl«, fragte ihr Chef.

»Das stand so nicht in meinem Schlachtplan... äh... Einsatzplan.«

Abwechselnd erzählten die beiden Polizisten, was passiert war.

»Und wissen's Chef, grad als ich beim Schafkopf die Schellen-Sau auf den Tisch knallen wollte, sprang der Franze auf und rannte raus«, begann Kröninger.

»Und dann ist der Ewald auf den Beifahrersitz gesprungen«, fuhr Schlegl fort.

»Gesprungen?« fragte Ebenhöh verwirrt.

»Wie ein junger Knabe«, sagte Schlegl.

»Und dann hat der Franze das Fluchtauto gestoppt«, sagte Kröninger und zwinkerte seinen Kollegen zu.

»Stark und schnell wie ein Löwe!«

»Wie ein Löwe?« Ebenhöh musterte Schlegl zweifelnd.

»Und Ewald hat ihn entwaffnet ...«

»Und der Franze hat ihm die Handschellen ...«

"You go and see, Ewald!" Franz called to his colleague. When Kröninger opened the lid of the trunk, he caught his breath. Before him there lay numerous bundles of banknotes, which had spilled out from a burst cardboard box. It just kept getting crazier. Also, his back was hurting more and more.

"Which bank did you rob?" he shouted to the captive.

"That is counterfeit money," the young man gasped out. "They forced me to distribute the money among the cattle dealers."

"Well, well, well... so that's who you are!" said Schelgl. "And who are they?"

"I can't ... They will kill me..."

"You can tell us about it at the police station!" Kröninger said.

Meanwhile, the patrol car, which Schlegl had requested for backup, had arrived. Unceremoniously, the officers dumped the smuggler into the [patrol] car. From a second car, Ebenhöh emerged.

"Now, pray tell me what you are doing here, Kröninger and Schlegl!" their boss asked. "That's not how it was written in my battle plan... ahem... plan of action."

Taking turns, the two policemen recounted what had happened.

"And you know, chief, just when I was about to plunk the ace of bells [diamonds] onto the table, Franz jumped up and shot out the door," Kröninger began.

"And then Ewald jumped into the passenger seat," Schlegl continued.

"Jumped?" Ebenhöh asked, confused.

"Like a young boy," Schlegl said.

"And then Franz brought the getaway car to a stop," Kröninger said and winked at his colleague.

"Strong and fast, like a lion!"

"Like a lion?" Ebenhöh regarded Schlegl doubtfully.

"And Ewald disarmed him ..."

"And then Franz put the handcuffs ..."

»Und dann hat ihm der Ewald ein Bein gestellt...« Schlegl grinste. »Wie ...«

Ebenhöh schüttelte unwirsch den Kopf. »Lassen Sie den Unsinn! Wir sehen uns später auf dem Einser. Und...«

Jetzt zeigte sich endlich so etwas wie Zufriedenheit in seinem Gesicht. »Danke. Gut gemacht.«

Kröninger und Schlegl fuhren zurück zur Gaststätte. Das hatten sie sich redlich verdient. Kröninger sehnte sich nach Roswithas Schlammwickel, aber erst musste er noch etwas erledigen.

Franze hielt seinem Freund die Tür auf. Kröninger lächelte dankbar und humpelte zum Stammtisch.

»Geh weiter.« Er sah in die Runde. »Wo sind meine Karten? Wehe ihr habt neu gemischt, ihr Sauhund...«

Schnabel schob ihm das alte Blatt rüber, als wäre nichts gewesen. Endlich konnte der Hauptwachtmeister mit der Schellen-Sau einen Stich machen.

"And then Ewald tripped him up..." Schlegl grinned. "Like..."

Ebenhöh gruffly shook his head. "No more of this nonsense! I'll see you later at the One. And..."

Now, finally, something like satisfaction showed on his face. "Thank you. [That was] well done."

Kröninger and Schlegl drove back to the tavern. They had honestly earned that. Kröninger longed for Roswitha's mud wraps, but before that there was something he had to take care of.

Franz held the door open for his friend. Kröninger smiled gratefully and hobbled to the regulars' reserved table.

"Let's go." He looked around the table. "Where are my cards? You better not have shuffled the cards anew, you dirty rotten scoundrels..."

Schnabel pushed his old hand over to him, as if nothing had ever happened. Finally, the chief sergeant was able to take a trick with the ace of bells [diamonds].

IRIS KLOCKMANN

Iris Klockmann was born in Lübeck, northern Germany, where she resides with her family. She worked in the medical field for several years before embarking on a career as a writer. Although she has been passionate about writing for a long time, she has managed only recently to earn a living as a freelance writer.[1]

In 2007, she published her first novel for young adults, *Ana und das Tor nach Looanaru* (*Ana and the Gate to Looanaru*). In the story, a young Irish girl is sent on a quest to recover three sacred stones—love, truth, and wisdom—required to open the gates separating the magical worlds from the real. Reviews of that first novel were optimistic, attesting to the author's skill in creating nuanced characters set within a gripping plot.

Also around 2007, Klockmann teamed up with fellow author Peter Hoeft to write and publish under several pseudonyms. Their successful collaboration resulted first in the publication of a historical novel, *Die Frau aus Nazareth* (*The Woman from Nazareth*, 2009) under the pen name Jonah Martin. Then, under the pen name Gerit Bertram, Klockmann and Hoeft published a set of historical novels: *Die Goldspinnerin* (*The Gold Spinstress*, 2010) and its sequel, *Das Gold der Lagune* (*The Gold of the Lagoon*, 2012), set in the fourteenth century in,

---

[1] "I have always wanted to write, but became able to realize my dream only a few years ago." Translated from: Eva Maria Nielsen, "Autoreninterview—Jonah Martin: Gespräch mit dem Autorenteam von 'Die Frau aus Nazareth,'" *Suite101.de,* 23 Aug. 2009, 20 Aug. 2011 <http://www.suite101.de/content/autoreninterview-jonah-martin-a60548>.

among other places, Klockmann's hometown of Lübeck. They also co-wrote the historical novel *Das Lied vom Schwarzen Tod* (*The Song of the Black Death*, 2014), which is set in sixteenth-century Nuremberg and counts among its cast of characters a fictionalized Albrecht Dürer, regarded as the greatest artist of the Northern Renaissance.

Iris has a very successful solo career as a bestselling author for Blanvalet, a German imprint of Random House. Under the pseudonym Anna Levin, she writes stories that deal with the prehistoric roots of indigenous folk in the locales in which her novels are set and that also show a deep concern for the environment. Her debut novel *Das Korallenhaus* (*The Coral House*, 2013) was an instant bestseller.

For many years, Iris has been traveling to faraway lands, driven by a desire for and a curiosity about other cultures and their prehistoric roots.

The story "Der Kuss des Todes" ("The Kiss of Death") is set in seventeenth century Venice, the city of cities, also known as the "Bride of the Sea."

IRIS KLOCKMANN

IRIS KLOCKMANN

Der Kuss des Todes
Venedig, anno 1640

Mein lieber Freund,
 siehst du auch die wundervollen Lichter, die sich auf der Lagune spiegeln, wenn du hinaussiehst? Wie so oft stehe ich auf unserer Terrasse über den Dächern Venezias und lasse den herzzerreißend schönen Anblick auf mich wirken. Der Schein der Öllampen in den Fenstern der Palazzi leuchtet gleich einem wogenden Meer auf der Wasseroberfläche. Hinter den Häuserreihen und Hinterhöfen kann ich noch die Silhouetten von San Michele und das Kuppeldach seines Klosters erkennen. Die vielen Lichter locken, verführen und flüstern von verborgenen Welten, die jeden Abend, mit Anbruch der Dunkelheit, neu entstehen.
 Von unten dringt ausgelassenes Gelächter zu mir herauf. Gestalten bahnen sich ihren Weg durch die Gassen. Sie sind auf dem Weg zur Piazza San Marco. Ich sehe Piraten mit ausladenden Hüten, prächtig gekleidete Kurtisanen mit Fächern in den Händen, Engel mit riesenhaften Flügeln, die im seichten Wind bei jeder Bewegung beben, und Kreuzritter mit wallenden Umhängen. Sie alle tragen weiße Masken.
 Carnevale.
 Nebenan im Salon sind Männerstimmen vernehmbar, Vater hat seine Kontoristen zu Gast. Vor einem Jahr haben wir unsere Heimatstadt Lüneburg verlassen, weil er eine aussichtsreiche

IRIS KLOCKMANN

The Kiss of Death
Venice, in the year 1640

My dear friend,

Do you also notice the miraculous lights that reflect in the lagoon when you look out over it? As so often, I am standing on our terrace above the roofs of Venice, and allowing the heartbreakingly beautiful evening to have its effect on me. Resembling a heaving ocean, the light of the oil lamps in the windows radiates on the surface of the water. Behind the rows of houses and backyards I can still see the silhouettes of San Michele and the domed ceiling of its monastery. The many lights beckon, tempt, and whisper of secret worlds which come into being anew every evening, at nightfall.

From below, boisterous laughter penetrates upwards; shapes shoulder their way through the alleys. They are on their way to the Piazza San Marco. I see pirates with wide hats, splendidly attired courtesans with fans in their hands, angels with gigantic wings which tremble with every movement in the the shallow breeze, and crusaders with voluminous cloaks. They all wear white masks.

Carnevale.

In the parlor next door I can hear men's voices; father is entertaining his accountants. We left our hometown of Lüneburg[2] half a year ago because he had been offered a

---

[2] A town in the German federal state of Lower Saxony, about 45 km southeast of Hamburg.

Stelle als Mercator im Fondaco dei Tedeschi angeboten bekam. Als tedesco im mondänen Venezia gehört es zum guten Ton, sich von Zeit zu Zeit mit einem rauschenden Fest oder einem vornehmen Trinkgelage der Verbundenheit seiner Dienstleute zu versichern.

Weintrunkenes Gelächter dringt bis in meine Kammer, die am anderen Ende des Flures liegt. Mutter trägt an diesem Abend ihr samtenes Gewand, muss jedoch die Gäste wie eine Magd bewirten. Ansonsten hat sie sich still zu verhalten. Vater liebt es nicht, wenn sie sich ins Gespräch mischt.

Immer mehr Menschen strömen aus ihren Häusern und streben der Piazza oder einer der Campi zu, auf denen die Spektakel stattfinden. Wie schade, dass du nicht bei mir sein kannst. Von unserem Haus aus sind es genau fünfundachtzig Schritte bis San Marco. Ich habe sie gezählt, mit diesem unbändigen Sehnen in mir, das mich Tag und Nacht begleitet. Denke doch nur, wir könnten uns unter die Masse von Leibern mischen, Masken würden unsere Gesichter verbergen. Wir wären frei.

Ich streife mir das eng geschnittene, schwarze Gewand über, das ich gestern im Bezirk Canareggio in Adolfos kleiner Schneiderei erstanden habe. Das Kostüm der Schwarzen Witwe sitzt wie eine zweite Haut. Vor dem Spiegel setze ich die Perücke auf und zupfe mir ein paar Locken in die Stirn. Meine Lippen male ich nach, mit dieser Farbe, die so gut zu meinem dunklen Haar passt. Etwas Kajal für die Augen, ein wenig Puder auf meine Wangen, mehr brauche ich nicht. Die mit zarter Malerei gefertigte Maske unterstreicht noch meine geheimnisvolle Aufmachung. Zufrieden übe ich vor dem Spiegel einen sinnlichen Augenaufschlag, grinse und werfe mir selbst eine Kusshand zu. Ich wüsste so gern, ob ich dir in dem Kleid gefalle. Aber alles was mir bleibt, ist Zwiesprache mit dir zu halten.

»Liebling, was machst du da?«

Da steht Mutter plötzlich in der Kammer. Sie sieht blass aus. Wenn du sie jetzt sehen könntest, mit diesem erschreckten Ausdruck im feinen Antlitz, aus dem Sorge, aber auch Enttäuschung zu lesen ist. Glaube mir, ich würde mich am liebsten in Luft auflösen.

promising position as Head Accountant at the Fondaco dei Tedeschi. As a *tedesco* [a German] in the highly fashionable Venezia, it is *bon ton* to assure the solidarity of one's employees with an occasional jamboree or sophisticated drinking bout.

Laughter merry with wine reaches into my chamber, which is at the other end of the hallway. Mother wears her velvet dress this evening, but has to serve the guests like a handmaid. Otherwise, she has to behave quietly. Father does not like it when she joins the conversation.

More and more people pour from their homes and head for the Piazza or to one of the fields in which the spectacles will be taking place. What a pity that you cannot be with me. From our house it is exactly eighty-five steps to San Marco. I counted them, with this overpowering yearning in me which accompanies me, day and night. Just think about it—we could intermingle with the masses of bodies; masks would conceal our faces. We would be free.

I slip on the tightly cut, black dress which I acquired yesterday in Adolfo's little tailor shop in the Canareggio District. The costume of the Black Widow fits like a second skin. I bewig and pull a few locks down my forehead. I touch up my lips with the color that goes so well with my dark hair. A touch of kajal for my eyes, a little powder for my cheeks—I don't need more. The mask which is created with delicate painting even gives emphasis to my mysterious makeup. Satisfied, I practice a sensuous look, grin, and blow myself a kiss before the mirror. I would so very much like to know if I meet with your approval in the dress. But all that is left to me is to have a dialogue with you.

"Dearest, what are you doing there?"

Suddenly, mother is standing in my chamber. She is looking pale. If you could see her now, with this frightened expression on her delicate face, in which I can read apprehension but also disappointment. Believe me, I would like most to disappear into thin air.

»Was ist das für ein Aufzug?« Sie flüstert, trotzdem kommt es mir vor, als schalle ihre Stimme bis in die letzten Winkel unserer Wohnung. »Ziehe dich sofort um!«

»Mutter, es ist Carnevale. Schau doch nur, die Stadt feiert wie im Taumel. Hörst du nicht die Trommeln, den Gesang? Bitte, lass mich gehen! Vertraue mir, in zwei Stunden bin ich wieder daheim.«

Ich umfasse ihre Taille und ziehe sie an mich. Schmal ist sie geworden, dabei hatte sie früher so schöne runde Hüften und Augen wie glänzende Murmeln. Sie riecht nach dem teuren, viel zu süßen Duftwasser, das Vater ihr zum letzten Christfest geschenkt hat. Zu ihr passt etwas Leichteres, Duftiges, aber Geschmack hat er ja nie besessen.

Sanft löst sie sich von mir. »Pass auf dich auf.«

»Mache dir keine Sorgen, ich trage doch meine Maske.« Da ist er wieder, der gequälte Zug um ihren Mund, den ich die letzte Zeit so häufig gesehen habe. »Vater wird sowieso noch eine Weile mit seinen Gästen beschäftigt sein.«

Sie nickt ernst. »Ich muss gehen, er ruft mich. Bald wird er mir auftragen, dass ich die Herren mit dem Leierspiel unterhalte. Warte, bis die Musik einsetzt.« Sie seufzt, streicht mir über den Arm und eilt hinaus.

Ihre Schritte verhallen auf dem Flur. Ich lege mich aufs Bett, lausche in die einsetzende Stille. Alles in mir ist in Aufruhr. Was wäre ich ohne Mutters Verständnis? Mein Blick wandert zu der alten Uhr auf der Kommode. Kennst du das, mein lieber Freund, wenn die Zeit einfach nicht verstreichen will, wenn der Sand der Uhr in schier unsäglicher Folter an derselben Stelle zu verharren scheint?

Endlich ist es soweit. Aus einem Versteck unter meinem Bett hole ich die roten Schuhe mit dem modischen Absatz hervor und lege sie in meinen Lederbeutel. Noch ein rascher Blick in den Spiegel, dann schleiche ich zitternd und auf Zehenspitzen zur Tür.

Doch meine Angst ist unbegründet. Niemand bemerkt mich, während ich barfuß die Treppen hinunter eile. Die Luft ist klar, verheißungsvoll. Der leicht brackige Geruch, der dem Canal entströmt, verbindet sich mit dem Duft von bratendem Fleisch.

"What kind of attire is that?" She whispers, but nevertheless it appears to me as if her voice were echoing from even the last corners of our apartment. "Change immediately!"

"Mother, it is Carnevale. Just look—the city is celebrating as if in rapture. Don't you hear the drums, the singing? Please, let me go! Trust me; I'll be home again in two hours."

I encircle her waist and pull her to me. She has grown slender, and yet she used to have such nice round hips, and eyes like shining marbles. She smells of the expensive, much too sweet toilet water which father gave her last Christmas. For her, something lighter, more aromatic would be appropriate, but, after all, he never has had taste.

She frees herself softly from me. "Take care of yourself."

"Don't worry; after all, I am wearing a mask." There it is again, the tortured line around her mouth which I have seen so frequently lately. "Anyway, father will be busy with his guests for a while longer."

She nods seriously. "I have to go; he is calling me. Soon he will instruct me to entertain the gentlemen by playing the lyre. Wait until the music begins." She sighs, strokes my arm, and hurries out.

Her steps fade away in the hallway. I lie down on my bed, listen to the ensuing silence. Everything in me is in turmoil. What would I be without my mother's understanding? My gaze wanders to the old hourglass on top of the chest of drawers. Do you know that, my dear friend, when the time simply does not want to pass, when the sand in the hourglass seems to remain in the same place, in almost unspeakable torture?

Finally, the time has come. From a hiding place under my bed I take out the red shoes with the fashionable heels and put them into my leather bag. Another quick glance into the mirror, then I sneak to the door, trembling and on tiptoes.

My fear, however, is unfounded. Nobody notices me as I hurry barefoot down the stairway. The air is crisp, full of promise. The slightly brackish smell, which escapes from the Canal, joins with the aroma of roasting meat. The leather shoes alone

Die Lederschuhe allein genügen, um mich wieder lebendig zu fühlen. Mein Atem hinterlässt kleine Dampfwölkchen in der kalten Luft, während mich die glitzernde Welt der Maskerade lächelnd empfängt.

Mein Freund, könntest du nur die Erlebnisse mit mir teilen! Noch in diesem Moment, da ich wieder auf dem Heimweg bin, ist mein Herz voll von all den betörenden Empfindungen. Wie viele Augenpaare mir anerkennend beim Tanz folgten. Ich weiß, dass mein schlanker Körper zur Musik seine ganze Weiblichkeit zeigt, dass die Art, wie ich meine Hüften wiege, die Begehrlichkeit vieler Männer weckt. Ihre Blicke haben auf meiner Haut geprickelt. Hände haben sich in der Menge nach mir ausgestreckt, sie liebkosten meinen Hals, den Schwung meiner Hüften. Ein weiches Lippenpaar senkte sich plötzlich auf meins. Zunächst war ich erschrocken, aber … der Kuss der schönen Fremden war pure Versuchung. Unmöglich, ihm zu widerstehen. Oh, wie sehr ich jeden Moment genossen habe! Gleich darauf erscholl ein Oh und Ah von überall her. Ich traute meinen Augen kaum! Auf einer der Bühnen bauten Akrobaten eine menschliche Pyramide und führten halsbrecherische Kunststücke vor. Ihre fantasievollen Kostüme glitzerten in der klaren Nacht. Nie zuvor habe ich Ähnliches gesehen.

Da hält mich eine Gestalt in einem blauen, mit Goldfäden durchwirkten Umhang zurück. Der Schein einer Fackel beleuchtet ihre goldene Maske und einen breitkrempigen Hut. »Gestatten. Mein Name ist Marcello, ich bin der beste Hellseher von ganz Venezia. Reiche mir deine rechte Hand, meine Schöne, und ich erzähle dir, welche Wunder das Leben für dich bereithält.«

Der Maskierte murmelt etwas Unverständliches, während er die Linien auf meiner Hand angestrengt betrachtet. Bei jeder seiner Bewegungen steigt mir der durchdringende Geruch von Weihrauch entgegen, dem ich mich allzu gern entziehen würde.

Zischend lässt Marcello die Luft aus den Lungen entweichen. Der Blick aus dunklen Augen ist verhangen, als er sich kerzengerade aufrichtet. »Schwarze Witwe, du hütest ein delikates Geheimnis. Aber sei unbesorgt, dir wird Gerechtigkeit widerfahren. Und nun geh«, stößt er heiser und mit ungewöhnlich heller Stimme hervor, »mehr habe ich dir nicht zu sagen.«

suffice to make me feel alive again. My breath leaves tiny little clouds of steam in the cold air, while the glittering world of the masquerade receives me, smiling.

My friend, if only you could share the experiences with me! Even in this moment, while I am on my way home again, my heart is full of all the beguiling sensations. How many pairs of eyes followed me appreciatively while I was dancing. I know that my slim body shows its full femininity during the music, that the way I swing my hips awakens the lasciviousness of many a man. Their eyes tingled on my skin. Hands reached out for me in the crowd; they caressed my neck, the swing of my hips. Suddenly, a soft pair of lips lowered onto mine. At first, I was frightened, but ... the kiss of the beautiful, strange woman was pure temptation. Impossible to resist it. Oh, how much I enjoyed each moment! A moment later, there was oohing and aahing from everywhere. I hardly trusted my eyes! On one of the stages acrobats were building a human pyramid and demonstrated their breakneck stunts. Their fanciful costumes glittered in the clear night. Never before have I seen anything like it.

That is when a figure in a blue cape with interwoven golden threads detains me. The glow of the torch shines a light on the golden mask and a broadbrimmed hat. "Allow me. My name is Marcello; I am the greatest clairvoyant in all of Venice. Give me your right hand, my beautiful one, and I will tell you which miracles life has in store for you."

The masked man murmurs something incomprehensible while he intensely considers the lines on my hand. At each of his movements, the pervasive smell of frankincense, which I would only too willingly evade, wafts toward me.

With a hiss, Marcello allows air to leave his lungs. The look from his eyes is veiled when he stands up as straight as a post. "Black Widow, you are guarding a delicate secret. But don't worry; justice will be done to you. And now go," he pants out, croaky and with an unusually high voice, "there is nothing more I can tell you."

Seine Worte lassen mich schaudern. Wie einfältig von mir! Dabei sind die Machenschaften der Scharlatane hinreichend bekannt. Vage Behauptungen stellen sie auf, wirkungsvoll in Szene gesetzt. Aber ich gestehe ohne Umschweife, Marcello hat seine Rolle hervorragend gespielt. Du und ich, wie sehr hätten wir uns über ihn und die kuriose Situation amüsiert! Geräuschlos husche ich ins Haus zurück und verstaue Perücke, Maske und Schuhe in meinem Lederbeutel. Mit einem seligen Lächeln auf den Lippen erreiche ich den obersten Stock. Die Glocken vom Campanile schlagen.

Dann liegt wieder Stille über dem Haus.

Ich öffne die Tür.

Vaters massiger Körper nimmt mir das Licht. Wie zur Salzsäule erstarrt, nehme ich jede seiner Regungen überdeutlich wahr. Mit verzerrtem Gesicht drückt er mich gegen die Wand. Ich stöhne innerlich auf.

»Wo kommst du her, Lorentz?«

Die Lippen fest aufeinander gepresst, starre ich zu Boden.

Vater tritt näher und zwingt mir seinen Blick auf. »Ich habe dich etwas gefragt!«

»Vom Ca ... Carnevale«, ist alles, was ich herausbringe. Hilfe, mein Freund, wo bist du?

»Hattest du meine Erlaubnis?« zischt er.

»Nein.«

Seine Finger krallen sich um meinen wollenen Umhang. Ganz langsam zieht er mich zu sich heran. »Das wird ein Nachspiel haben.«

Hinter mir spüre ich schmerzhaft den Türgriff im Rücken, mein Schlüssel steckt noch. Schweißperlen tropfen mir in den Nacken. Weißt du, wie Angst riecht? Sie brennt wie die Hölle.

»Wieso hast du dich als Weib verkleidet? Kein ehrbarer Mann trägt Weiberfummel. Du versündigst dich!« bellt er, und ein Schwall seines weingetränkten Atems streift mich. »Treibst du es etwa mit Kerlen? Raus mit der Sprache!«

Gewiss wüsstest du in diesem Moment eine passende Antwort. Ich jedoch bleibe stumm. Was soll ich auch entgegnen? Dass mich allein das Gefühl, den weichen, weiblichen Samt auf der Haut zu spüren, unendlich glücklich macht? Dass es für mich

His words make me shudder. How silly of me! Though the manipulations of the charlatans are sufficiently known. They make vague claims, staged effectively. However, I admit without ceremony that Marcello played his role magnificently. You and I, how much would we have been amused by him and the strange situation!

Without making a sound, I scamper back into the house and store away the wig, the mask, and the shoes in my leather bag. With a blissful smile on my lips, I reach the top floor. The bells from the Campanile chime.

Then the house lies in silence again.

I open the door.

Father's bulky body blocks the light for me. As if turned into a pillar of salt, I am hyperaware of each of his movements. His face contorted, he pushes me against the wall. Inwardly, I heave a groan.

"Where are you coming from, Lorentz?"

My lips pressed together tightly, I stare at the floor.

Father steps closer and forces me to meet his eyes. "I asked you something!"

"From the Ca... Carnevale," is all I manage. Help me, my friend, where are you?

"Did you have my permission?" he hisses.

"No."

His fingers clench around my woollen cloak. Very slowly he pulls me toward him. "This will have consequences."

Behind me, I feel the door handle in my back, causing me pain; the key is still in the lock. Beads of perspiration drip down my neck. Do you know how fear smells? It burns like hell.

"Why did you dress up as a women? No honorable man wears drag. You are committing a sin!" he snaps, and a wave of his wine-drenched breath touches me. "Are you doing it with men? Out with it!"

Unquestionably, you would have had an appropriate answer in this moment. However, I remain silent. After all, what should I say? That simply the feeling of the soft, feminine velvet on my skin makes me infinitely happy? That for me it is as if I slipped

ist, als schlüpfe ich in mein wahres Wesen, meine ursprüngliche Identität? Es fühlt sich so richtig an. Doch das verstehst nur du.

Verzweifelt versuche ich, mich aus Vaters Umklammerung zu winden. Aber sein Griff bleibt unerbittlich.

»Nein, ich treibe es nicht mit ihnen!« bringe ich schließlich hervor, erstaunt über den festen Klang meiner Stimme. Ich bin weit mehr als alles, was du vermutest, flüstert es in mir. Nur wie soll ich das einem Menschen erklären, für den ein makelloser Ruf und eine gut gefüllte Geldkatze die einzigen Götter sind, denen er zu dienen bereit ist?

»Wisch dir gefälligst die Farbe aus dem Gesicht, und dann troll dich!« Damit lässt er mich ruckartig los. Als er auf den Salon zusteuert, schwankt er. Mutter steht davor, die Augen geweitet. Sie öffnet den Mund, Vater unterbricht sie mit einer einzigen Handbewegung, und sie folgt ihm.

Mit weichen Knien flüchte ich auf meine Kammer. Sie streiten, wobei Mutters Kommentare durch die dicken Wände kaum vernehmbar sind.

Ich liege wach, zu aufgewühlt, zu hin und hergerissen bin ich zwischen dem Zauber der Nacht, Marcellos Prophezeiung und Vaters abfälligen Worten. Du fehlst mir.

Ausgerechnet nach dieser durchwachten Nacht wollen die Rechnungen und Berichte, die sich auf meinem Schreibtisch im Fondaco dei Tedeschi stapeln, kein Ende nehmen. Ich habe dir doch berichtet, dass ich bei Herrn Ullrich Wolfhart Buchführung und Buchhaltung erlerne?

Als ich endlich das ehrwürdige Gebäude verlasse, dämmert es bereits. Entsinnst du dich, wie wir im Spätsommer in einem der geheimen Gärten spazieren gegangen sind? Du hast mir gezeigt, wie ich das seltene Kleinod trotz seiner schützenden Mauer erreichen kann. Im Schatten hoher Bäume haben wir gesessen und verfolgt, wie die letzten Sonnenstrahlen die üppig blühenden Rosenstöcke und den Lavendel mit warmen, beinahe unwirklichen Farben beschenkten.

Du bist mein, für alle Zeit, waren deine Worte. Ich warte auf den Augenblick, an dem ich dir meine Liebe endlich beweisen kann, habe ich dir geantwortet. Doch wann wird das sein? Wenn sie uns entdecken, riskieren wir den Tod.

into my true character, my original identity? It feels so accurate. Although, only you understand that.

Desperately, I try to wriggle myself out of father's clutches. However, his grip remains unrelenting.

"No, I don't do it with them!" I eventually call forth, surprised over the firm sound of my voice. I am much more than anything you suspect, it whispers inside me. Only, how am I supposed to explain this to a person for whom an impeccable reputation and a well-filled money pouch are the only gods whom he is willing to serve?

"Kindly wipe the color off your face, and then off with you!" With these words, he suddenly lets go of me. As he heads for the parlor, he is swaying. Mother is standing in front of it, eyes wide. She opens her mouth; father stops her with one single move of his hand, and she follows him.

With weak knees, I escape to my chamber. They argue, although mother's comments are hardly audible through the thick walls.

I lie awake, too much in turmoil, too much torn between the enchantment of the night, Marcello's prophecy, and father's derisive words. I miss you.

The bills and reports which pile up on my desk at the Fondaco dei Tedeschi seem to not want to come to an end, after this sleepless night of all times. You remember that I told you about studying accounting and bookkeeping with Master Ullrich Wolfhart, don't you?

When I finally leave the venerable building, dawn is already breaking. Do you remember when we were strolling through the hidden gardens in late summer? You showed me how I could get to the rare jewel in spite of its protective wall. We were sitting in the shade of tall trees and witnessed how the last rays of the sun lent warm, almost unreal colors to the exuberantly blooming rosebushes and the lavender.

You are mine forever, were your words. I am waiting for the moment in which I can finally prove to you that I love you. Yet, when shall that be? Should they discover us, we will risk death.

Meine Schritte führen mich wieder zu unserem geheimen Treffpunkt. Ein steinerner Brunnen zwischen zwei Häusern verbirgt den Zugang zu dem schmalen Pfad. Nun sitze ich unter unseren Bäumen und sauge die Schönheit des verwunschenen, winterlichen Gartens in mir auf.

Ein Entenpaar verharrt bewegungslos zwischen den Gräsern, die den Teich in der Mitte bewachsen. Es wartet auf den Frühling, wie du und ich.

Wenn ich etwas vermisse, dann ist es das dichte Grün meiner Heimat, das fröhliche Gezwitscher der Vögel in den Bäumen. Die leichtfüßigen Rehböckchen, die in unseren Wäldern durchs Geäst springen, unsere duftenden Torffeuer, an denen wir uns an kalten Tagen wärmen. Die hübschen Backsteinhäuser von Lüneburg. Deshalb hast du mir den Garten gezeigt, nicht wahr? Du weißt, wie du meine aufgewühlte Seele besänftigen kannst.

Hinter mir knistert das vom Frost erstarrte Laub. Ich wirble herum, suche zwischen Büschen und Sträuchern, die den geheimen Pfad säumen. Nichts. Aber da ist jemand! Ganz deutlich fühle ich Augen auf mich gerichtet, die jede meiner Bewegungen beobachten. »Hallo? Wer ist da?«

Schritte, sie kommen auf mich zu. Kalter Schweiß bricht aus meinen Poren. Furcht frisst sich jäh durch meinen Leib. Glaubst du, ich verliere allmählich den Verstand?

Ich laufe, meine Füße berühren kaum den Boden. Ein paar gut gekleidete Bürger recken die Hälse nach mir. Als ich wieder im Bezirk San Marco bin und mich die vertrauten Eindrücke wie in einen Kokon hüllen, getraue ich mich endlich zu verschnaufen.

Nun, da ich mich besinne, sehe ich klarer. Natürlich waren es nur ein paar Vögel, die auf dem verharschten Boden nach Futter suchten. Die Begebenheiten der letzten Nacht müssen meinen Geist verwirrt haben.

Je weiter ich mich unserem Heim nähere, umso zögernder werden meine Schritte. Die Zwillinge mit den dunklen Zöpfen aus dem Nachbarhaus spielen vor der Tür. Sie stecken die Köpfe zusammen. Eine der beiden zeigt auf mich und kichert. Was hättest du in dem Fall getan? Ich beschließe sie zu ignorieren, frage mich jedoch, was an mir so anders sein soll, dass man

My steps lead me again to our secret meeting place. A stone fountain between two houses obscures the entry to the narrow path. I am now sitting beneath our trees and drink in the beauty of this enchanted, wintry garden.

A couple of ducks are poised motionless among the grasses that grow in the center of the pond. They are waiting for spring, as do you and I.

If I miss anything, then it is the thick green of my native country, the merry twittering of the birds in the trees. The nimble-footed little roebucks which jump through the branchwoods of our forests, our aromatic peat fires which warm us up on cold days. The pretty redbrick houses of Lüneburg. That was the reason why you showed me the garden, wasn't it? You know how to comfort my agitated soul.

Behind me the leaves rustle, stiff from the frost. I whirl around, look among the bushes and the shrubbery which line the clandestine path. Nothing. Nevertheless, someone is there! I definitely feel eyes focused on me, which observe every one of my movements. "Hello? Who is there?"

Steps, they are advancing toward me. I break out in a cold sweat. Fear is suddenly eating through my body. Do you think that I am gradually losing my mind?

I run; my feet hardly touch the ground. Several well-dressed citizens crane their necks looking after me. When I am back in the San Marco District and the familiar impressions envelop me like a cocoon, I finally dare to pause for breath.

Now, that I recollect myself, I can see clearly. Obviously, these were merely a couple of birds which were looking for food in the crusted-over ground. The events of last night must have addled my brain.

The more I get closer to our home, the more halting my steps become. The twins with the dark braids from the house next door play in front of the door. They put their heads together. One of them points at me and giggles. What would you have done in such a case? I decide to ignore them; however, I ask myself what is so different about me that people look at me in

mich immer wieder abschätzig betrachtet. Dabei bemühe ich mich täglich nach Kräften um einen männlichen Gang. Nur wenn ich mich ungestört fühle, wage ich, meinen Körper sich bewegen zu lassen, wie es ihm natürlich erscheint. Es ist, als spräche er eine andere Sprache, folge seinen eigenen Gesetzen. Auch du wurdest in einer falschen Hülle geboren. Obgleich du es nie erwähntest, fühle ich diese unumstößliche Wahrheit. Warum sonst habe ich mich dir sogleich verbunden gefühlt, schon bei unserer ersten Begegnung?

Mutter empfängt mich mit einem traurigen Lächeln und geschwollenen Augen. Der Anblick tut mir weh. Vater nickt nur knapp. Wir essen schweigend, das Klappern unserer Löffel auf den Tellern zerrt an meinen Nerven.

»Wir haben zu reden!« kommt es schließlich von Vater.

Um es kurz zu machen: Vater verbietet mir für die nächsten Wochen jeglichen Ausgang. Mutter sitzt bleich neben ihm, ihr Blick wandert zwischen ihm und mir hin und her. Vater stopft sich mit unsicheren Bewegungen eine Tonpfeife. Er will wissen, ob ich öfter Frauenkleider trage.

Ich ringe um Worte. Wo sind nur meine sorgfältig einstudierten Antworten geblieben ... Mutter schüttelt unmerklich den Kopf. Aber es drängt mich ohne Unterlass, die Zeit der Lügen und Ausflüchte endgültig zu beenden, ihm mein wahres Wesen zu offenbaren. Aber meine Angst malt mir die grausamsten Bilder. Du und ich im Kerker, auf die Hinrichtung wartend. Glaub mir, mein Freund, für die Wahrheit bin ich zu feige.

»Nein, natürlich nicht, Vater. Nur an Carnevale habe ich ein Kleid getragen«, antworte ich endlich. Jedes einzelne Wort der Lüge schmerzt.

Wenn ich nur wüsste, wie ich mich morgen heimlich aus dem Haus schleichen soll.

Vater beobachtet mich. Ich fühle mich wie auf einer Anklagebank, und er spielt den Richter. Natürlich könnte ich ihm erklären, wie sich alles entwickeln hat. Wann ich mir eingestanden habe, dass ich nicht nur Spaß an der Verwandlung habe, sondern dies ein Teil von mir ist. Ein mächtiger, schillernder Teil.

a disparaging way, time and again. At the same time, every day I make every effort to [assume] a manly gait. Only when I feel undisturbed do I dare let my body move the way that feels natural to it. It is as if it were talking in another language, following its own laws. You also were born in the wrong shell. Although you never mention it, I sense this irrefutable truth. Why else did I feel immediately connected to you, even at our first encounter?

Mother receives me with a miserable smile and swollen eyes. The sight hurts me. Father merely gives a brief nod. We eat silently; the rattling of our spoons on the plates tugs on my nerves.

"We have to talk!" father says finally.

To cut a long story short: father prohibits me from any excursions whatsoever during the following weeks. Mother sits next to him, [looking] pale. Her gaze wanders hither and thither between him and me. With unsteady movements, father fills a clay pipe. He wants to know if I frequently wear women's clothes.

I struggle with the words. Where in the world did my carefully rehearsed answers go... Mother shakes her head imperceptibly. But I feel this constant urge to end this time of lies and excuses once and for all, to reveal my true nature to him. However, my fear paints the most brutal pictures. You and I in the dungeons, waiting for our execution. Believe me, my friend, I am too much of a coward for the truth.

"No, of course not, father. I wore a dress only on Carnevale," I finally reply. Every single lie hurts.

If I only knew how to sneak away secretly from the house tomorrow.

Father watches me. I feel as if I were in the prisoner's box, and he is playing the judge. Obviously, I could explain to him how everything came about. At what time I admitted to myself that I not only enjoy the metamorphosis, but that it is a part of me. A powerful, glittering part.

Er fuchtelt mit der Hand, als ob er eine lästige Fliege verscheuchen will, und zieht ein finsteres Gesicht. »Das ist einfach nur lächerlich, Lorentz! Ich glaube dir nicht!« Er beugt sich tiefer über den Tisch und bleckt die Zähne. »Ich verbiete dir, jemals wieder in Weibersachen herumzulaufen! Sonst gnade dir Gott!«

»Lass Gott aus dem Spiel, Vater! Er sieht uns an und nicht unsere Gewänder«, entwischt es mir.

Er holt aus, und im nächsten Moment brennt meine Wange von seiner Ohrfeige.

Erbost springe ich auf, die Hände hinterm Rücken zu Fäusten geballt. Wenn du wüsstest, welch schandhafte Antwort ich auf den Lippen habe. Lediglich mein Verstand lässt mich innehalten. Deshalb drehe ich mich auf dem Absatz um und laufe auf meine Kammer.

Anders als befürchtet stürmt er mir nicht hinterher. Ich werfe mich aufs Bett, umklammere mein Kissen. Papier raschelt. Und dann entdecke ich den versiegelten Brief mit deiner geschwungenen Handschrift.

Morgen zur ersten Abendstunde, lese ich.

Glücklich vergrabe ich das Gesicht in meinem Kissen. Du kannst nicht ahnen, dass ich das Haus abends nicht mehr verlassen darf. Wochenlang haben wir einander nicht gesehen, und ausgerechnet jetzt ... Als wäre das Versteckspiel nicht schwer genug, erlässt Vater noch diese unsinnige Strafe. Glaubt er wirklich, er kann mich von dir fernhalten, oder ändern, was mir in die Wiege gelegt wurde? Soll er meinetwegen versuchen, mich einzusperren. Stets werde ich einen neuen Weg finden, um mich von seinen Fesseln zu befreien. Weil das zweite Wesen in mir schön und voller Sehnsucht ist. Weil du es liebst.

Mutter kommt ins Zimmer und bittet mich zu Tisch. Also schiebe ich Unwohlsein vor und sage ihr, dass ich nicht hungrig sei.

Mit besorgter Miene setzt sie sich zu mir. »Eins der Zwillingmädchen von nebenan hat mir heute früh eine Nachricht für dich gegeben. Hast du sie gefunden?«

Ich setze mich auf. »Ja, Gott segne dich, Mutter.«

Sie sieht mich lange und forschend an. »Du wirst dich Vaters Anweisungen widersetzen, nicht wahr?«

He waves his hand about, as if he wanted to shoo away an annoying fly, and scowls. "That is simply ridiculous, Lorentz! I don't believe you!" He bends farther down onto the table and bares his teeth. "I forbid you to run around in women's clothes ever again! Or, may God have mercy on you!"

"Leave God out of it, father! He is looking at us, not at our clothes," escapes from my mouth.

He raises his hand, and in the next instant my cheek burns from the slap to my face.

I jump up, incensed; the hands behind my back clenched into fists. If you knew what disgraceful reply I have on my lips. Only my wits make me pause. Therefore, I turn around on my heels and run up to my chamber.

Contrary to what I feared, he does not chase after me. I throw myself on the bed, clutching my pillow. Paper is rustling. And then I discover the sealed letter in your curved handwriting.

Tomorrow, at the first hour of the evening, I read.

I bury my face in my pillow. You cannot guess that I am not allowed anymore to leave the house in the evening. We haven't seen each other for weeks, and now of all things... As if playing hide and seek were not already hard enough, father has to impose this absurd punishment. Does he really believe that he can keep me away from you or make a change to how one was born? So, let him try to lock me up, I don't care. I will always find another way to free myself from his shackles. For the other creature inside me is beautiful and full of longing. Because you love it.

Mother enters the room and asks me to come to the [dinner] table. So I pretend to be unwell and tell her that I am not hungry.

With a worried expression, she sits down beside me. "One of the twin girls from next door gave me a message for you this morning. Did you find it?"

I sit up. "Yes. God bless you, mother."

She looks at me, long and inquiringly. "You are going to disregard father's orders, are you?"

Ich schweige. Je weniger sie erfährt, umso besser.

»Lorentz, du kannst mir nichts vormachen.«

Wir umarmen uns.

»Lass Vater nicht warten«, mahne ich leise. »Du weißt, wozu er in dem Zustand fähig ist.« Mutter tätschelt mich. Alsbald bin ich wieder mit mir allein.

Während ich am nächsten Tag meinen Dienst in der Schreibstube versehe, schweifen meine Gedanken ständig zu dem Plan ab, den ich in der Nacht geschmiedet habe. Mutter hat mir aufgetragen, ein Bündel mit Tuchwaren für sie abzuholen, das sie bei ihrem Schneider Pandolfo bestellt hat. Ich weiß nicht, ob sie ahnt, was ich vorhabe. Aber mein Plan wird gelingen! Mein geliebter Freund, spürst du auch, wie stark und unzerstörbar unsere Verbindung ist?

Heute fällt mir das Rechnen schwer, ich darf keinen Fehler begehen. Herrn Wolfhart ist meine Zerstreutheit nicht entgangen, denn er lässt mich mehrfach Kostenrechnungen nachprüfen. Wenngleich Vaters Schreibstube in einem anderen Seitenflügel liegt, wäre es ihm ein Leichtes, sich jederzeit nach mir zu erkundigen. Deshalb gebe ich vor, noch die Monatsbilanz fertigstellen zu wollen, weshalb mir mein Lehrherr anerkennend auf die Schultern klopft. Als er die Schreibstube verlässt, atme ich auf.

Schließlich verberge ich mich in einer Nische hinter dem Portal und beäuge den immerwährenden Trubel vor dem Kontor. Vollbeladene Fuhrwerke, von Ochsen und Eseln gezogen, stehen in Reih und Glied. Kaufleute aus aller Herren Länder begehren Einlass in die stolze Stadt, um ihre Waren feilbieten zu können. In der von Regen kündenden Luft sind die Ausdünstungen von Mensch und Tier geradezu ekelerregend. Kleine Kinder greinen, und die erschöpften Lasttiere scharren mit den Hufen. Es gibt kaum einen günstigeren Moment, sich davonzustehlen.

Aus der Wäschekammer beschaffe ich mir einen Umhang, einen dunklen Hut und den dazugehörigen weißen Kragen, den die höhergestellten Kontoristen zuweilen tragen. Die Kleider sind mir an den Armen und Schultern zu groß, aber sie erfüllen ihren Zweck. Gesenkten Hauptes husche ich hinaus. Meine

I remain silent. The less she finds out, the better.

"Lorentz, you are unable to pull the wool over my eyes."

We embrace.

"Don't make father wait," I remind her quietly. "You know what he is capable of in this condition." Mother pats me. Soon I am again alone with myself.

While I am completing my tasks in the office the next day, my thoughts invariably wander to the plan which I forged during the night. Mother told me to pick up a bundle of cloth goods for her which she ordered at her tailor, Pandolfini's. I don't know if she has an inkling of what I have planned. But my plan will succeed! My beloved friend, do you also feel how strong and indestructible our connection is?

Today I have a hard time with the calculations; I must not make any mistakes. My absentmindness did not escape Master Wolfhart because he has me check the cost accounting several times. Although father's office is in another wing of the building, it would be easy for him to inquire about me at any moment. Therefore I pretend to complete the monthly balance of accounts as well, which is why my master claps me on the back approvingly. When he leaves the office, I breathe a sigh of relief.

I finally hide in a corner behind the portal, eying the constant hustle and bustle in front of the trading station. Fully laden carts, drawn by oxen and donkeys, stand there in rank and file, seeking admittance to the proud city in order to be able to offer their goods for sale. In the air, which heralds rain, the odor of humans and animals is nothing less than nauseating. Small children whine and the exhausted pack animals paw the ground. There is hardly a better moment for stealing away.

From the laundry room I requisition a cloak, a dark hat, and the corresponding white collar, which is worn off and on by higher-level accountants. The clothes are too big for me in the arms and shoulders, but they serve their purpose. With my head bowed, I scurry outside. My feet want to run as fast as they can,

Füße wollen laufen, so schnell sie es vermögen, doch das würde mich nur verdächtig machen. Unauffällig ziehe ich den Hut tiefer in die Stirn, zwinge mir einen gemäßigten Gang auf und schlängele mich durch die Menge. Nur nicht umsehen. Als ich die letzte Brücke zur Piazza San Marco überquere, zerrt eine heftige Windbö an meinem Hut. Wenn ich ihn nur nicht verliere. Die Rufe der Gondolieri und die allgegenwärtigen Schreie der Seevögel klingen auf einmal wie von weit her.

Gleich habe ich in unseren Garten erreicht. Folgt mir ein Augenpaar, oder ist es nur meine Hysterie, die mir einen Streich spielt?

Erst als ich die Schatten der Arkaden vom Palazzo Ducale erreiche, getraue ich mich, meine Lider wieder zu heben. Männer mit Handwagen überqueren lauthals singend die Piazza, während eine Schar Kinder den Tauben kleine Brotkrumen zuwirft. Dicht hinter mir meine ich Schritte zu vernehmen. Hastig springe ich in einen Hauseingang. Dem Allmächtigen sei Dank, es sind keine bekannten Gesichter unter den Passanten zu erkennen.

Im Garten begrüße ich die Abenddämmerung mit einem stummen Gebet. Das Licht ist sanft und zeichnet Muster auf den mit trockenem Laub bedeckten Boden. Wie friedlich es hier ist. Ich setze mich auf eine Bank unter einer Akazie, deren letzte Blätter im sanften Wind rascheln. In Momenten wie diesen träume ich davon, dir meine Heimat zu zeigen, wenn sich die Heide im Herbst in ein Meer aus weißen, rosé- und violettfarbenen Blüten verwandelt. Dabei würde ich dir – leise, um den Zauber nicht zu zerstören – die Geschichte von dem Bauernmädchen erzählen, das vor einiger Zeit vom Moor verschluckt wurde. Rätselhafte Laute sollen seitdem des Nachts dort zu hören sein.

Mir scheint, auch du hütest Geheimnisse. Stets bist du es, der mir Nachrichten zukommen lässt. Warum weiß ich nur so wenig von dir? Du musst ungefähr Anfang Dreißig sein, bist also etwa doppelt so alt wie ich und nennst dich Dante. Das mag ein vornehmer Name sein, mir gefällt er jedoch gar nicht, weshalb ich ihn selten benutze. Deine Kleidung ist schlicht, aber von ausgesuchter Qualität, dein Kinnbart sorgfältig gestutzt.

but that would only make me [look] suspicious. Without attracting attention, I push my hat lower down on my forehead, force myself into a moderate pace, and weave my way through the crowd. Just don't look around. When I cross the last bridge to the Piazza San Marco, a fierce gust of wind pulls on my hat. If only I don't lose it. The calls of the gondoliers and the omnipresent cries of the seabirds all of a sudden sound as if from far away.

Moments later, I have reached our garden. Is there a pair of eyes following me or is it merely my hysteria playing a trick on me?

Only after I have reached the shadows of the arcades of the Palazzo Ducale [the Ducal Palace] do I dare to raise my eyelids again. Men with handcarts, singing loudly, cross the Piazza, while a horde of children throws small breadcrumbs to the pigeons. Close behind me, I think I hear steps. Hastily, I jump into a house entrance. Thank the Almighty, I can see no familiar faces among the passers-by.

In the garden, I welcome the dusk with a silent prayer. The light is soft and paints patterns onto the ground, which is covered with dry leaves. How peaceful it is here. I sit down on a bench under the acacia whose last leaves rustle in the soft wind. In moments like these I dream of showing you my home country, where in autumn the heath transforms into a sea of white, rose-colored, and violet flowers. In the course of this, I would tell you—quietly, so as not to destroy the magic—the story of the farmer girl who was swallowed by the moor some time ago. Since that time, mysterious noises have been said to be heard there at night.

It seems to me as if you also are guarding secrets. Invariably, it is you who sends news to me. Why do I know so little about you? You must be in your early thirties, approximately; that makes you twice as old as I am, and you call yourself Dante. That may be a nobleman's name, but I don't like it all; that is why I rarely use it. Your clothes are simple, but of exquisite quality; your goatee is carefully clipped. You skillfully evade my

Meinen Fragen, wer du bist und wo du lebst, weichst du geschickt aus. Einmal habe ich unter deiner Schaube einen Ring aufblitzen sehen. Du wirst Gründe haben, warum du dein Leben geheim hältst, beruhige ich mich zum ungezählten Mal. Bitte verzeih – aber in manch beunruhigendem Traum sehe ich dich in leidenschaftlicher Umarmung mit anderen. Doch sobald sich dein Blick in meinen senkt ist es, als ob sich meine Zweifel wie Seifenblasen in der Luft auflösen. Dann schäme ich mich gar für meine niederen Gedanken.

Mit einem Seufzen luge ich zum Pfad hinüber.

Ein Geräusch lässt mich erstarren. Über mir öffnet sich unvermittelt eins der bemalten, bleiverglasten Fenster. Entsetzt presse ich eine Hand vor den Mund, damit mir nur kein Laut entschlüpft.

»Vergiss nicht die Rahmen blank zu putzen«, höre ich die gestrenge Stimme einer Frau. »Die Herrschaften dulden keine Nachlässigkeit! Also eile dich. Morgen gegen Mittag werden sie zurückerwartet.«

»Natürlich«, antwortet eine helle Jungmädchenstimme.

Hoffentlich blicken die Zofen nicht hinaus. Wenig später wird das Fenster wieder geschlossen. Ich springe auf, um mich an die Mauer eines Seitengebäudes zu drücken.

Es ist schon spät, und ich darf keinesfalls versäumen, Mutters Tuchwaren rechtzeitig vom Schneider abzuholen. Vater ist ohnehin wachsam, sein Argwohn ist beinahe körperlich spürbar.

Mit einem Brennen in meinem Inneren mache ich mich auf den Rückweg. Wenig später betrete ich das Handelskontor durch einen Hintereingang. Die Wäschekammer ist verriegelt. Mit einem leisen Fluch auf den Lippen verstecke ich die geborgte Kleidung in einem Stall, der den Lasttieren der Reisenden vorbehalten ist.

Plötzlich presst sich eine Hand auf meinen Mund, und vor Schreck fällt mir Mutters Tuchbündel zu Boden. Warmer Atem streift meinen Nacken, der vertraute Duft von Sandelholz kitzelt lockend meine Sinne.

»Ich bin's.« Der Griff lockert sich.

questions about who you are and where you live. On one occasion I saw a ring flash underneath your overcoat. You will have reasons why you keep your life secret, I reassure myself for the umpteenth time. Please forgive me—but in many a disquieting dream I see you in a passionate embrace with another. However, as soon as your gaze loses itself in mine, it is as if my doubts dissolve into air like bursting bubbles. Afterward I am even ashamed at my base thoughts.

With a sigh I peek over at the path.

A sound makes me freeze. Above me, all of a sudden one of the painted, leaded windows opens. Terrifed, I press a hand over my mouth so that not the slightest sound can escape.

"Don't forget to clean the frames to a shine," I hear the strict voice of a woman. "The lady and the lord of the house don't tolerate any negligence. So, hurry up. We expect them back tomorrow around noon."

"Yes, ma'am," the bright voice of a young maiden replies.

I hope the maids are not going to look outside. A little later, the window is closed again. I jump up to squeeze against the wall of an annex.

It is late already, and I must not fail to pick up mother's cloth goods in time from the tailor. Father is watchful as it is; his suspicion is almost physically palpable.

With a burning inside, I set out on the way home. Shortly afterwards, I enter the trading station through a back entrance. The laundry room is bolted. With a quiet curse on my lips I hide the borrowed clothes in a stable which is reserved for the pack animals of the travelers.

Suddenly, a hand presses over my mouth and, terrified, I drop mother's bundle of cloth goods on the ground. A warm breath touches my neck; the familiar scent of sandalwood tickles my senses enticingly.

"It's me." The grip loosens.

Da stehst du vor mir, mit einem Ausdruck in den dunklen Augen, den ich nicht zu deuten vermag. Über deinem Gesicht liegen Schatten, und ich kann dem Drang, dich zu berühren, kaum widerstehen.

»Was machst du hier? Hat dich jemand gesehen?« frage ich leise und blicke mich nach allen Seiten um.

»Keine Sorge. Wir sind allein.«

Du trittst näher, und mein Herzschlag beschleunigt sich. So war es von Anfang an, und so wird es wohl für immer bleiben.

Voller Freude streiche ich mit den Fingerspitzen über deine Hand, einmal mehr von der Zartheit deiner Haut überrascht.

Wir halten uns umfangen. Du zitterst. Und während wir den kostbaren Moment stumm in uns aufsaugen, blicke ich zu dir auf. »Woher wusstest du, dass ich hier bin?« Kaum hab ich das ausgesprochen, erkenne ich die Wahrheit. »Du warst schon vor mir dort.«

»Ja. Es tut mir leid, dass ich dich im Unklaren lassen musste. Mir erschien es zu gefährlich, mich im Garten zu erkennen zu geben.«

Dein Lächeln ist liebevoll wie immer, als du jede Linie meines Gesichts erkundest, dennoch schwingt Traurigkeit in deiner Stimme mit. »Was ist mit dir, Dante?«

»Was mit mir ist? Sieh dich nur an! Du musst deine schönen Formen unter derben Männerkleidern verstecken. Welch Jammer!«

»Wir müssen hinnehmen, was uns nicht zu ändern gegeben ist«, antworte ich, obwohl meine Worte nur wie eine leere Phrase klingen. »In ihren Augen sind wir Sünder. Aber wir beide wissen, dass zwischen uns nichts ist außer reiner Liebe.«

Du schweigst. Mutters Bündel liegt noch auf dem Boden. Mein Hals ist plötzlich wie zugeschnürt. »Ich muss gehen. Ich bin schon viel zu lange fort. Mein Vater …«

»Bitte.« Dein intensiver Blick hält meinen fest. »Schenke uns noch ein wenig Zeit, bevor wir uns voneinander verabschieden. Jeder Moment ist kostbar, ganz im Gegensatz zu all den Jahren vorher und jenen, die noch folgen.«

There you are in front of me, with an expression in your dark eyes which I am unable to interpret. Across your face lies a shadow and I can hardly resist the urge to touch you.

"What are you doing here? Did anybody see you?" I ask quietly and look around me in all directions.

"Don't worry. We are alone."

You step closer and my heartbeat speeds up. That is how it has been since the beginning, and that's probably how it always will be.

Full of delight, I run the tips of my fingers over your hand, once more surprised by the softness of your skin.

We stay in the embrace. You tremble. And while we silently drink in the precious moment, I look up at you. "How did you know that I was here?" Hardly have I said this, when I realize the truth. "You were already there before me."

"Yes. I am sorry that I had to leave you in the dark. It appeared too dangerous to me, to make myself known in the garden."

Your smile is affectionate as always, as you explore every line in my face; all the same, a sadness resonates in your voice. "What is wrong with you, Dante?"

"What's wrong with me? Just look at you! You are forced to hide your beautiful shape under rough men's clothing. What a pity!"

"We have to accept what is not given to us to change," I reply, although my words sound merely like an empty phrase. "In their eyes, we are sinners. But we both know that there is nothing between us but pure love."

You remain silent. Mother's bundle is still on the ground. Suddenly, my throat feels constricted. "I have to go. I have already been away much too long. My father ..."

"Please." Your intense gaze locks with mine. "Give us a little more time before we take leave of each other. Every moment is precious, in stark contrast to the years before and those that follow."

Wie recht du hast. Letztlich wird es auf ein paar Minuten mehr oder weniger nicht ankommen. »Gut. Versprichst du mir, dass wir uns bald wiedersehen?« frage ich dich heiser.

»Nein. Diesmal wird es ein Abschied für immer sein.«

In meinem Innersten krampft sich alles zusammen. »Wieso denn?« stoße ich hervor und mustere deine liebgewonnenen Züge. »Ah, jetzt verstehe ich! Du gehst auf Reisen, nicht wahr? Dann warte ich eben auf dich. Die Zeit geht vorüber, irgendwie.«

Du schüttelst nur den Kopf.

»Du bist verheiratet. Ist es das?« frage ich bange, meine Nägel in deinen Mantelstoff gekrallt. »Ich ahne es schon länger. Sag mir die Wahrheit, ich kann sie ertragen!«

»Nein, für mich hat es immer nur dich gegeben, Lorentz. Du bist mein Schicksal, dem ich mich nicht zu entziehen vermag.«

Gefangen in dem würzigen Duft von Sandelholz, das du stets benutzt, rüttele ich dich. »Du sprichst in Rätseln! Was ist mit dir!«

»Ich habe wirklich versucht, es zu verstehen«, flüsterst du und schließt kurz gequält deine Augen. »Gott allein weiß wie sehr. Aber es ist mir nicht möglich, dir zu verzeihen, zu tief hast du mich verletzt.«

Entsetzen bemächtigt sich meiner. »Ich? Wie könnte ich dich verletzen?«

Dein Mund verengt sich zu einem schmalen Strich, deine mahlenden Kieferknochen treten scharf hervor, und mich überläuft unvermittelt ein Frösteln.

»Entsinnst du dich, wie ich dir im letzten Jahr meine Liebe schwor? Du bist mein, für alle Zeit, sagte ich zu dir.« Du hebst mein Kinn. »Sag, Lorentz, was hast du darauf erwidert?«

»Dass ich auf den Augenblick warte, an dem ich dir meine Liebe beweisen kann«, antworte ich wahrheitsgetreu.

»So ist es.« Du nickst grimmig. Auf einmal entdecke ich in deinen Augen einen Schimmer, der mich an das Glitzern von Eiskristallen erinnert. »Und was hast du mit deinem Versprechen angefangen?« zischst du, und ich schnappe bestürzt nach Luft. »Mit Füßen getreten hast du es! Damit hast du alles, was zwischen uns war, zerstört!«

How right you are. Ultimately, a few minutes more or less won't matter. "All right. Do you promise me that we shall see each other again soon?" I ask you huskily.

"No. This time, it will be a farewell forever."

Deep down inside me, everything is convulsing. "Why is that?" I gasp out, and study your facial features, of which I have become fond. "Ah, now I understand! You are going on a journey, aren't you? Then I shall just wait for you. Time will pass somehow."

You merely shake your head.

"You are married, that's it?" I ask anxiously, my [finger]nails clawing the fabric of your coat. "I already suspected that for some time. Tell me the truth; I can take it!"

"No, for me there has always been only you, Lorentz. You are my destiny which I am unable to escape."

Caught in the spicy aroma of the sandalwood, which you always use, I shake you. "You are speaking in riddles! What is wrong with you!"

"I have really tried to understand it," you whisper, and briefly close your tortured eyes. "God alone knows how much. But I am unable to forgive you; you hurt me too deeply."

Horror takes possession of me. "I? How would I be able to hurt you?"

Your mouth narrows into a small line; your gnawing jawbones jut out sharply and suddenly I begin to shiver with cold.

"Do you recall how I swore my love to you last year? You are mine, I said to you, for all time." You are lifting my chin up. "Tell me, Lorentz, what did you reply to that?"

"That I am waiting for the moment when I can prove my love to you," I reply truthfully.

"That's right." You nod grimly. All of a sudden, I discover a shimmer in your eyes which is reminiscent of the glittering of ice crystals. "And what have you done with your promise?" you hiss and I gasp for air, aghast. "You stepped on it! By doing that, you destroyed everything that existed between us!"

Deine Worte sind wie Keulenschläge. Blinzelnd versuche ich zu verstehen, es will mir jedoch nicht gelingen. »Zerstört? Was habe ich dir getan?«

»Das fragst du noch? Betrogen hast du mich! Es war eine Frau. Eine Frau, Lorentz!« Deine Hände auf meinen Armen sind wie Schraubstöcke, vor Schmerz verziehe ich das Gesicht.

»Sag nicht, du hast die reizvolle Zigeunerin mit den roten Haaren vergessen, von der du dich so inbrünstig hast küssen lassen.«

Geradezu maskenhaft, bar jeden Gefühls wirken deine Züge nun. Maske ... Da taucht in meiner Erinnerung das Bild der Rothaarigen vor mir auf. Ihr sinnlicher Kuss. Hände, die sich nach mir ausstreckten und mich liebkosten.

»Aber Liebster, komm zur Besinnung, und lasse mich bitte los! Du tust mir weh«, antworte ich und lächle, doch es gerät schief. Gleich darauf lockerst du deinen Griff, und ich reibe mir die schmerzenden Stellen. »Das war nichts als eine flüchtige Begegnung im Carnevale«, fahre ich fort, meine Stimme hohl vor Fassungslosigkeit. »Sie hat mich überrascht, Dante! Es ging alles so schnell. Außerdem war es doch nur ...«

Auf einmal sind da schlurfende Schritte, das Schnauben von Ochsen. Rasch schlüpfen wir in eine im Dunkeln gelegene Ecke. Die Geräusche nähern sich, ich halte den Atem an. Als die Laute wieder verstummen, lehne ich mich schwer gegen die Wand. Nachdenklich kehrt mein Blick zu dir zurück. Noch während ich dich betrachte, schießt mir ein Gedanke blitzartig durch den Kopf. »Wie hast du eigentlich von meinem Besuch beim Carnevale erfahren?«

»Ich habe dich gesehen.«

»Du konntest überhaupt nicht wissen, dass ich mich an jenem Abend aus dem Haus schleiche.«

»Ich habe jeden Abend vor dem Haus auf dich gewartet.«

»Moment.« Unzählige Gedanken huschen durch meinen Geist, doch sie sind wie Irrlichter – mal hier, mal dort und nicht einzufangen. »Jeden Abend? Wieso?«

Du hebst eine Braue. »Ich war allzeit in deiner Nähe. Weil du mein bist und ich auf mein schönes Vögelchen achtgeben muss, damit es nicht seine Orientierung verliert.«

Your words are like blows with a club. Blinking, I am trying to understand, but I am unable to do so. "Destroyed? What did I do to you?"

"You have the nerve to ask? You betrayed me! It was a woman. A woman, Lorentz!" Your hands on my arms are like vices; my face contorts in pain.

"Don't tell me that you have forgotten the charming gypsy woman with the red hair whom you allowed to kiss you so fervently."

Your expression appears almost masklike, devoid now of all emotion. A mask... That is when the image of the redhead surfaces in my memory. Her sensuous kiss. Hands which reached for me and caressed me.

"But, my beloved, come to your senses and please, let go of me! You are hurting me," I reply and smile, but it turns out crooked. Immediately, you loosen your grip and I rub the aching spots. "That was nothing but a fleeting encounter in the Carnevale," I continue, my voice hollow with bewilderment. "She surprised me, Dante! Everything happened so quickly. Besides, it was only..."

Suddenly, there is the scuffling of feet, the snorting of oxen. Quickly we slip into a dark corner. The sounds are approaching; I hold my breath. When the sounds have fallen silent, I lean against the wall heavily. Pensively, I turn my gaze back to you. While I am still looking at you, a thought shoots through my head like lightning. "Actually, how did you find out about my visit to the Carnevale?"

"I saw you."

"You couldn't know in the first place that I was going to sneak out of the house on that evening."

"I waited for you in front of the house every evening."

"Just a moment." Countless thoughts flit through my mind, but they are all like will-o'-the-wisps—one moment here, the next moment there, and you cannot catch them. "Every evening? Why?"

You lift a brow. "I was near you at all times. For you are mine and I have to watch my pretty little bird so that it won't lose it's orientation."

Durch meinen Schleier von Verwirrung dringt ein ungeheuer-
licher Gedanke zu mir durch. »Dann bist du es gewesen, dessen
Schritte ich hörte? Du hast mich beobachtet?«

Das Schmunzeln auf deiner starren Miene wirkt wie ein
Lichtstrahl in der Finsternis. »Wie klug du bist.«

Schönes Vögelchen ... Die Erkenntnis trifft mich mit eiserner
Härte. Seit dem Streit mit Vater habe ich insgeheim ihn ver-
dächtigt, mir gefolgt zu sein. Allmächtiger. Ich kann spüren,
wie mir das Blut aus dem Kopf weicht. »Wir hätten gemeinsam
auf die Piazza gehen können, Dante«, presse ich hervor, als ich
glaube, meine Fassung wiedererlangt zu haben.

Deine steife Haltung, die Kälte, die du ausstrahlst, all dies
scheint zu einem Fremden zu gehören. Nicht zu dir, dem
Menschen, dem ich am meisten vertraue.

»Wir, gemeinsam?« höhnst du. »Du bist es, der nicht begreift!
Aus deinen Worten spricht die Unerfahrenheit eines Frischlings.«

»Aber wenn du ebenfalls auf der Piazza warst, wieso hast du
mich nicht angesprochen?« Bittend will ich deine Wange berühren, doch deine verengten Augen lassen mich innehalten.

»Das habe ich.«

Das Blut rauscht mir in den Ohren. »Das ist nicht wahr,
Dante!«

»Und ob!« Du bist mir jetzt so nahe, dass ich die Wärme
deiner Haut deutlich wahrnehmen kann. »Trete nur näher,
Schwarze Witwe, und ich verrate dir, was das Schicksal für dich
bereithält«, kommt es mit heller Stimme von dir.

Ich kann dich nur anstarren. »Du warst es? Du warst
Marcello, der Hellseher?«

»Ja.«

Unfähig zu begreifen, schüttele ich den Kopf.

Du ziehst mich in die Arme und liebkost die feinen Haare in
meinem Nacken. Hilflos beäuge ich die Stalltür vor mir. Wäre
da nur jemand, der mir helfen könnte! Ich muss mich aus deiner
Umarmung befreien, aber meine Glieder wollen mir nicht
gehorchen. »Du hast deine Stimme verstellt, damit ich dich
nicht erkenne«, flüstere ich nach einer gefühlten Ewigkeit.

»Außerdem habe ich meinen Umhang über Weihrauchdampf
gehängt, um den Duft von Sandelholz zu vertreiben«, ergänzt

Through my veil of confusion, a monstrous thought gets through to me.

"Then it was you whose steps I heard? You watched me?"

The smile on your frozen countenance seems like a ray of light in the darkness. "How clever you are."

Pretty little bird... The realization hits me with an iron force. Since the fight with my father I had secretly suspected him to be following me. Almighty God, I can feel how the blood seeps out of my head. "We could have gone together to the Piazza, Dante," I utter, after I think I have regained my composure.

Your rigid posture, the coldness which you exude—all this seems to belong to a stranger. Not to you, the person whom I trust most.

"We, together?" You scoff. "You are the one who does not understand! Your words attest to the inexperience of a newcomer."

"But if you also were in the Piazza, why didn't you approach me and talk to me?" Pleadingly, I attempt to touch your cheek, but your narrowed eyes make me pause.

"That's what I did."

Blood is rushing in my ears. "That is not true, Dante!"

"Yes, it is!" You are now so close to me that I can clearly feel the warmth of your skin. "Come closer, Black Widow, and I will reveal to you what fate has in store for you," he says in a bright voice.

I can only stare at you. "That was you? You were Marcello, the clairvoyant?"

"Yes."

Unable to understand, I shake my head.

You pull me into your arms and caress the fine hairs at the nape of my neck. Helplessly I look at the stable door in front of me. If there were only someone who could help me! I have to free myself from your embrace, but my limbs don't want to listen to me. "You altered your voice so that I would not recognize you," I whisper after what seems like an eternity.

"Besides that, I hung my cloak over the smoke of incense in order to dispel the aroma of sandalwood," you add airily.

du leichthin. »Dann weißt du gewiss auch noch, was Marcello, der Hellseher, dir prophezeite?«

Fieberhaft versuche ich mir die Worte ins Gedächtnis zu rufen, sie wollen mir jedoch nicht einfallen.

»Ich helfe dir gern auf die Sprünge, Geliebter«, raunst du und streichst mit den Fingerspitzen über meine wild klopfende Halsschlagader. »Wie erregt du bist. Marcello sagte: Du hütest ein delikates Geheimnis. Aber sei unbesorgt, dir wird Gerechtigkeit widerfahren.« Deine Finger verharren an meinem Hals, um dann die Linien meiner Lippen nachzuziehen. »Du warst die Schönste in jener Nacht, wie eine kostbare, exotische Blume. Wie schade, dass unsere gemeinsame Zeit schon zu Ende ist. Glaube mir, ich werde dich bis zu meinem letzten Atemzug vermissen.«

»Ich ... ich verstehe ... dich nicht.« Mehr bringe ich nicht heraus.

»Es ist ganz einfach, Lorentz.« Du schließt die Augen und schmiegst deine Wange an meine.

»Ein Leben lang habe ich jemanden wie dich gesucht. Jemanden, der ebenso Mann wie Frau in sich vereint. Du warst die Erfüllung meiner Träume.« Du küsst mich, zunächst fragend, zärtlich. Ich möchte dir widerstehen, aber ich kann es nicht, zu lange habe ich mich nach diesem Augenblick gesehnt.

»Glaube mir, ich teile dich mit niemandem! Lieber werde ich dafür in der Hölle schmoren! Hier und jetzt erfüllt sich die Prophezeiung.«

Wie von ferne nehme ich eine rasche Handbewegung wahr, dann jagt ein scharfer Schmerz durch meinen Oberkörper. Ich blicke an mir herunter. Ein Dolch steckt bis zum Schaft in meiner Brust. Mit weit aufgerissenen Augen sehe ich noch dein melancholisches Lächeln, die Träne, die dir über die Wange läuft. Herr, erbarme dich unser. Durch meine schwindenden Sinne schieben sich gellende Schreie. Sie rufen meinen Namen. Wie eigentümlich, ich fühle keinen Schmerz mehr. Es ist, als schwebe ich. Um mich wird es dunkler. Aus der Stalltür lösen sich ... die Umrisse zweier Gestalten ... Vater. Mutter. Vergebt mir.

Ende

"Then you certainly remember what Marcello, the clairvoyant, prophesied to you?"

Feverishly, I try to recall the words, but they don't want to come back to me.

"I will gladly put you on the right track, beloved," you murmur and run the tips of your fingers over my wildly throbbing carotid artery. "How excited you are. Marcello said: You are guarding a delicate secret. But don't worry; you shall meet with justice." Your fingers rest on my neck, only to move on to follow the outline of my lips. "You were the prettiest one that night, like a precious, exotic flower. Too bad that our time together has already come to an end. Believe me, I shall miss you until my last breath."

"I... I do not ... understand you." I am unable to produce more.

"It is very simple, Lorentz." You close your eyes and press your cheek to mine.

"My whole life, I have looked for someone like you. Someone who unites in himself a man and a woman. You were the fulfillment of my dreams." You kiss me, first wonderingly, tenderly. I would like to resist you, but I am unable to do so; I have ached for this moment for too long.

"Believe me, I shall share you with nobody! I'd rather burn in Hell! Here and now, the prophecy shall be fulfilled."

As if from afar, I notice a quick movement of a hand, then a sharp pain races through my upper body. I look down on myself. A dagger is stuck in my chest, to the hilt. With my eyes wide, I notice also your melancholy smile, the tear which is running down your cheek. Lord, have mercy on us. Through my waning senses, I can hear shrill screams. They call my name. How strange, I don't feel pain any longer. It is as if I were floating. Around me, it is getting darker. Coming from the stable door... the outlines of two shapes... Father. Mother. Forgive me.

The End

Fondaco dei Tedeschi: Deutscher Handelskontor in Venedig
Tedeschi: Deutscher
Schaube: ein weiter, vorne offener Überrock, der ohne Gürtel getragen wurde
Geheime Gärten: Von 1600 bis 1800 war Venedig die Königin der Gärten, besaß sogar einige botanische Gärten. Die Gärten der venezianischen Patrizier waren der Öffentlichkeit allerdings nicht zugänglich und von meterhohen Mauern umgeben, damit die Reichen ungestört ihren Vergnügungen nachgehen konnten.
Mercator: Kontorleiter
Kontorist: Buchhalter.

Glossary:

Fondaco dei Tedeschi: German trading post in Venice

Tedeschi: Germans

Schaube: A loose overcoat, open to the front, which was worn without a belt.

Hidden Gardens: From 1600 to 1800, Venice was known as the Queen of Gardens; it even had a few botanical gardens. The gardens of the Venetian Patrician were not open to the public, however, and were surrounded by walls several meters high, which allowed the rich to pursue their pleasures undisturbed.

Mercator: Accounting Manager

Kontorist: Accountant

EDITOR/TRANSLATOR PROFILE

A native of Germany, M. Charlotte Wolf has lived in the United States for almost twenty years. Before coming to the U.S., she conducted her undergraduate work in American Studies and German language and literature at two German universities. In the U.S., she completed an M.A. in German and a Ph.D. in Interdisciplinary Studies (Literature and Women's Studies), among other areas. Since 1985, she has worked as a freelance translator and editor of English and German. Her expertise is in Literature, Linguistics, and Women's Studies. In addition, she has had a successful career in education as an administrator, teacher, and trainer for German, English, ESL, and yoga. In her free time she is a passionate reader of multilingual literature, watches movies (foreign and film noir), travels, and writes poetry.

Charlotte is happily married to Martin Tobias who, after a long career in electrical engineering, has now turned to photography.